GINGER STREET

Ginger Street

Anne Douglas

PIATKUS

All the characters in this book are fictitious and any resemblance to real
persons, living or dead, is entirely coincidental.

Copyright © Anne Douglas 2002

First published in Great Britain in 2002 by
Judy Piatkus (Publishers) Ltd of
5 Windmill Street, London WIT 2JA
email: info@piatkus.co.uk

The moral right of the author has been asserted

A catalogue record for this book is available from the British Library

ISBN 0 7499 0622 7

Typeset in Times by Palimpsest Book Production Limited,
Polmont, Stirlingshire
Printed and bound in Great Britain by
Butler and Tanner Ltd

Author's Note

This story of Italian and Scottish families set in Edinburgh is a work of imagination. Apart from certain wartime figures, all the characters are fictional and Ginger Street itself does not exist. The background, however, is real, and in my researches for that I acknowledge a deep debt of gratitude to Dr Terri Colpi's definitive studies on the Italian communities in Great Britain, both listed below. My thanks also go to Mrs Lydia Leighton, of Edinburgh and Rome, for her help in checking the Italian in the novel, and to the staff of the Edinburgh Room and the Scottish Library, Edinburgh City Libraries, for their unfailing assistance.

Works consulted:

Colpi, Terri, *The Italian Factor*, Mainstream, 1991
Colpi, Terri, *Italians Forward*, Mainstream, 1991
Mileham, P.J.R., *Scottish Regiments*, Spellmount, 1988
Mullay, Sandy, *The Edinburgh Encyclopedia*, Mainstream, 1996
Nimmo, Ian, *Scotland at War*, Archive/Scotsman, 1989

Part One

Chapter One

The children of Ginger Street were coming home. No one met them from school. The streets on that November afternoon in 1929 were safe enough, though dark between the gas lamps. There were lights in the shops, though, and in the jolting trams, and in the tenements.

Ginger Street, on the south side of Edinburgh, where Newington meets St Leonard's, was all tenements. Built in the nineteenth century to one plain design, they lacked the height and faded grace of the Old Town houses. There were no cornices or plaster ceiling roses here; no reminders of past glories when the quality had shared houses with the poor. On the other hand, none of the Ginger Street tenements had fallen down, unlike one or two in the Old Town.

Walking home to Number Twenty-Four with two friends and her sister, Ruth Millar did not think of herself as one of the children. She was fourteen and would be leaving school at Christmas; was already feeling rather apart from the others: her sister, Sylvie, Millie MacAllan and Vi Smith, who were only twelve. They could still get excited looking at the sweeties in the Italian shop window, whereas she had to think about finding a job.

Still, she didn't mind stopping with the others, to look in at Signor Rietti's display. There were the usual dummy boxes of chocolates, looking pale in the gaslight, and the tall glass jars of Scottish boilings, 'soor' plums and humbugs, buttered brazils. Looking was all they could do, for they hadn't a ha'penny amongst them. Ruth and Sylvie got sixpence pocket money on Saturdays, threepence of which had to go into their moneybox, where it stayed. Millie and Vi, who came from large families, only got a few coppers when they could be spared.

'Och, I'm away,' said Millie, at last.

'Me, too,' said Vi. 'No point in looking when you canna buy.'

'I wish it was summer,' murmured Sylvie, as she and Ruth stood alone, still with their noses pressed to the shop window. 'Then I'd buy an ice-cream.' She read aloud the notice on the shop-door. 'Cornets, one ha'penny; wafers, one penny.' Ruth gave a short laugh, as she blew on her gloved fingers. 'Even if it was summer, you still couldn't buy anything. You've no money.'

'When you get a job, Ruthie, you could buy me something.'

'Got to find the job first, and then I won't be earning much.'

No, it wouldn't be much, and she didn't want it anyway, for she would rather have stayed on at school and taken her Leaving Certificate like Signor Rietti's son, Niccolo – Nicco, as his family called him. He was at the Catholic secondary school and said to be clever, his father wanted him to do well. But so was Ruth clever and had been selected to work for the certificate but, as her mother said, her father only earned 'buttons' working in a grocer's in Nicholson Street, while Nicco's father had his own shop. That was the difference, you ken. It wasn't possible for Ruth to stay on at school, whereas Nicco could.

'Now, if your dad should ever get his own shop,' Isa Millar had said comfortingly. 'We could think again, eh?'

If Dad ever got his own shop! That was a joke. What was he going to buy it with? Those 'buttons' he earned at Tomlinson's? There was nothing for it but to comb the job adverts every night for something Ruth could try for, but jobs were getting hard to find, even for badly paid young people. Somebody had said there could be two million unemployed by next year. 'Will I be one of them?' wondered Ruth.

Like Sylvie, Ruth was considered attractive rather than pretty. Both girls had large, blue-grey eyes, though Ruth's bobbed hair was dark and Sylvie's fair, and both had turned-up noses inherited from their mother that they would have liked to change. Their

4

seventeen-year-old brother, Kester, who worked in a biscuit factory, had their father's good straight nose. Now why had that nose not come to them? In the women's magazines their mother bought when she could afford them, Ruth had read that turned-up noses were never snub, always 'tip-tilted'.

'There you are, Sylvie,' Ruth said, laughing. 'Our noses don't turn up, they're tip-tilted!'

'Who says ma nose turns up, anyway?' cried Sylvie hotly.

She knew and Ruth knew that however their noses were described, they were never going to look like the beautiful Marilena, Nicco's sister, who was dawdling down the pavement at that moment, while her cousin, Renata, told her to get a move on, it was too cold to hang about. Marilena's face was a perfect oval, her eyes dark and lustrous, her nose classically straight. At only thirteen, she must surely have had all the boys at the Catholic school dancing round her, but she would know better than to encourage any boys. Why, her mother didn't even let her play in the street with girls, never mind boys! And she was never allowed to go to the Saturday morning cinema shows that everyone else would die rather than miss, and were certainly not missed by Renata, the daughter of Signor Rietti's brother, who owned a little café at the end of Ginger Street. But, then Renata was a rebel, a fiery girl with a mane of black hair she was always threatening to have bobbed and a wide scarlet mouth. It was said her parents didn't know what to do with her, and had enough trouble, anyway, with her brother, Guido, who was rumoured to be 'wild', though what Italians called wild and what the Scots called wild might be two different things. He sold his father's ice-cream in the summer and worked in Gibb's biscuit factory with Kester in the winter, but Kester never said what he got up to, if anything.

'Are you no' coming in?' Marilena asked, hugging Sylvie, with whom she was 'best friends'. Her accent, like all the young Italians away from home was Scottish. At home, they spoke something else, an Italian dialect that came from their original village in the mountains. 'It's so cold out here!'

'No money,' said Sylvie, who was certainly shivering.

'Ah, come on into the warm! *Papà* will give us all some sweeties. Renata, are you coming in?'

'Sure, if there are some sweeties going!' Renata gave her wide smile to Ruth, who smiled back. She very much admired Renata.

The girls all followed Marilena as she pushed open her father's shop-door, ringing its bell, and called in their home dialect:

'*Papà, Papà*, I'm home!'

Chapter Two

The shop was a little bit like home for the Millar girls, too, for they had come here so often and knew it so well. To begin with, of course, their mother had been disappointed when they'd flitted from a close off the Canongate to Ginger Street. It was a step up, was Ginger Street; they'd two bedrooms here and their own lavatory. But the corner shop was Italian, would you credit it? Isa's brow had darkened and the corners of her mouth had turned down.

'Now, Jack, how I'm going to manage, unless you bring everything back from Tomlinson's?' she had demanded, to which placid Jack had said he would bring everything back from Tomlinson's and with a discount too, so what was she complaining about?

'Well, you ken very well, every woman runs out of something from time to time, eh? And they'll no' have ma sugar or ma flour or ma eggs at an Italian shop! Why, they only sell spaghetti and ice-cream! I bet you canna even get a packet of tea!'

What slander! Signor Roberto Rietti stocked everything a Scottish housewife could wish for, together with – and these were what the girls loved to smell closing their eyes – all manner of other things they didn't meet anywhere else. Herbs and garlic, pungent onions on strings, creamy white cheeses, strong dark sausages, streaky hams, and beautiful, golden, crusty bread that came up from an Italian bakery in Leith. Even Isa had been won round in the end, grudgingly admitting that it was a grand show the Riettis put on and the vegetables were certainly very fresh. 'Just as long as your dad brings me ma proper messages.' She'd always add, to get the last word, and the girls would knock each other's ribs and smile.

On that dismal November afternoon, the shop seemed especially warm and welcoming. If there was a slump on the way and men being laid off everywhere, at least for the moment things seemed as normal, with plenty of Italian and Scottish customers ready to buy. Not sitting at the counter, waiting to give their order as they did at Tomlinson's, but sorting things out themselves from the tall wooden shelves and putting them together, to be paid for when the signore had time to add them up.

Marilena's father was a handsome man, but rather thin. He had a high forehead, from which sprang a shock of black hair, and his eyes were large and melancholy.

'Why do Italians like Signor Rietti look so sad?' Ruth once asked her mother. 'As though they're missing something?'

'Well, they are missing something. They're homesick. For Italy.'

'But, Ma, they've lived here for years! Some were born here!'

'Still exiles, you ken. For a country they've never seen.'

'I've heard they sometimes go back.'

'When they get the money together.' Isa had been thoughtful, considering how they might do that and wondering if Jack might do the same. 'Some do make money, specially in the catering trade.'

Now Signor Rietti was smiling at his niece and including Ruth and Sylvie in the smile, as Marilena hung round his neck, wheedling sweeties out of him, and only leaving him alone when he turned to open up the glass jars behind him.

'What would you like?' he asked in English, coughing a little, and placing the cigarette he had been smoking on a tin ashtray. 'Come and choose.'

'Smoking, Uncle, and in the shop, too?' asked Renata, shaking her finger at him. 'You'll be in trouble if Aunt Carlotta catches you!'

He put his own forefinger to his lips, and sent a dark gaze skywards, for his wife was in the flat upstairs.

'Not a word,' he whispered, and gave the girls their sweeties, brushing aside their thanks. 'Maybe I'll put my cigarette out, eh? Before Nicco sees it, too.'

'He never comes out as early as us,' said Renata, who always brought Marilena home. 'Those secondary school folk have to work too hard, if you ask me. I'm glad I'm not staying on!'

'Nicco's's a clever boy, it's no trouble to him, Renata.' Signor Rietti screwed the lids back on his jars. 'I want him to be an accountant, something good in a profession, not working in a shop like me.'

'Why, *Papà*, I thought you wanted him to help you,' said Marilena. 'It's the family shop.'

'Have to keep things in the family,' Renata agreed.

'Maybe I'll ask Guido, then. Who knows?'

'Guido! He'd be hopeless! Anyway, he has to help with the ice-cream when he's not at the factory.'

'All this is just talk,' said Signor Rietti, turning to attend to a customer. 'Renata, don't forget to take the cheese for your mother, it's the Bel Paese she likes.' As the shop bell rang again, he looked up and smiled. 'And here's Nicco, anyway! Marilena, run up and tell your mamma to make him his coffee.'

The tall young man stood in the doorway, taking off his hat and shaking moisture from his coat. His eyes were as dark and brilliant as his sister's, he had his father's good looks without the melancholy, but that evening seemed weary, as though the day had been long for him and had brought its own burdens. Though Ruth envied him, she also felt sorry for him. It was well known that his mother doted on him and watched him like a hawk, and though she watched Marilena in the same way, Isa said that would end when Marilena was safely married and producing bambinos. With Nicco, it would probably never end, whatever he did. And if his father, too, was watching him, expecting him to do well, no wonder he seemed weary, poor Nicco!

He greeted them all cheerfully enough, however, with special smiles for Ruth and Sylvie, and held the door open for them when they said they had to go; for, like his father, he was very well mannered. Then his eyes went to the back of the shop, and theirs followed. Signora Rietti was descending the stairs.

Though she seemed old to the Millar sisters, she was in fact not yet forty, a woman in her prime, with the straight nose and oval face she had passed to her daughter. Her fine eyes were a little shadowed now, and she was beginning to put on weight, but everyone in the shop looked at her, and she responded by holding her head with even more grace and treading each step carefully, as though she were a grand personage. It was her way, they all knew it, and when she reached the shop counter they relaxed and stopped watching, but then the signora leaned forward, sniffed, and let out a series of cries in her own dialect, followed by: 'Roberto! Roberto!'

'Oh, dear,' whispered Renata. 'Poor Uncle Roberto's for it now, Aunt Carlotta's smelled his cigarette! He's not supposed to smoke, you know, doctor's orders, he has a bad chest.'

'Quick, Renata, empty the ashtray!' whispered Marilena.

But it was too late. The signora had seen the cigarette end and as she turned her accusing eyes back to her husband and he began to make excuses, Nicco, Marilena, and Renata all joined in, expostulating and waving their hands, while the customers looked on with interest and the Millar sisters, exchanging quick looks, slipped out of the door and made for home.

'Aren't Italians noisy?' asked Sylvie, as they reached their own stairs and ran up lightly to their door. 'Why do they all talk at once?'

'Ever heard Ma get going with the neighbours?' Ruth countered. 'But they do seem noisier than us, it's true. Maybe it's their language.'

'I like their language,' Sylvie said dreamily. 'Do you no' think it's prettier than ours?' She flung out her arms. '*Bellissima! Prego! Grazie!*'

'Hey, what's all this?' asked their brother, Kester, thundering up the stairs after them. 'Have I come to the wrong house? Oh, *scusi, Signorina, per favore!*'

'Is that what Guido taught you to say?' cried Sylvie. 'No teasing!' But he bundled her through the door, laughing, and said he wanted his tea.

10

Chapter Three

The Millar girls had seen enough poor dwellings to know that they were lucky to live in the flat in Ginger Street. It wasn't just the second bedroom and private lavatory that made the difference, though they were deeply grateful for both, but the way their mother kept things. It was as though she'd never forgotten her time in service and had to keep to the same routines in her own home. The range was riddled and cleaned and blackleaded every morning and the rooms swept and dusted. The laundry was done on Monday in the downstairs wash-house, whether or not there was any hope of getting it out to dry. Ironing was done on Tuesday, bedrooms turned out on Wednesday, living room on Thursday and all floors thoroughly scrubbed every Friday after baking day. On Saturdays Isa did her sewing and mending, and on Sundays she cooked the joint that Jack bought at reduced price from a butcher he knew. No one went to the kirk. Jack and Isa were not religious, though they brought the children up to know what was right and what was wrong. That was what mattered, eh?

'And where've you two girls been?' their mother asked now, when the sisters and Kester took off their damp coats and hats and went to the range to warm themselves. The table was already set for the meal, though that was Sylvie's job, and the vegetables prepared, though that was Ruth's job. Kester, of course, did not have a household job, because he was a worker. But when I go out to work, I bet I'm still peeling the potatoes when I come in,

11

thought Ruth, I'm sure that votes for women are never going to change that.

'We just went to the Italian shop,' said Sylvie, rubbing her fingers together. 'Marilena's dad gave us sweeties.'

Isa clicked her tongue in exasperation. She was now thirty-eight; attractive without good features, in the way of her daughters, with wavy brown hair recently bobbed, and quickly darting brown eyes.

'Eating sweeties just before your tea! Now, woe betide you if you leave that haddock I'm frying! And why could you no' have bought the sweeties, anyway?'

'Spent their pocket money,' said Kester, grinning. 'Same as I used to do. Never had two coppers to rub together by Wednesday!'

'What a way to go on!' Isa began bustling about the way she liked to do before a meal; calling on the girls to wash their hands, then help her get the vegetables on, flour the fish, put the plates to warm, their dad would be in before they knew it!

Everything was ready by the time Jack Millar, big and heavy-faced, came stamping in, shaking his coat, towelling his fair hair and cheering them all by his vitality, as he always did. Dad's like a fire you can warm your hands at, thought Ruth, as her mother dished up the haddock. No one else in the family was like him, it was a sort of gift, she supposed, and hoped suddenly, fiercely, that he would get his shop, and turn out to be as lucky as he always said he was. But she thought it wasn't likely.

'And how was Mr Rietti?' her mother was asking. 'I may be wrong, but that feller never looks very well to me.'

'He's got a cough,' Ruth told her. 'But he's always in the shop, so he can't be too bad.'

'Got into trouble tonight,' said Sylvie, giggling. 'Signora Rietti found out he'd been smoking. You should have heard the racket she made!'

'That signora!' Isa said sharply. 'Thinks far too much of herself. Has that whole family right under her thumb.'

'Italian mothers are like that,' Jack remarked, finding more mashed potato in the pan and scraping it on to his plate. 'They're the ones that say what's what.'

'Oh, well!' Isa laughed. 'Maybe that's no' a bad thing, eh?'

When the meal was over and the girls had washed up and made tea, Jack took up his evening paper and Kester said he'd go out for a bit, with one or two of the 'lads'.

'No' drinking?' his mother asked sharply.

'Och, what's a pint or two, Ma? A feller's got to go out sometimes!'

'Lucky to have the money,' Jack remarked. He tapped his paper. 'Seen the latest unemployment figures?'

Kester's face darkened. 'Aye, I feel bad. But what can I do? I mean, it'll no' do the unemployed any good if I just sit around at home, will it?'

Jack looked at his wife. 'Seventeen,' he murmured. 'Canna blame the laddie, Isa.'

She shrugged. 'All right, then, Kester. But no' coming in when we're all asleep and being sick all over the place, mind.'

He leaped up, grinning. 'You'll no' hear a thing, Ma, I promise, and I'll no' be sick because I canna afford to drink enough for that.'

'Just as well!' she called after him, as he grabbed his coat and was away before she could change her mind.

'Kester always gets his own way,' said Sylvie, after a pause. 'Boys are always the favourites.'

'What rubbish!' cried her mother, picking up her knitting and beginning to count stitches. 'Where'd you get these daft ideas?'

'Marilena says it's the same for her. Nicco can do just what he likes but she's no' allowed to do anything.'

'Nicco's older than Marilena, that's why he has more freedom.'

'I'm no' so sure,' said Jack, lighting his pipe. 'Italian girls are kept on a pretty tight rein. Their folks seem terrified of letting 'em out o' their sight. That's why they marry 'em off young, so they needn't worry any more.'

'Well, you two girls are no' marrying young, if I've anything to do with it,' said Isa. 'See a bit o' life first, eh?' Her face changed,

13

as she bent over the heel of the sock she was turning. 'If you can,' she added, after a moment.

There was a silence while they all thought of girls seeing life and of how unlikely that was. Even Sylvie, at twelve, knew that you needed money to see a bit of life, and money was what no one had. No one they knew, anyway.

'Are there any jobs in that paper, Dad?' asked Ruth, clearing her throat.

'Ah, Ruthie, you're no' really going out to work?' Jack was hunting for the adverts page. 'I think of you as a wee lassie, still.'

'She is a wee lassie,' said Isa. 'But you ken how things are.'

'I don't mind about no' staying on at school,' Ruth murmured without truth. 'Plenty of girls are leaving at my age. Renata's going to work in her dad's café. She's looking forward to it.'

Isa's brown eyes filled with sudden tears. 'Renata's different from you, Ruth. She's been looking forward to leaving school since she started. But you could've done well. Been a secretary, or a teacher or something.'

'I might still do that later on.' Ruth began looking down the jobs column with her father. 'Let's see what there is, anyway.'

Jack stabbed his forefinger at a couple of items. 'Shop vacancies there. How much are they paying?'

'Experience required' read Ruth aloud. 'Minimum age, sixteen. No good to me. The offices usually ask for sixteen-year-olds, as well.'

'There's a kitchen maid wanted,' said Sylvie, reading over her shoulder 'You could always be a maid, Ruth.'

'Over ma dead body!' cried Isa. 'Och, I'm no having a daughter of mine running herself into the ground for some daft rich woman! A factory job'd be better than that!'

'Well, I don't leave school till December,' said Ruth. 'I'll be sure to find something by then.'

'Aye, sure to.' Isa folded up her knitting and stood up. 'But away to bed with you girls, now. You've school in the morning.'

Jack put his pipe in an ashtray and yawned. 'How about another cup of tea, then, if you're putting the kettle on?'

'If I'm putting the kettle on!' she cried fondly. 'Och, Jack, you're a devil for tea!'

'Better than beer.'

'Aye. Oh, now you've made me think about Kester. I worry about him, Jack. He drinks more than you ever did.'

'He's young, it's what all young lads like to do. Give over worrying.'

'You know what can happen if a fellow takes to drink.'

'He's not going to take to drink, Isa. Now you go and put the kettle on and give us one of thae shortbreads you made, eh?'

'I was thinking you could take 'em over to Aunt Addie. It's your Sunday for going.'

Once a month, Jack visited his aunt in Glasgow. She was his mother's only sister and his only relative, for his parents had died when he was a boy and his brothers, less lucky than Jack himself, had not come back from the Great War. Very occasionally, he would take the family with him to Glasgow, but that was five rail fares instead of one, and Aunt Addie these days was a wee bit crotchety and said young folk got on her nerves. It was better all round if he visited her himself, and that suited her, he'd always been her favourite.

'Ah, come on,' he said now. 'You can spare a coupla bits, eh? I'd get wrong for saying it, but your baking's better than anything we sell, Isa.'

'Oh, best butter, you know what to say!' she cried, laughing, and went to make his tea.

'Do you no' wish we had a bathroom?' asked Sylvie, as she and Ruth shiveringly prepared for bed.

Ruth said she did wish it. There was nothing more fiddling and tedious than having to help Ma fill the hip bath every Friday night with water that was never really hot. Kester had Saturday, Ma and Dad had other nights, och, there was always somebody pulling that old bath around the flat!

'When I grow up,' Sylvie said with decision, 'I'm going to marry a man with a bathroom in his house. The Italians have got one, you ken.'

'Oh, well, maybe you'll marry Nicco!' Ruth said with a laugh.

Sylvie laughed, too. She couldn't imagine marrying Nicco, or anyone, really. 'No, but if they can have one, why can't we?'

'I suppose we might one day. When our ship comes in.'

'What ship?' asked Sylvie.

It was some hours later that Ruth, suddenly waking, heard Kester coming home. There now, he'd banged the door and the Dougalls on the ground floor would be sure to complain! Never missed a chance, did they, to come up and start moaning to Ma about something her family'd done? Ruth sat up, listening to her sister's quiet breathing. She couldn't tell whether her brother had been sick or not, but one thing was for sure, he'd fallen up the stairs.

Chapter Four

Guido Rietti called in early the next morning, to see if Kester was ready to go to the biscuit factory. He often liked to come in, see them all, pull the girls' hair ribbons and treat Isa to a display of courtly manners. Sylvie was of the opinion that he was handsomer than his cousin, Nicco, and perhaps he was, with curly black hair and the strangely blue eyes he'd inherited from his mother, but Ruth thought him a bit – well, she didn't know. Couldn't find the right word. 'Flashy?' suggested Kester, and that was it, that was the word. But Kester and Guido got on well enough, even if they were not particularly close. Guido, for instance, had not been one of Kester's drinking companions the night before, and could not help grinning at Kester's white face and refusal to look at his porridge.

'Serves you right!' cried Isa. 'Coming in late and waking us all up and getting me in the wrong with the Dougalls again!'

'Aye, should learn to hold your drink,' said Jack, who was walking about, still shaving. 'See Guido here, he'd never over indulge, eh?'

'He drinks plenty, only it's wine, no' beer,' muttered Kester, pulling on his coat. 'Och, I'll away. Maybe I'll feel better in the fresh air.'

'No' want a cup of tea, Guido?' asked Isa, smiling at him, but Guido said, no, they'd probably be late clocking on as it was. The two young men left the flat, Guido lightly running down the stairs on dancer's feet (he loved dancing), Kester following, more slowly and more painfully, as Guido grinned.

'Come on, old man, shall I take your arm?' he asked, as Kester scowled, but then a knock on the outer door made him halt 'and wipe his brow.

'Postie,' he muttered. But it was, in fact, a telegraph boy.

Ever since the Great War, telegrams had struck fear into everyone's heart, and Kester, though he could remember very little of the war himself, still felt a pang of dread as he looked at the boy on the doorstep.

'Who's it for?' he asked hoarsely.

'Millar,' sang the boy. 'Telegram for Millar.'

Kester looked at Guido. 'Who could be sending us a telegram?' he asked, knowing it was a foolish question, and as Guido shrugged, the boy laughed.

'Couldnae tell you!' he said impudently. 'Come on, mister, I've no' got all day. Want to send an answer?'

'Watch the lip,' snapped Kester, reluctantly taking the little orange envelope. 'Guido, you'd better get on, I'll have to give this to ma dad.'

'Don't worry, I'll be late with you.'

'Wait there,' Kester told the boy.

Up the stair, Jack had finished shaving and was eating porridge with the girls, while Isa sliced bread and set out jam. 'Back again?' she asked irritably, as Kester appeared, but at the sight of the telegram in his hand, turned pale.

'What's that?' asked Jack, though he could see perfectly well what it was. He stood up, as Ruth and Sylvie stared, spoons suspended, and Guido hovered in the doorway.

'Telegram, Dad,' said Kester. 'The boy's waiting for an answer.'

'It must be Addie,' Isa whispered. 'I mean, who else?'

'Why would Addie send us a telegram?' asked Jack, holding it. 'Something must have happened.'

'Open it, Dad!' cried Sylvie. 'Tell us what it says!'

'Here's a knife, slit it,' said Isa as Jack hesitated, but he opened the envelope with his large thumb and slowly lowered his eyes to its short message.

'Regret to inform you,' he read, and Isa put her hand to her heart, remembering the war. Her brother, Sam, had been killed on the Somme only a week after Jack's older brother, Don. And then there'd been Ian, only a year younger than Jack – he'd died at the third battle of Ypres. Never a day passed without Isa thinking it would be Jack's turn next, but he'd come though without a scratch. Lucky Jack. Except when he thought of those white crosses that were not his.

'Regret to inform you,' Jack said again, clearing his throat. 'Mrs Collier died yesterday.'

'Aunt Addie, did I no' tell you?' cried Isa, as the others looked at one another. 'What else does it say, Jack?'

'Please contact at your earliest convenience.' Jack raised his eyes. 'That's all. It's signed Fordyce. He's the lawyer.'

'Aunt Addie had a lawyer?' asked Kester, astonished.

'Aye. Well, it was Uncle George who took him on, when he sold the dairy, but that was years ago.' Jack smiled wryly. 'Used to think some of that money would've come to me, but poor old Addie lived too long, eh? Kester, slip down and give that boy a copper or two. Tell him no answer.'

'Where's the coppers, then?' asked Kester.

The girls didn't want to go to school, it was all too exciting. Of course, they were sorry about Aunt Addie, but she was a shadowy figure to them, and so old maybe she wasn't sorry to depart. And now there was the telegram and talk of lawyers and Dad having to think how he could get to Glasgow.

'Will we have to wear black?' asked Sylvie, who was always interested in what she wore.

'Of course not!' her mother told her. 'I'll wear ma black coat to the funeral, but black armbands'll do for you.' She looked at Jack, who had left his breakfast and was striding up and down the living room, thinking things out. 'Will there be enough for the funeral?' she asked in a low voice.

'Och, I should think so. She'll have had a bit put by, eh?' Jack ran his hands through his thick fair hair. 'Folk do, you ken.'

'You should've asked her, Jack. Discussed things.'

'You ken what she was like. Never one for talking about her affairs.'

'Well, if there's nothing, we'll just have to do the best we can. Girls, get your coats on! Have you made your piece for break-time?'

'I'm no' having her buried on the council,' said Jack, with a sudden sob, as his daughters stared in alarm. Dad crying? The tears came to their own eyes. 'She was ma mother's sister and always good to me.'

'Aye, she was.' Isa went to him and put her arms round him. 'Like I say, we'll do what we can. When'll you go to Glasgow?'

'I could go today. It's early closing. Best get things started, eh? Besides, I want – I want to see her.'

Amongst the children progressing along Ginger Street on their way to school, Ruth and Sylvie spotted Millie MacAllan and Vi Smith. They hurried after them, bursting to tell their news.

'Our auntie's died!' cried Sylvie importantly. 'We're going to wear black armbands.'

Millie, who had not yet had her hair bobbed, swung her dark plait to and fro and stared with interest at the sisters, while Vi, large, fair and solid, asked:

'What's she die of?'

That was a poser. Ruth and Sylvie realised that they didn't know.

'She just slipped away,' answered Ruth, who had heard the phrase and thought it sounded very peaceful and right for Aunt Addie. 'She was quite old.'

'Think she'll leave you onything?'

'Shouldnae be so nosey, Vi!' cried Millie. 'Aye, but will she?'

'She might,' Sylvie replied coolly. 'Our dad's going to Glasgow to see the lawyers.'

Lawyers. The girls fell silent. They didn't know much about lawyers, except that where they were was money.

'Must've had something to leave,' said Vi, at last.

'There's Marilena and Renata!' cried Sylvie, running ahead.

'And Nicco!' called Ruth, following.

In the harsh wind, even the handsome noses of the Riettis were slightly red and their faces blue, as they waited for the sisters to reach them.

'Our auntie's died, we're going to have black armbands,' Sylvie burst out again.

'Oh, how sad!' the Italians cried, with a sympathy that Ruth knew was genuine. She had learned that the family was all important to Italians and that any death within it would be cause for true grief. Black was worn for long periods at a time, in fact widows often wore it all their lives, and funerals were very elaborate.

'Please give your mother and father our deepest sympathy,' Nicco said gravely. 'We'll be thinking of them at this time. When is the funeral to be?'

'We're no' sure. Dad's gone to Glasgow to arrange it.'

'We'll all be going, though,' Sylvie said hastily. 'Even if we have to have a day off school.'

'Of course you will go!' cried Renata. 'Why, they can't refuse, when it's a funeral!'

Feeling rather a fraud, Ruth said quietly that Aunt Addie was their great-aunt, they hadn't known her very well.

'No matter,' said Renata firmly. 'You have to pay your last respects, it's only right.'

'We must go,' said Nicco, 'But please don't forget to give your parents our sympathy, will you?'

He was looking at Ruth, rather than Sylvie, his dark eyes so soft and gentle, she felt uneasy taking his compassion. Still, it was true, she had lost a relative and, apart from her mother's sisters in Canada, that relative was the last one her family had. The Italians would scarcely be able to understand that. They had family just down the road at the café, as well as many relations still in Italy, Marilena said, and kept up with them all. Would I want so many relatives? Ruth wondered. She had a sudden image of the family as something warm and comforting like a scarf around your neck. But what if it were too warm? Too comforting? What if you wanted to loosen it sometimes? She made a little face, as she and Sylvie watched the Riettis hurrying away. To have just Ma and Dad, Kester and Sylvie, that was enough. Until she married, of course. If she married. There were a lot of unmarried women about, since the Great War took all the men, but they were of an older generation. Ruth had never really thought about it before, but now she felt sure she would marry. What a strange time to think of it, though, with Aunt Addie dead! Especially when she should be thinking about a job.

Chapter Five

Kester came home early that afternoon, complaining that he didn't feel well, but his sisters knew that he was really wanting to see if Dad was back from Glasgow. He wasn't.

'He won't be back yet.' Isa explained, setting out the ingredients for dumplings. They could already smell the simmering stew all over the flat. 'He's that much to do, you ken, and the train to catch.'

'So, what train do you think he'll get?' asked Kester.

'How can I say? What's all the interest, anyway?' Isa gave her son a sharp glance. 'That lawyer's never going to tell your dad anything today!'

'He did ask Dad to see him at his earliest convenience,' said Kester, looking round the kitchenette for something to eat. 'Any biscuits, Ma?'

'And you work in a biscuit factory? Why'd you no' bring some of the rejects back, then?'

'Sorry, couldn't face them. Feel better now. Is there any short-bread, then?'

Isa's face puckered a little. 'I made it for poor Addie,' she murmured. 'Makes you realise, eh? She'll never eat ma short-bread again.'

'I'll just have a cup of tea,' Kester said hurriedly. 'While we're waiting.'

'Yes, well, if it's your dad you're waiting for, as I say, he might have nothing to tell you.' Ida went into the living room with her teapot and made the tea from the kettle singing on the range. 'And

23

I don't like this hanging round, waiting to see what poor Addie's left. It's no' seemly, Kester.'

'Aye, that's true.' He sighed and took up the teapot to pour himself tea. 'Probably hasn't left us anything, anyway.'

'Left your dad anything, you mean. And how about giving us some tea, while you're at it, Kester?'

'Ma,' exclaimed Ruth 'I think I hear Dad!'

'Jack!' cried Isa. 'Is that you?'

'It'd better be,' he answered, standing in the doorway, a tall, golden man in a damp overcoat, carrying his hat in his hand. 'Else some stranger's got our key.'

'Dad, how'd you get back so soon?' asked Kester, as the girls ran to hug their father and take his coat.

'Just managed to catch the early train.' Jack was still standing in the same spot, looking at his family as they looked back at him. There was something different about him, they couldn't say what. Perhaps it was his eyes that were shining, or even glittering. Or it might have been that he was very slightly trembling. When before had they ever seen their father tremble? Why didn't he speak to them? Tell them what had been happening?

'Well,' asked Isa, wiping her hands on her apron. 'Did you see her, then?'

'Aye, I saw her.'

'And how was she?'

'Very peaceful. It was a very peaceful death. She just slipped away in the night.'

Ruth's face went red and she bit her lip. How had she known? She hadn't known, of course, it was just a guess, that that was how Aunt Addie had died. Yet it had been so right for her.

'And did you see the lawyer?'

'Aye, I did.'

'Oh, for heaven's sake, Jack, can you no' spit it out?' cried Isa. 'What did he tell you? If anything?'

'He told me I was executor and sole beneficiary.' Jack suddenly began to walk up and down the living room, as though powered by some outside force, rubbing his hands together, shaking his fair head. 'Did you hear me, Isa? Sole beneficiary!'

'What's a beneficiary?' whispered Sylvie.

'It means I get everything ma poor aunt had to leave,' Jack told her, suddenly swinging round. 'Me, alone.'

'And did she have anything to leave?' asked Isa fearfully.

'She did.' Jack stood still again. He ran his hands over his face. 'She had seven hundred and fifty pounds. Aye, that's the sum. Seven hundred and fifty pounds. Can you believe it?'

'Ma,' said Kester, 'Here's a chair. You look like you're going to faint.'

Some time went by before they could all take it in. Jack said of course the will had not been officially read, but as he was the only one concerned, the lawyer had told him he might as well know what was in it, in case he'd had any worries about funeral bills, or anything of that sort.

'No worries now!' exclaimed Jack, and Isa echoed, 'no worries,' though she didn't yet look happy.

'I just canna think where Addie got it from,' she moaned, as the girls stood quietly together and Kester slumped back on the couch, for all the world as though they'd had bad news instead of good. Jack sat down and took Isa's hand in his.

'It was Uncle George's money. Came from the sale of the dairy when he retired. Remember? I thought Aunt Addie would've spent it by now. She never did. The lawyer invested it for her, and she only spent the interest.'

'That's what she's been living on, all these years?'

'Aye, that and her pension. Never needed much, she told Mr Fordyce.' Jack looked down at Isa's hand and turned her wedding ring round and round. 'Feel bad, Isa. I wish she'd had a bit of fun with some of that money.'

'She was never the sort for fun, Jack. Everybody said your Uncle George was a catch, with his own dairy and that, but she was happy just living a quiet life, eh? I always said, money was of no interest to Addie, and seems I was right. Because she kept it all for you.'

'I just wish I could thank her,' said Jack, after a pause. 'Och, I'm away—'

Taking out his handkerchief, he went out of the living room, striding along in that strange, jittery way he seemed to have adopted, and they heard him go into the bedroom and close the door.

'It's the shock,' said Kester. 'That's what's hit him.'

'It's grief,' Isa corrected. 'Aye, he was fond of Addie, you ken. It gives you mixed feelings, eh? To lose somebody and take their money?'

They were all very subdued, as they went about the business of getting tea ready, with even Kester giving a hand, but when the stew and dumplings were on the table and Jack was back, looking more his old self, even if his eyes were red, they began to accept what had happened to them.

'We're rich!' cried Kester.

'I'd no' say that,' said Isa. 'No' *rich*.'

'Rich for us, I mean.'

'I'll be able to buy ma shop now, anyway,' said Jack. 'And have something over, all right.'

'Dad, your shop!' cried Ruth. 'I never realised!'

'Aye, ma ship's come in, at last.'

'So that's what folk mean,' Sylvie murmured. 'When your ship comes in, you're rich.'

'And how often does it happen?' asked Isa. 'Jack, you are lucky, eh? Just like you always say. But I keep thinking of all the poor bairns out there, with their dads out of work.'

'Aye. No' much we can do, Isa.'

'We should do something, Jack.'

'Let me get ma shop sorted out first.'

'It's a poor time to be starting out, Jack, when we're in a depression.'

'I'll make a success of it, Isa. Leave it to me. I'll be like Sir Thomas Lipton. He started out with nothing and ended up with millions. A string of shops, a knighthood, racing yachts, the lot! Aye, you'll see! Sir Jack Millar, that'll be me! No, Sir John, of course, that's ma real name. And you'll be Lady Millar, Isa. No, I'm serious. It could happen, eh?'

'Best get your one shop first,' said Isa dryly, but then she burst into tears and hugged him, and the girls shed a few tears too, while Kester pretended his lip wasn't trembling, but had to get a hankie anyway. They were finally thinking about going to bed, though they knew they wouldn't sleep, when Denny Mowat from the top floor knocked on their door and said did they no' ken there were some flowers for them on the stair?

'Flowers?' Ida repeated, looking at the spray of white chrysanthemums wrapped in tissue paper. 'Who can have sent us flowers, then?'

'Ma, there's a card,' said Ruth, and read it aloud:

'To the Millar Family, from the Rietti Family, with deepest sympathy.' She looked at her mother, with more tears welling in her eyes. 'Ma, is that no' kind? We told Nicco and Marilena about Aunt Addie and their mother must have got these for us.'

'Ah, it's lovely, Ruth, it's just lovely! I feel bad now I ever said anything about the signora. Sylvie, find me a jar to put these in, will you?' Isa blew her nose. 'What a day this has been, eh? Shall we ever forget it?'

'I shan't forget Addie,' said Jack, in a low voice.

'We'll none of us forget Addie,' Isa told him.

Chapter Six

It was difficult for the Millars to believe the next morning that they hadn't dreamed the whole thing, but of course they couldn't all have dreamed the same dream, could they? No, it was true, all right. Jack had the figures from the lawyer, written down on headed paper for them all to read, and they did read them, over and over again, to make sure. There was no doubt about it, they were no longer have-nots, they were haves. They were privileged, they were lucky, or, at least, Jack was lucky, and his luck was their luck. As they ate their breakfast and went through their usual morning routines, his family thought their father seemed more golden than ever.

The only snag was that he had sworn them all to secrecy. They were not to tell anyone what had happened, until he said the word. Isa didn't mind, she could bide her time, before seeing the astonishment on the faces of Mrs Dougall and the rest, when they heard she'd come into money. But the young people were bitterly disappointed.

'Ah, Dad!' cried Kester, who had been looking forward to stunning all his colleagues at the factory with his news. 'That's too cruel!'

'Dad, I'll burst, if I have to keep it all a secret!' wailed Sylvie.

'Me, too,' said Ruth. She had been imagining what everyone would say, Millie, Vi, Renata, and all the girls at school, when they heard she was an heiress. Well, as good as. 'Why do we have to keep quiet, Dad?'

'Because I just want to wait until everything's all signed, sealed and delivered. Until probate's been granted and the money's legally mine.'

'Another new word,' sighed Sylvie. 'What's probate?'

'Like I say, it's when everything you've been left is legally yours. Handed over to you, with everything checked up and no doubts possible. That's when we can tell people.' Jack put on his coat, for he was going to work as usual. 'And when I'll tell Tomlinson's, and all. I'm no' going to tell them before, or I might be out on ma ear before I'm ready!'

'Could they sack you, just for inheriting some money?' cried Isa.

'No, but for thinking of opening a rival shop, they could. And I've always said that's what I'd do, if I ever came into anything.' Jack combed his hair at the little mirror by the door. 'Not that I'll be opening up in this area. I'd never be such a fool as to set maself up against Tomlinson's!'

'So, we'll be looking further afield?'

'Sure, we will.' Jack smiled back at his family. 'Remember, you folks – never a word to anyone!'

Ruth helped Sylvie to clear the table, her eyes troubled.

'What did you and Dad mean, about going further afield?' she asked her mother.

'Why, you know very well what we meant! Dad explained it. He'd no' be keen to set up in this part where he'd be up against Tomlinson's.'

'So, where's he planning to go?'

'He's got to find the right place. Could be anywhere.' Isa was rattling dishes by the sink. 'Is that table cleared, Sylvie? Where's the jam? I canna see the jam.'

'Here's the jam,' said Sylvie. 'Shall we do our piece now?'

'Never mind our piece,' cried Ruth. 'I want to know if we have to leave Ginger Street?'

'Honestly, what a girl! I thought you were supposed to be the bright one, Ruth! Of course we'll be leaving Ginger Street! Dad wants to find premises with a flat above and be right on the spot. That's the best way.'

'I don't want to leave Ginger Street,' Ruth said, after a pause.

'I bet you don't want to, do you, Sylvie? All our friends are here.'

Sylvie considered. 'I wouldn't mind if we had a really nice flat at the new place. With a bathroom!'

'But what about Marilena and everyone? You'd never see them again.'

'Of course you'd see your friends again,' said Isa. 'You could come over any time to see them.'

'It wouldn't be the same, Ma, you know that.'

Isa gave an exasperated shake of her head. 'Honestly, Ruth, I'm surprised at you. Here's your dad got the most wonderful good fortune, and all you can do is whinge on about Ginger Street. It's just a street like any other. You'll soon get used to the new place, 'specially when you make friends at the new school.'

'What new school?'

'Well, have you no' realised you'll be able to stay on at school now? Aye, now there's something you wanted, eh? You'll be able to take your Leaving Certificate and get a good job, so perhaps that'll stop you looking like a wet weekend!'

Ruth stared at her mother, in baffled dismay. She felt that what she wanted was being given to her with one hand, and taken away with the other. To stay on at school, not to have to look for a job, yes, that would be wonderful. But to have to leave Ginger Street, leave the school she knew, start again somewhere else – she didn't see how she could face it.

'You never told me I could stay on at school,' she said slowly.

'No, I was meaning to, though. Stands to reason we can do without your bit of money now, and it was what you wanted, eh? To do your certificate?'

'It's just what I wanted. I'm really happy, Ma.' Ruth kissed her mother's cheek, then stood back. 'But I still don't see why I can't get the tram to my old school from the new place. I'm pretty well grown up now, after all.'

'Grown up!' scoffed Sylvie.

'Well, old enough to leave school! That's what I was going to do, wasn't it? So why should I no' be old enough to go on the tram?'

'Your dad and me don't want you trailing across the city every day, Ruth, and there's an end to it. If we did manage to stay near here, well, that'd be different, but I can tell you now that your dad's thinking of Trinity.'

'Trinity? That's miles away!'

'Aye, but he wants a good area, some place where folk'll want quality stuff and there'll no' be too many out o' work. There's some nice parts to Trinity, I reckon he could do well. Now, no more arguing.' Isa sighed. 'I've enough on ma plate without arguments. I've to go to Glasgow today, to start making arrangements for the funeral.'

The funeral was held a week later, on a wild, gusty day that sent the trees round the Glasgow kirk bending and creaking, and blew the veiled top hat from the head of one of the undertakers. It could have been comical, to see him chasing after it amongst the gravestones, but no one felt like laughing. Jack and Isa, as chief mourners, were weighed down by grief and a certain guilt, that they had done so well out of poor Addie's death. The young people, in their black armbands, were too overcome by the solemnity of the occasion to find relief in anything. This was the first funeral they had ever attended and they found it all too harrowing. The solemn words, the doleful music, the thought of little Aunt Addie going into that plot with her dead husband, and with only three wreaths to comfort her, too.

'Only three wreaths, Isa,' Jack murmured. 'Doesn't seem much of a send-off for a lifetime.'

'Well, there was one from us, one from the lawyer, and one from her neighbours. I don't think that's too bad, Jack. A lot of her friends have already passed away.' Isa looked around at the other mourners. 'And quite a few folk turned up, Mr Fordyce and all. Could have been worse, you ken.'

'I suppose so,' muttered Jack. 'At least our wreath was a big one.'

'The best we could get.' Isa felt for his hand. 'It's nice we've been able to do things right for her. Try to think of that.'

After the burial, there were refreshments laid on at a small hotel near the kirk. Most people came back, glad to be in somewhere warm out of the biting wind and to enjoy the tea, sandwiches and fruit cake that so cheered up Kester and his sisters. They were amazed to see the difference in the mourners, once the ceremonies were over. How they talked, and even laughed, as they tucked into the food, had more tea, accepted eventually a glass of sherry, and only reluctantly took their departure.

'Why, it's just like a party!' cried Sylvie. 'Nobody's crying!'

'Aye, folk cry more at weddings than funerals,' said her mother. 'Doesn't mean they're no' sad, they're just easing off because the funeral's over. Terrible strain, you ken.'

'That's true,' said Jack with feeling.

On the train home he told them that, even though probate was some way off, he might start doing some preliminary looking round for premises.

'In Trinity?' Ruth asked mournfully.

'Maybe. But I'm keeping an open mind.'

'I wish you'd keep an open mind about Ginger Street.'

'Ruth!' warned her mother, 'don't start!'

She picked up an evening paper that someone had left, and pointed to the latest dismal news, of firms closing and men being laid off. 'You should be grateful for what you have, Ruth.'

'I know, I am.' Ruth lowered her eyes. 'It's just that I'm scared, thinking of moving to a new school and everything.'

'It'll be the same for me!' cried Sylvie.

'Aye, it's difficult,' agreed Jack. 'Nobody likes being new. But, doing your certificate, Ruth, that means a lot, eh?'

'Yes, it means everything. I'm sorry, I won't say any more.'

Jack glanced at his son. 'And I've been wondering, Kester, if you'd be interested in coming in with me, when I get ma shop?'

'You mean, give up the biscuit factory?' asked Kester.

'You'd no' want to?'

'I'd do it like a shot!' Kester grinned. 'When do I start?'

Jack beamed. 'Soon as I find what I want. Pass me that paper, Isa. Let's see if there's anything in the adverts today.'

Ruth, looking at her own reflection in the compartment window, listened to the clickety-click of the train and brooded over what her mother had said. Of course she was grateful for what she had, and specially for what Dad had, too, but she couldn't help feeling as she did about leaving Ginger Street and her school and her friends. Why could Ma no' see that? It was true, then, what Renata sometimes said. Parents didn't understand.

'Anybody want a butterscotch?' asked Kester.

'Oh, did you bring some?' cried Sylvie. 'Yes, please!'

'I wouldn't mind,' said Ruth.

Taking comfort in the butterscotch, she looked out now beyond her reflection into the darkness of the landscape travelling past. How nice it would be if she could have just told Nicco that she would be staying on at school, working for her Leaving Certificate as he was. Would he be pleased for her? Ma said Italians thought girls ought not to have careers, but just stay at home until they got married. Ma wasn't always right, though. She'd once said Italians kept themselves to themselves, yet look how friendly they'd always been in Ginger Street! Look at the flowers the signora had sent in sympathy! Ruth finished the butterscotch and yawned, suddenly realising that she was very tired. It had been a tiring and rather frightening day, and she was glad it was almost over.

'Edinburgh!' cried her father's voice, very loud, at her ear, and she sat up with a start. 'Come on, Ruthie, no sleeping till we get home!'

Such was the change that had come to their lives, Jack took a taxi for them from the station. A taxi! Sylvie was beside herself. Oh, how she wished it wasn't dark and people in Ginger Street could see them coming home by taxi!

Chapter Seven

Shortly after Hogmanay, Jack found what he wanted: a grocer's shop in Fielding Road, in the centre of the Trinity area of the city, rather run-down as its elderly owner was failing in health and ready to retire, but with excellent potential. Close to a chemist's and a butcher's, it was also close to good solid property – semi-detached villas and privately owned flats – from where Jack could expect the kind of customer who would patronise his style of high-class grocery. For that was what he had in mind, he told Isa. Not just your ordinary run-of-the-mill stuff, but best quality hams and bacon, teas, coffees, speciality cheeses, all the kind of thing you could get at Logie's in Princes Street, but at lower prices. Millar's was going to be a famous name in Edinburgh provisions, no doubt of it!

'What's the flat like?' asked Isa. 'There is a flat, over the shop, I hope?'

'There is, Isa. You just come and see it!'

She was impressed. They all were, even Ruth, who had made up her mind not to be, whatever it was like. Old Mr Cameron, who owned it, had already departed, but Jack had the keys from the lawyer and showed them round. There was a long living room, with a proper fireplace instead of a range, which was in the kitchen. There were two good sized bedrooms and a small one that would do for Kester. And there was a bathroom!

'Oh, Ma, it's lovely!' cried Sylvie. 'Dad, can we come? Can we really live here?'

'We can, we can.' Jack's eyes were on Isa, who was walking round, opening cupboards, sniffing the air for damp.

'What do you think, Isa? he asked cautiously.

'Needs a good clean, Jack. When did anybody blacklead that range? But it's no' bad. Better than I thought.' She smiled. 'In fact, it's nice. I like it.'

'I like it,' Kester declared. 'I think it's grand. A step up from Ginger Street, eh?'

'We used to think Ginger Street was a step up, too,' said Ruth. Her father looked at her.

'So what do you think of this place, then?' he asked softly.

She hesitated, not wanting to give in too quickly. But what could she say? It was perfect.

'I like it, too,' she said at last. 'It's just right for us.'

'There you are,' cried Isa. 'I knew you'd see sense in the end!'

'But what about the schools?' Ruth asked quickly. 'Where can we go to school?'

'There's a junior school for Sylvie and Fielding Secondary for you,' Jack said eagerly. 'Just round the corner from the shop, couldn't be nearer.'

'I bet there's a tram stop round the corner as well,' said Ruth. 'I could easily get the tram to my old school.'

'Oh dear, oh dear, you don't give up, do you?' sighed Isa. 'Never mind the tram, Ruth you'd need two, anyway. This is a grand place to live, and the school'll be a grand school, too. You'll see.'

'You will, Ruthie,' added Sylvie, taking her sister's hand.

Everyone was looking at Ruth and her face was flushing, her lower lip trembling. She knew she'd lost and felt rather a fool, for here was Sylvie, two years younger than she was, and not minding at all about facing a new school. But then school didn't mean as much to Sylvie as it did to Ruth; she would be leaving just as soon as she could.

'All right,' Ruth said at last. 'I'll go to Fielding Secondary. It'll be easier.'

'There's ma Ruthie!' cried Isa and hugged her tightly, while Jack, grinning in the background, rattled coins in his trouser pocket, and said he'd take them all to the Fielding Café. That was round the corner, too.

*   *   *

'But will our offer be accepted for the shop?' Isa asked anxiously, as she poured tea in the café. 'There might be other folk in for it.'

'No, it's been on the market a while. The lawyer says I can get it cheap. Old Cameron's already bought his bungalow in Corstorphine.'

'So, why's it been sticking?' asked Kester, buttering a scone. 'Hard times, eh?'

'I suppose so.' Jack glanced at Isa. 'All right, I know this is the wrong time for new ventures, but I've got the money now to do what I want to do. I canna pass this chance up, and that's all there is to it.'

'All right, Jack, we understand,' said Isa soothingly. 'Folk'll always want groceries, whatever happens. At least, some folk will. Try the scones, they're nearly as good as mine.'

'When do we get this probate through?' asked Kester. 'I mean, when can we tell folks about the money?'

'The lawyer says all the paperwork'll be finished this coming week.' Jack smiled. 'Then you can tell your pals, Kester.'

'And I can tell Marilena!' cried Sylvie.

And Renata, thought Ruth. And Millie and Vi and Nicco. She didn't know why, but she felt quite a little stab of excitement at the thought of telling Nicco.

Chapter Eight

In fact, Ruth and Sylvie didn't tell anyone. At least, not about the money. They were all ready with their news, almost had the words in their mouths, as they caught up with Millie and Vi, trudging to school, until they saw that Millie had been crying.

'What's up?' asked Ruth, feeling a knot already tightening in her stomach.

'Her dad's lost his job,' said Vi curtly.

Millie found a damp hankie in her coat pocket and wiped her eyes. She didn't look at anyone, but stared straight ahead down Ginger Street. Vi took her arm, but Millie shook it away. Ruth and Sylvie exchanged glances. They knew that Millie's father had worked in a small factory off the Dalkeith Road, and that, like the Millars, the family had moved to their present flat as a 'step up'. Now, what would happen? Millie would be leaving Ginger Street, too, but not for better things. There was nothing that could be said to comfort her. Nothing that would take away the dead look from her eyes, or lift her shoulders, hunched in her big sister's coat.

'He's sure to find something else,' Ruth said, knowing her words sounded hollow, knowing that they were.

Vi sniffed, and Millie gave her one sharp, disgusted glance, then returned to her study of Ginger Street. They all walked on in silence, the sisters longing, cravenly, to see someone else they knew but seeing no one, which was just the way of things when usually the street was filled with friends. As Millie and Vi trailed on through the slush, Ruth dropped back and caught Sylvie's arm.

'Don't say anything,' she said fiercely. 'Don't tell them about the money.'

'I wasn't going to!' cried Sylvie.

'No, well, maybe we'd better no' tell anyone just for now. We'll just say that we're flitting, eh?'

Sylvie nodded, her attractive little face looking pinched with cold and insight into other people's woes.

'I feel so bad for Millie,' she whispered. 'Don't you?'

'Yes.' Ruth was remembering her mother's words again. Told me to be grateful, she thought. Now I know what she meant. Because Millie wasn't one of those faceless people out there, the unemployed. She was Millie, their friend, and her dad had lost his job. Oh, but could she bear to feel grateful, not to be like Millie? Could she bear to be lucky? It was a relief when the bell began to ring and they were called into school.

At the end of the day, back in Ginger Street, they looked for Marilena and Nicco, but didn't see them. Ruth said she'd go and see Renata, who was now working in her father's café.

'You tell Ma that I'll be a bit late,' she told Sylvie, who of course said she wanted to come to the café too. No, Ruth was firm, they'd better not both be late.

'You can help Ma and sweeten her up. I really do want to see Renata. Not to tell her about the money, just that we're leaving. She is a special friend, after all.'

Sylvie having agreed to oblige, with ill grace, Ruth ran down the street as fast as she could, though the slush was still lying and was in fact beginning to freeze, now that the temperature was dropping again. Ahead of her was Vittorio Rietti's café, as bright as a beacon in the January gloom, a place she liked as much as Roberto Rietti's shop, though it was only since Renata had begun work there that she had come to know it well. Now she pushed open the door and was at once absorbed into warmth and light and the delicious smell of sauces and pasta, garlic, and Italian sausages. What a splendid place to be on a cold January night, thought Ruth, and other people thought so too, for the café was packed, mostly with Italians. Though young Scots office workers were customers at lunchtime, evenings were the time when Italians liked to bring their children, for no alcohol was served, and the atmosphere was very different from the usual Scottish pub, where children would not be accepted in any case and women weren't particularly welcome either.

Why don't we ever come here? Ruth wondered, as she watched the children twirling their spaghetti and laughing, but she knew her folks would never eat Italian food, never in a million years. Italians were one thing, their food quite another.

'Ruth!' cried Renata's mother, Brigida, catching sight of her. 'How are you? *Come stai?*'

She and Renata were trying to teach Ruth a few words of Italian, and Ruth, after a moment or two, shyly replied,

'Er – *Molto bene, grazie.*'

'Very good, very good!' Brigida clapped her hands. She was a slim, live-wire of a woman, not at all Italian looking, for her hair was reddish-brown and her eyes – those eyes she had passed to Guido – were vivid blue, but then Renata, who had her father's dark good looks, said many Italians were fair and light-eyed. 'We are not all the same, Ruth, just as you Scots are not all the same. How boring that would be!'

'Is Renata here?' asked Ruth, smiling at Signor Vittorio Rietti, who had just appeared from the back with a tray of glasses and a plate of rolls.

'Ruth, hallo! You wish Renata? I will call her!' He shouted over his shoulder, 'Renata! Renata! Come quickly! Now, you have a drink, Ruth? You have lemonade? Tea?'

'*No, grazie,*' Ruth answered. 'I must go home.'

'Ah, some other time,' said Brigida. 'Here is Renata! Now, tell me, Ruth, what do you think of her hair?'

There had been a tremendous family row when Renata, true to her word, had taken her first wages and gone off to have her hair bobbed. Her mother had wept, her father had said it was the worst day of his life, to see his daughter's beautiful hair chopped into a boy's haircut. Guido had said a girl should look like a girl, and Aunt Carlotta hadn't spoken to her niece for a week. But as Renata came bouncing towards her, Ruth honestly thought that she had the right sort of face for the new cut, and that it matched her character as well as her face.

39

'I think Renata's hair looks lovely,' she told Brigida. 'The style really suits her.'

'Of course it does,' Renata said briskly. 'Hallo, Ruth! What brings you here?'

'The thing is, her Aunt Carlotta blames me!' cried Brigida, before Ruth could answer. She struck her breast. 'Me! As though I could stop my daughter doing what she wanted! Renata has never listen to me, never!'

'Yes, I do listen to you, Mamma,' Renata said, putting her arm around her mother's shoulders. 'I just don't always do what you tell me. Ruth, I've got to take some ravioli to that table – wait for me, eh?'

As she expertly moved between tables with her tray, Ruth watched with admiration and some envy. Already, Renata seemed to have grown up, grown up and away, from a schoolgirl like herself. Was this what work did for you? But Ruth was staying on at school.

'I won't keep you, you're busy,' she told Renata quickly as soon as she arrived back at the counter. 'Now you're at work, I never see you, but I wanted to tell you that we're flitting from here.'

'Oh, no!' Renata's eyes were large on Ruth's face. 'Where to? Why?'

'Ma dad's got a grocery in Trinity. We're going to live over the shop.'

'Trinity? That's miles away!' Renata turned to her mother. 'Mamma, do you hear, Ruth's moving! Her dad is going to a shop in Trinity!'

Brigida widened her dazzling eyes. 'Ah, no, no! Ah, we shall miss you. Vittorio, Ruth's family is leaving Ginger Street! They are going to Trinity.'

He was taking an order, but turned to shake his head and murmur regrets. So far? To Trinity. Two tram rides, eh? But Ruth would come back? Come back to see them?

'Yes, yes, you will come back.' Renata put her hand on Ruth's shoulder. 'Or, we'll meet? On my half day? What about a job? Will you look for something round there?'

'I'm staying on at school,' Ruth answered, with some hesitation. 'Ma thinks they can let me, now.'

'Staying on at school?' Renata's eyes were bright with sudden intelligence. She knew about Aunt Addie's death, of course, and probably guessed that there had been some sort of inheritance, but she made no comment, only said that she was glad for Ruth, getting what she wanted.

'Me, I never wanted more school. I'm like Guido, just wanted to be out earning a few bob.'

'Where is Guido?' asked Ruth. 'He's no' helping tonight?'

'Helping? No! He says he's done enough at Gibb's, but I've worked all day too.' Renata shook her head in exasperation. 'Like he always is, he's down at the *fascio*. I love our club just like he does, but when do I get the chance to go?' She glanced at two new customers who had just come in and were studying the hand-written menu pinned on the door. 'Look, I have to serve these people, but you'll keep in touch, eh? And you'll come in to say goodbye?'

'Oh, yes, we'll no' be going for a few weeks.' Ruth gave Renata a hug and waved to her parents. 'I just wanted to tell you what was happening. Now, I'd better go, Ma's going to kill me, anyway, for being so late! *Arrivederci*!'

'*Arrivederci*!' the Riettis cried, and several diners waved and grinned as well, before Ruth let herself out into freezing Ginger Street and ran all the way home.

'What a time to come home!' cried Isa. 'I hope you've no' been eating anything at that café, Ruth, and spoiling your tea! What did you want to see Renata for, anyway?'

'Just to tell her we were leaving. No, I never had a bite and I'm starving, Ma. Can I do anything?'

'No, we've done everything,' Sylvie snapped. 'You're so late, Ruth! Kester's already in and Dad'll be here any minute.'

'And I suppose you told Renata about the money, did you?' asked Isa, as Ruth washed her hands and slowly dried them. 'Aye, it'll be all over the street in no time.'

'I never told her about the money. I've no' told anyone.'

'Nor me,' said Sylvie.

Their mother stared at them, truly astonished for once.

41

'Why, I thought you were dying to tell folk! I thought it was all you wanted to do!'

'Millie MacAllan's dad has lost his job,' Ruth said, after a pause. She hung up the towel on its nail. 'We didn't feel like saying anything.'

Isa turned away, biting her lip. 'There's your dad's step,' she said quietly. 'I'll dish up.'

Chapter Nine

Ruth and Sylvie still hadn't told Nicco or Marilena that they were leaving, for they never seemed to see them.

'Since Renata's left, Marilena must be waiting to come home with Nicco,' said Ruth, as they stepped gingerly over the pavements ribbed with ice that cracked underfoot. Their fingers in the gloves their mother had knitted for them felt damp and stiff, their feet in wellingtons quite numb, which at least was better than the pain of chilblains that would come as soon as they thawed out. When they reached Signor Rietti's shop, they stopped to look around, but there was still no sign of Marilena or her brother.

'You're right, they must be coming back later,' Sylvie agreed. 'Let's go inside and wait for them. I've still got some pocket money left, we can buy something.'

The shop bell gave its usual sharp little ting, but the man at the counter looking up was not Signor Rietti. It was Nicco.

'Why, Nicco, you're here!' cried Ruth, thinking she must sound ridiculous. 'I mean, you're working. You're no' at school.'

He arranged a few packets of cigarettes on the counter in front of him. 'I've left school,' he said quietly.

'Left?' Ruth glanced at Sylvie, who was looking round for Marilena. 'But you were staying on for your certificate, Nicco! Why have you left?'

'My father's not well. He's been told to rest.'

'Oh, I'm so sorry! Oh, that's such a shame.' Ruth was flushing, feeling perhaps she had no right to pry, but pressing on, because, as she realised now, she cared what happened to Nicco. 'But why have you to leave, Nicco? I mean, when your dad gets better, you could go back, couldn't you?'

A customer wanted vegetables weighing and Nicco was occupied for some time. When he was free, he pushed his black hair from his brow and shrugged a little.

'I've said I'd take over to put my mother's mind at rest,' he said, after a pause. 'She's been worrying, in case my father tries to keep on, so as to let me go back to school.'

'Could your ma no' look after the shop?' asked Sylvie. 'Plenty of ladies work in shops.'

'It's hard work, she couldn't do it alone.' Nicco shook his head. 'I wouldn't want her to, anyway. It's better for me to take it on.'

'But I thought your folks were keen for you to get qualifications,' said Ruth. 'Have a career.'

'It was *Papà* who wanted that for me, my mother's always thought I should run the shop.' Nicco smiled. 'It was my grandfather's. He walked to Scotland from Italy long ago, sent for my grandmother and Uncle Vittorio after he'd settled. Eventually he managed to buy this place and when he died, it came to my dad.'

'Didn't your uncle want it?' asked Sylvie, rather cheekily, Ruth thought, but Nicco was polite, as usual.

'He wanted to keep on his café. I expect they settled things somehow. Anyway, you can see it's always been in the family and Mamma thinks I should carry it on.'

'Fancy your grandfather walking so far!' exclaimed Ruth. 'I've heard Italians used to have to do that, just to find work.'

She thought of Millie's father. How far would he walk to find work? Just as far as the Italians, probably, with all the other unemployed. There was already talk of Scottish women organising a march to London, for bread for their bairns.

'Our dad's just bought a shop,' said Sylvie cheerfully. 'It's in Trinity. We're flitting when everything's settled.'

'Oh, Sylvie!' Ruth whispered. 'We weren't going to say!'

'About flitting? 'Course we were!'

'About buying the shop.' Ruth looked up at Nicco, whose eyes were fixed on her.

'You're leaving Ginger Street, Ruth? I'm sorry. We'll miss you. We'll miss you all.'

'Yes, well, I don't really want to go, but what can I do?' Ruth hesitated. 'They're going to let me stay on at school, only it'll be a new school. I'm no' sure how I'll get on.'

Nicco leaned across his counter. 'You'll do well,' he said softly. 'I'm very happy for you. But you won't forget us, will you? You'll come back to Ginger Street?'

'Where's Marilena?' interrupted Sylvie. 'Why do we never see her now?'

Nicco stood back. 'Now that Renata and I can't go with Marilena to school, Mamma's taking and bringing her home.' He laughed, a little apologetically. 'You know Mamma, she doesn't walk very fast!'

The sisters laughed, too, thinking of Marilena trying to hurry along the stately signora. Oh, what a trial parents were!

'I will come back,' Ruth said quickly, looking into Nicco's face. 'I won't forget Ginger Street. I won't forget anyone.'

'And I won't,' said Sylvie, then gave a squeal of excitement. 'Here's Marilena!'

Suddenly the shop was revolving again around the signora, as she came sailing in, with Marilena in tow. All the customers greeted her and she bowed her head, taking off her dark cape and her gloves but retaining her elaborate hat. As Nicco hurried round the counter to kiss her cheek, Marilena and Sylvie rushed off into a corner to whisper together.

'Here's Ruth, Mamma,' said Nicco. 'Come to tell us she's leaving. Her family's moving to Trinity.'

His mother's fine eyes went over Ruth. She said nothing, but had she understood?

'I'm so sorry to hear that Signor Rietti is not so well,' ventured Ruth. 'Please give him our best wishes.'

'*Grazie*, you are very kind,' Signora Rietti answered. (So she had understood!) 'Now, I must go to him.' She moved to the stairs at

45

the back of the shop, where she paused to look back. 'Marilena!' she called, and Marilena jumped.

'I want to see *Papà*,' she said to Sylvie. 'Oh, but I'm so sorry you're going. Come in to say goodbye, eh?'

When she and her mother had vanished up the stairs, the shop seemed strangely empty. There was nothing else for Ruth and Sylvie to do but leave, for Nicco was busy serving people now and could only smile briefly as they hovered to say goodbye. Outside in the street, the cold air hit them again, and they put their gloved hands over their noses and would have liked to walk fast but did not dare.

'What did you think of that, then?' asked Ruth. 'Signor Rietti being ill and poor Nicco having to leave school?'

'I don't think he minded. He never said so.'

'He's putting up with it, for his mother's sake. She could run that shop if she wanted to, she just wants Nicco at home.'

'And gets what she wants,' said Sylvie, then gave a cry of anguish.

'Ruth, we didn't buy anything! And I had ma money all ready!'

'Never mind, we can get something tomorrow.'

They both knew there wouldn't be many tomorrows left for them to shop in Ginger Street.

Chapter Ten

Yet their leaving seemed to be taking so long!

'If I'm going, I like to go,' Isa said irritably. 'Why are these lawyers taking all this time to give us possession?'

'You know how it is,' Jack said easily. 'There's searches and formalities and this and that to check. The main thing is the shop is ours and I can get on with buying ma stock.'

'So, here it is, nearly the end of February. When'll we get in?'

'March. Middle of March. They've promised me.' Jack gave his wife a good-humoured hug. 'Come on, you'll have plenty to do, anyway, if I know you.'

'That's true,' she answered, pleased at the thought of all there was to be done, for she hated to be idle. Apart from cleaning the present flat from top to bottom, so that no new tenant could criticise her when she'd gone, there was a bed to buy for Kester at the sale room, because his little recessed bed would no longer do, and then it would be nice for the girls to have a single bed each, so she'd try for them, as well. There was matting to order for the new living room and curtains to make, because Mr Cameron's were falling apart, his wife'd been dead for years and if he'd ever so much as shown thae curtains a drop of water, it would be hard to believe. Still, what could you expect of a man? Och, she'd plenty to do, to get things to rights. She just wished it was all done and they were on their way to Trinity, she'd had enough of Ginger Street.

Ruth's feelings, of course, were the reverse. Every extra day they waited to leave was another day at her old school. And another chance to see Nicco. Every afternoon now, she looked in at the shop, pretending that she was only accompanying Sylvie, who wanted to see Marilena, sometimes buying some little thing, sometimes just searching the shelves, but always keeping her eye on Nicco, who seemed ready to keep his on her. They'd always been friends, that went without saying, but had now become very special friends, and Ruth wasn't sure how it had happened. All she knew was that time was running out, slipping away quickly like sand in an hour glass, and that one day the letter would come from the lawyers and they would be on their way. Then what would happen to this very special friendship?

Occasionally, she would see Guido in the shop. He'd arrive to deliver fresh ice-cream, now that the weather was better, then help himself to a cornet or a soft drink, lean against the counter and hold forth on Mussolini. This seemed to infuriate Nicco, who, though calm on the whole, could be as passionate in argument as his cousin when roused. Ruth didn't know the ins and outs of it, but it seemed that Guido was all for Mussolini, who was the leader of the Italian people, even though they had a king as well, and Nicco wasn't. They would talk together in their own language, Guido's blue eyes spitting fire, Nicco's dark ones returning it, while the customers listened and sometimes joined in, and once Nicco's father shouted downstairs that that was enough! Down came the signora, with a face like a thunder cloud, and the two young men subsided, muttering apologies for upsetting Signor Rietti. Finally, Guido took himself off, and Nicco, his face mottled red, became his usual calm self again.

'What's it all about?' Sylvie whispered to Marilena, but Marilena only shrugged. Nicco and Guido often argued these days, but her mother said it was political talk, they should take no notice.

'I never knew Nicco could get so worked up,' Sylvie said, with a glance at Ruth.

'We are Italians,' Marilena answered. 'We always get worked up.'

'You're sweet on Nicco, aren't you?' Sylvie asked Ruth, on their way home.

'No, I'm not! We're friends.'

'Remember when you said to me, I might marry Nicco?' Sylvie giggled. 'So might you!'

'I'm a bit young yet for thinking about marrying!'

'Marilena says Italian girls often marry young. Sometimes only sixteen.'

'Well, I'm no' Italian, and I'm going to get myself a good job. No chance of me getting married at sixteen.'

'I think Guido is much better looking than Nicco. If I was getting married, I'd choose him.'

'Sylvie, you do talk rubbish sometimes. You're only a little girl.'

'Well, I'm only saying.' Sylvie took her peever stone from her pocket and slid it along the pavement. 'We're playing peevers tomorrow at school. Can I have your stone, Ruth, if you don't want it? It's better than mine.'

'I might no' be getting married, but I'm too big for peevers,' Ruth said with a laugh. 'Yes, you can have it, Sylvie, if you don't say anything to Ma about me and Nicco.'

'I'd never say anything, Ruth! Anyway, what could I say? If you're no' sweet on him?'

'I just don't want to talk about him to Ma, that's all.'

'You are sweet on him!' Sylvie cried triumphantly. 'Oh, poor old Ruth, when you're going away!'

The day came in late March when postie brought the letter they'd been waiting for. Contracts were exchanged, searches complete, if Mr Millar cared to call in at the lawyer's office, a date for possession and handing over keys could be arranged.

'Thank the Lord!' cried Isa, who already had a duster round her head, ready for more spring-cleaning. 'That's a weight off ma mind!'

'Do I give notice now at the factory?' Kester asked his father.

'Aye, it's going to be all hands to the pumps when we move in,' Jack said, his eyes shining. 'I'll need all the help I can get.'

'Dad, could you no' give Mr MacAllan a job?' Ruth asked suddenly. 'He hasn't found anything yet.'

'Bob MacAllan? He's a factory worker, Ruth, no' a shop assistant. Besides, I've got Kester.'

'You just said you needed all the help you could get.'

'Aye, well, at the start.'

'Could you no' take him on at the start, then?'

'Oh, Jack, I wish you could!' cried Isa. 'Sarah MacAllan's got five bairns to feed, and you ken what the dole is.'

'You'll need somebody when I'm out delivering stuff,' said Kester. 'You'll no' be able to manage on your own, Dad, if we're busy.'

'If we're busy, aye, there's the catch. I've to be good and busy before I can afford another man's wages.'

'You will be busy, you're going to be a success,' Isa told him. 'Remember, Sir Jack Millar?'

He laughed, running his hands through his hair. 'I'll think about it. I'll see what I can do.' As they clapped their hands, he re-read his letter again. 'I'll away, then, to fix up this date, then I'll have to confirm ma own notice to Tomlinson's. They've been good, you ken, wished me luck.'

'What is the date, Dad?' Ruth asked. 'When do we go?'

'Well, old Cameron'll go along with anything we suggest. I'd say, a week from now. What do you think, Isa?'

'Fine. We can be ready by then.'

Not me, thought Ruth. But she said nothing, of course.

Chapter Eleven

If only she could see Nicco on his own, just once, to say goodbye! But in the shop there was always someone with him – his mother, or customers, or Marilena. Even if he did happen to be alone, Ruth herself had Sylvie tagging along, and she could think of no possible way to lose Sylvie. Day after day in the short time that was left to her, she racked her brains to solve her problem. It was not until two days before the flitting that she managed it, and then only by a stroke of luck.

Because Sylvie was leaving so soon, Signora Rietti suddenly permitted Marilena to ask her up to the flat over the shop for tea and Italian cake. This meant that not only was Sylvie out of the way, but the signora too, and Ruth would have her chance to speak to Nicco. Provided she could avoid the customers! Of course, he might not agree to meet her, but she would not even think of that.

When Sylvie had ecstatically followed Marilena up the stairs that Tuesday afternoon, Ruth hovered round the shelves, waiting for an opportunity to catch Nicco alone at the counter. When it came, she darted forward, and all in one breath, the words tumbling out so fast she wondered if he would understand her, asked him to meet her the following afternoon after school in the Meadows. It was early closing, his half day, and she would make some excuse to her mother and Sylvie, say she was going to the café to see Renata, or something, anything, as long as she was sure he would be there.

'The Meadows?' he repeated. His gaze, on her face, was intent, but it seemed to her that he was mystified, unable to understand what was so clear, that they should be able to say goodbye on their own, away from the shop, away from family. She began to waver. How must she appear to him? Just a kid, a schoolgirl, with a turned-up nose and a ribbon in her hair. And he was composed, good looking, not much older than she was, but seeming so much more adult, who might after all only be thinking of her as a child. Perhaps, she'd got everything wrong? There was no special friendship at all?

Then he said quietly, 'I'd like to go to the Meadows,' and she felt her heart leap.

'You would?'

'Yes, but what of your mother, Ruth? What will she think? And you must tell her. It's not something you should do, walk with a young man in a park.'

'Yes it is! People go to the park all the time!'

'Not Italian young men and girls.'

No, well she'd heard that and knew that Marilena, for instance, would never be allowed to go out with a boy without a chaperone. But she, Ruth, was a Scottish girl. Italian rules need not apply to her. All the same, she knew she wasn't going to tell her mother.

'It's all right, Nicco,' she said earnestly. 'We'll no' be gone long. It's no' as if we're going to the pictures, or anything. I needn't tell my mother.' She added quickly, 'And you needn't tell yours.'

He flushed and glanced upwards, as though the signora might be listening.

'I'd rather you did speak to your mother,' he said firmly. 'I'd feel better, if you did.'

'All right, I'll tell her!' Ruth cried recklessly. 'If you say you'll be there.'

'What time?'

'Four o'clock? Ten past? I might be a bit late, depending what time we get out of school.'

'Where?'

'At the bowling green. That's easy to find.'

Nicco licked dry lips, and again looked round the shop, then up at the ceiling.

'I will try to be there, Ruth.'

'Try?'

'I will be there.'

Their eyes locked, then Ruth backed away, opened the door and fled.

She must have looked strange when she reached home, for her mother asked her if she had a headache. Ruth said she was quite well, but wanted to say she might be late back tomorrow.

'Off to the Riettis' café again?'

'Yes,' Ruth answered gratefully. 'I'm going to say goodbye to Renata and her ma and dad.'

'Well, be sure no' to be too late back. We're making a start on the packing.'

'Oh, I won't.'

Ruth went to her room and sat on the bed that was soon to be sent to the sale room. She felt bad, deceiving her mother, but she had no choice. Ma would never let her see Nicco on her own. Somehow she knew that. Ma liked him, liked his family. But, if Ruth were to ask if she could go walking with him in the Meadows, Ma would just say no. After a time, she got up and poured some water into a basin from the jug on the washstand, and splashed her face with her hands. Then she looked at herself in the washstand mirror, looked at her nose again. Tip-tilted? No, just turned up. She ran her finger down it, as though she could straighten it, and turned away. Time to help Ma with the tea, not that Sylvie would want anything.

'Ma! Ruthie!' There was Sylvie now, coming in, flushed and excited, bursting with details of Marilena's home. 'So Italian, Ma. Has all little lamps burning under photos and holy pictures, and lace the signora's made, and shawls and things, but all very nice and comfortable.'

'And what was the tea like?' asked Isa, all ears, for none of them had ever been inside the Italian flat. 'Was there proper tea, or what?'

'It was proper tea, poured out of a teapot,' Sylvie answered loftily. 'And we had sweet biscuits and special rolls and a great big cake that the signora had baked herself, it was like a teacake, all sugary, with marzipan. I loved it!'

'So you'll no be wanting tea with us, then?'

'Och, no, I'm full.' Sylvie was dancing around the room, too excited to keep still. 'Ma, when we move can we invite Marilena over?'

'Aye, one day, but it'll be some time before we're straight. How did you get on with Marilena's mother, then? Was she nice?'

'Oh, yes, and her dad was, too, though you can tell he's no' well.' Sylvie had stopped to take breath. 'Her ma wanted Nicco to walk me home, because she never lets Marilena out on her own, you ken, but I said I'd be fine.'

'Well, I should think so, seeing as we're just up the street!' cried Isa. 'The signora wraps that girl in cotton wool!'

'Fancy thinking Nicco should walk you home,' said Ruth, with a desperate attempt at a casual tone.

'Fancy,' Sylvie repeated, her eyes sparkling. 'Ma, while you're having your tea, shall I start on the packing?'

'Yes, if you just pack what I put out. I'll lay it all ready for you now.' Isa bustled away, and Sylvie shook her head at her sister.

'Better be careful, Ruthie, you were nearly blushing then, talking about Nicco.'

'No, I wasn't!'

'Yes, you were.'

'Well, never mind now. Listen, tomorrow I'm going to say goodbye to Renata, so you come on home on your own, eh?'

'Why shouldn't I say goodbye to Renata? I know her too.'

Ruth tried to keep calm. 'You can see her some other time, and her folks. I want to see them by myself.'

Sylvie looked at her knowingly. 'Are you really going to the café?' she asked. 'Why have I to come home alone, then? We can walk together as far as here.' As Ruth frantically sought for an explanation, Sylvie leaned forward.

'If you're going to meet Nicco, I promise I'll no' say anything, Ruth, but you ought to stop telling all these lies.'

'Just come home on your own,' Ruth said with stiff lips. 'And say nothing.'

'I said I would do that, didn't I?'

Chapter Twelve

Was it worth it? To run like this, till her chest was sore and her side had a stitch, just to be on time? To tell all those lies and lie awake half the night, worrying in case Sylvie let out what she suspected? Ruth, on her way to the Meadows after school the following day, was beginning to think she'd made a terrible mistake. This could so easily go wrong. For a start, she should never have told her mother she was going to the café to say goodbye, because now she must do that as well as seeing Nicco, for if she didn't, Renata might come round to try to say goodbye to her, and then there would be trouble. Real trouble, not just for meeting Nicco, but for lying to Ma. Until now, Ruth had been lucky, her parents had never laid a finger on her. But there was always a first time and this could be it, couldn't it? Sweat was breaking on Ruth's brow by the time she got to the Meadows and looked for Nicco.

And there he was, walking up and down by the bowling green, a strange, almost exotic figure against the background of the slowly moving players, in their hats and cardigans and extra jumpers. Tall, black-haired, rather pale, with dark eyes – and looking for her.

'Ruth!' He had seen her and came to her, and as she took his hand, all her worries fell from her mind.

'I can't stay long,' she said, catching her breath. 'I have to go to the café to say goodbye to Renata.'

'Shall I walk with you, then?'

'Yes, it might be better. Oh, but I must sit down first, I've run all the way.'

'Poor Ruth,' he said softly. 'Look, there's a bench here. Have a little rest.'

She sank down, loosening her hand from his, and pulled the ribbon from her hair so that she might look older. 'Feel a terrible mess,' she said, still gasping a little.

'You look very pretty, Ruth, you always do.'

She shook her head and they sat in silence for a minute or two.

'Did you tell your mother you were meeting me?' he asked at last.

'No, I didn't.'

'Oh, Ruth!'

'I didn't want to talk to her about it, I wanted it to be just between us. Our goodbye.'

'Well, it was a nice idea. To meet like this,'

Ruth watched the bowls players. 'You'd never have asked me to meet you, though, would you?'

'You know why. I did explain.'

'Would you've liked to ask me?' She turned her head to look at him, and he met her eyes with deep, fond sincerity.

'Yes, I would.'

'You don't think I'm too young?'

He hesitated, looking about him. He's uneasy, Ruth thought, he doesn't think he should be here with me, in spite of all I've said.

'You are young,' he answered at last. 'Well, I suppose I am, too, but you're—'

'I know, a schoolgirl. I might've had a job by now, Nicco, don't forget that!'

'I just feel a bit responsible. Letting us meet like this. It's not that I don't want to, you know that.'

'We are friends, that's the point, Nicco. Special friends, so why should we no' meet to say goodbye?'

'You're right.' He suddenly took her hand. 'I did say it was a nice idea.'

'I'll come back to see you,' she said earnestly, looking down at her hand in his. It was the first time there had ever been such contact between them, and she could scarcely believe it was happening. 'I'll come back to Ginger Street, I promise.'

'Maybe.'

'Why'd you say that? Do you no' think I will?'

'To begin with, Ruth, then you'll forget.' His eyes were very kind. 'People do.'

She looked at him for a long moment, taking in that kindness, reading in his face all that he wasn't saying. Because he was kind.

She wanted to say she would never forget him, but other words were trembling on her lips, words she couldn't say, hadn't even known until this moment were true. 'I love you.' Oh, how silly, how pathetic! She was just like the girls at school, who fell for teachers for a week or two. Just like herself, come to that, for hadn't she done the same? There'd been that time she'd followed a teacher round like his shadow, until one day she'd suddenly wondered what it'd all been about. Was her feeling for Nicco only that? Was he right? She'd forget him? She'd certainly forgotten that teacher, who was now working in Glasgow. Mr —, Mr —, Crawford was it? One thing was certain. Whatever her feelings were for Nicco, he didn't return them. As she had seen, he was just being kind, coming to meet her that day. The friend she'd always said he was. She felt a little sick.

'Got to go,' she said, loosening her hand from his and jumping to her feet. 'Got to go to the café.' She was resolutely not looking into his face.

'I'll come with you,' he said eagerly.

'You needn't.' She was already walking away.

'To Ginger Street, Ruth. Why not?'

'All right.'

She led the way, hurrying, but Nicco, with his long legs, easily caught up with her. He seemed to want to speak to her, but she guessed he didn't know what to say and hoped he wouldn't say anything. She didn't want any more kindness or gentleness. Didn't want any understanding, or promises for the future that she would soon forget him. Her whole being felt open to pain; she was a wound, stinging with rejection and the knowledge that she'd been a fool. At least, she was going away! She need never see Nicco again.

'Here's the shop,' he murmured, at the corner of Ginger Street.

'Do you want me to come with you to the café? Or would you like to say goodbye on your own?'

'Oh, I want to say goodbye on my own!' she answered, bursting into tears. 'I want to say goodbye to everybody.'

For some time, he watched her running away from him down Ginger Street, then he turned and knocked on the shop door, which was always locked when the shop was closed. It was opened by Marilena.

'Where've you been, Nicco? Mamma wanted you to play cards with *Papà*.'

He made no reply, but locked the door behind them and followed her up the stairs to where his parents were waiting.

Chapter Thirteen

The following morning, one of cold wind and promised showers, a van drew up at Number Twenty-Four for the Millar's flitting. It was considered rather grand in Ginger Street, to have a van with packers and tea chests and such, when most folk moving house still managed with a horse and cart, or even a handcart. But the Millars had a respectable collection of furniture and could certainly afford a proper van now, so there it was, parked and open at their door, while small children who did not have to go to school stood around, watching, hoping for handfuls of pennies, as though the flitting were a wedding.

Kester and Jack had gone on ahead to Trinity to open up the flat, while Isa was left to enjoy herself, ordering the removal men around, making cups of tea, finding things for the girls to do, who were really only in the way.

Sylvie, of course, was aware that things had gone wrong for Ruth yesterday. She could hardly have missed Ruth's tears during the night, and if Isa had not been so preoccupied with the move, she would not have missed their signs the next morning. As Sylvie, feeling the weight of Ruth's misery, didn't dare to say a word, Ruth thanked the Lord for her luck and lived for a little longer in her own sad world.

During the morning, various neighbours looked in. Mrs Dougall, Mrs Mowat, Mrs Smith, mother of Vi, and Mrs MacAllan, mother of Millie. On went the kettle, out came the biscuit tin, that Isa kept with her at all times in case the men packed it before she was ready, and the women sat on the remaining chairs discussing Isa's good fortune, for of course, news of the inheritance had now leaked out. If some were envious, Sarah MacAllan was not. All she felt was gratitude for the job Jack had given her husband, which made Isa feel bad, as she filled the teacups that were still to be packed. She was no Lady Bountiful, was too worried about the future to take pleasure in acting out that role, though it eased her conscience about having money to see Sarah's relief.

'I canna tell you, Isa, what it means,' Sarah was murmuring. 'Bob was that low, you ken, going out seeking work every day, coming back wi' nothing, and us living on the dole.' She gave a thin smile. 'You ken how much that is? One pound thirteen shilling a week for the seven of us. Aye, and some begrudge it us and all!'

The women shook their heads in sympathy and cheered themselves with more tea and biscuits, until the men put their heads round the door and wanted the chairs, which meant they had to depart.

'All the best, hen!' they cried, as Norrie Mowat went up the stairs and the others went down, calling, 'Take care, now!' 'Come back and see us, eh?'

As her ex-neighbours left her, Isa shooed away the waiting children with a ha'penny or two, then stood for a moment, watching the removal men put the last chairs into the van.

'That you?' she called.

'Aye, that's us, Missus. We're away.'

'Wait, wait, I'll let you have a few last things!'

She ran back up the stairs, calling to the girls to rinse the cups and find some paper to wrap them in, quick now, the men were waiting. The kettle could be left, it went with the range and there was another at Trinity, but Isa took the biscuit box, running back to the van, while the girls followed with the carton of cups wrapped in newspaper.

'You've got the address, now?' Isa shouted at the men, as they secured the back of the van and took their seats in the cab.

Aye, they'd got the address, they'd see her husband there.

'OK, missus!' they called out of their window. 'Stand back now, we're away.'

Isa and the girls stood in silence, as the van moved off, bearing their possessions to Trinity, a home on the move, waiting to be created all over again.

'That's it, then,' Isa murmured. 'Get your coats, girls, and we'll away for the tram.'

'Fancy having to go by tram,' grumbled Sylvie. 'Why could we no' have had a taxi again?'

'We may have come into a bit o' money, but we need it all,' Isa told her. 'We're no' frittering it away on taxis, when we can go for coppers on the tram. Hurry, now, I want to lock up and get off. Canna leave your dad to tell those removers where to put things, he's sure to get it wrong.'

But Ruth was stiffening on the step and Sylvie was jerking her mother's arm.

'Ma, here's Signor Rietti, and Nicco! I think they want to speak to you.'

'Signor Rietti?' Isa turned in surprise, to see Nicco's father, leaning on Nicco's arm, slowly approaching her. 'Signor Rietti, whatever are you doing out in this cold wind? You'll catch your death!'

'No, no.' He looked frail and yellowish, his black hair firmly tucked under his cap, a great muffler round his throat, but he smiled and bowed. 'It is almost spring and I'm better, I'm much better. When Nicco told me you were leaving, I said I wanted to come to say goodbye. You were good customers of ours. My wife and I, we wish you the best of luck.'

'Oh, Signor Rietti, I don't know what to say!'

This was true. Isa was overcome, partly because she had never felt herself a true customer of the Italian shop, and partly because at one time she had been pretty free with her criticism. Now, here was this dear man, making the effort to come to say goodbye, and she not knowing where to look!

'Girls, girls,' she called, to cover her confusion. 'Come and say goodbye to Signor Rietti. He's so kind, come to wave us off, eh? And Nicco, too. You're very good.'

Nicco had been standing at his father's side, as watchful as a nurse. Now he bowed and took an envelope from his pocket, which he presented to Isa.

'This is a copy of a photograph my father once took,' he told

61

her. 'It shows Sylvie and Marilena outside the shop. We thought you'd like it.'

'A photo of me?' cried Sylvie. 'Oh, let me see, let me see!'

'Hush now,' said Isa. 'I'm worried about your dad standing, Nicco. I'd ask you up the stair, but all the chairs have gone—'

'I'm quite all right, thank you, Mrs Millar, please do not worry,' said Signor Rietti, as Sylvie pored over the snapshot of herself and Marilena standing in front of the shop window, both smiling into the camera, with the handsome face of the signora behind and Nicco next to her, his hands on the girls' shoulders. Ruth, studiously avoiding looking at either the photograph or Nicco, was keenly aware that he was looking at her.

'I'm sorry, Ruth, it doesn't show you,' he said quietly. 'I can't think where you were.'

'At home with tonsillitis!' cried Sylvie. 'I remember it all as clear as clear. Ruth wasn't at school and I came home on ma own, and there was Marilena, and her dad said he'd one last shot in the camera and took us all at the door! Oh, it's lovely, eh!'

'A lovely memory,' said Isa. 'The shop and all of you, and your dad for taking it. Isn't it nice to have it, Ruth? Sylvie, let Ruth see the picture.'

'It's very nice,' Ruth agreed. She raised her eyes and met Nicco's, so full of sympathetic feeling for her, the colour rose to her face and she turned away.

'Now, we'd better go,' Nicco's father was saying. 'You'll keep in touch?'

'Och, yes, of course we will! We'll no' forget Ginger Street, eh, girls?'

'Goodbye, Mrs Millar,' said Nicco. 'Goodbye, Sylvie. Goodbye, Ruth.'

He was beseeching her to part on a friendly note, and why shouldn't he expect that? It wasn't his fault he didn't feel as she did, she'd just been foolish to think he might.

'Goodbye, Signor Rietti,' Ruth said clearly. 'Goodbye, Nicco. Thank you for coming.'

'Aye, we appreciate it, we really do,' called Isa, as the Italians began their walk back to the shop, Nicco again taking his father's arm and watching over him every step of the way. 'And thanks for the photo!' added Isa.

'Thank you!' echoed Sylvie, who was still gazing at herself in the snapshot with a gratified smile. 'I'll keep this for ever,' she told Ruth. 'To remind me of Ginger Street.'

Ruth said nothing. As they put on their coats and hats, and watched their mother lock the door of Number Twenty-Four for the last time, she knew she needed no reminders. But maybe she wouldn't mind looking at that photograph again. One day.

Part Two

Chapter Fourteen

The meeting with Renata was for lunch, at John Johnson's department store restaurant. Poached eggs on toast, they would have, thought Ruth, running from Princes Street towards the North Bridge, or else something with cheese. Didn't matter, anyway, it would be just so lovely for the two of them to meet again. It was lucky that Renata, writing from London, had suggested a Saturday for the rendezvous, for that was Ruth's half day and meant she wouldn't have to rush back to the lawyer's office where she now worked as a junior clerk. She could wander round JJ's after lunch, take Renata to see Sylvie in the millinery department, try on all the hats and have a really good old gossip. And how Ruth was looking forward to that! It was now August 1935 and she hadn't seen Renata since 1931, when she'd departed for London after the death of her Uncle Roberto.

The Millars had been deeply grieved to read of Signor Rietti's death in the local paper. They'd debated for some time over attending the funeral, not wanting to intrude, yet fearing that the signora might think it remiss if they stayed away. In the end, they'd joined the large congregation at the local Catholic church, and had felt that the signora had appreciated their presence. Though she was overcome with grief, she had pressed their hands as they filed out afterwards and inclined her head in greeting, whereas Ruth sometimes wondered whether Nicco had even known who they were, his eyes had seemed so glazed, so blank. Her heart had gone out to him, although her old feeling for him had died long before. Almost as soon as she left Ginger Street, in fact, just as he had prophesied. She had rarely gone back, had grown quite away. If she met Renata occasionally it was usually in town, and then of course Renata had gone down to help her mother's cousin run her ice-cream business in Clerkenwell, and had only returned for flying visits to her family. Now she was coming home to be married in September to a long-term admirer, a young man whose family came from the same Italian village as the Riettis, a perfect match.

'I am a changed woman!' Renata had written. 'I am the darling of the family!'

Ruth, marvelling, thought she would believe the change in Renata when she saw it. She felt that she herself had not changed so very much, except, perhaps in looks, for the strange thing was that she and Sylvie had suddenly become quite pretty. Seemed it didn't matter about their turned-up noses after all! But neither was in any hurry to be walking down the aisle. Sylvie was having too good a time, and though Ruth occasionally went to the pictures or dancing with young men, they didn't mean much to her and she was really more interested in having a career before she married. She'd done well at school and was ambitious to be something more than a clerk; had even, in fact, begun to think of taking the Civil Service exam, though at twenty she'd have to wait a year to do that and might have to move to London if she passed.

Och, who knew what she'd do? It was lovely to have plans, even though Kester, working for her father, thought her considering the Civil Service was a bit of a joke, just as her dad said it would all be a waste of time, because when she got married she'd only have to resign. And wasn't that a piece of nonsense, anyway, that married women couldn't keep professional jobs? At least Ma was all for her studying. If she'd had the chance herself, she'd have done the same.

Renata was waiting outside the main entrance of John Johnson's, a large store on the North Bridge that spanned the railway line to Waverley Station. Not so expensive as some of the Princes Street shops, JJ's sold everything from drapery and furniture, to clothes, pots and pans and china, as well as teas and light lunches. Sylvie worked in the millinery department, but had her lunch in the staff canteen; Ruth had said they'd see her later.

'To try on hats, I suppose?' Sylvie had asked cheekily. 'It's amazing how many folk try on hats and never buy!'

'Come on, it's fun. Everybody does it.' Ruth hesitated. 'And some people have no money to buy, anyway. They come in to get off the street.'

That was true enough. It was well known that there were always folk drifting round the store because they'd nowhere else to go except home, where no news was bad news and they couldn't face admitting again that they'd found no work. The economic situation had not improved as the 1930s had progressed. Ruth and Sylvie had not forgotten the faces of the unemployed as they marched through Edinburgh not so long ago.

'Renata!' cried Ruth now, flinging her arms round her friend, whose striking looks cancelled out that last memory of her, pale and weeping, all in black, at her uncle's funeral. Today she was a blaze of colour in a red calf-length dress, with matching jacket and small hat tilted over glossy dark hair that was longer than Ruth remembered. When Ruth had been shown the engagement ring and admired it, she told Renata she looked wonderful, but hadn't she grown her hair? What had happened to that bob she'd been so desperate to have?

Renata made a face. 'To please Mamma, for the wedding, I agreed to grow my hair. Did I not tell you I was a changed woman? But so is your hair longer, Ruth, and it suits you.'

'I hope so!' Ruth laughed, as they made their way to the lift for the restaurant. 'I spend enough time messing about with it. Sometimes I think I'll have a perm.'

'No, no, it's lovely as it is.' Renata's gaze went over Ruth's face, her bright eyes, her cheeks flushed with hurrying, and she smiled. 'You're really pretty, Ruth, do you know that?'

'Don't sound so surprised.' Ruth was embarrassed. 'Anyway, you should see Sylvie.'

'I want to. Ah, but I can see you following in my footsteps, Ruth. Don't tell me there's no young man around for you?'

'No one special. I'm happy working, at the moment.'

Renata rolled her eyes. 'Happy working? Ruth you are the strangest girl in the world!'

They ordered eggs on toast, followed by tea and pastries, for one shilling and sixpence per person, special offer, Ruth saying she hoped Renata didn't mind not eating Italian, Renata saying she had tried all sorts of food in London and liked everything. Oh, she had really enjoyed London! Her mother had not wanted her to stay on so long, but it was true that poor old Cousin Sofia could do with her help and Renata had absolutely refused to come back until Federico had persuaded her. There'd been so much to see and do, so much more freedom away from the café, and after all, what harm could there be, seeing the city, going out to the *fascio*, having fun?

'Don't you have one of those clubs here?' Ruth asked, as the waitress brought their order.

'Oh, yes, there's one here, there are *fasci* everywhere, but I couldn't go very often. Not like Guido. Remember how I used to complain? Now, in London, things were different.' Renata gave a triumphant smile. 'Cousin Sofia was very understanding about letting me go out!'

'Yet you've still come back, Renata? How did Federico make you change your mind?'

Renata shrugged. 'I suppose I just felt – well, like getting married. I do love him. He may be Mamma's choice, but he's mine, too. He has a good job – works for his father making ice-cream machinery. I think we'll be happy.'

'That's wonderful. And I can see it's true, you really are a changed woman.'

But Renata laughed. She bit into her pastry with strong white teeth, and flicked away a crumb from her lips. 'Just wait till there's no baby in the first year and see what Mamma and Aunt Carlotta say! My aunt will be more than ever glad I didn't marry Nicco.'

Ruth stared over the rim of her teacup. 'Marry Nicco? Were you going to?'

'Well, if Federico hadn't appeared, Mamma would have been all for it. She was always so scared I'd marry out, you see, and people do sometimes, because there aren't so many Italians in Edinburgh. Not compared with Glasgow, say.'

'Would it matter? If you married out?'

Renata's dark eyes widened. 'Are you joking? Every Italian parent here wants their sons and daughters to marry the right person from the right part of Italy. It's like you Scots. Would your parents want you to marry a foreigner?'

Ruth hesitated. 'If I loved him, I'm sure they'd understand.' She looked down at her plate. 'But surely Nicco's mother would have been happy to have you as a daughter-in-law?'

'Me? She'd never have wanted me to marry Nicco. I'll tell you the truth, she will never want anyone to marry Nicco. Marilena, yes, she'll want her to be married and pretty soon, too. Probably to Guido. Oh, yes, that would be a very suitable match. But Nicco, no. I don't see anyone being good enough for him. Especially now that poor Uncle Roberto's gone and Aunt Carlotta's alone.'

'It's hard for her, Renata.'

'Yes, but my aunt has a talent for making things hard for everyone else, too.' Renata searched in her bag and took out an envelope. 'Now, can you guess what I have here, Ruth?'

'Oh, Renata, the wedding invitation?'

'Yes, for you and your family. Mamma's just sent the one, she hopes you will think it correct.'

'Correct?' Ruth smiled a little as she studied the invitation, beautifully produced on pale blue paper decorated with a sprig of flowers and the word '*Nozze*'. 'I don't know what's correct, Renata. Folk I know don't send formal invitations much.'

'With us, everything is formal. If it's important, it has to have ceremony.' Renata waved her hands expressively. 'You know, weddings, christenings, funerals – there's the right way to celebrate them all. So we think.'

'And I think you're right. We have some ceremonies, too. They mark things, don't they?' Ruth began to read aloud the Italian words of the invitation. '"*Il Signore e La Signora Rietti annunciano il matrimonio della figlia Renata Brigida con il Signor Federico Martinello*" – och, that sounds so grand! And I see you've put the English underneath. "*Il Signore e La Signora Rietti* announce the marriage of their daughter etcetera." That's handy for us.'

'Well, we are inviting a lot of Scottish people, too.' Renata laughed. 'We are inviting everyone, the Cathedral will be packed, and my poor father bankrupt. But I told him, if he wants me taken off his hands, he'll have to pay. Ruth, you'll be coming to my wedding, won't you? You and your family?'

'Of course! Nothing will keep us away. Sylvie works Saturdays usually, but I know she'll take a holiday, she wouldn't miss it for the world.'

'And your parents, too? I'm sorry, I haven't asked after them. How are they? How's the shop?'

'Well, it was a bit shaky to begin with, but it's doing well now.' Ruth smiled. 'You know my dad, he's always so optimistic, always talking about expanding, and Kester's the same, fancies being manager in some new shop, but Ma keeps their feet on the ground. You know Ma, too!'

'I hope I'll see them all at the wedding. I want to see everyone, I want all my friends around me!' Renata leaped to her feet and took Ruth's arm. 'Let's go and see Sylvie, let's look at her hats. I might want to buy one, you know, for my going away.'

They spent a delightful hour or so in JJ's millinery department, while Sylvie, very fair, very slender in a black dress with a white collar, brought out everything in the shop for Renata, and Renata tried everything on. In the end, she settled for a cream confection with veiling that would go with the cream suit she was making for her going away outfit. The wedding dress, made by her mother, was already finished, and Sylvie hung on Renata's every word as she described it. The collar, so – buttons on the long sleeves, so – buttons on the bodice, so – and then the sweeping train, the narrow waist.

'Oh, it sounds gorgeous!' Sylvie whispered, her eyes alight. 'It'd be almost worth getting married, to have a dress like that!'

'Hardly the right reason for getting married,' Ruth said crisply.

'No, and sometimes I think, why don't we just elope and be done with it all!' cried Renata. 'Ah, but I mustn't spoil Mamma's fun. She's having the time of her life, arranging everything. Only my father is looking glum. Now, I'd better go before I spend any more money. Sylvie, you be sure to come to my wedding, eh?'

Sylvie, hugging her, was already lost in thought, and Ruth whispered to Renata as they made their way from the store, that she was probably already planning her own outfit for the wedding.

'She's mad about clothes, you ken. Clothes and her appearance, that's our Sylvie!'

'Well, she's certainly turned into a very pretty girl, Ruth. I wish I could have had you both for bridesmaids, but I'm not having bridesmaids. Just a married couple, friends of the family, who act as attendants – we call them *compari*.'

'You couldn't have had Marilena and Nicco?'

'Well, it's more usual to choose people who are married. I wish I could have had Marilena, the poor little prisoner! Always wanting to escape. Her time will come, when she marries Guido.'

'Is that definite?'

Renata shrugged. 'If Aunt Carlotta wants it, you can be sure it will be definite. Ruth, I must run for my tram.'

They arranged to keep in touch and Ruth, watching her friend cleaving through the shoppers on the pavement, her red hat the last of her to be seen, thought that to say goodbye to her was to lose a little light, a little colour, from a drab, grey world. Marriage wouldn't change her, as it changed some women. She would not be dragged down into drudgery and child-bearing. Hadn't she just said there would be no baby in the first year? Trust Renata to know how to manage that! Ruth, on her way to her own tram, wondered what you had to do, but as she wasn't getting married herself for years and years, she needn't worry about finding out just yet.

Chapter Fifteen

Isa was much impressed with Renata's wedding invitation and showed it to Jack and Kester when they finally came up from the shop.

'Look at this, is it no' grand? The Riettis are putting on a fine show, eh, for their girl?'

Jack, yawning, said, Aye, it was grand, was tea ready?

'Just waiting on the tatties.' Isa, a little plumper but otherwise unchanged from the days of Ginger Street, passed the invitation to Kester, who was lighting a cigarette and shaking the teapot that was cold. 'Kester, you want to see? That's Renata Rietti's wedding invitation. They want us all to go. It's good of them to think of us, eh?'

'Did you no' make us any tea, Ma, to be going on with?' Kester glanced at Sylvie. 'Away and put the kettle on, Sylvie.'

'Put it on yourself. I've been working too.'

'And me,' put in Ruth.

'Thought it was your half day.' Kester, letting his cigarette hang from his lip, cast his eye quickly over the invitation, said, yes, it was very pretty, but if nobody was going to make any tea, he supposed he'd have to make it himself. Thing was, he was exhausted, been on his feet the whole long day, seeing as Bob MacAllan had been out on deliveries.

'Och, are we no' all exhausted?' cried Isa, snatching the invitation from him. 'Now, don't you get ash on this, Kester, I'll be keeping it for the mantelpiece, so's folks can see. Ruth, give thae tatties a prod, will you, while I make some tea?'

'Honestly, talk about spoiling boys!' Ruth murmured, but went

74

into the kitchen to prod the potatoes anyway. 'Are you going, then?' she called over her shoulder. 'Going to the wedding?'

Jack, opening his evening paper, pursed his lips and shook his head.

'Think I'll have to say no. Canna leave Bob all day on his own, eh? Kester, you could go, mebbe.'

'I'm no' one for weddings, Dad.'

'Plenty to drink,' said Sylvie teasingly at which Kester shrugged.

'It's an Italian wedding, they'll be drinking wine.'

'It'll be a lovely do, whatever they drink,' snapped Isa, as Ruth came in with a tray of cups. 'Och, when I think back to ours, Jack! 1911, it was, and we'd no' a penny piece to our names, then that old devil I worked for went and gave me five pounds. Five pounds! I nearly died. Bought a cake and drink and a whole lot of food and invited all the neighbours. Your Gran was alive, then, and she made me ma dress on Mrs Beith's sewing machine, she was the only one that had one, you ken, and what a lovely dress it was. Do you remember it, Jack?'

'Aye, it was blue.'

Isa flushed with pleasure. 'It was, it was. Fancy you remembering, Jack!'

'There's plenty I remember,' he said with a grin. 'You don't need to spend a mint to have a good time at a wedding, that's what I remember.'

'Well, the Italians like to make a splash, so I've heard. The more they spend, the better they're thought of, you ken.'

'And isn't that the same with most people?' asked Ruth, pouring the tea. 'Folk do go by what you've got.'

After their meal, Jack fiddled with his new wireless, trying out different stations in a way that Isa said set her nerves on edge, while Sylvie announced that she was going to the pictures with a fellow who worked in Soft Furnishings. Ruth said she'd some reading to do, she'd be in her room.

'When you've finished, mebbe we could look through ma patterns?' said Isa. 'See what there is for the wedding? I fancy a nice two-piece, eh? But we've no' got much time.'

'I can get us all something smart at discount from JJ's,' said Sylvie, from the doorway. With full make-up and a new (reduced price) dress, she was looking very attractive. 'Like a million dollars' as the fellow from Soft Furnishings was later to tell her, in a phrase he'd picked up from the films. 'I'm no' keen to mess about doing dressmaking when I can get things ready-made.'

'To think I'd ever hear a daughter of mine talking like that,' sighed Isa. 'Well, off you go, and mind you're no' late back, eh?'

When Sylvie had clattered down the stairs in her high heels, it became obvious that Kester was also preparing to go out, though the way he hung around the door made his mother instantly suspicious.

'Are you out drinking again?' she cried.

'No. As a matter of fact, I'm away to the pictures, too.' Kester flushed a little. 'Got a new girl.'

'Another?' asked Jack, grinning. 'Seems like there's a new one every week, Kester.'

'This one's special. I met her at that Merchants' dance you gave me a ticket for, Dad. She was with some friends, I was on my own, we sort of hit it off. Ruth'll know her father, he's a teacher at Fielding Secondary. She comes from a nice home.'

'A nice home?' cried Isa, bridling, 'As though you don't? What's this society girl's name, then?'

Kester's flush deepened. 'Fenella,' he said in a low voice. 'Fenella MacMenzies.'

'I remember her and her dad,' said Ruth, without enthusiasm. 'Bit of a mouthful, her name.'

'Och, it's nice!' cried Kester.

'So it is,' Jack agreed. 'There was a girl called Fenella at school, I remember. Pretty lassie, and all. Had two long red plaits.'

'Did she?' sniffed Isa. 'Well, Kester, if you're going, you'd better go, eh?'

'Aye. See you later, then.'

His relief as he left them was like something you could touch, thought Ruth, and wondered how long he'd been worrying over telling Ma about his new girlfriend. Somehow, she had the impression that this one might be different from all the others he'd taken out, he really seemed keen. Might even be the one for him, then maybe there'd be another wedding coming up soon. Imagine Kester married! Impossible. To please her mother, who was looking downcast, Ruth said she'd look through the dress patterns, though she secretly thought she'd follow Sylvie's example and get something at JJ's. But then her father left the wireless, sat down, began cleaning his pipe and clearing his throat, a sure sign that he had something important to say.

Oh, no, thought Ruth, he's going to buy a new shop!

She was right. As soon as Isa had given him one of her sharp enquiring looks, Jack declared:

'Isa, I'm going after another shop. In Marchmont.'

'Och, you're not!' she cried. 'Jack, I'm no' having it. Look how long it took you to get going with this one! You'd to spend far more than you ever meant to, eh? And now you want to risk all the profit in another shop where the same thing'll happen all over again. Are you barmy, or what?'

'It'll no' happen again,' he said patiently. 'When I opened here, I never realised how much competition there was. I thought folk'd want ma quality stuff and come to me, but they stuck with the old shops and it took me a year or two to build up. But I've found just the right place this time, no' too many other grocers around, plenty of customers in the flats, and the good houses in the Grange just up the road. There's this fellow selling up—'

'Just like a fellow was selling up before!'

'It's a grocery, but no' so good quality as mine, and there'll be a gap that I can fill.' Jack leaned forward. 'Be reasonable, Isa. This is ma chance to expand, and I've always said that's what I'd do. The way I see it, I canna go wrong!'

'Canna go wrong, with this country the way it is? Thousands out of work, hunger marchers everywhere – is it the time to be expanding at all, Jack? You could risk losing all we've got.'

Ruth, looking from one to the other of her parents, couldn't help feeling her mother was right, yet knew her father wouldn't be the man he was without his vision for the future. He was lucky, he felt that in his bones. Things had always worked out for him, he was sure they always would, and could no more bear to stay where he was than an explorer could bear to stay at home.

'Everybody has to take risks in business, Ma,' she ventured, and was rewarded with a grateful look from her father, but her mother was shaking her head.

'No' in these times, they don't. And you tell me what we can do if we go under? Go on the dole?'

'We are not going on the dole!' cried Jack. 'I've still got money put by.'

'Aye, and you'll be spending it. Och, I've no patience with you, Jack! There's Kester and Bob MacAllan to consider as well, you ken.'

'I am considering them! It's Kester I want to manage the new shop, and he's as keen as me. Then Bob can stay on here and I can take on other fellows to help Kester. I'll be giving work to men who want it, Isa. You should remember that.'

'For how long?' Isa leaped to her feet. 'Och, I'll away to find ma patterns, I've had enough of this.'

Jack exchanging glances with Ruth, as Isa bounced out of the room, gave a rueful grin.

'She's never one to let a fellow run his own business,' he said, after a pause.

'She's worried, Dad.'

'Been worried ever since we met.'

'That's because she's had to be.'

Jack drew his fair brows together. 'I've given her a pretty good life lately, Ruth. Damn' sight better than most.'

'Yes, but I'm thinking of the old days.'

'Aye, she was poor in the old days.' Jack began the ritual of lighting his pipe. 'So was I. Doesn't stop me from trying to better maself.'

'I know, Dad. I suppose it's seeing all these folk looking for work. Selling shoelaces, and that.'

'Aye.' Jack puffed on his pipe. 'Well, I'm trying to do ma bit to get things moving again, in ma own small way. You have to do what you think is right, Ruthie, and I'm no' just thinking of maself.'

She smiled and would have touched his hand, but her mother came marching in with a stack of leaflets and magazines in her arms.

'Made up your mind what do to?' she asked coldly.

'You know I want you to be happy,' Jack answered quietly. 'I want us to be together in what we do.'

'And if I'm no' happy?'

He was silent for some time, smoking his pipe. 'I think you'll have to let me make the decisions,' he said, at last.

'The decisions? This decision!'

'Aye.'

Isa tossed her head. 'So much for wanting us to be together!'

'Look, will you try to understand? I know what I'm doing.'

'All right, we'll say no more. You go ahead. See what happens.'

'Think of Kester. It'll be good for him to have some responsibility.'

'Very expensive way to give him responsibility!'

'He's like me, he's keen, wants to get on.'

'You had to make your own way.'

'Had some good luck, though. Now I want ma son to have a bit of luck, too.'

'Aye, all right, let's see how it goes. Maybe it'll all be as grand as you say, Jack.'

He stretched out his hand and took hers. 'You're softening, Isa, I can see it, you're coming round. You always do.'

'Great soft thing, that I am,' she whispered, putting her fingers round his. 'I can never stand us having arguments, Jack.'

'Nor me. That's why you always win.'

'As though we were talking about a war!' she cried, and Jack stood up, with a placid smile.

'I think I'll have another go at finding Hilversum on the wireless. Good tunes on that station, you ken.'

As Isa breathed a heavy sigh, Ruth said cheerfully.

'Let's have a look at your patterns, then, Ma, see what there is.'

Chapter Sixteen

Renata's September wedding day dawned fine and clear, with even a little sunshine by the afternoon, as the time of the ceremony drew near.

'Aye, it's a good omen,' Isa commented, as she and the girls, with Kester bringing up the rear, approached Saint Mary's, the Roman Catholic cathedral at the top of Broughton Street. 'Happy the bride the sun shines on, eh?'

'Another damn' silly old wives' tale,' grunted Kester, who was wearing his Sunday suit and looking morose. 'You're saying every bride that gets rained on is going to be unhappy?'

'Now don't start picking me up, Kester,' Isa said sharply. 'It's just a saying. And even if you don't want to come today because your Fenella's no' here, try to look a bit more cheerful. Canna expect to be with her all the time, remember!'

He coloured furiously. 'I know you don't like her, Ma, but she's important to me, that's the thing.'

'I never said I didn't like her,' replied Isa, who had said it frequently, though not to Kester. 'Let's no' get involved in arguing. We're supposed to be going to a wedding!'

'Think Kester will be next?' Sylvie whispered to Ruth, who shrugged but admitted she'd been thinking he might be. They'd all met the tall Fenella MacMenzies and had not taken to her cold good looks, or the way her blue eyes had swept over their flat and themselves in a way that seemed to find everything wanting. Yet, as Jack had pointed out with his usual good nature, she must be fond of their Kester, or she wouldn't have agreed to go out with a fellow who was just a grocery assistant. To which Isa had retorted that their Kester was as good as anyone else she could have found, and better than most! Whatever the truth of that, there was no doubt that Kester was head over heels in love with Fenella, and dying for his father to complete the deal for the new shop so that he could be made manager and have something better to offer her. As the deal was certainly going ahead perhaps it would turn out to be true, that he would be married next, though his mother and his sisters preferred to put that thought from their minds.

'Here we are, nice and early,' said Isa, looking round with interest at the guests gathering outside the cathedral. 'So we can see if there's anybody we know.'

'Seem to be mainly Italians,' murmured Sylvie. 'All very well dressed.'

'Why, so are we well dressed,' replied Isa, who was looking attractive and quite youthful in a pale blue hat and a two-piece she had made herself from one of those old patterns of hers. Ruth was in dark blue, with a small hat of blue flowers, both bought at discount price from John Johnson's, as was Sylvie's pink dress and stylish hat.

'You all look pretty as pictures,' Jack had told them, before he returned to the shop he had decided not to leave. 'So, no talking to strange men at this wedding, eh?'

'Chance'd be a fine thing,' laughed Isa. 'I'd like to know who's going to be talking to me.'

'Get away with you!' cried Jack. 'You look no older than your daughters. I'll have to tell Kester to keep a watch on you.'

But that was when Kester had turned up with his long face and his dark suit, and Jack had said he might as well have been going to a funeral. 'Don't drink too much,' he had warned him. 'We'll no' want your sisters to be carrying you home.'

To which Kester had by coincidence made the same reply as his mother.

'Chance'd be a fine thing.'

Now he looked without interest at the chattering guests, mostly Italians, as Sylvie had remarked, but with a good sprinkling of

Scots, too, and suddenly brightened as he caught sight of a face he recognised.

'Hallo, there's Guido! Hey, Guido, over here!'

The young man turned, raised his dark eyebrows and came over. They had seen him only briefly at his uncle's funeral and had had no conversation with him then, but he hadn't changed since the old days, and in his formal suit with a white flower in his buttonhole, was as handsome as ever.

'Mrs Millar, how are you?' He bowed over her hand, as she smiled delightedly. 'And is this Ruth?' He smiled into Ruth's eyes. 'Where's that hair-ribbon I used to pull?'

'Hello, Guido,' she said calmly. 'I've got past the hair-ribbon stage, I'm afraid. So's Sylvie.'

'Sylvie? Where's Sylvie?'

'Come on,' said Sylvie, laughing. 'You know who I am, Guido.'

But he was gazing into her face as though she were indeed a stranger.

'I wouldn't have known you,' he said quietly. 'You are – quite different.'

'Never mind her,' said Kester, striking Guido's shoulder. 'How about recognising me? I used to work at the biscuit factory, remember?'

'I'm sorry,' Guido murmured, 'I must go, I'm supposed to be showing people to their seats. You will be coming to the reception?' He spoke to them all, but was looking at Sylvie. 'There will be dancing, you will save me some dances?'

'Oh, yes, you can count on it,' said Kester irritably. 'And if you're showing folk to their seats, where do we go? We're on the bride's side, if you're interested.'

The organ was playing, the guests were seated inside the cathedral, a nineteenth-century building with high altar and wide nave, decorated today with white flower arrangements and tall candles. Everyone was waiting for the bride, yet first came members of the Rietti and Martinello families to take their places in the front pews. Federico's parents escorted by Guido led the way, followed by Marilena, exquisite in lilac, walking with Brigida, who was already dabbing tears from her eyes with a lace handkerchief. Finally, in a large hat of pansies but a dress of black, came Carlotta, leaning on the arm of Nicco.

So that's Nicco, thought Ruth, remembering him at his father's funeral, when he had seemed smaller than he used to be. Now, he appeared taller. Taller and thinner, but elegant in his dark suit. Elegant, and handsome. Not in Guido's way, but his own way. And Ruth remembered that, too.

The large, fair-haired bridegroom was now waiting with a man and a woman, the *compari*, at the head of the nave, the priest and servers were waiting on the altar, everyone in the congregation was waiting and whispering, when, suddenly, the organ began to roar out an entry march and the radiant Renata appeared on the arm of her father. The wedding was about to begin.

Chapter Seventeen

It was time for the dancing at the reception. The excellent meal had been eaten, the speeches made, the toasts drunk, and now the floor had been cleared and Renata, without her veil, was waltzing with Federico, as the guests cried: 'Ah!'

Soon, other couples were dancing, too, while other guests talked at small tables. Ruth could see Nicco's mother, sitting with Federico's parents, Marilena at her side, and Nicco, leaning against one of the ballroom pillars, not as yet making any effort to ask anyone to dance. But Guido was already on the floor, and with Sylvie. He had not wasted a moment. As soon as the band had struck up, he had appeared, hovering, at Sylvie's side. As soon as Renata and Federico had circled the floor, he and Sylvie were on it, clasped in each other's arms.

Of course, they were both beautiful dancers, Guido well known for his style and fancy footwork, Sylvie for her skilful following, for the way she could seem as one with her partner, almost a part of him. So much so, that Ruth had on occasion seen young men at the end of a dance appear quite bewildered at finding themselves alone on the floor, with Sylvie already moving off with someone else. Not Guido, though. When the band finished a number, he did not wait, but simply snatched Sylvie back into his arms, without looking at anyone else, without even considering, it seemed, that he should do his duty and perhaps ask the bride to dance. Or, Marilena.

Even across the room, Ruth could see that Marilena's eyes were already smouldering, but there was nothing she could do to help, especially as Renata's affable bridegroom had already come to claim her for a dance. And when that dance was finished, there at her side was Nicco.

'May I have this dance, Ruth?' he asked politely, and there was the old kind look in his eye. But as they moved into a foxtrot, surprise replaced the kindness and Ruth, gratified, knew he was thinking she had changed.

'You are looking very pretty today,' he observed, and it occurred to her that while men made that sort of remark all the time, women rarely did. When would she ever, for instance, say to him, 'You are looking very handsome today, Nicco'?

'But then you always were pretty,' Nicco added. 'Back in Ginger Street.'

'I don't think so.'

'I do think so. And now, of course, you're older. Quite grown up. What are you doing these days?'

'I'm a clerk in a lawyers' office. MacRobbie and MacRobbie.'

'I always thought you'd do well.'

'Nicco, I'm a junior clerk!'

'I have this feeling you'll go far.'

'Well, I might. I want to. And you're still running your shop, Renata told me. I was very sorry, you know, when your dad died.'

'I know. You came to the funeral. We appreciated that very much.'

'You remember us? You remember me?'

'Of course. I said, it meant a lot.'

They continued their progress round the ballroom. Though they could not equal Guido and Sylvie, they both danced well together and were enjoying themselves in a quiet, relaxed sort of way. I'd quite like another dance with Nicco, Ruth was thinking, when without warning, Marilena appeared, inserting herself between them, pushing Ruth out of her way, pouring out a stream of Italian, as other dancers stared, amazed.

'Marilena, what do you think you are doing?' Nicco cried, in English, taking her to the side of the dance floor. 'How can you be so rude, pushing Ruth away like that? Please apologise at once!'

'I'm sorry, Ruth,' Marilena said distractedly. 'But I am so hurt,

I am horribly hurt, I hurt here!' She put her hand to her breast, and her dark hair fell around her lovely face, as her tragic eyes moved between Ruth's face and Nicco's. 'It's Guido. He has humiliated me, he has shown me up before all our friends and relations at Renata's wedding. He is supposed to be engaged to me, but he has not been near me, he has never spoken to me, he has never danced once with me, only with Sylvie. All the time, Sylvie! Mamma says you must do something, Nicco, you must do something now. I tell you, I will not be treated like this, I will not!'

'Dear God,' said Nicco, turning pale. His gaze went instantly to his mother, as did Ruth's. The signora's face wore the look of thunder they all knew and feared, and her eyes, fixed on Guido still dancing with Sylvie, oblivious of everyone, were carrying the lightning.

'Guido is not officially engaged to you,' Nicco said, turning back to Marilena. 'Even he would not treat a fiancée like this, and people here don't even know about the understanding.'

'I know!' cried Marilena. 'And Mamma knows. She is arranging our betrothal. She says you must go at once and tell Guido to stop humiliating me. You must stop him dancing with Sylvie.'

'Go and ask her to dance yourself,' Ruth urged Nicco. 'You know, as though it were an excuse-me.'

'Someone else has had the same idea,' Nicco observed. 'Kester is dancing with Sylvie.'

'You mean, someone else's mother has had the same idea,' Ruth answered, as she watched her brother and sister dancing together, while Guido stood alone in the middle of the floor, brushed by other dancers staring at him. Her gaze moved to Isa, who was standing stiff as a ramrod, watching her son and daughter on the floor, her face as dark as the signora's. It was she who had sent Kester to separate Sylvie and Guido, and from the look of her, there would be words on the way home.

'Will you excuse me, Ruth?' asked Nicco, 'I must go and speak to Guido.'

But Guido's father was already threading his way through the dancers towards him, followed by Brigida, Carlotta and Marilena, whose hand was to her eyes, and the guests were falling back, preparing for trouble. Oh, what a terrible end to Renata's lovely wedding day! What could be worse than a family row? We'd better go home, thought Ruth, as Vittorio ordered Guido off the floor and Sylvia and Kester hurried off, too. We'd better get Sylvie right out of this.

As she tried to find her mother, Renata herself, flushed and emotional, still in her bridal gown, put her hand on Ruth's arm.

'Ruth, you're not going? Oh, there's no need, no need!'

'Renata, I don't know what to say.' Ruth was stammering in embarrassment. 'It's been lovely, really lovely, and you look beautiful, but I think Ma will want us to go home, it'll be easier, you ken.'

'Oh, trust Guido to cause trouble, even at my wedding!' Renata cried in fury. 'I saw him dancing with Sylvie, I knew what would happen, and now Marilena is in a state, and Aunt Carlotta will be blaming me—'

'How can she possibly blame you, Renata?'

'Well, it's my wedding where it all happened, so it must be my fault, but of course it's all Guido's. As usual!'

'That brother of yours,' said Federico appearing and putting his arm around Renata's waist. 'I think I must have a word with him, man to man.'

'You're not the only one wanting to have a word with him, man to man, or woman to man, come to that.' Renata pointed to where her parents, Nicco, Marilena and the signora were all talking to Guido at once, fiercely waving their arms to emphasise their words, while he stood without speaking, his face expressionless, his eyes sliding from one face to the other, settling nowhere.

Ruth embraced Renata and shook Federico's hand. 'Look, I have to go, but I'll be in touch, soon as you come back, I promise.'

'No, I will be in touch. I'll send you a postcard from my honeymoon.' Renata kissed Ruth's cheek. 'It's a secret where we are going, of course, but I can tell you, it's wonderful. Federico's father is paying for it, and we are very, very lucky people, aren't we, Federico?'

'We are,' he answered, his arm going back to her waist.

'Now, don't you worry about Sylvie, Ruth –' Renata went on, '– and tell your mother not to be too cross with her, because she's not to blame.'

'I don't know about that,' cried Isa, emerging from a crowd of guests with a defiant Sylvie and embarrassed Kester in tow. 'Renata, I canna get near your folks to thank them, so will you say thank you for me and tell them we had a wonderful time and we're aye grateful for being asked?'

'Of course, I will, Mrs Millar, and I want to thank you for your beautiful tablecloth,' Renata said smoothly. 'I'll write you a little note, as soon as I can.'

'Nae bother, Renata, nae bother. Och, I feel that bad, I canna tell you! Causing all this trouble, and on your special day and all. Whatever will your folks think of us? And yours, Mr Martinello? Just say that ma girl was thoughtless—'

'Thoughtless?' cried Sylvie. 'What did I do that was thoughtless?'

'Don't say a word,' Kester told her. 'Thank the bride and let's go.'

'Aye, we'll away,' said Isa, setting her hat straight and trying to smile. 'All the best, Renata – and Mr Martinello?'

'Federico,' he said kindly.

'Federico. And have a lovely time, wherever you're going. Sylvie, come on. Ruth, where's your hat? Kester, have you thae coppers I gave you for the tram?'

'But have you got the *bomboniere*?' cried Renata. 'You must not go without your leaving presents, you know!'

Yes, someone had given Isa their beautiful little presents – tiny flower vases for the ladies, cuff-links for the gentlemen, all so exquisitely wrapped and addressed in the bride's own hand. Thank you again, thank you, keep in touch, all the best, *arrivederci*!

'Oh, thank God, we're away!' cried Isa, as she and her family ran from the reception, keeping their heads down as though they feared being recognised.

'I never felt so ashamed in my life,' Isa told Sylvie when they were all seated together on the wooden seats of the tram, clutching their presents. 'With all thae Italians around, seeing you and Guido behaving like – well, I canna say what, but it wasn't good. And that poor girl, Marilena, so upset. What were you thinking of, Sylvie? What got into you?'

'Ma, we were only dancing!' Sylvie answered in a fierce whisper. 'What's wrong with that? Why is everybody making so much fuss?'

'You know very well why,' said Ruth, glancing round at the other passengers, all studiously reading their evening papers, but clearly eavesdropping with interest. 'Mebbe we should talk about this at home.'

'A fellow doesn't dance all the time with the same girl at a wedding,' Kester told Sylvie. 'He's supposed to be polite and ask the bride and the relatives. Guido didn't even ask Marilena and he's supposed to be engaged to her.'

'He is not engaged to Marilena!' Sylvie flashed. 'He told me himself, it's all been dreamed up by their mothers. There's nothing in it at all!'

'He should still have asked her to dance,' said Isa. 'But he preferred to make a spectacle of himself with you, Sylvie, and showed you up at the same time. And then there was that awful argument! What a carry on at poor Renata's wedding, and her looking so lovely! All I wanted, was to get away.'

'Well, we are away,' muttered Sylvie. 'So I hope you're happy.'

'Wait till I tell your father about this,' said Isa. 'He'll have something to say, I promise you!'

'You're going to tell Dad?' Sylvie gave a bitter laugh. 'Anyone'd think I was six years old!'

'Behave like it sometimes,' said Isa.

It was a miserable end to a splendid day. When they got home, they changed out of their smart clothes, put on ordinary things and felt worse, because when they'd dressed earlier, everything was to come and they were looking forward to it. Now it was all over and there had been unpleasantness, and Sylvie had been to blame, or partly to blame, and Marilena made unhappy and her mother furious, and that was all they would remember about poor Renata's wedding day.

Jack, of course, was mystified by the whole affair, when Isa tried to tell him what had happened over the inevitable pot of tea.

'Sylvie danced with Guido and Marilena was upset? Well, it's no' the end of the world, is it?' he asked, gratefully drinking the tea and eating ginger cake, for who knew when there'd be a meal ready at this rate?

'Just what I say!' cried Sylvie. 'It's no' the end of the world! If Marilena hadn't thrown hysterics, no one would have noticed!'

'Think not?' asked Kester. 'Everyone was watching you two showing off like you were a floorshow, or something. I was listening to what folk were saying, and I can tell you they were noticing, all right!'

'Well, don't say any more for now,' said Ruth. 'What's done is done. It's right what Ma said, Sylvie just didn't think.'

'No, and I'm still no' thinking I did anything wrong!' cried Sylvie. 'Guido's just a beautiful dancer and I liked dancing with him and I didn't want to stop, that's all there is to it! Now, I'm away to bed. I've got a terrible headache, thanks to all you folk going on at me. Goodnight!'

They sat in silence, as she slammed from the room, then Kester took a large slice of cake and solemnly worked his way through it.

'I'm glad Fenella wasn't there,' he said, when he'd finished. 'What would she have thought?'

'Whatever she'd have thought, don't you dare go fixing up a wedding yet a while,' snapped Isa. 'We've had all we want of weddings for now, thank you very much.'

'Sylvie, are you awake?' asked Ruth, tiptoeing into the bedroom some time later.

'No,' sniffed Sylvie. 'I'm sound asleep.'

'Oh, Sylvie, I'm sorry things went so wrong today,' said Ruth, sitting on her sister's bed. 'It was all a bit public, that was all, eh?'

Sylvie sat up, putting her hair back from her flushed, tear-stained face. 'It's true what I said, Ruthie. Guido isn't engaged to Marilena. She had no right to go on like she did.'

'I've heard Italian girls take what they see as slights very seriously, and so do their families.'

'Aye, but this wasn't a slight, Ruth. He never even thought about her!'

'I'd say that was something of a slight,' Ruth said with a smile.

'No, I mean, he never thought he should be dancing with her.'

Sylvie leaned back against her pillows. 'He's awful handsome, eh, Ruth? I think he's better looking than when we knew him in Ginger Street.'

'He's OK.'

Sylvie hesitated. 'He's asked me out, you know. Asked me to go dancing next week at the Palais.'

Ruth stood up. 'Are you going to go?' she asked evenly, wondering what on earth their mother would say.

'Of course I am! And don't look like that. I needn't tell Ma.'

'Sylvie, that'd no' be a good start, would it?'

'Who's starting anything?' Sylvie suddenly got up and draped a cardigan around her shoulders. 'I'm starving, I've just realised, I never had any tea.'

'Ma's sending Kester out for fish and chips,' Ruth told her. 'She says she can't be bothered to cook anything tonight.'

'Fish and chips! Oh, Ruth, tell Kester to get some for me, eh? And I think I might as well get dressed again.'

'Honestly, Sylvie!' Ruth stood, laughing at her sister, but Sylvie only began throwing on clothes.

'I saw you dancing with Nicco,' she remarked, running a comb through her hair. 'You seemed to be getting on very well. Will you be seeing him again?'

'Nicco?' Ruth was genuinely surprised. 'No, I don't think so. Why should I?'

Chapter Eighteen

She did see him again. It was on the following Wednesday, at five o'clock. The office workers of the firm MacRobbie and MacRobbie, Writers to the Signet and Commissioners for Oaths, were going home, running up the steps from the basement entrance of the Queen Street premises, some already lighting cigarettes, for Mr Joseph MacRobbie, the senior partner, did not approve of smoking during working hours. Ruth was with a friend of hers, a typist named Hattie Brown. They were discussing a Greta Garbo film they might go to see later in the week. When Ruth turned her eyes from Hattie's face, she saw Nicco.

For a moment, he didn't really register with her. He looked different, anyway, in a sports coat and a trilby hat, and why would Nicco be in Queen Street, the heart of the New Town, when he should be in Ginger Street? Then she remembered that this was Wednesday, his early closing day, so this could be Nicco, in fact, was Nicco, and after the second or two it had taken for her mind to work it all out, she was smiling and saying, 'Hello, Nicco, what are you doing here?'

His eyes went to Hattie, who smiled knowingly and walked on, calling, 'Goodbye, Ruth. See you tomorrow.'

'Oh, yes. 'Bye, Hattie!'

Nicco, touching his hat, relaxed a little. 'I wanted to see you again,' he said disarmingly.

'Oh.' Ruth, taken aback, tried to recover herself. 'You didn't say anything at the wedding.'

'You know what happened at the wedding.'

They began to walk slowly along Queen Street, past the tall New Town houses that had once been private homes and were now mainly offices of the grander kind. Nicco was looking at Ruth cagily, trying to guess her response, but all she was feeling was surprise. When she'd been fourteen, the appearance of Nicco like this would have seemed the answer to a prayer. But she was no longer fourteen and didn't pray.

'I'm really surprised to see you here,' she said, after a pause. 'I mean, taking the trouble to come to the office. The thing is, I'm just on my way home.'

'You think I shouldn't have come?'

They had reached the corner that turned into Hanover Street and had stopped. Nicco was looking down into Ruth's face; she was looking away, at the crowds of city workers going home. Just up the road was the stop where she caught her tram. Already quite a queue was forming.

'Ruth?' Nicco said gently.

She looked up, smiling uncertainly. Why was she behaving like this? Really, she was pleased he had come to seek her out, wasn't she? She didn't know, wasn't sure what she thought. There was just the feeling of surprise, that was all. So many years had passed. They were both different people from those youngsters in Ginger Street.

'No, I'm glad you've come,' she told him. 'Only thing is, I have to get home. Ma gets worked up if we're late.'

'I don't want to make you late. I thought if I came today – my half day, you see – I could ask you to meet me some other time.'

'When, though? You don't have much time off.'

'I could come earlier next Wednesday and we could have a bit of lunch somewhere. If you'd like that.'

'I would. It'd be lovely.'

'If I were to meet you at your office at one o'clock, say, we could go to a place I know off Dundas Street. It's a little Italian café. I know the men who run it. One of them looked after the shop for me on Renata's wedding day.'

'One o'clock, Wednesday, then. All right, I'll look forward to it.'

'You'll come?' He seemed surprised and relieved. 'That's good, that's wonderful. Shall I see you to your tram?'

It was strange the way it happened, but somehow, as the tram moved off, Ruth found Nicco still with her on the upper deck. They'd got the last two seats and there he was, next to her, his long thin fingers folding the tickets he'd bought, his eyes on her.

'What are you doing, Nicco?' she asked, laughing. 'You're coming home with me? You could. You could have your tea. Ma always makes plenty.'

Nicco laughed, too, but wryly. 'I don't think so, Ruth, thank you. I don't think your mother would want to see me at the moment.'

'Because of Guido? But Ma likes him! She thinks he's wonderful, the way he pretends to kiss her hand and all that.'

'Things are a bit different now.'

'Ma blames Sylvie as much as Guido for what happened. Anyway, they didn't mean any harm, they were just happy, dancing together.'

'I still think I'd better keep our of your mother's way.'

'So, what are you doing on this tram?'

'I wanted a little more time with you.'

Ruth looked out of the window. They were passing the gates to the Royal Botanic Gardens, some way from her stop. More time for Nicco to be with her. More time for her to be with him.

'I don't like to say this,' she said quietly. 'But I bet I'm no' popular with your mother, either.'

Nicco was silent.

'Isn't that true, Nicco?'

'Well, I haven't told her about meeting you,' he admitted. 'Things are difficult just now.'

'Why ever did you decide to come seeking me, then?' Ruth cried spiritedly. 'You're asking for trouble!'

'I have a right to see you,' he said, in a low voice. 'I decided that the other night, after the wedding.'

'Why? What happened?'

After Renata and Federico had left for their honeymoon, the Riettis

94

had all gone back to Vittorio's café, which was empty, having been closed for the day. Earlier, Brigida had stopped them all from shouting at Guido – it was Renata's wedding, she would not have it spoiled by a family row. After the newly-weds had left, that would be the time to speak to Guido, and would be best done back at the café, over a bottle of wine and something to eat. Naturally, Federico's parents would not be invited. This was Rietti family business only.

Nicco, next to Ruth in the rattling tram, re-lived that time in his uncle's living room, where his aunt had set out the red wine and the cold meats, olives, hardboiled eggs and tomatoes, while his mother sat like something carved and his weeping sister studied her blotched face in Brigida's mirror and wept even more. Only Guido had appeared unmoved, though he was tossing off the wine pretty quickly.

'Now, Guido, what have you to say for yourself?' his father asked uneasily. 'It is a question of Marilena's honour, you understand. You are her betrothed.'

'Excuse me,' Guido interrupted. 'I am not Marilena's betrothed.' He turned to Marilena herself. 'You know that's true, don't you, Marilena?'

She shook her head. 'It is not true, Guido. Mamma arranged everything some time ago. She told me I was to marry you, and it would be a wonderful match.'

'But I never said I would marry you!' he cried, his composure for the first time beginning to crack. He turned to Brigida. 'Mamma, be honest! This is something you fixed up with Aunt Carlotta, isn't it? But when did I ever say I'd go along with it? I love Marilena, she's my cousin, she's family, but I don't want to marry her. And I bet she doesn't want to marry me. She's a beautiful girl, she could marry anyone? Why me?'

Carlotta's dark eyes flashed. 'You know why!' she stormed. 'You have just said, you are family. So, you are from the home village. You understand our feelings, you understand what our own place means to us, our village and the bell tower, the spirit of the bell tower! Renata has been lucky, she has found a young man who understands that, too, but Marilena might never find anyone. How can she marry out? There is only you, Guido, and your mamma and I, we thought you were happy about it, we thought you wanted Marilena! Now you have humiliated her before everyone and you must make amends.'

'I did not humiliate her,' Guido answered, with desperation. 'All I did was dance with another girl. How am I supposed to make amends?'

'Nicco, you're Marilena's brother, you should be telling Guido what to do,' Vittorio muttered, finishing his wine. 'But Guido's my son, so I'll tell him, if you can't.' He looked at Guido. 'You must marry Marilena as soon as possible.'

'That's right,' Brigida said eagerly. 'Carlotta can announce the engagement in the paper tomorrow, make it all formal, then we'll begin to make arrangements—'

'No,' Guido said flatly. 'I won't do it. I have the right to marry as I choose. I have the right to dance with Sylvie Millar if I choose. And I have the right to take her out, if I choose. And I'm going to do that.' He stood up. 'Believe me, I don't want to upset you, and I'm really sorry if I've hurt you, Marilena, but I have to live my own life as I see it.'

There was a stunned silence, then his father said:

'You want to live your own life as you see it? Guido, that's nonsense. All our lives depend on other people's. You cannot live your life just for yourself.'

'And it's not even true!' Brigida cried shrilly. 'Guido, you know you care as much about the family as anyone. You follow Mussolini, Il Duce, who tells us to revere the family and our country and all our traditions. All that's happened is that you've fallen in love. Or, think you have.'

'In love!' Carlotta boomed contemptuously. 'What does it mean, in love? An excuse to hurt your family!'

'You have fallen for Sylvie Millar, fallen for her fair hair,' Brigida went on tremulously. 'Isn't that true, Guido? Isn't it?'

'All I want is to take her dancing,' he said firmly. 'And that's my right.'

And Nicco, who did not usually admire his cousin, admired him then. Guido had had the courage to face his family for something he believed in, and it took courage to face the family, by God it did. Would I have that courage? thought Nicco. Should I have it? Ruth's face came into his mind, a face he had always liked to look at, even years ago when she had been too young for him to think of as anything except a child. But she was not a child now and he had found her again and wanted to see her again. Would see her again, if she were willing.

He looked at her now as the evening sunlight filtered through the tram windows and shone on her fine, open face, on those blue-grey eyes he remembered so well, that turned-up nose he'd always found so endearing.

'I'll explain sometime,' he said lightly. 'But now, aren't we nearly at your stop?'

When they left the tram, he walked with her almost as far as her father's shop, then halted.

'Better not go any farther, Ruth.'

'I hate all this secrecy, Nicco.'

'Are you planning to tell your folks you're seeing me next week?'

Ruth lowered her eyes. 'I don't think I need.'

'Well, then, your dad needn't see me, either.'

She shrugged. 'Might be best.'

'You do want to see me next week?' he asked quickly. 'You're not thinking you'd be better off out of it all?'

'I don't want to cause trouble. I mean, what will you say to your mother when you come next week?'

'I often have things to do on my half day. See the suppliers and that sort of thing. It'll seem no different.'

'It will be different, though.' Ruth gave Nicco a long, grave look. 'But I suppose it'll be all right, for once.'

'For once?'

'Nicco, let's see how things go, shall we?'

He bit his lip. 'There was a time when you wouldn't have been so cautious.'

'You said yourself, I'm older now. Quite grown up.' She suddenly reached up and brushed his cheek with her lips. 'We're different people, Nicco, we're starting from scratch.'

97

'As long as you're not ruling me out of the race.'

They both laughed, both pleased, Nicco because she had kissed him, Ruth because she'd made him happy.

'Till next week,' Nicco said, and left her, walking fast to the next tram stop, stopping once to look back, then hurrying on. When she could no longer see him, Ruth turned and went home, going through the shop where her father and Kester were still working and Bob MacAllan was just in from his deliveries.

'Are you late?' asked Kester. 'You look as though you've been running. Your face is red.'

'Aye, blushing,' said Bob, with a grin. 'What've you been up to, then?'

'Nothing,' said her father, also grinning. 'When's our Ruthie get up to anything?'

'I knew Nicco was sweet on you!' cried Sylvie, when Ruth, rather against her better judgement, told her she would be meeting him the following week. 'It was just the way he was looking at you, that time you were dancing. Remember, I asked if you were seeing him again?'

'I'm no' sure I should be seeing him again,' Ruth said slowly. 'It's like I said to him, we could be asking for trouble. Don't say anything to Ma, will you?'

'As though I would! I've got secrets of my own to worry about.'

Chapter Nineteen

When Sylvie arrived at the *Palais de Danse* on Saturday evening, she found Guido already waiting. He had wanted to collect her from home, but had understood, of course, that that would not have been a good idea.

'When will your mother like me again?' he murmured, as Sylvie came to him, after hanging up her coat and putting on her dancing shoes. 'She always used to have a soft spot for me.'

'Och, she'll soon forget all that trouble at the wedding,' Sylvie said easily. 'It never meant anything, anyway.'

Guido's blue eyes flickered. He knew how much it had meant. 'I'll get the tickets,' he told Sylvie. 'You know, I can't believe we're together like this, just the two of us. And you look so pretty, Sylvie. *Una bellissima ragazza!*'

She smiled, relieved that she had managed to meet him at all, for it had not been easy to work out a lie that her mother would accept. In the end, she had said she was going to the dance with girls from JJ's, but there had been a strange look in her mother's eye, as though she did not altogether believe her. It was true, of course, that it was unusual for Sylvie to be going out with girlfriends, and then she had taken so much trouble getting ready, putting on her latest dance dress, working on her make-up, fiddling with her hair. All this for girlfriends, Isa wondered?

'Ma, I'm hoping to dance with young men, no' my girlfriends,' Sylvie had said brightly. 'And I always like to look nice.'

'Well, have a good time, then,' Isa said at last. 'Remember, I don't want you coming home after eleven, or on your own. Wait, I'll give you something for a taxi.'

'I can share one with one of the girls. She lives in Trinity, too.'

But as Isa began looking in her purse for a shilling, Sylvie, eaten up with guilt, said, no, no, she could pay, and avoiding Ruth's cool gaze, ran for the tram. Why ever should Ruth look so disapproving? She was going out with Nicco and keeping that a secret, wasn't she? It occurred to Sylvie that she and her sister were both getting into deep water, meeting these Italian cousins, but it was too late now to back out from meeting Guido. Anyway, she wanted to meet him. He excited her more than any other man she knew. To be in his arms again, moving to his guidance, feeling his body against hers – she wasn't going to give that up. At least, not tonight.

It was all just as she had dreamed, when they were dancing together. All the magic she remembered from the wedding came back, and in a way was more intense, because the people around them were strangers, they could almost feel they were alone. Guido's blue eyes scarcely left her face, as they covered the floor, and she knew that as he exerted the power of his dancing over her, she herself was captivating him. The knowledge thrilled her, so much so she didn't want the dancing ever to end, but of course the band had to have an interval and beer, and the dancers had to rest.

Guido brought soft drinks to their table, fixing his eyes again on Sylvie, who pretended to be interested in looking round the ballroom, but was well aware of that strong, passionate gaze never leaving her face.

'You know, it is strange,' he told her. 'If you were an Italian girl, you would never be here with me like this.'

'Oh, I know. They aren't allowed out much, are they?' Sylvie sipped her lemonade. 'Poor things. What are their parents frightened of?'

'It is the custom. An Italian girl will not go out alone with a young man unless she is engaged to him. Sometimes, not even then.' Guido laughed. 'And if a young man calls, it's pretty well considered enough for an engagement, anyway. If he doesn't follow it up, he is accused of dishonouring her.' He drank his lemonade. 'I tell you, Sylvie, men have a difficult life.'

'Sounds to me it's the women who have a difficult life.'

'You know I have been accused of dishonouring Marilena? Because I didn't dance with her at the wedding?'

Sylvie shook her head. 'I think our way of managing things is better. More casual.'

'Yes, but then there is the other side of things.'

'What other side?'

He hesitated. 'Well, when an Italian man marries an Italian girl, he knows that for her, he is the first. She will not have been out with other men, she will not even have kissed anyone else or held hands, or anything like that.'

Sylvie raised her eyebrows. 'And you think that's good?'

'Of course! It is what men want.'

'But the girls won't expect the same from you?'

'No. It is different for men.'

'I think that's terrible, Guido! Really unfair!'

'So, you do not mind going out with young men?' he asked quietly.

'I've been out with one or two fellows, yes.'

'And your parents don't object?'

'They trust me, Guido.'

'These young men, they kiss you?'

Sylvie flushed. 'That's none of your business!'

'I'm sorry.' He lowered his eyes. 'You can't blame me for asking. You are very important to me.'

'Important? This is the first time we've been out together.'

'You will come out with me again, though, won't you?'

She didn't at once say yes. It was true he was more exciting to be with than any other man she knew, but on the other hand, going out with him would have its difficulties, and she was one who liked an easy life. Her eyes went to the platform to which the members of the band were returning, her heart leaped a little and her feet began to tap at the thought of the music starting up again. She was about to tell Guido she would go out with him another time, when a tall young man with light hair and a broad, friendly face paused at their table.

'Hello, Sylvie!' he said cheerfully. 'How are you?'

'Hello, Mark. Fine, thanks.' Sylvie glanced at Guido. 'This is Mark Imrie, Guido. His brother was at school with Kester. Mark, this is Guido Rietti.'

The two men murmured a greeting.

'I know Kester,' Guido said, pleasantly enough, but his eyes on Mark were watchful. 'We worked together at Gibb's biscuit factory.'

'Is that right? I'm in the police myself. A sergeant.' As the band suddenly struck up with a quick-step, Mark smiled down at Sylvie. 'How about a dance, Sylvie? I'm all on my own tonight. You don't mind, Mr – er – Rietti?'

'As a matter of fact, I do mind,' Guido answered, rising. He took Sylvie's hand. 'Sylvie is dancing with me, Mr Imrie, and only me. Good evening.'

Mark Imrie's smile had become contrite. 'My mistake – shouldn't have asked. Nice meeting you, Sylvie. Give my best to Kester.'

As he left them, making for the bar, Guido's gaze on Sylvie was hard. 'You know that fellow? You've been out with him?'

'No, I told you. He has a younger brother who was at school with Kester. I don't really know him at all.'

'Why should he ask you for a dance, then?'

'Well, he's been to our flat a couple of times. Just when the lads were going to a football match, or something.'

'And that gives him the right to think he can ask you to dance?'

'Honestly, Guido, what's all the fuss about? He's just come to the dance on his own, the way fellows do. Where's the harm in asking me for a dance?'

'It is not the way to do things.' Guido's face was pale, and as he took Sylvie's arm to take her on to the dance floor, she could feel him trembling. 'Men can get angry when someone behaves like that.'

'I wasn't going to say yes, anyway.'

'Weren't you?'

'No. I didn't mind being asked, but I'm with you. I want to dance with you.'

He smiled, all his charm returning, and as he looked down at her, his gaze softened. 'And I with you, Sylvie. Only you.'

They moved away together and for Sylvie that was enough to wipe out the memory of the last little unpleasantness. Being with Guido like this could perhaps make her forget anything, but that thought didn't worry her. It was true that she liked an easy life, but she also liked to live for the moment. And this moment was sweet.

At the end of the evening, it was Guido who ordered a taxi to take her home. Sylvie, sitting close beside him on the back seat, giggled a little.

'When I was little, I thought going in a taxi was the best thing in the world!'

'Still think that?' he asked softly.

'No,' she answered, equally softly.

He paid the taxi off a little way from Sylvie's home, as Isa would be looking out for her, and they stood in the shadows, Guido holding Sylvie by the shoulders, looking into her face.

'I don't like to think of those other men kissing you,' he said, with sudden curtness.

'Did I say they kissed me?'

'They did, didn't they?'

'All right, they did. Goodnight kisses, that's all. Nothing to get excited about.'

'I tell you, I can't bear to think about them.'

'Don't think about them, then,' she answered shortly. 'I told you before, this is none of your business.'

'If we go out together, it is.'

She moved from his grasp. 'So, we needn't go out together.'

'Sylvie, don't say that! Please!'

'Well, it's no' very nice for me, is it, if you're going to find fault with me all the time? Just because I've kissed one or two fellows goodnight? I bet you've kissed plenty of girls from the biscuit factory, eh? Kester said you took plenty out.'

When he made no reply, Sylvie laughed triumphantly.

'There you are! You've kissed other people, I've kissed other people, I don't mind, why should you?'

'I'd like you to mind,' he said at last. 'It would mean I was important to you. As you are to me.'

'I told you, I can't be. Not yet. We don't really know each other.'

'Well, will you come out with me again? We needn't go dancing, we could just go to the pictures, or something.'

'If we go out again, you must promise no' to criticise me, Guido.'

'Oh, God, I promise, Sylvie.'

She looked up into his face, revelling in her power, then kissed him on the lips. 'A goodnight kiss,' she whispered. 'But that one's for you.'

When she let herself into the flat, she was smiling to herself, thinking of the effect her kiss had on Guido. He, who was so experienced with other girls – as long as they were not Italians, of course – had been knocked sideways by one kiss from herself. He had scarcely known what to say to her, and had made no attempt to kiss her back, but when she had said she must go home, had held her hands in a strong dry grip and made her promise to meet him at one of the cinemas. What was on? Who cared? She must just agree to see him again, or he couldn't leave her. All right, she had promised and he had left her, or, rather, he had walked away, looking back all the time, and she had run quickly back home. And here she was, smiling and trying not to, for she knew enough to know that her smile would be tell-tale and she couldn't afford that.

They were watching the door as she came in – her mother, her father, and Ruth, but not Kester.

'I'm on time!' she called, as the kitchen clock struck eleven. 'Got a taxi back, like you said, Ma.'

'With that girl from Trinity?' asked Isa, putting some sewing away.

'There were a couple of us,' Sylvie answered obliquely.

'You're looking very nice,' observed Jack. 'Bet the fellows were around, eh? Whyn't you go too, Ruth?'

'Mebbe next time,' Ruth answered.

'I notice Kester's no' back,' Sylvie remarked, to take attention from herself. 'He comes home when he likes.'

'It's different for men,' Isa murmured, yawning. 'Och, I'm away to ma bed.'

'Me too,' said Sylvie.

*   *   *

104

In their room, she cried in exasperation to Ruth:

'If I hear one more time that something or other is different for men, I think I'll scream!'

'Guido been saying that?' asked Ruth.

'Sort of.' Sylvie took off her dress and hung it up. 'Said a lot of things.'

'How did you get on with him, then?'

'Well, he's a beautiful dancer.'

'I already knew that,' Ruth said dryly.

Sylvie shrugged. 'He's pretty intense, to tell you the truth.'

'Intense? I thought he was all charm. A real ladies' man.'

'He can get worked up.' Sylvie put away her dancing shoes in her half of the wardrobe, then sat on her bed in her slip. 'Tell you who I saw – Mark Imrie. You know, Ron Imrie's brother?'

'Big policeman?'

'That's right. He asked me to dance and Guido was furious. Said I was only dancing with him.'

'You were with him, Sylvie.'

'I know, but some fellows wouldn't have minded so much. Anyway, I didn't dance with Mark, so Guido was happy. Till he started thinking about the other young men I'd been out with.'

Ruth, who had been turning back her bed, gave her sister a quick, sharp look.

'Sylvie, are you seeing Guido again?'

'Just to go to the pictures.'

'I'm wondering if you should get mixed up with him. He sounds as though he could be difficult. Jealous.'

'Och, no. Anyway, I can handle him.' Sylvie unrolled her stockings. 'He's exciting, that's the thing. Different from other fellows.'

'That's the problem, Sylvie. And you're very young, remember, you might no' be able to handle him, as you call it.'

'You're going out with an Italian, aren't you?'

'Nicco's very different from Guido.'

'Well, you run your life, Ruthie, and I'll run mine.'

Ruth was silent for a moment, then went to the door and

looked out. 'Bathroom's empty,' she told Sylvie. 'Do you want to go first?'

'Yes, please.' Sylvie yawned and stretched. 'Ruth, isn't it grand having a bathroom? You remember that old tin bath we used to have?'

'Sylvie, are you going to tell Ma about going out with Guido?'

'Are you going to tell her about Nicco?'

Ruth hesitated. 'Mebbe later.'

'I'll say the same. Listen, there's the door. That'll be Kester back from seeing Lady Fenella. Wonder when he's going to pop the question?'

'That's called changing the subject,' said Ruth, but Sylvie had already gone.

Chapter Twenty

Jack and Kester were in the shop the following Wednesday morning. It was early, they weren't yet open, and Bob MacAllan was outside, sweeping the front. Jack was whistling, as he checked the till, pleased with himself, pleased with his shop that looked so grand. You wouldn't find a better stocked shop than his wherever you looked in the city, and folk knew that as well as he did. They came to him for the best bacon and hams, high-class coffees and teas, wines, preserves, and every kind of grocery item you could wish for. Why, he kept four kinds of rice, and five kinds of sugar! Ladies would come and put their orders in – see, there were the chairs they sat on at the counter – and they would talk with him, and even flirt, some of them, then they'd leave the orders with him for delivery and take themselves off, maybe carrying a little packet of coffee tied up with a bow, just to show they'd been shopping. Och, he really enjoyed himself, doing his job so well for them, and for the ordinary customers who came in too, and he did have ordinary customers who just liked to see something different. Everyone got the same service, whether they shopped with him all the time, or came in for a treat, and it was his attention and devotion, he was sure, that had kept his head above water in spite of the recession. Now, it was all paying off, because he'd long recovered from his shaky start and was getting ready for his new shop, when Kester would have the chance to do as well as his old dad!

'Dad,' said Kester, in a low voice. 'Can you let me have any money?'

Jack's eyebrows rose. He closed the till and looked at Kester.

'Money? How much?'

'I'm no' sure.' Kester's eyes were on the door, watching out for Bob's return. 'I want to – I want to buy Fenella a ring.'

Jack straightened a display of preserves at the side of the counter. 'Never knew you'd got that far,' he said, after a pause. 'I mean, asking her to marry you.'

'I've no' asked her yet.' Kester was embarrassed, twisting the string of his white apron in his large hands. 'I'm pretty sure she'll say yes, though, when I do. We've – talked about the future.'

'So you want to have the ring ready?'

'Aye.'

'How much do you need?'

Kester licked his lips. 'I'd like to get something good, Dad, if possible. It'd make a lot of difference.'

'Well, come on, how much do you want? I'm no' a mind reader, Kester!'

'Mebbe – twenty pounds?'

Jack's eyes started from his head. 'Twenty pounds? Kester, are you crackers, or what? I canna spare that kind o' money! And if that girl wants you, she'll take you whether you can afford a ring or not. Your mother never had an engagement ring, it was all I could manage to buy the wedding ring.' Jack shook his head. 'Soon as I get turned round with the new shop, mebbe I'll get her a ring, a dress ring, you ken, if she'll take it, but she's no' much interested. I'm sorry, Kester, I canna help.'

'But Dad, you got all that money from Cousin Addie! And this shop's doing well, you're opening the new one—'

'All that money I got has been spoken for, Kester. You know I'd to spend more than I thought when we came here, and now I've to think of the new place. I canna do everything, can I?'

'I'd pay you back, Dad,' Kester said eagerly. 'So much a week. I'm no' asking for a gift.'

'Aye, even so.' Jack was looking at the clock. Nearly opening time. 'See if Bob's finished outside, Kester.'

'Dad, will you just think about it? You'll no' be out of pocket, if it's a loan!'

'Mebbe you could find something cheaper, then?'

Kester hesitated. 'I'll try, I'll look around. It's just that Fenella knows I'm going to be manager at Marchmont, and if I can give her a nice ring as well, that'd show her folks I'm right for her.'

Looking into his son's pleading eyes, Jack bit his lip. 'Och, I'll think about it. But I'm making no promises.'

'No, Dad! Thanks, Dad!' Kester was visibly relaxing, his face beaming, when Ruth came hurrying through the shop on her way to work. 'Hallo, Ruth. You're looking smart today, what's on?'

'I always look smart,' Ruth answered quickly. But it was true, she was wearing her best jacket and skirt of blue-grey tweed to match her eyes, with a small blue hat and matching gloves.

'You got an interview, or something?' her father asked fondly.

'No, it's just such a nice morning, I thought I'd wear my suit. Why's everyone taking so much interest?' Ruth's cheeks were a bright pink that turned to red, when Bob MacAllan came in with his broom and grinned.

'Och, lassie, is that you blushing again?'

'I'm away for the tram!' cried Ruth and ran from the shop, banging the door behind her so that its bell jangled loudly and the men laughed.

Travelling into the city on the same old route she knew so well, Ruth felt furious. Not only with Bob, for his teasing – she knew he meant no harm – but also with herself for dressing in such a way as to attract notice. Wearing her best suit to work! It was lucky her mother hadn't spotted it, but then she'd been careful only to put on the jacket after she'd left the flat. Why had she dressed up, anyway, just to meet Nicco for a snack lunch? Deep down, that was the thing that worried her most. Was she wanting to get involved? She'd be crazy, if that were true. Like Guido, he was surrounded by difficulties as thick and impenetrable as a hedge of thorns. Sylvie would soon find that out, if she didn't know it already, and Ruth, who didn't need to find it out, was mystified by her own actions. Agreeing to meet, putting on her best clothes, wanting to look her best. For Nicco? He belonged to the past.

But when, after the strangely long morning, she ran up the steps to the street and saw him waiting there, wearing the same trilby hat and sports coat as before, his dark eyes brightening, a stab of the old excitement he had once inspired stung her as though it were yesterday. Nicco might belong to the past, but here he was in the present, waiting for her, admiring her – for she could tell he was admiring her, and knew that that was why she'd worn her best suit – to see that look of admiration in his eye. Oh, Ruth, she told herself, as she walked beside him down Queen Street, tread carefully. You're on dangerous ground.

Chapter Twenty-One

Valdo's, off Dundas Street, sold cigarettes and sweets, delicious bread and a few groceries, but there were also tables set inside and outside for those who wanted the snacks Rodrigo and his brother, Domenico, served all day.

'This is what I want to do,' Nicco told Ruth, hanging up his hat as they arrived. 'Have tables and serve a little food.'

In Ginger Street? thought Ruth, who couldn't picture it. Still, she said it was a good idea. Workers might come from the offices in the main streets, it could work out.

'*Buon giorno*, Nicco!' cried the Valdo brothers, who were young and good looking, if not quite as good looking as the Rietti cousins. Their large, liquid dark eyes went at once to Ruth, and she knew they were wondering why she was with Nicco when she wasn't Italian.

'This is Signorina Millar,' Nicco said in English. 'She knows my shop in Ginger Street.'

'Ah.' The brothers smiled. A customer, then, not a girlfriend.

'Ruth, meet Rodrigo and Domenico,' Nicco went on. 'I owe Domenico a great thank you. He took care of my shop when Renata was married.'

'Renata!' Domenico cried, and kissed his fingers. 'I lose out there, yes? She is married and on her honeymoon!'

'In Italy,' said Nicco. 'Federico's father paid for it. Ruth, what would you like? Something quick?'

They settled for funghi ripieni, which Nicco said was just stuffed mushrooms served on toasted Italian bread, but very delicious, and sat down at an inside table.

'Renata has gone to Italy, Nicco?' asked Ruth. 'I didn't know that – haven't had her postcard yet.'

'A secret, wasn't it?'

But Ruth was astounded. To go abroad! No one she knew had ever been abroad. Abroad was for other people, society people, folk with money. Sometimes, Ruth had looked at posters in travel agents' shops and sighed over the pictures of the great liners and the famous trains. Even the names were enough to transport you to other worlds. The *Mauretania*, the *Aquitania*, the Blue Train, the Orient Express. Imagine sailing away, all flags waving! Or, boarding the boat train. Having porters put your luggage in your wagon-lit and knowing what to tip. Taking dinner in the restaurant car, where there'd be little lamps over the tables and views of mountains and lakes and deep, dark forests. She'd seen it all on the films, read about it in books. Travel with a capital T! But the idea of anyone she knew travelling that way was something she couldn't quite take in.

'No wonder Renata said they were lucky,' she said slowly. 'Federico's father must be doing well, to give them such a honeymoon.'

'Yes, and now everyone knows he is doing well,' Nicco replied, smiling. 'That's the advantage for him.'

'Whereabouts in Italy have they gone?'

'Why, to our own village, in the south, in the mountains. It's where we'd all like to go. See where our forebears came from – we all dream of that. Some dream of staying.'

'Do you, Nicco?'

He shrugged. 'I can't imagine going home for good, but I'd like to see Italy. One day.'

Their mushrooms arrived, stuffed with bacon and tomatoes, garnished with mozzarella cheese, and served by Rodrigo with a flourish. Afterwards, they would like ice-cream? They said they'd just have coffee. Ruth had wangled another half hour for her lunch-hour by promising to work late the following day; even so, they couldn't linger.

Over the little meal, which was a welcome novelty to Ruth, Nicco talked of his fellow Italians. How most of the Edinburgh community came from a certain province, and those in Glasgow from another. All over the United Kingdom, there would be Italian communities with loyalties to particular places back home.

'We call it *campanilismo*.' Nicco grinned. 'Don't look so scared, Ruth! It only means the spirit of the bell tower, and that's just the spirit of place. It's a way of putting it all together. Family feeling. Love of home.' He drank the coffee Rodrigo had brought. 'Loyalty to what we all know.'

'I see,' said Ruth, thinking that the more he said, the further he moved away. It was just as well she had been careful to remind herself of the dangers of getting involved. *Campanilismo*! What Scot could compete with that? No wonder Nicco's mother wanted Guido for Marilena. He was probably the only one that would fit the bill. As for Nicco – Ruth couldn't imagine who would suit for him. She drank coffee, too, and looked gloomily into space.

'Of course, there are so few of us in Edinburgh, things are difficult for the older generation,' Nicco was saying. 'I mean, young people sometimes have to marry out, as we say, and then the parents get upset.'

'That would be your mother,' said Ruth.

He looked down into his cup. 'Yes, that would be Mamma,' he agreed.

It was on the tip of Ruth's tongue to say, 'So, you'd never be able to marry out, then?' but she stopped herself in time. To ask a question like that would be getting involved, and she had decided against that.

They had to go, time was ticking by.

'Mustn't be late,' said Ruth, rising, and Nicco paid the bill, after some argument with Rodrigo and Domenico, who wanted their lunch to be on the house. It seemed to her that the brothers' eyes were puzzled as she said goodbye. Maybe they were thinking she was, after all, Nicco's girlfriend? They must have known that wasn't likely. They knew the signora, didn't they?

On the way back to Queen Street, Nicco asked Ruth if she liked her job.

'Yes, but I'm thinking of doing something else. Mebbe trying for the Civil Service examination.'

'What would that mean?'

'Well, I'd sit the exam when I was twenty-one, and if I passed I'd go to one of the departments.'

'In Scotland?'

'Might be London.'

'I see.' Nicco was keeping his handsome face expressionless. 'I said you'd do well, Ruth.'

'Haven't passed the exam, yet. Might never pass.'

'You've got another year.' He suddenly smiled. 'So we've got another year.'

That was a joke? Ruth wasn't certain how to react, so she laughed. She couldn't see herself and Nicco going out for a whole year, when even this first planned meeting had been difficult enough to arrange. Nicco, his smile fading, stood still and made her stand with him, stand very close.

'You laugh, Ruth, but I would like to be with you for a year – or, any time.'

'Nicco, we've only just met.'

'Met again. We knew each other before.'

'I didn't mean anything to you before.'

He gently ran his hand down her face. 'So, now you take your revenge?'

'That's silly talk, Nicco. That's a piece of nonsense.'

'Yes. I'm sorry. Maybe you just don't want to be involved, then?' He sighed. 'I wouldn't blame you.'

They began to walk on, Ruth's cheeks flaming at the words that had found their target. She couldn't deny them, she did want to be safe. Yet, at the thought of not seeing Nicco again, the future appeared to her as unaccountably grey. She would have her studies and they were important, she would have the chance of meeting some 'nice Scottish boy' who would please her family, she need never cross swords with Signora Rietti. Oh, God, but she wanted Nicco! Yes, now she knew. It hadn't taken long for the old feelings to resurface, and all her self-deception was as bubbles blowing in the wind before them. About as solid. About as real. Her hand found Nicco's and felt instant response. He looked down at her, she smiled up at him.

114

'Shall we try to meet again?' he asked quietly.

'I don't know when it could be. You only have Wednesday half day, I only have Saturday.'

'What about Sunday? Sunday afternoon?'

'You could manage that?'

He shrugged. 'I'd think of some excuse.'

Ruth hesitated. To meet on Sunday afternoon would mean she too would have to make excuses to her mother. Make excuses? Tell lies. She didn't feel ready.

'Why don't we meet again like this? Next Wednesday?'

'So little time, Ruth. I want to be with you without looking at the clock.'

'I know, but we needn't go to the café. We could get sandwiches, we could walk in Princes Street Gardens.'

He nodded. 'Wednesday, then. As long as I see you sometime.'

They had reached Queen Street and the offices of MacRobbie and MacRobbie. It was the end of their time together.

'Oh, Nicco, I wish I'd had the afternoon off!' Ruth sighed.

'Not as much as I do, *cara*.'

'I was thinking, I could perhaps come over to Ginger Street on Saturday afternoon, buy something at your shop?'

A look of doubt swam into his eyes, though he said at once, 'Yes, you could.'

'But you don't want me to?'

'It's just, Marilena will be there.'

'And won't want to see me? I understand, I'm Sylvie's sister.'

'She's pretty low, Ruth. Knows Guido is taking your sister out.'

'Couldn't she go out somewhere herself? That Italian club Guido goes to?'

He shook his head. 'Mamma's not in favour.'

'I wish there was something I could do.'

'She'll be all right, Mamma will find her somebody.'

Their thoughts moved from Marilena to themselves, and they held hands and said goodbye, though didn't dare to kiss. Not in Queen Street.

'Till next week, then,' said Nicco, at last drawing away. 'Same time?'

'Same time.'

*　　*　　*

Sitting at her desk, back at the office, Ruth felt the pang of parting. 'Sweet sorrow', was it? Vague memories of school Shakespeare floated into her mind. Perhaps there was a sweetness about saying goodbye, if you knew it wasn't really goodby, if it held all the promise of the next meeting. A little smile curved her lips, as she looked down at her work, and Hattie Brown, sitting opposite, gave a smile too, at the thought of Ruth's finding one of Mr Joseph's conveyance files amusing.

Chapter Twenty-Two

Guilt. That was the price the Millar sisters were paying for their relationships with the Rietti cousins as the autumn advanced. The guilt was caused by the secrecy they both felt they had to preserve, and every time they looked at their parents when they went out to meet the Italians, they wished they could just admit the truth and get rid of their burden. Just say, 'I'm seeing Nicco today,' or, 'I'm seeing Guido.' Why not? Why shouldn't they do that? It was true that Italians weren't popular at the moment, since Mussolini had invaded Abyssinia and upset Britain and the League of Nations, but Nicco and Guido weren't just any Italians. They were known to Isa and Jack, their families had been friends. Until Renata's wedding, anyhow.

But now Renata was back from her honeymoon, full of all that she'd seen. Black-shirted fascists in Rome, the home village in the mountains, all their relatives and friends, the bell tower! Yes, she and Federico had been welcomed into their own past, touched their own community, and had had a time they would never forget, but the point was, they were back, the wedding was long over, it was time to forget what Guido had done. That was Sylvie's view. And if Guido could be forgiven and accepted, so could Nicco be accepted. That was Ruth's view. Yet, they both held back from telling their parents, and by parents they meant their mother, that they were seeing the Rietti cousins.

How they envied Kester! Everything so simple and straight-forward for him in his relationship with Fenella. He'd even got the ring, from one of Jack's customers, a jeweller, who had offered an elegant little Victorian ring of three small diamonds in a gold setting for less than the twenty pounds Kester had wanted to pay. Jack had agreed to lend the money, Fenella had expressed herself delighted, and before anyone could adjust to the idea, the announcement had appeared in the paper and Kester was an engaged man.

'I canna believe it,' sighed Isa. 'Our Kester, leaving the nest!'

'Not yet,' Jack replied. 'He canna afford to get wed before I open the new shop and that'll be some time yet. After Hogmanay, anyway.'

'They're thinking of a spring wedding,' Sylvie said morosely. Like the rest of the family, she had not been pleased at her brother's engagement, and had particularly not wanted to see a pretty diamond ring on Fenella's finger. Isa, too, had called the purchase of the ring a shocking waste of money, when you thought of how many bairns could be fed for the cost of it.

'Och, it's no' Kester's job to feed other people's bairns!' cried Jack, laughing. 'Have a heart, Isa.'

'Well, I never had a ring!' she cried spiritedly. 'And I never wanted one, either. A wedding ring was enough for me and should be enough for that bean-pole Kester's marrying, too.'

'I suppose she is on the tall side,' said Ruth. 'But she's attractive. Lovely hair.'

'Blonde,' said Isa. 'All men like blonde hair.' She glanced at Sylvie. 'I bet that's why Guido was after you at Renata's wedding, eh?'

Sylvie blushed scarlet and Ruth asked hastily if they'd be having the MacMenzies family back, now that Fenella's mother had had them all over one Sunday afternoon. Isa groaned and said she supposed she'd have to ask them, but it would only be for afternoon tea, because that was what Mrs MacMenzies had given them and would be only fair. She'd do egg and cress sandwiches, a few scones and one of her fruit cakes, that'd make a nice enough spread. Thinking about it, she'd go and check the dried fruit for the cake now, so that if she needed more, Jack could bring some up from the shop.

'Why didn't you tell Ma about Guido just then?' Ruth asked

118

Sylvie, when their parents were out of the way. 'It's time she was told.'

'About Nicco, too, then.'

'Yes.' More than anything, Ruth wanted to tell her mother about Nicco, for her snatched lunch-time meetings with him were becoming more and more difficult to bear. She knew he felt the same, was longing to take her somewhere where they could be alone, could kiss and caress as lovers do, even though Nicco said he'd feel bad about it, for really they should be married. And though they had never put it into words, they both knew that marriage was for them. It was true that Ruth had her studying to do, for Nicco was firm that she should take her exam, he would not be the one to take that away from her, but what she would do if she passed was something she hadn't yet faced. All that mattered was to have time together and both were approaching the state of mind when they could think of nothing else. They would have to meet on Sundays, go somewhere for the afternoon, but to move forward like that, Ruth felt she must be honest with her mother, whether or not Nicco was the same with his.

'I do want to tell Ma about Nicco,' she said fervently. 'I need to be with him, that's the thing, and I don't mean in Princes Street Gardens!'

'You're really in love, aren't you?' Sylvie asked curiously. 'What's going to happen?'

'How do you mean?'

'Well, are you thinking you'll marry Nicco?'

Ruth hesitated. 'There's nothing decided.'

'But will you? Come on, you must know what you want!'

'I do know.' Ruth's face was scarlet. 'I do know, Sylvie. I want to marry Nicco.'

Sylvie was silent for a moment. 'It'll no' be easy,' she said at last. 'I think I'm glad I'm not in love with Guido.'

Ruth, relieved that Sylvie's interest had passed from herself, studied her sister. 'You've been out with Guido often enough.'

'I know. It was exciting at first, but now – well, I think he's too keen. He isn't what I thought.'

'What did you think he was?'

119

'Sort of like me, just wanting to have a nice time. Go dancing, you ken, mebbe to the pictures, have a few kisses.'

'I thought that's how he'd be, too.'

'Aye, with other girls, no' with me. Right from the start, he's kept telling me I was important and wanted me to think he was, too. And then, when we're out together, if I see anyone I know, he never wants me to speak to them, and if I do, he wants to know all about them, and if they were the ones I went out with before, and if they kissed me and all of that.' Sylvie shook her head. 'I tell you, I just don't dare look at any guy now, in case it starts him off. It's getting me down, Ruth, and that's a fact.'

'I told you he was jealous, Sylvie.'

'Aye, well, I've had enough of it. I'm going to have to tell him that I don't want to see him any more. It's a good job I never said anything to Ma about him. The next time we go out together will be the last.'

Cold fingers touched Ruth's spine. 'How d'you think he'll take it, Sylvie?'

'He won't like it, but what can I do? I know he wants to marry me, but I don't want to marry him. I don't want to marry an Italian, anyway. There'd be too many problems.'

'You're right, you're no' in love with him, so it'd be best to stop seeing him. But, be careful, Sylvie, eh? Let him down lightly.'

'Oh, yes,' Sylvie agreed. 'I'll be very kind.'

Oh, God, thought Ruth.

Chapter Twenty-Three

A few days later, when Sylvie was returning to Millinery from her lunch break, she saw a policeman. A sergeant, tall and fair, carrying his hat, and smiling at her. What a relief! She had just been wondering what crime she might have committed, when she'd realised the policeman was Mark Imrie.

'Mark! What are you doing here? And in your uniform, too!' Sylvie laughed. 'Am I in trouble?'

'Of course not.' Mark laughed with her, a strong easy laugh that made her feel good, she didn't know why. 'Just want your advice. Need you to help me find a present for my mother, it's her birthday.'

'When?'

'Tomorrow.'

'Now isn't that typical of a man, leaving it to the last minute? But why ask me?'

'Remembered you worked here, knew you'd find me something.' Mark looked up and down the carpeted corridor with a desperate gaze. 'Must be something, eh? I mean, somewhere in this shop? It's my lunch break, I've only got half an hour left.'

Sylvie smiled. 'Well, I'm supposed to be back at work, but I daresay I could spare a few minutes, as you're a customer. How much d'you want to spend?'

He shrugged. 'Few bob?'

'Well, let's go and look at the scarves and gloves. You can get a nice silk scarf for about five and eleven.'

When an interested colleague had produced a fine selection of scarves, Sylvie sorted through them and Mark watched. 'Of course, I don't know your mother,' Sylvie reminded him. 'What colours does she like?'

'Colours?' He was gazing into Sylvie's eyes. 'Er – I can't be sure. Think she likes blue. Or, could be pink.'

Sylvie and the other assistant exchanged glances.

'What about this?' asked Sylvie, taking up a Paisley patterned scarf. 'I think this would suit anyone.'

Mark put a large hand towards it, then withdrew. 'Better be careful with that, eh? Looks just right, though. How much is it?'

'Five shillings,' said the assistant. 'Special offer.'

'I'll take it,' Mark declared. 'What a weight off my mind! Where do I get some wrapping paper?'

'Miss Monro will wrap it for you. She's got some really nice tissue and she'll put a ribbon on for you.' Sylvie winked at her colleague. 'You can do that, eh, Agnes?'

'Anything to oblige! Would you pay at the cash desk, sir?'

'I can't thank you enough, Sylvie,' Mark told her, as they left the scarf and glove department, Mark gingerly carrying his small parcel, Agnes smiling after them. 'I knew you'd be my saviour. Can I give you a cup of tea or coffee or something?'

'I'd like to say yes, but I'm due back at Millinery.' Sylvie stopped to look up into Mark's face, which was rather a long way from her own. 'Hope your ma has a lovely birthday.'

'She's laying on a tea and all the works.' Mark touched Sylvie's hand. 'Listen, what's all this about Kester getting engaged, then? Are you going to be bridesmaid?'

'There's no date for the wedding yet.'

'How about you?'

'Me?'

'Are you getting engaged to that Italian guy I've seen you around with?'

'No, I am not. Whatever gave you that idea?'

'So, there's hope for me, then? I mean, to ask you out?'

'Maybe.'

'All right, I'm asking, then.'

Sylvie hesitated. 'Can we leave it for a bit?'

'I thought we might go dancing.'

'Yes, that'd be nice.'

'So, when can I ask again, then?'

'Next week? I take my lunch between twelve and one.'

'Funny, I do too. Or, I can make sure I do.'

As she left him, swaying self-consciously on her high heels, she was aware of his eyes following her until she'd entered the swinging doors of Millinery.

'You're late,' said the departmental manager.

'Sorry, Miss Colley. I had to help a customer choose a scarf.'

'We sell hats here, Miss Millar.'

'Yes, Miss Colley.'

Silly old cat, thought Sylvie, putting woollen berets into a deep drawer, but really she didn't give a damn for Miss Colley, not when she remembered Sergeant Imrie.

Chapter Twenty-Four

On Friday evening, she was in Guido's arms again, dancing a quickstep round one of her favourite dancehalls, in Leith. It had a splendid floor. Sylvie felt she could have danced on it for ever, and for a moment or two even regretted that this would be the last time she would have Guido for a partner. The regret soon passed. As she kept her own eyes averted from his that were fixed as usual on her face, she knew she wanted peace of mind, and peace of mind didn't come with Guido. Dancing with him was like dancing in a minefield – at any moment, he might explode, taking her with him.

'You're very quiet tonight,' he murmured, putting his face close to hers. 'Anything wrong?'

'No. I'm a bit tired, that's all.'

She wasn't in the least tired, she felt strung up with nerves and a terrible excitement, for tonight was the night. Though she wasn't looking forward to saying goodbye to Guido, she was drawing on all her reserves to get the ordeal over. In all these weeks, she had been a prisoner of his obsession with her. Now she could scarcely wait to be free.

When the interval came, Guido found them a table and went for their drinks as he usually did, while Sylvie defiantly lit a cigarette – Guido did not like her to smoke – and turned her head. Mark Imrie was standing at the bar. He was with a group of friends and did not see her, but she drew in her breath with apprehension and ducked her head down in case he did. His presence was the last thing she wanted on that particular evening.

When Guido returned with their lemonade, he gave her a melting look and said softly:

'Now tell me what's the matter, *cara*. Come on, I know there's something.'

It wasn't the right place to talk to him, surrounded by other people, but where was the right place? Standing shivering in the street? At the pictures? They were never really alone, though sometimes when dancing they'd thought so. But she couldn't say what she had to say when they were dancing.

'It isn't easy –' she began, not looking at him, but feeling his body stiffen all the same. There was something of the cat about him, something precise and quiet in his movements, something quick and alert about his senses, and now she knew he was sensing danger. But any Scottish laddie might have been as quick, she supposed, hearing her tone of voice. Lovers were always quick.

'Go on,' he said quietly, when she stopped.

'I've been thinking, Guido, maybe we shouldn't see each other so often.'

'So often? Once a week? What are you trying to say?'

When she didn't at first reply, he caught her wrist and held it. 'Tell me what you mean, Sylvie.'

'I mean – I think you're getting too fond of me.'

It was his turn for silence and she stole a look at him. He had turned pale, so pale his blue eyes seemed dark by contrast; dark and glittering, they made him a stranger. She tried to pull her wrist away from him, but he held it still.

'Sylvie, I thought you were fond of me,' he said slowly. 'I thought you loved me.'

'I know you did,' she whispered. 'But I never wanted you to think that. I never did anything to make you think that.'

'Coming out with me? Dancing with me? Letting me kiss you? That didn't mean anything?'

She jerked at her wrist and he let it go. 'Not what you thought.'

'So none of my love meant anything to you?'

'I really like being with you, Guido, dancing with you and all that, I could dance with you for ever!'

'I see. I am a dancing partner.'

'No! Och, I don't know how to put things, Guido, I'm no' clever, I can't explain what I feel, but you are the most exciting man I've ever met, you're very special.'

'But you do not love me?' Guido's mouth twisted. 'You know, an Italian girl would not have treated me this way. Played with me.'

'I never played with you!'

'Yes, be honest. You led me on. You let me think you cared for me.'

'No, I didn't, I didn't! Guido, you're no' listening!' Sylvie was frantic. Everything was going wrong, sliding away from her. She had thought she could 'handle' Guido, get away with anything because he loved her, but his very love was preventing her from doing what she wanted and she hadn't bargained for that. 'All I thought at the beginning was that you wanted a nice time, going dancing, and that sort of thing. I never realised you wanted to be serious, or I'd never have agreed to go out with you.'

'Is there someone else?' he asked coldly. 'Tell me now, for I shall find out anyway.'

'There's no one else, I promise. I'm no' ready to be married, and you wouldn't want to be married to me anyway. You'd rather have an Italian wife, wouldn't you? Somebody your family'd accept and be happy with?'

'Yes, I would,' he said frankly. 'But it is too late for that now. You are the one for me, Sylvie, and I am not going to let you go. You'll come to understand that and until you do, I'll wait. But we will not say goodbye.' Guido leaned forward, his eyes fixed on Sylvie's face. 'Not even *arrivederci*.'

She was staring at him, hypnotised by the force of his speech, the power of his dark blue gaze, when Mark Imrie came strolling across to stand at their table.

'Hallo there! We meet again, eh?'

'What do you want?' asked Guido, quickly rising to his feet.

'What I wanted before. Just a dance with my friend there. Sylvie.'

'Sylvie is with me.'

'I think she'd agree to a dance with me.'

'You will not ask her!'

'You don't own her, Mr Rietti.'

'You will not ask her to dance,' Guido repeated. 'If you do, I will knock you down.'

'You will?' Mark laughed. He bowed low. 'Miss Millar, may I have the honour of the next dance, please?'

'Mark, for heaven's sake, just go!' Sylvie cried, but it was too late. Guido had already landed a punch on Mark's chin that sent him staggering, and as the blood spurted from his cut lip, Guido took Sylvie's hand and led her from the hall.

'Hey,' one of Mark's friends, who had been watching events, shouted after him. 'You've torn it! Did you no' ken he was in the polis?'

'Get your coat,' Guido told Sylvie in the vestibule of the hall. 'We are leaving.'

'I am not leaving, Guido. Not with you.'

'I am ordering a taxi. We are leaving together.'

'No,' said Mark, appearing at Sylvie's side, holding a handkerchief to his lip. 'If you'll just quietly depart, Rietti, I'll forget about pressing charges, but Sylvie stays here, anyway.'

'You are going home with him?' Guido asked Sylvie, his voice trembling.

'I am going home alone,' said Sylvie. 'I don't want anybody.'

'Are you leaving?' Mark asked Guido. 'Or, do I call the manager?'

Guido hesitated. He was still very pale and looked ill, but he had taken command of himself, as though he would not let himself show weakness before Mark. He turned his eyes on Sylvie, whose face had become blank as a doll's and who was leaning against the wall. She too looked ill.

'If you are not going home with him, Sylvie, I will leave you. But I will see you again soon. That was arranged, I believe.'

'When? When was it arranged?'

'When I said you would understand what I'd been saying to you. But I will not discuss anything before this man, so I will see you some other time. Look out for me.'

As she closed her eyes and turned her head away, Guido walked swiftly towards the exit, pulled open the door and went through.

Mark ran after him, out into the street where he looked up and down, but there was no sign of him.

'He's gone,' he said, breathing hard as he came back to Sylvie. 'But I don't trust him, Sylvie, he's a madman. I can't let you go home alone.'

'I said I wouldn't go home with you and I meant it,' she said wearily. 'Will you ring for a taxi?'

'One of the guys here has a sister with him. I'm going to ask her to go home with you. Just wait there a minute, eh?'

'I don't want anyone, I tell you! What could I say? What would she think?'

'You're no' feeling well, that's what you say.'

'She'll have seen what happened. Oh, God, I feel so bad! I feel so guilty! This is the worst day of my life, Mark.'

'Just stay there, I'll get Vera.' Mark put his hands on Sylvie's shoulders. 'This isn't the worst day of your life, Sylvie. You've done nothing wrong, you've no need to feel guilty.'

'You don't know anything about it.' She shook her head. 'I've broken his heart, Mark, that's a terrible thing to do.'

'Hurt his vanity, you mean. He's insulted, that's all. He'll get over it.'

But his words brought no comfort to Sylvie. She didn't believe them. And as she went home in the taxi with the sympathetic Vera, she could not forget what Guido had said to her. 'Look out for me.'

'Are you OK?' asked Vera, as Sylvie left the taxi at the shop in Trinity.

'I'm all right, thanks.'

'I'll take the taxi back, then. Dinna worry, Mark's given me the money. What a nice fella, eh?'

'Very nice. Goodnight, Vera, thanks for coming with me.'

'Goodnight, Sylvie. Take care, eh?'

Oh, yes, she would take care, thought Sylvie, trying to pull herself together before facing her mother. Take care never to see poor Guido again. How she would do that, she had no idea.

Chapter Twenty-Five

It was just as well that Isa was madly cleaning the flat in preparation for the visit of the MacMenzies family, otherwise she might have noticed that there was something wrong with Sylvie. In fact, no one except Ruth noticed that Sylvie seemed afraid of her shadow, but then Ruth was the only one who knew that the shadow was not hers.

'He's still following you?' she asked Sylvie fearfully.

'Oh, yes,' answered Sylvie, who was always pale these days and looked, as her mother might have said, as though she was 'coming down with something'. 'He stands in the doorway of Millinery, just looking at me, and I know Miss Colley's wondering about him and I'm so scared she'll tell me off. Mebbe give me the sack or report me or something.'

'Why should she do that? It's no' your fault, Sylvie.'

'Well, Mark's been coming into the shop as well, trying to get me to go out with him, but I told him I wouldn't, I daren't, and he's given up just now.' Sylvie fixed Ruth with large frightened eyes. 'Supposing Guido had seen him! I don't know what he'd have done!'

'Can't you speak to Guido? Ask him to stop?'

'I've tried. Sometimes he's outside our canteen, wanting to take me to lunch, but when I've tried to tell him that it's no good him following me around, he's no' going to get anywhere, he just laughs and says he's prepared to wait for me for ever.' Sylvie shook her head. 'The worst is when I get off the tram at night when it's dark, and I think he might be there, waiting for me outside the flat.'

'Has he ever been there?'

'Once. Ruthie, I was so scared, when he came out of the shadows! I don't think he'd ever attack me, but he can look so strange, with his eyes shining and that, he frightens me to death. I don't know how much more I can take.'

'It can't go on,' Ruth murmured. 'We'll have to tell Dad.'

'No! No, I don't want to tell Dad, or Ma. I don't want to make things worse than they are.' Sylvie's voice was shrill. 'I just want to be left alone!'

'Mark could do something. He's in the police. There must be ways of stopping a fellow from trailing you like this.'

'I don't want to involve Mark, either. That could be dangerous. But mebbe you could ask Nicco to say something? I know they don't get on, but Guido might listen to him.'

'No, Nicco's already spoken to him. Guido just laughed in his face. He says he'll try again, but Guido's in such a state, he'll need to be careful.'

'Careful, yes!' Sylvie laughed hysterically. 'That's what I'm being. Very very careful, but it's no' doing me much good!'

'I'm going to speak to Renata,' Ruth said firmly. 'I have an idea she might be the best one to sort this out.'

Renata and Federico had just moved into their new ground floor flat, two streets away from Vittorio's café, where Renata was still working.

'Well, how are things?' Ruth asked, finding a chair in Renata's living room that was still filled with boxes waiting to be unpacked, while Renata poured their tea. 'What's it like, being married?'

'Wonderful! I can recommend it. Going to bed, it is amazing!'

'Oh, yes?' Ruth, blushing, hastily drank her tea. No one she knew ever mentioned bed in a marriage connection, but then Renata was Renata.

'Yes, I'm really happy with Federico.' Renata passed Ruth a plate of biscuits. 'He is the sweetest man in the world. And generous! He'd give you anything he had, just like his father. How those two run a business, I can't think.'

'I like good-hearted people like that.'

'Only thing is, I have to say it, Federico's very easily led. I worry about him sometimes.'

'How d'you mean?'

'Well, you know, he listens to people. Guido, for instance. Guido talks away about Il Duce, next thing, Federico is a fascist. His father isn't, but Guido's more persuasive. Makes Federico think his father's too set in his ways to understand new ideas.'

'Doesn't he listen to you?'

'Oh, yes, but I haven't got involved in politics so far. Maybe Il Duce is everything they say, I don't know, I haven't made up my mind. But if I want my own way, I tell you, I get it!'

'I can believe that, Renata.'

'Take this flat. If it had been left to Federico, we'd still have been living with his parents. Then I'd have had his mother watching me all the time, telling me what to do, just like Aunt Carlotta!' Renata laughed, throwing back her dark hair. 'Would I put up with that? Never! So, here we are, with our own place, and I work at the café to help out. Federico's folks are like everybody else, keep wondering when the baby is coming, but I let them wonder! Now, that's enough about me, let's talk about you.'

'Oh, I'm all right.'

'You are?' Renata gave Ruth more tea. 'Well, I can tell you have something on your mind, all the same. Is it Nicco?'

'Nicco's always on my mind, but it's Guido I want to talk to you about. You knew he was seeing Sylvie?'

'Know it? I never hear anything else from Mamma! I tell you, I truly believe she is lighting candles in the church to make Guido give up Sylvie and turn to Marilena.'

'Well, her prayers have been answered, in a way. Sylvie has broken with Guido herself, but he won't accept it.'

'Oh, my God, that's Guido for you!' cried Renata, when Ruth had told her the story. 'He's been spoiled all his life, never refused a thing. Now he'll never be able to believe that Sylvie doesn't want him. It will seem impossible to him, so he'll think he just has to wait and she'll change her mind.'

'The thing is, he has been hard hit, Renata. I'm sure he is truly in love with Sylvie, and she did encourage him. Mebbe without realising it, you ken, but he might have thought she cared more than she did.'

'It would never have worked out, Ruth. Sylvie would never have been able to cope with our family, even if she had cared for Guido. She's well out of it all.'

'Is she?' asked Ruth.

'Oh, it will be different for you,' Renata said quickly. 'You are not Sylvie, and Nicco is not Guido. You'll fit in very well.'

'If I ever get as far as that. The way things are going, I don't know if I will. But I'm thinking about Sylvie at the moment. Guido is following her around and it's getting her down. She's afraid of what he might do.'

Renata sat back, staring into space. 'He won't hurt her,' she said at last. 'I'm certain she's no need to worry about that.'

'It's Mark Imrie she's worrying about. She'd like to go out with him, but daren't because of Guido.'

'He's the fellow Guido punched at the dance? And he's a policeman? Couldn't be worse, could it?'

'Can you think of anything we can do? I mean, to make Guido stop following Sylvie?'

'We'll have to think of some way he can forget her and save his face at the same time.' Renata heaved a sigh. 'But how? If he were to go away, maybe?'

'To Italy?'

'Couldn't afford it.' Renata suddenly smiled. 'But there's London, eh, where I went? To Cousin Sofia's? He could afford that.'

'Would he go?' Ruth asked doubtfully.

'I think he would. I think it might be the perfect excuse for him to give up trying to get Sylvie back. And it would really get her out of his head, if he got to know new people. Fascists, probably – there are plenty in London. All Sir Oswald Mosley's black shirts.'

Ruth shivered. 'I'm glad Nicco isn't mixed up with anyone like that.'

'Got more sense. Look, I'm going to put this London idea to Guido as soon as possible.'

'I'd be truly grateful if you would.'

'Better still, I'll get Cousin Sofia to write to him, say he can help her with the business, the way I did. It'd be better coming from her.'

'Oh, I knew you'd come up with something!' cried Ruth. 'What can I do to thank you? Wash the cups? Unpack these boxes?'

'Come and see me again soon.' The two young women hugged, then Ruth put on her coat and hat and said she'd better get back home. They were having Kester's future in-laws to tea next day and Ma needed moral support. Renata smiled and said she knew all about what happened to mothers when in-laws were coming. Hadn't Brigida had the whole flat painted before Federico's parents came to celebrate the engagement, even though she already knew them well?

'Shall we ever be like that?' asked Ruth.

'Never! Well, probably. Look, if you ever need anyone to talk to, I mean about Nicco, or anything, you come to me, eh? I'll help you all I can.'

'I know that. Thank you, Renata.' Ruth pressed her friend's hand. 'For everything.'

'Well, we'll see how things work out. In the meantime, take a good look at my hair and say goodbye.' Renata spun round, putting her hands through her thick, rich mass of hair. 'I'm having it cut again next week.'

'Renata, you're not!'

'Yes. I grew it to please Mamma for the wedding, but now I am sick of it and away it goes!'

'What will Federico think?'

'He will like it. He likes anything I do. Of course, Mamma will throw another fit, but this is my little gesture of defiance, to say I am as I am. It is no good trying to please everyone, Ruth. Sometimes you have to please yourself. Remember that.'

'You're right, of course,' said Ruth.

'I'm always right, *cara*.'

Sylvie perked up like a watered flower when Ruth told her that Guido might be persuaded to leave Edinburgh.

'Oh, Ruth, do you think he would? Oh, I'd be so glad, I'd be so happy!'

'It'd no' be for ever, if he did go, Sylvie, so don't get too excited.'

For the first time in days, Sylvie's cheeks were pink and her eyes bright, as she contemplated life without Guido, even if it were only a temporary freedom.

'You don't know what it'd mean to me,' she said in a low voice. 'Just to have a break from looking over my shoulder. Oh, Ruthie, isn't Renata wonderful?'

'Yes, but we'll have to wait and see if her idea works. Guido might just refuse to go to London.'

'I think he'll go, I think he'll be glad to get away.' Sylvie gave a radiant smile. 'Och, I feel so good, I'm even going to be nice to Fenella tomorrow.'

'Don't get carried away,' Ruth answered, laughing. 'Just remember what it's going to be like. Best cups, best cloth, best everything, and Ma on the hop and Kester on pins.'

'Ruth, it'll be lovely.' Sylvie was dancing round their room. 'The way I feel, everything's lovely.'

Chapter Twenty-Six

Fenella's parents were a little older than Jack and Isa. In fact, her father, Walter MacMenzies, was quite grey, and so cold-looking Isa said after their first meeting, that he looked as if the frost had caught him. His pupils at Fielding Secondary would probably have agreed with her, for he was an unpopular master, well known for his acid tongue and habit of hurling chalk at any child who annoyed him. His wife, Alison, was more colourful, with blue eyes and the golden hair she had passed to her daughter, though Isa said she had her doubts about that gold today. See the tell-tale parting? Och, good luck to her, if she fancied trying to look young, but if Kester wanted to know what his future wife would look like when she wasn't young, he'd only to look at Mrs MacMenzies. And if he was impressed, the rest of his family wasn't!

As Ruth had foretold, their home had been cleaned and polished as though for a regimental inspection, and everything that was kept for best had been brought out for this casual Sunday afternoon tea. 'I'll just do this' and 'I'll just do that', Isa had said, but her family knew that she'd expended all her energy and skill to put on a good show for Kester's future in-laws, because she hadn't forgotten how he'd said when he first met Fenella, that she came from 'a nice home'. She'd show them all who came from a nice home, so she would!

To give them credit, Fenella's parents were very pleasant and polite. Indeed, quite complimentary over the flat and the tea and Jack's business, which they knew was superior to the usual grocery store. Why, Mrs MacMenzies even shopped there herself, or at least put an order in, so as to avoid the embarrassment of being served by Kester, and her husband ordered wine.

'We're so pleased to hear that the new shop will be in Marchmont, practically in the Grange, Mr Millar,' Mrs MacMenzies observed, accepting a third cup of tea. 'Such a nice area, isn't it? And then Kester will be in charge? That's very good news.'

Kester gave a bashful smile and turned to Fenella, whose cool gaze was sizing up Sylvie's new jumper suit and Ruth's jacket and skirt.

'Aye, I wanted to give the lad responsibility,' said Jack. 'And I know he'll do well, you can count on it.'

'He's got a good head on his shoulders,' said Isa. 'All my children have.'

'You work in John Johnson's millinery department, don't you?' Mrs MacMenzies asked Sylvie. 'Now, Fenella was considering teaching.'

'Why, I thought you worked in a flower shop!' exclaimed Ruth.

'That was only temporary,' Fenella replied. 'I was waiting to go to Moray House for teacher training. Daddy said I'd make a very good teacher.'

'Waste of time now,' her father said shortly. 'Have to give up on marriage.'

'That's so unfair!' cried Ruth. 'Why should married women no' be able to keep professional jobs?'

'Because they take men's jobs away from them, and men are the breadwinners.' Mr MacMenzies gave Ruth the full benefit of his grey stare. 'You're a bright girl, Ruth, I remember you from Fielding. I'm sure you can see the point of the argument.'

'Yes, I can see the point, but what it means is that a lot of women can never have careers of their own, and that seems to me to be wrong.'

'Ruth's going to try for the Civil Service when she's old enough,' Isa said proudly. 'She's working for the exam.'

'The Civil Service!' cried Mrs MacMenzies.

'Why not?' asked Ruth.

'I'm surprised,' said Fenella smoothly. 'I thought you'd be getting married yourself pretty soon.' She laughed. 'After I saw you in

Princes Street Gardens the other day with that terrific looking fellow!'

'Who's that, then, Ruth?' asked Isa. 'One of your friends from the office?'

'I thought he might be Italian,' said Fenella. 'He had beautiful dark eyes and hair.'

All eyes went to Ruth, whose face was dusky red. As she sat as though struck dumb, Sylvie, next to her, was willing her to say, yes, it was a friend from the office, that's all, just a guy from the office. Go on, Ruth, say it! But Ruth by her very silence was already telling them all that the man she'd been with in Princes Street Gardens was not a friend from the office.

'Mrs Millar, this has been so nice,' Fenella's mother said, covering the moment. 'Thank you so much for asking us, but I think perhaps we ought to be on our way.'

'Weren't we going to discuss the wedding?' asked Fenella, frowning.

'Another time, I think, dear.' Mrs MacMenzies rose, nodding to her husband, who also stood up. 'I've already made some enquiries at the hotel and maybe you and Kester should see the minister at the kirk next week. Goodbye, Mrs Millar, Mr Millar – we've really enjoyed ourselves, haven't we, Walter? Goodbye Sylvie, goodbye, Ruth.'

'Goodbye,' said Ruth tonelessly.

It seemed to take endless time before the MacMenzies had left and the Millars were on their own again, but the time was not long enough for Ruth, for as soon as the door had closed on the guests, her mother turned to her.

'Who was that fellow yon girl was talking about, Ruth? Who've you been seeing in Princes Street Gardens?'

'Is Ruth no' allowed to see a fellow these days?' cried Sylvie.

'Of course she is!' Isa's eyes were flashing. 'But I don't expect her to keep her young men a secret. Who was it, Ruth?'

'You've guessed already, haven't you?' asked Ruth. 'It was Nicco.'

There was a short silence. Isa and Jack exchanged glances.

'Nicco Rietti?' asked Jack.

'There's only one Nicco,' Ruth replied.

'Why'd you no' say you were seeing him?' asked Isa.

'I thought you mightn't approve. After what happened at Renata's wedding.'

As Sylvie coloured and looked down at her hands, Isa nodded her head. 'You're right, your dad and me wouldn't have approved, but no' because of that. We don't want you going out with an Italian, anyway.'

'An Italian?' Ruth stared angrily at her mother. 'What do you mean, calling him AN Italian, as though he was a stranger? We're talking about Nicco! He was born here, he could say he was British, and you like him, don't you? You liked his father, too!'

'Aye, I liked Nicco's dad and I like Nicco, but I don't want you going out with him. He might have been born here, but he's no Scot, is he? He's part of the Italian community. Now you know as well as I do, Ruth, that if you go out with a fellow, it can lead to marriage and marriage with an Italian would no' be suitable.'

'No' suitable,' agreed Jack.

'No' suitable? cried Ruth.

'We're no' saying Italians aren't as good as us, Ruth, we're only saying they're different. They've a different religion, they've different customs, and different views.'

'Aye, that's why Italians like to marry Italians,' said Isa. 'And quite right, too. You'd never fit in, Ruth, you'd be very unhappy. You just imagine what it'd be like, having the signora for your mother-in-law! I'll bet Nicco's keeping you a secret, eh? Just like you've kept him a secret from us.' She stared at the table still laden with tea things, then sat down and suddenly burst into tears. 'It's the deceit I mind about! It's our Ruth going out to meet Nicco and never saying a word! How could you do that, Ruth? How could you?'

'I never wanted to, Ma,' Ruth said, weeping, too. 'I hated keeping it a secret.'

'And so did I,' said Sylvie. 'Och, you might as well know, Ma, I've been going out with Guido. I never told you because I thought the same as Ruth, you'd never approve. I've given him up now, but if you're going to go on at Ruth, I want to tell you, I did the same.'

'Sylvie!' Isa gave a cry of anguish. 'You and Ruth the same? Both keeping secrets from your dad and me! Oh, it's too much! Jack, is it no' too much? Why should our girls treat us this way?'

Jack shook his head, as though he could find no words; his face was stony. But Kester's face was scarlet and his eyes were angry.

'What's the matter with you two?' he shouted, staring from Ruth to Sylvie. 'Here we've had a grand day, with my girl and her folks coming to tea and Ma putting on a lovely show, and you two have to go and spoil it! Going out with Nicco and Guido behind Ma's back! I'd like to knock your heads together, so I would!'

'Kester, that sort of talk does no good,' said Jack curtly.

'And it was Fenella who spoiled everything!' cried Sylvie. 'She was the one who mentioned Nicco when she shouldn't have done. She spoke out of turn.'

'You leave Fenella out of this!' Kester replied. 'She'd a right to say what she did. Now we all know about Ruth and Nicco.'

'Well, what have you got against him?' cried Ruth. 'You liked him when we lived in Ginger Street.'

'I know, I still like him, he's a good chap, but it's true what Ma says, he's too different from us. There'll only be trouble if you take up with him, Ruth, and we don't want trouble.'

'There needn't be any trouble. I love him and I'm going to marry him.'

Silence fell, as Ruth's words made plain how much farther her plans had gone than her parents had ever dreamed. What had seemed only an unsuitable possibility had suddenly become nightmare reality; for a moment, neither Jack nor Isa could take it in.

'You canna do that,' Isa said at last, a shaking hand at her lips. 'You're no twenty-one, we'll no' give permission.'

'I don't need to be twenty-one,' Ruth answered swiftly. 'I'm over sixteen, that's all that matters.'

'Never!' cried Isa. 'That canna be true! Jack, it's no true, is it?'

He hesitated. 'I think it is, Isa. Folk don't need parents' consent to be married in Scotland. That's why the English sometimes come up here to wed when they elope, and no' just to Gretna Green.'

'I don't believe it!' cried Isa. 'Parents must be able to have a say!'

'Ma, I know the law from cases there've been at the office,'

Ruth said quietly. 'I can get legally married and you can't stop me. But why would you stop me? Why wouldn't you want me to be happy?'

'Have you no' been listening to a word I've said? I've told you why you won't be happy marrying Nicco, and if you go ahead with this crazy plan, you'll do it without ma blessing or your Dad's!' Isa got to her feet and put a hand on a chair to steady herself, the knuckles showing white. 'Aye, and you'll do it away from this house and all, because you'll no' marry him from here and you'll no' even see him from here. If you canna give Nicco up, you'll give up your home instead, and that's all there is to it!'

'Ma!' Ruth's face was paper-white, her eyes enormous, as she gave a single agonised cry, while Sylvie reached for her hand and Kester wiped his face and shook his head. Jack stood up and ran his hands through his hair.

'Isa, you're no' throwing the lassie out?' he asked huskily. 'You're no' meaning that, eh?'

Tears were spurting again from Isa's eyes and her mouth was working, but she said nothing.

'Ma, I can't afford to pay for a room,' Ruth said brokenly. 'What can I do?'

'You can give up Nicco. Sylvie's given up Guido, so you can do the same. It's for your own good, Ruth, I'm telling you, you'll never be happy. Can you no' see what it'd be like for you, if you married into Nicco's family? I'm no' letting you do it!'

'I love him, Ma. I'll never give him up.'

'Well, then, you ken what you can do.'

'Ma, you can't put Ruth out!' wailed Sylvie. 'You can't!'

'No, you can't, Ma,' Kester muttered. 'Nobody wants that. It'd be wrong.'

'It isn't going to happen,' said Jack. He stood up. 'Ruth's staying here.'

'Jack!' cried Isa.

'My decision, Isa. I don't want Ruth to marry Nicco any more than you do, but until she does marry, she stays here, where she belongs.'

'Even if I still see Nicco?' whispered Ruth.

140

Her father looked at her. 'I'd like to suggest that you stop seeing him for a bit. Think this whole thing through.'

'I don't know if I can, Dad.'

'Give it three months, eh? Then see how you feel. Whatever happens, you've no need to worry, we'll no' be showing you the door.'

'You speak for yourself, Jack!' cried Isa.

'Come on, now.' Jack put an arm round his wife's shoulders. 'You ken very well, when it came to it, you'd never put our Ruthie out. We're no' that sort.'

'I'll never agree to her marrying Nicco, Jack.'

'She's no' marrying him yet. Let's give over arguing, and see how things go. In three months, she might be feeling quite different.'

'That's true.' Isa shot a glance at Ruth, whose eyes were cast down. 'Ruth, will you do what your dad says? Will you give Nicco up for three months and see how you feel then? For all our sakes, and Nicco's too.'

'It'd do no good, Ma.'

'Well, will you try?'

'All right, I'll try.'

Isa relaxed, letting her shoulders slump and the bright hard light in her eyes die. She gave a ritual sniff, as though to say she'd done all she could and had achieved all that could be expected. 'Thank God for that, at least. But Ruth, you just remember Sylvie. She soon got tired of Guido. Come on, now, away with thae dishes! Put the kettle on, Kester, we could do with some more tea.'

'Or something stronger,' he murmured. 'I could do with a drink.'

'Just as well you can't have one,' Sylvie told him. 'You drink too much, Kester. What's Fenella going to do with you?'

They went off to the kitchen, carrying plates and arguing, while Ruth stood where she was, like someone slowly recovering consciousness. She felt as though she'd been lifted by a whirlwind, battered and buffeted, and dropped home to earth. Only home had changed, and meeting her mother's eye, Ruth was terrified her mother had changed too. She hadn't of course, she hadn't meant anything she'd said, but as they stared warily at each other, then slowly hugged and drew apart, each knew that for a little while Isa had seemed willing to let Ruth go.

Chapter Twenty-Seven

There was a mist from the Forth the following Wednesday. It was not the weather to walk in the gardens, or anywhere, in fact, for you could scarcely see the grass or the trees, or the Christmas decorations that were going up in Princes Street.

'Let's have lunch at Valdo's,' Nicco suggested. 'You look so cold, Ruth.'

'I'd rather go some place where no one knows us.'

His eyes were thoughtful on her face, seeing beyond its pallor to something that pierced his heart with fear.

'You want to talk to me?'

She nodded, and he took her arm. 'There's a café in Rose Street, always full, no one'll even see us.'

'You can never be sure of that,' said Ruth.

They ordered something, didn't care what, and sat hunched over a small table in the Rose Street café, where the air was so thick with steam and cigarette smoke, it was probably true that no one amongst its crowd of patrons could see them.

'What's wrong, then?' asked Nicco, keeping his voice down. 'I can see there's something.'

'My folks know,' Ruth answered. 'About us, I mean.'

Nicco's dark eyes never left her face. 'How?'

'Kester's girlfriend saw us. Described you to Ma and everyone.'

'And your folks were upset? Because of Guido? Or, because they don't like me?'

'They do like you. And they weren't thinking of Guido.'

'Why, then?'

Ruth looked away. 'Because you're Italian.'

'I see.'

'Oh, Nicco!' She pressed his hand where it lay on the table. 'It's their version of that bell tower thing you talked about. Campan – whatever it was.'

'*Campanilismo*?' Nicco smiled faintly. 'Well, why should that just be for Italians? They want a Scot for you, is that it?'

'I suppose so. But the other thing is they think I wouldn't fit into your family.'

'And I wouldn't fit into yours.'

'But you would, if they gave you a chance. I just can't understand their attitude.'

'They're right,' he said quietly. 'I don't know about me, but about you. It would be very difficult for you to come into my family. I lie awake every night, wondering if I should ask you to do it.'

Ruth gave a shaky laugh. 'You never have asked me, Nicco.'

His eyes widened. '*Cara*! I have!'

'No' in so many words.'

'You know I love you and want to marry you.'

'Yes, I know.' She touched his hand. 'And I want to marry you. I want to be a part of your family, be with you, you've no need to worry.'

He looked down into his cup of pale coffee. 'When I haven't even dared to talk to my mother about you?'

'You don't want to upset her, just like I didn't want to upset my folks.'

'Which shows the problem, *cara*. There is something to be upset about.'

'There needn't be. If we're strong enough.'

He shook his head. 'Doesn't just depend on us.'

Ruth stared at him for a moment, then leaped to her feet. 'I'm going to order some more coffee – this stuff's like dishwater!'

After some persuasion, the waitress, who said that the café was no' the Caledonian and what did they expect for one and ninepence all included, brought them some strong black coffee, which they drank as gratefully as though they were suffering from hangovers.

'Tell me the worst,' Nicco said when they had set down their cups. 'I know you haven't told me yet. Have they forbidden you to see me?'

'My mother wanted to do that. She was going to ask me to leave home.'

Nicco went white. 'Oh, God, no! Ruth, that's terrible. You could lose your home? Because of me?'

'She didn't mean it,' Ruth said quickly. 'And Dad said I could stay, anyway.'

'If you don't see me?'

'They want me to stop seeing you for three months.' Ruth smiled wryly. 'See if I can forget you. I told them I'd try, but I won't, it's just impossible.'

Nicco was silent.

'Isn't it?' She pressed. 'How could we stop seeing each other? I couldn't bear it.'

'Shall we go now, Ruth? Shall we walk back to your office?'

Her gaze on him was apprehensive. 'You couldn't do that, could you, Nicco? Stop seeing me?'

'I'm trying to think what's best. You get your coat, I'll pay the bill.'

Outside, the dankness of the mist met them and folded itself around them with long wet fingers as they walked arm in arm towards Queen Street. Traffic was muffled, footsteps strangely hollow; people hurrying past seemed in disguise, scarves round their mouths, hats pulled down. The Christmas decorations had quite disappeared.

'You don't mean you won't see me again?' Ruth asked Nicco, trying to see the expression on his face, but he too was a stranger, with the brim of his trilby over his brow and only the tip of his fine nose showing above his turned-up collar.

'I just think it might be fairer to you.'

'How can you say that? All I want is to be with you.'

'But, think about it, Ruth. What's your future going to be with me? Living over the shop in Ginger Street, my mother and my family thinking of you as a stranger? Your chance of a career gone?' He pressed her arm. 'That's what your folks are seeing for you, isn't it? I feel bad because it's all I can offer you.'

'It's all I want, Nicco!'

'Maybe you think that now, but if we were apart for a while, you might think differently. And I don't want you to regret anything, you see. I want you to be very sure of what you're doing.'

'I am sure, I am. Anyway, we agreed, I can still take my exam.'

'If we were to marry, you couldn't take a job. Not a Civil Service job.'

'IF we're to marry, Nicco?'

'Your folks'll never agree.'

'Nor will your mother, but it doesn't matter. We can marry without their consent, if we have to.'

Nicco's head drooped. 'It would be a dreadful thing, to do that.'

'I know, but we might have no choice.'

'I'm not sure I could do it.'

'Nicco!'

'Ruth, I'm an Italian. To marry a girl without her parents' blessing – it would seem so wrong to me.'

'Wrong? You're saying you don't want to marry me?' He stopped and drew her close. She felt the moisture dripping from his hat, and her own tears falling.

'I think we should do as your parents say,' he said gently. 'I'd feel better about things.'

'Better?' She laid her head against his damp coat.

'Yes, because if we part for a while and we still feel the same, we'll know we're doing the right thing.'

'I know anyway!'

'Your folks don't agree. This would show them. Then they might accept me.'

'And what about your own mother?'

He hesitated. 'I'll tell her, when we were sure. When we've proved we're sure. Ruth, will you do it?' He held her tightly against him. 'It'll be hard, but it'll be worth it. And you won't have to tell lies to your mother. You know you were never happy about that.'

'No.' She heaved a long sigh. 'Well, we'd better say goodbye. If it's what you want.'

'For God's sake, it is not what I want!'

'It's what my folks want and we don't have to do it.'

'I've explained why I think we should.'

'I know. I'm just trying to face it.'

'Ah, Ruth!'

Their mouths met in a long, last kiss, then Ruth drew away.

'When do we meet again, then?'

'I don't know. What do you think?'

'Don't ask me!'

'Three months? Could we stand it?'

She shrugged, walking on. He ran to catch up with her.

'Ruth, you do understand, why we're doing this? Say you do!'

'I do.' She paused at the top of the steps leading to the basement entrance of MacRobbie's and fingered the brass plate on the railings that was running with water. Her eyes went to Nicco's white, tormented face. 'But it never would've been my idea.'

'You'll see, it'll be worth it. Nobody can say we haven't done all we can to be sure.' He put his hand on her arm. 'Better go in, Ruth, you're wet through.'

'Goodbye, Nicco.'

'*Arrivederci, cara.*'

She did not wait to watch him go, but hurried into the warmth of the office, where she took off her wet things and hung them up.

'Heavens, you're soaked!' cried Hattie. 'You should never have gone out today.' She smiled. 'It's Wednesday, though, eh?'

'I shan't be going out next Wednesday,' Ruth said coldly and sat down at her desk.

'Ah,' murmured Hattie, and wisely disappeared to do some filing.

Ruth, alone, bowed her head and let the tears fill her eyes again. To think of not seeing Nicco for three months! It would seem a lifetime, and he'd inflicted it on them. Even though she knew why, a knife turned in her breast when she thought of it. But they'd get through, they must get through, and Nicco was right, it would be worth it.

146

'Ruth,' called Hattie from the door. 'There's someone to see you. He's in the front office.'

'Who? Who is it?'

'Why not go up and see?'

Ruth flew up the stairs to the reception office, where a damp, forlorn figure stood waiting for her.

'Nicco?'

'Ruth – just wanted a word.'

Miss Berry, the receptionist, cleared her throat and busied herself with papers on her desk. Nicco moved a little away, with Ruth following, her eyes alight, his beseeching.

'Just wanted to say, if you really feel we can't do it – you know, what we said – maybe we needn't.'

'I can do it,' she whispered, feeling amazing strength, because she'd seen his weakness. 'It's the right thing, Nicco. I see that now.'

'Are you sure?'

'Yes, I'm sure.'

'All right, then.'

'Now, you'd better get home, Nicco, you're wet through, too.'

'The mist's lifting, it's not so bad, now.'

'That's good. *Arrivederci*, Nicco.'

'Goodbye, Ruth.'

When he had left her, Ruth glanced at Miss Berry, whose eyes were kind.

'Hope he doesn't get pneumonia!' she said brightly.

'So do I,' said Ruth.

Chapter Twenty-Eight

Three months. Yes, it was a lifetime. And, of course, when she actually had to face the separation from Nicco, Ruth's new strength faded. Every Wednesday, she still found herself wandering in Princes Street Gardens in the December weather, hoping Nicco might have come anyway, jumping at the sight of any tall figure that might have been his, falling into despair when it wasn't. Sometimes, she thought of going back to the shop in Ginger Street, buying Italian cheese or ham, just so that she could speak to him, maybe even touch his hand when he wrapped up her purchase. But she'd suggested that before and he hadn't wanted it. There was Marilena to think about, and worse, the signora. Imagine those dark eyes looking through her! Ruth scrapped that idea, and went instead to look into the windows of Valdo's, for you never knew, Nicco had to go somewhere on his afternoon off and the Valdo brothers were friends of his. But as soon as Rodrigo raised his head, or Domenico's eyes moved to the window, Ruth pulled her hat down over her brow and ran away like some sort or criminal.

It didn't help that her sister and her brother were so happy. Naturally, she was glad that all was going well for them but, by contrast, her own situation was made worse when Kester talked incessantly of Fenella, and Sylvie's eyes kept lighting up at the mention of Mark Imrie.

As Renata had prophesied, Guido had leaped at the idea of going to London. 'Went off like a shot from a gun,' she reported back to the Millar sisters. 'Said goodbye to the biscuit factory, made

148

Mamma stop weeping long enough to pack his bag, and took the first train down from Waverley. Now he's having a wonderful time, fund-raising for the Abyssinia campaign, going to the *fascio*, and doing a bit of work for Cousin Sofia when he feels like it.'

'When's he coming back?' Sylvie had asked nervously.

'Who knows?' Renata had shrugged. 'Oh, he will come back eventually, but by then I think he'll have definitely got you out of his system, Sylvie.'

'I hope so.' Sylvie had shuddered, then smiled. 'Because Mark Imrie's asked me out and I'm going to go.'

That was the way of Mark's entry into Sylvie's life, and her mother couldn't have been happier about it. Such a nice, steady Scottish boy, eh? His father was an ironmonger in Corstorphine and was a bit like Jack, had had the same tenement beginnings, his mother, too, so no nonsense there about being 'better class', or showing off or anything like that. And Sylvie said he was doing really well in the police. Already a sergeant, but tipped for inspector, and then what? Could end up being a top man in the force, who'd be able to give Sylvie a very good life indeed, a nice, calm life, which was what she needed. Forget Guido's Italian fireworks that Isa had now heard all about. If you asked her, Sylvie had had a very lucky escape, and all Isa wanted was for Ruth to make that escape, too. Not that Nicco was like Guido. No, he was a nice fellow, but Italian, so there'd be all the problems Isa had already put into words, you couldn't deny them. At least Ruth was trying to forget him, as they'd asked her to do, but you only had to look into her great sad eyes to know she'd not forgotten him yet.

In January, Jack opened his new shop in Marchmont and Kester was installed as manager. Acting like a dog with two tails, Sylvie said, but in truth it was not the best of times for the new venture, with George V having recently died and a pall of mourning hanging over the country. Nor was there any sign of the depression coming to an end, though, of course, Jack was hoping that his new customers were not too worried about that. They must have been worried about something, though, for the new shop's start was just as shaky as that of the shop in Trinity. Jack said not to worry, takings would pick up when word got around about the quality of his stock, and those customers who'd gone elsewhere when the old shop closed, would be coming back in droves.

'I hope you're right,' said Isa. 'With Kester getting married, and all.'

'At least, we've no' to pay for his wedding,' said Jack cheerfully. 'But I've got my eye on Sylvie. That girl's going to come in with a ring on her finger one of these days.'

He was right about that for, one evening in February, a rapturous Sylvie and a self-conscious Mark came to ask his permission to become engaged.

'Fancy asking!' cried Jack, practically swelling with pride. 'There's no' many bother to do that these days!'

'I like to do things the proper way,' said Mark, as Sylvie hugged Isa and Ruth and accepted a kiss from Kester. 'And I can let you know what I've got, Mr Millar. Some savings in the post office, and my pay, which isn't too bad as a sergeant. Then my father's going to give me a bit of cash, too, so I think I can support Sylvie all right.'

'Sure you can,' Jack told him. 'I ken well you'll take care of Sylvie and make her a fine husband. She's a bit young, mebbe, but she'll be a good wife to you, I can promise you.'

'I'm no' too young!' exclaimed Sylvie. 'Mark, show them the ring.'

The solitaire diamond ring was produced and placed on Sylvie's finger, there were more kisses and hugs, followed by celebration drinks when Kester returned from the off licence with a bottle of sherry and a few beers.

'This is the happiest day of my life!' Sylvie declared, her eyes glistening with tears, but she did not look at Ruth. 'We'd like to get married in August, if that's all right?'

Isa looked at Jack and nodded. 'As long as you're no' expecting a big do. I daresay Mrs MacMenzies'll be putting on something grand for Fenella—'

'I don't know about grand,' cried Kester.

'Well, we won't be competing, anyway. Or with Renata's, come to that.'

'Let's no' talk about Renata's wedding,' Sylvie said hastily. 'I know mine'll be lovely, and just what I want.'

'Aye, we'll do the best we can,' Isa said fondly, and Ruth thought, of course they would, with Sylvie marrying just the right sort of fellow, the perfect Scottish bridegroom. Then she felt a little ashamed of standing aside from the family's joy, and gave Mark a kiss and said how glad she was to welcome him as a brother-in-law.

'Don't forget, I can get things at discount,' said Sylvie, thinking at once of what they would all wear. 'I'm going to look at the wedding dresses tomorrow morning. Och, I can't wait to see Miss Colley's face when I tell her I'll be leaving to get married!'

'You know, I thought you weren't so keen on getting married yet,' Ruth said to Sylvie later, when the sisters were going to bed. 'You used to say you were having too good a time.'

'That was before I met Mark.' Sylvie turned her new ring on her finger. 'I feel so safe with him, Ruth, and I need to feel safe. He's like a big rock I can lean on.'

'There's more to marriage than safety, Sylvie.'

'Yes, well, I love him, too. I always knew he was the one for me, and I thought, if I've found Mr Right, why should I wait?'

'Why indeed?' asked Ruth, and Sylvie's hand flew contritely to her mouth.

'Oh, Ruthie, I'm ever so sorry! Here's me going on about Mark, and you no' even allowed to see Nicco! I feel terrible!'

'It's all right. I want you to be happy.'

'Have you really no' seen him since December?'

'He sent me a Christmas card.' Ruth smiled briefly. 'We've kept our promises, all right.'

'What'll happen next, then?'

'I don't know. I expect he'll turn up one day.' Ruth got into bed and lay against her pillow, staring into the distance. 'Sylvie, supposing he doesn't?'

'He will,' said Sylvie firmly.

He did. On the last Wednesday in March, Ruth saw him again. She

151

had been running up the steps from the office at lunch time, not planning to go to the gardens, for she'd long ago realised that there was no point in that, when she saw his tall figure at the railings. Her heart leaped, but she kept her composure; she was determined to do that.

'Hello, Nicco.'

'Hello, Ruth.'

He had lost weight, or at least his face was thinner. Look at his cheekbones! There were shadows under his eyes, too, as there were under her own. Anyone would think we'd been ill, thought Ruth. What have we done to ourselves?

He took her hand in a strong dry clasp. 'The three months are up,' he said huskily. 'How do you feel?'

'Feel?'

'About me. Do you feel the same?'

She had thought she'd make a joke, say, 'Oh, no, I've changed, I don't feel the same at all,' but the look in his eyes told her she couldn't do that.

'What do you think?' she asked gently.

'I don't know, I'm too afraid to think.' He smiled. 'Nearly didn't come.'

'I've been waiting three months, Nicco.' She began to pull him along the pavement. 'I've been desperate for you to come.'

He smiled. 'To tell you the truth, I've been coming every week. Wanting to, but you said we should give a separation a try, so I stuck it out.'

'Nicco, it was you who said we should give it a try! Do what my folks said!'

'Was it? I must have been crazy, then. I've been crazy this past three months, I know that.'

'Me, too. Crazy and ill.'

'Ill?' His look sharpened. 'You've been ill, Ruth?'

'No, just felt it. And looked it. So do you look ill, Nicco, as though you've had the flu.'

'Well, you look beautiful. The best sight for my eyes in three months!'

They stopped, as they usually did, at the corner where Queen

Street joined Hanover Street, to decide where they would go. The gardens? A café? They didn't care, they were together.

'We're sure now, aren't we?' Ruth asked. 'We can make plans.'

'We're sure.'

'I'm going to tell my folks tonight,' Ruth said confidently. 'Will you tell your mother?'

'Yes.' He took her hand, to cross the road, and to mask his only tiny hesitation. 'I'll tell my mother as soon as I get home.'

Chapter Twenty-Nine

Everything was quiet in the flat over Nicco's shop when he came back from his meeting with Ruth. He had begun to look his old self when he was with her; now, as he caught sight of his face in the glass at the top of the stairs, it seemed to him that he looked ill again. Convalescent, at best. It was strange his mother had never noticed. Or, perhaps she had and had chosen to say nothing, for reasons of her own. He knew his nerves were getting to him and he straightened his shoulders, smoothed down his hair, before going into the living room.

For a moment, he saw it as it might appear to Ruth. An Italian room in a Scottish flat. A little light beneath the photograph of his father, flowers under the picture of the Virgin Mary; handmade lace and crochet work, elaborate cushions, rugs, heavy curtains. And there, in her chair, was the Italian lady responsible for it all, his mother, Carlotta, so very handsome still, though looking older since his father's death, with two white wings cleaving her dark hair. Nicco saw her too with Ruth's fresh eye, and knew she might seem formidable. Oh, God, she seemed so to him!

'Nicco, you're back early!' she said now, in their own speech, and rose to go to the kitchen. Though she didn't know it, she had something in common with Isa Millar there, believing that men always needed something to eat or drink the minute they stepped in the door. If women needed anything, of course they could get it themselves. 'You would like tea? Coffee?'

'Thanks, I don't want anything.' Nicco took a chair and made his mother sit down. 'Where's Marilena?'

His mother frowned. 'I let her go to Millie MacAllan's. Millie has the same half day, and wanted Marilena to help her with some sewing. Can you believe, she scarcely knows how to thread a needle herself?'

'There aren't many as skilful as Marilena.'

'No.' Carlotta sighed heavily. 'But she should be sewing her wedding dress, Nicco. Did I ever dream she would still be unwed at nineteen!'

'Plenty of time, Mamma.'

'I don't agree. Marilena should be married and starting a family, then she would not be so unsettled. I have a difficult time with her, Nicco. It comes of mixing with all these Scottish girls.'

'It's only natural for her to want to go out.'

'She must be protected, until she marries.' Carlotta shook her head. 'But who can she marry? Guido is in London. Will he ever come back?'

'Of course he will. This is his home and Uncle Vittorio needs him.'

'I will speak to Brigida, see what she knows.'

There was a little silence, during which Carlotta studied Nicco, and he thought, she is going to say something about how tired I look, and if she does, I can say – what? What can I say? He ran his hand across his brow that was sweating and tried to take command of himself. What sort of a man was he, then, if he was afraid to speak to his mother? He did not want to hurt her, that was his problem, and she would be hurt. Mortally wounded, even. He kept his eyes down under her scrutiny.

'Is anything wrong, Nicco?' she asked, at last. 'You seem on edge.'

He cleared his throat, dragged his eyes to hers. 'I have something to tell you, Mamma. I'm afraid – it will upset you.'

She nodded her fine head. 'I knew there was something. I've known for a long time.'

'You never said.'

'I waited for you to tell me.' His mother folded her hands across her black skirt.

He drew a long breath, held his hands together. 'Mamma, I have been seeing Ruth Millar.'

A scarlet colour swept across her face and receded, leaving her frighteningly pale. As her eyes, dark and terrible, rested on him, he knew, whatever she had expected, it wasn't this.

'Seeing?' she repeated. 'When?'

'On Wednesday afternoons.'

'All those Wednesdays? Mother of God!' She rocked herself in anguish. 'All those Wednesdays when you had to go places, you were seeing her? Nicco, Nicco, how could you?'

He bowed his head.

'How could you do that, Nicco? Meet the sister of the girl who took away Marilena's happiness? Meet a Scottish girl behind my back?'

'I didn't want to hurt you, Mamma.'

'Hurt me? What are you doing now?' His mother put a hand to her heart and caught her breath. 'Nicco, you are not telling me that you want to marry this girl? Dear God, that couldn't be true! You wouldn't marry out, Nicco, away from our community? You wouldn't marry a girl who knows nothing of what matters to us?'

'People do marry out, Mamma. Especially here, where there are so few of us.'

'Never in this family!' she cried. 'There has never been any-one in this family who has turned his back on the bell tower of home!'

'I am not turning my back on anything, Mamma. I love my homeland, I love all the things that matter to us. But I love Ruth, and I can't live without her.'

'Love, love, love!' Carlotta leaped from her chair. 'Why do all you young people talk of love? It is meaningless, to say, "I am in love"! Love comes with marriage and years together. It comes with marrying the right person, so that you share everything and know everything about the family and what matters. The sort of love you think you have for Ruth Millar would never last. It isn't real, it is something you imagine. Tell me how she would manage

156

in our family! She isn't even Catholic! How would you go to church together? Where would your children be christened?'

Her words were like a great cascade flowing over him, he wanted to cover his ears, shut them out, and began to walk up and down the room, twisting his shaking hands, as she continued to hurl arguments at him, taking such rattling breaths, he thought she might have some sort of attack and turned and tried to calm her.

'Mamma, that's enough. You will make yourself ill, going on like this. Please, be quiet and let's discuss this sensibly.'

'Ill? Yes, I am ill, Nicco! You have made me ill, my only son, my first-born. What mother would not be ill, to hear what you have said?' Carlotta caught her breath, as a new thought came to her. 'And what do Ruth Millar's parents think of this? Has she told them about you? Are they happy?'

He was silent.

'I see, they are not happy! How could they be? It is the same for them, Nicco, as for me. They will want a Scottish boy for her, someone who is the same as they are. That is what all parents want, a son-in-law, a daughter-in-law, who can be one of the family.' Carlotta leaned forward. 'Have they forbidden her to see you? You have not been going out on your Wednesdays lately. Only today.'

'They asked us not to meet for a while, to make sure we really cared for each other.' Nicco glanced sharply at his mother. 'We didn't meet for three months, and you see, we feel the same. It is the real thing for us. We want to spend our lives together.'

His mother drew her lips together in a hard straight line. 'You will not spend any part of your lives together in this flat, Nicco. You own the shop, I own the flat. If you insist on marrying this girl, you will have to find somewhere else to live.'

He stood very still, taking in what she had said. It came to him, that she was the same as Ruth's parents, willing to use any weapon to force their child to do their bidding. Only they had backed down, at least for the time being, and his mother would never back down. Even if he had hurt her deeply, and he knew he had, it was terrible to him to think that she would be willing to turn him out of his home. How could she do that? She knew he had not the money to rent a good flat elsewhere. He was keeping his head above water, but only just, and Ruth, once she married, would have no income. It was possible that Mr MacRobbie might permit her to stay on, as he would not be subject to the same rules as the professions, but it was unlikely. A married woman was expected to be kept by her husband and her job made available for someone else.

'You would make me do that?' he asked in a low voice.

'Yes. I would. I will not have Ruth Millar as my daughter-in-law. I will not have her living in my house.'

'You know I can't afford another place to live.'

She shrugged. 'There are plenty of rooms in the Old Town.'

'And you'd be happy for Ruth and me to live in one of those rooms?'

'I am not happy for you and Ruth Millar to live anywhere!' she cried. 'It is your choice, Nicco, your choice! You have brought it on yourself!'

A door banged and a light footstep sounded on the stairs.

'Marilena,' whispered Carlotta. 'Now you must tell her what you are planning to do.'

He told her, he took her reproaches without a word, and when she and her mother had hurried away to tell his uncle and aunt of his disgraceful behaviour, he caught a tram to Trinity. He didn't know why, there was little point in standing outside Ruth's home, looking up at her windows, but he wanted to be near her, felt then that she was all he had in the world. The last thing he expected was that he would see her, but the spring evening was not yet dark and she spotted him as she stood looking out from her bedroom, her eyes full of tears.

'Nicco!'

She was down the stairs and out of the house like a bird in flight and in his arms before he disappeared.

'You're surely a mirage!' she cried, half laughing, half crying. 'When I saw you, I thought I must have conjured you up, because I felt so bad, so low!'

'Me, too,' he whispered. 'Oh, Ruth, it's been terrible!'

'I know, I know.' She was kissing his face over and over again, and he was kissing her back.

'My mother won't accept you, Ruth.'

'And my folks won't accept you.'

158

He touched the tears on her cheeks. 'You spoke to them?'

'Soon as I got back. I told them I'd done all they asked. I said I hadn't seen you for three months and I still felt the same and so did you. They said it made no difference, they still didn't want me to marry you.'

The disappointment had been so bitter, she could hardly put it into words. When she'd given up seeing Nicco for three long months and still felt the same, she'd been so sure her parents would see her love was the real thing. But if she hadn't changed, neither had they.

'We appreciate what you did, Ruth, we want you to know that,' her mother had told her. 'But we've been thinking and we still feel it's no' right for you to marry Nicco. It's your happiness that's at stake, you ken. Marriage is more than just thinking you're in love. You'd never be able to settle into Nicco's family, and they'd never want you.'

'I'd be marrying Nicco, no' his family!'

'Families are what count.'

'Aye, that's true,' said Jack.

Ruth looked at him, and he looked away. She knew, if he'd been on his own, she could have worn him down, but her mother was a different matter. She thought she knew best, she genuinely thought she was doing the right thing, saving Ruth from future unhappiness. What could be done to fight that?

'You know I can get married, anyway,' she had murmured at last, using her last weapon.

'Against our wishes?' cried her mother. 'You'd never do that!'

'You don't care about MY wishes,' Ruth had answered, and had run blindly to her room.

Now, she raised tear-filled eyes to Nicco's.

'What do we do now? I know you won't want to marry me.'

'Ruth, for God's sake!'

'Well, you did say you thought it would be wrong for us to be married without my parents' consent.'

He bit his lip. 'Did I say that?'

'You did!'

'The truth is,' he said slowly, 'I can't do without you. That's what

I've learned these past months. If your parents won't agree, we'll have to marry anyway.'

She gave a long sigh of relief and held him close.

'But I'm not even sure where we can live,' he said, reluctantly releasing himself. 'My mother won't let us share the flat.'

'We'll find a room somewhere.'

'Then there's your exam. What will you do about that?'

'I'll have to let it go.'

He groaned. 'I never wanted you to do that.'

'It's no' your fault. Anyway, you had to give up your education to run the shop, didn't you? These things happen.'

'Yes, but I don't like to think of you having to give up your career for me.'

Ruth shrugged. 'Women have to make that kind of choice – at any rate, at the moment.'

'And you've chosen me. I'll make it up to you, Ruth. I promise.'

'You've already made it up.' She kissed him passionately. 'Nicco, I'll have to go. Will you see me next week?'

'Oh, God, yes, next week. Ruth, I love you.'

'I love you, Nicco.'

They parted, as the dusk turned to darkness and lights sprang up in Trinity. Ruth ran into the flat, Nicco went home on the tram. Both felt they were striding clouds.

Chapter Thirty

If Isa thought that Ruth was still seeing Nicco, she kept her suspicions to herself, just as the signora never asked if Nicco was still seeing Ruth. But then, the signora said very little to Nicco, anyway. There were times when he thought he would just move out from home and take a room for himself, but even the small rent required for that would be a waste of money when money was going to be in such short supply. Stick it out, was Ruth's advice; the end was in sight. She was, after all, having to endure things herself, especially the weddings.

First, there was Kester's. She and Sylvie were bridesmaids, following the ice-cool Fenella in ivory satin, dancing at another reception, waving off the newly-weds when they left for a touring honeymoon in Mr MacMenzie's car. Kester was so happy, it hurt to look at him. Hurt Ruth, anyway, who didn't care about a smart wedding or a honeymoon, but just wanted her folks to want her happiness too.

Sylvie's wedding was even more of an ordeal, for Jack and Isa were fond of Mark, where they were not fond of Fenella, and welcomed him into the family in just the way Ruth would have liked to see them welcome Nicco. All through the summer, she'd had to put up with her mother's delight at planning the oh-so-suitable wedding for Sylvie, while the knowledge that she couldn't even say she was meeting the man she loved was like so much salt in a wound. And she was expected to be bridesmaid again? Of course she agreed, it would have looked odd if she hadn't, and submitted to yet more sessions of dressmaking by her mother, whose mouth seemed permanently full of pins and whose eyes on her were often bright and speculative, but who still said nothing.

She's hoping that my feeling for Nicco will burn itself out, thought Ruth, but that's not going to happen. Once or twice she found herself on the verge of telling her mother the truth, but always saved herself in time. Still, the thought of what lay ahead for herself and Nicco was all that kept her sane in the midst of her sister's bliss.

She left it to a week after the wedding. Let her folks savour the memory for a week, anyway. For, of course, it was a lovely wedding, with not a thing to spoil it. No disasters, no embarrassing incidents at the reception, no one getting drunk, or upsetting anyone. After all, the groom was a policeman! And Sylvie did look so pretty, and Mark looked so proud. Be happy, thought Ruth, watching a crowd of guests flinging confetti at her sister and her new husband as they squirmed and screamed and tried to get to their going away car, from which a JUST MARRIED banner was already trailing, along with several old shoes.

'Och, what a sight!' cried Isa. 'Whatever will thae folk get up to next?' She glanced quickly at Ruth. 'Will you no' say goodbye to your sister, then? This is something special for her, you ken, going off to be a married woman.'

'I've said goodbye,' Ruth whispered, looking down at Sylvie's bouquet, which she had caught.

Her mother suddenly touched her arm. 'I want the same for you, Ruthie. To be married like Sylvie. To the right man. You think I'm hard on you, but it's only because I want you to be happy, can you no' see that?'

'The car's going, Ma,' Ruth answered, her eyes full of tears. 'Wave, then, wave!'

'Aye, the lassie's gone,' cried Jack, joining them, and looking woeful. 'I canna believe it – little Sylvie, away on her honeymoon!' He put his arm round Isa and smiled down at Ruth. 'You got the flowers, Ruthie? Means you'll be next.'

Isa, clicking her teeth at his tactlessness, said sharply, that that wasn't always true. 'Away, now, we've the guests to see to, Jack. Let's hope they don't hang around too long.'

One week later, Ruth was in her bedroom, packing. It was Saturday morning and she was not at the office because she'd given in her notice. Everyone had been very kind and clubbed together to buy her a cut-glass fruit bowl, and Mr MacRobbie had said how sorry he was to lose her, but she did understand, didn't she, that her job should really be for someone unmarried, unless it was a man, of course, and he would need the money? Oh, and I don't? thought Ruth, but knew it was pointless to argue and in any case was in too much of a dream to be able to think clearly. Was she really doing this? Saying goodbye to MacRobbie and MacRobbie, telling everyone she was going to be married? Seemed it had been true, for here she was today, not at the office, but packing her case, ready to meet Nicco. Still seemed like a dream.

Her father was downstairs in his shop, her mother had gone to the butcher's. It was time to go. She looked at herself in the mirror, wearing her good suit, and remembered for a moment the brides she knew. Renata, Fenella, Sylvie. All so beautiful on their special days, all so lucky, with their parents' smiles upon them. Don't think like that, she told herself, think of Nicco. She put on her hat, picked up her case and her coat, and looked around her room for the last time. Already, it looked different. The dressing table empty of clutter, her bed and Sylvie's, stripped and flat, everything as neat and tidy as a hospital ward. She gave a sob. Brought it home, didn't it? Neither she nor Sylvie would ever sleep here again. This was an ending. And a beginning. Have to think of that.

Hurry now, hurry. Ma would be back soon. Prop the note by the clock in the living room, run down the stairs and leave by the back door, not through the shop. Oh, God, if her dad should see her! Or, Bob MacAllan? Ruth, with a suitcase! She halted for a moment, to check the watch she'd recently been given for her twenty-first. Nicco should be round the corner with the taxi by now. What if he weren't? Supposing he'd changed his mind? Sweat was trickling down Ruth's neck as she got herself out of the back door and began to run down the street. Then the worst thought of all came into her mind. Supposing she should meet her mother coming back from shopping? No, she wouldn't, she wouldn't. They'd fixed for the taxi to wait away from the shops her mother would visit. It was all right, all right. There was the taxi waiting. There was Nicco. Thank God.

His strong hands were taking her case, the driver was twisting round, looking at them, and they were looking at each other. Neither spoke, but their eyes were eloquent.

'Here,' said Nicco, at last, 'I got these.'

Two white carnations. They pinned them on.

'Where to now?' asked the driver.

'Queen Street Register Office, please,' said Nicco.

And they held each other in joy.

Chapter Thirty-One

Their witnesses were waiting. As the taxi drew to a halt outside the Register Office, Nicco gave a deep sigh.

'Thank God,' he murmured. 'They might not have been there.'

But they were. Federico in his best grey suit with a rose in his lapel, Renata in brilliant pink with a white hat and a corsage of carnations and sweet peas tied with maidenhair. Both were waving and smiling, and Ruth, leaving the taxi on trembling legs, felt sudden tears sting her eyes. Renata and Federico. These were all they had as family, she and Nicco. No parents, no brother or sister, to see them wed. Which hadn't seemed to matter when they'd planned their secret marriage, for they only needed each other. True, but as she was embraced by Nicco's cousins, kissed and held tight, Ruth knew deep down that she did want family, she did want her mother and father to be with her on this day and as that couldn't be, was so grateful to have Renata and Federico, she almost shed tears in earnest. Especially when a newly-married couple appeared from the open doors of the Register Office, followed by relatives and friends, all laughing and throwing confetti as they ran to waiting cars.

'Don't cry,' Renata whispered, reading her mind. 'You've got us, Ruth.'

'Us? She's got Nicco!' cried Federico, and Ruth smiled radiantly.

'I have, Federico, I have!'

Renata gave her another hug. 'And it'll be a lovely wedding, you'll see. You don't have to have all that fuss we had to have a great day.'

'I wish I could've worn a special dress, though.' Ruth looked down at her suit. 'I didn't dare, in case anyone saw me leaving.'

'You look beautiful, Ruth, you really do. Now, where's Nicco?'

He was still at the taxi, his hands shaking so much he could hardly find the fare and as the driver watched sardonically, Federico had to run to help him.

'Och, it's no' as bad as all that, is it?' asked the driver, laughing suddenly. 'Come away, then! I've been married fifteen year this Hogmanay and it hasnae done me any harm!'

Who would have thought we'd be so nervous, when we are so happy? thought Ruth, as Nicco joined her, smiling, but so pale. Yet most brides and grooms were nervous before the wedding, and she and Nicco had more to be nervous about than most. As Federico waved away the taxi and swung up their suitcases, Ruth straightened her hat, dabbed at her eyes, and took Nicco's hand.

'It's time,' she whispered. 'Let's go in.'

How easy it was, in the end, to get married! All their parents' opposition faded from their minds, as they went through the formalities with the registrar, and even the fact that their families were not present didn't matter any more, for it was their right to be doing what they were doing, and the registrar in carrying out his professional duties was so obviously accepting that. The fee was paid, the necessary documents examined, and then, after the short civil ceremony, the words were said that made Ruth and Nicco man and wife. Wearing their new wedding rings, for Nicco, like many Italian men, had opted to wear a ring too, their eyes met. They thought they could never look away, but the registrar was putting pens in their hands ready for their signatures on the marriage schedule and calling forward the witnesses. It was Renata's turn to shed a few tears, as, with Federico, she appended her name, and she laughed and shook her head.

'Why should I cry, when I am so glad for you?' she demanded, and the registrar smiled and said he'd never known a wedding where somebody didn't cry. Ruth by then was in such a daze, she was only dimly aware of shaking the registrar's hand, of kissing Nicco, and then Federico and Renata, and moving out into the golden light of

Queen Street. Golden? Oh, yes, it was. To think she had worked for so long in this very street and never seen it look so wonderful!

'Just a minute,' said Renata, as they stood on the steps of the Register Office, bathed in that strange light, and before they could stop her, had shaken paper rose petals over their heads.

'Oh, no!' gasped Nicco, laughing. 'Oh, Renata, you devil, you're not supposed to do this!'

'No, but everyone does. Don't think you can escape!'

'You can shake all that stuff off at our place,' Federico said kindly. 'We've got a cold meal all ready.'

'And champagne!' cried Renata. 'Let's find a taxi.'

All these taxis, thought Ruth. Wouldn't Sylvie have been thrilled! For a moment, she felt a stab of regret that her sister wasn't with her, but Federico was flagging down a passing taxi and Nicco's eyes were on her. They were on their way to their celebration and she had so much to celebrate. She put Sylvie from her mind.

'We can never thank you two enough for what you've done for us today,' Nicco said huskily, when they had eaten Renata's splendid cold meal and been toasted in champagne. 'You've made all the difference to our wedding. We'll never forget it.'

'Never,' Ruth chimed in eagerly.

'What did we do?' cried Renata. 'Signed our names? Provided some salad? It was nothing!'

'You know what you did,' Nicco said in a low voice.

'You were family,' whispered Ruth.

'Don't talk about it,' Federico murmured, embarrassed. 'Whatever we did, we were glad to do it.'

There was a silence, as they thought of those who might have been present and were not, then Nicco stood up and said it was time to go to the station, they mustn't miss their train.

'Away to honeymoon at last,' Renata said fondly. 'Oh, how lovely it will be!'

'We're only going to Fife,' Nicco told her, 'Not quite as far as you went.'

'Oh, just as far, Nicco, just as far!'

Yes, just as far, thought Ruth. For her, at least, a completely new life was beckoning, with no bridge that she could see back to her old one. Och, that was silly talk! Of course, her old life would still be a part of her. Ma and Dad would come round. Once she was married, they'd understand. Wouldn't they?

'I'd better get another taxi,' Federico was saying. 'We're coming with you to the station, you know. Got to see you safely off to wherever it is.'

'You haven't actually said where,' Renata remarked.

'It's no secret,' Nicco told her. 'We're going to Pittenweem, a little fishing village in the East Neuk.'

'Staying in a guest-house,' Ruth added. 'Just for five days. Domenico's going to look after the shop, but Nicco can't ask him to give up too much time.'

It was on the tip of Renata's tongue to ask what her Aunt Carlotta thought about all of that, but wisely she said nothing and occupied herself in brushing the rose petals from Ruth's hair and whispering in her ear that she would have a marvellous time that night, no need to worry!

'I'm no' worrying,' Ruth whispered back.

And a marvellous time it was. Close in each other's arms, under the fresh rough sheets of their guest-house bed and with the sound of the sea murmuring outside their windows, all the previous months of anxiety they'd had to endure were forgotten. They might have to face anxiety again when this was over, but they had five days away from everything and everyone they knew, and that was a lifetime. Tomorrow, as different people, married people, they would explore the little village with its whitewashed cottages and its fishing boats pulled up on the shore, but tonight they were teaching each other to love, and the lessons were easy.

In the morning, when the sun made crooked patterns on the ceiling and they could smell bacon cooking somewhere below, Ruth stretched herself and smiled contentedly. She wound her fingers in Nicco's black hair and looked long and devotedly into his eyes.

'Happy?' he asked gently.

'You know I am.'

He laid his face against hers. 'I want you to be happy, Ruth. Happy always.'

'Well, why shouldn't I be?'

'You know the problems.'

'Nicco, we're no' worrying about problems now. This is our honeymoon!'

He moved away from her, shaking his head. 'I feel bad, though, Ruth. Thinking of our parents – not giving their blessing. It should've been different for you, you should have had a wedding like your sister's—'

'I didn't want a wedding like Sylvie's, I was happy with what we had, Nicco.'

'And then there's the flat we've found.' Nicco's eyes were sombre. 'In the Old Town. Not what you're used to, and I can't give you anything better. I woke in the night, couldn't stop thinking about it—'

'Oh, Nicco, fancy waking and thinking about that flat!' Ruth was trying to laugh. 'On our wedding night.'

Nicco laughed, too. 'You're right, I was a fool. But, oh God, Ruth, you can see why I'm worrying, can't you? I want to make you happy, I want you to have no regrets for marrying me, that's all I want in the world!'

'I'll never have any regrets!' Ruth cried, throwing her arms around him. 'Never any regrets, Nicco. You're all I want, all I'll ever want, you just remember that!'

They were clinging together, lost to time and place and everything except themselves, when a knock sounded on their bedroom door.

'Breakfast in half an hour.' Came the stern voice of their landlady, Mrs MacRurie. 'If you'll be wantin' the bathroom, it's free.'

They looked at each other in a moment of stillness, then burst into laughter.

'I don't think she likes honeymooners,' Ruth whispered, leaping out of bed.

'Now how would she know we're honeymooners?' asked Nicco, opening his case and finding all his clothes interlayered with rose petals. 'Oh, Renata, wait till I see you again!'

In exactly the half hour they'd been given, they were both washed and dressed and downstairs eating eggs and bacon and resolutely avoiding the eyes of the other guests. No more was said of the future.

Part Three

Chapter Thirty-Two

It was 1937. A strange year for the British people, with a Coronation in May that had seen one King take the place of another. Of course, it had never been intended that George VI should ascend the throne, which belonged by right to his older brother, Edward, the darling of the people. But in December, 1936, Edward, who had succeeded George V, had shocked the nation by abdicating when he had been refused permission to marry Mrs Simpson, an American divorcee, and make her Queen. The Crown went to his brother, the Coronation was re-arranged, life went on. Or, seemed to. But the country had been deeply shaken all the same, and there were those who saw the Abdication as another aspect of an uncertain world. Civil war in Spain, Italian aggression in Abyssinia, Germany marching everywhere – no one felt safe, but there was nothing anyone could do, they had to leave things to the politicians. What a laugh, eh? As though they'd be able to solve anything!

On a warm day in September, Isa and Sylvie were walking down the High Street. They were not worrying about the international situation, which they preferred to put out of their minds, but were on their way to visit Ruth. Her daughter, Giovanna, known as Gina, was two weeks old and back from hospital, where, as Isa thanked the Lord, she'd been born, and not in that couple of rooms Ruth now called home. Oh, to think that her Ruthie was back in the Old Town, where Isa and Jack had started off married life, in a tenement no better than theirs!

'Och, when I remember what your sister could've been, Sylvie, it breaks ma heart to think what she's thrown away,' groaned Isa, as they reached the turning for Ruth's flat in Hebburn Place. 'I mean, she could've been a civil servant, she could've been somebody! And what does she do? She marries Nicco behind ma back and ends up here!'

'Never mind, Ma, you've forgiven her now,' Sylvie answered, gasping a little, for she was six months pregnant and already as she put it herself, as 'big as a house'.

'Aye, since the wean was on the way. Which is more than that signora's done, eh? Och, I told Ruth how it'd be, if she married Nicco, but she never took a blind bit of notice. I mean, he's a nice lad, but his family takes everything he's got. Look at that great splash of a wedding he'd to pay for, when Marilena married Guido! What's left for poor Ruth?'

'Ma, calm down,' said Sylvie wearily. 'We're there. Anyway, Nicco's mother did go to see Ruth in hospital.'

'Aye, and I bet she was as cold as Christmas!' Isa swung open the door to Ruth's tenement that was never locked. 'Well, it's like I say. Ruth's made her bed, now she'll have to lie on it.'

Thirty-Seven Hebburn Place, where Ruth and Nicco had been living since they returned from honeymoon was a typical Old Town building, several storeys high and in a precarious state of repair. Some of the rooms were large and elegant in their proportions, though so crammed with tenants any elegance was pretty well concealed. The entrance close and the stone stair were blackened from many years' of use, and if any paint had ever been applied to the internal doors, it was not in living memory.

'Och, what a place!' cried Isa, picking her way up the stair through a crowd of small children. 'If I could just take a bucket of hot water and a scrubbing brush to it all, eh?'

'It'd probably fall down,' Sylvie answered, then halted with her mother, as a door on the stair opened and a little woman in a long apron flew out.

'Mind thae bairns, eh?' she cried. 'They've to stay there till we get the babby born, dinna let them wander wi' you, now!'

'Someone's having a baby in there?' asked Sylvie, her face paling.

'Aye, Mrs MacSween. It's her sixth.' The little woman laughed. 'Has one every year, you ken. That's last year's babby there.'

Isa and Sylvie turned their eyes on a small damp bundle trying to crawl up the next flight of stairs. 'Oh, my God,' cried Isa, clicking her tongue and grabbing the child. 'Soaking wet,' she said to the woman in the apron. 'When I've seen ma daughter, I'll come in and give you a hand, Mrs—'

'Nisbet, hen, Mrs Nisbet.'

'Ma!' wailed Sylvie.

'Looks like you'll be minding a bairn yourself soon enough,' Mrs Nisbet told her cheerfully. 'Who're you seeking, then?'

As Isa began to explain that they were come to see her daughter up the stair, a shrill voice came from behind the door. 'Mrs Nisbet, Mrs Nisbet, come quick, come quick!' And the children, all dressed in a strange variety of clothes but without shoes, came clutching at Mrs Nisbet's skirts, crying for their mother.

'Is the babby born yet?' the oldest boy asked. 'We want in!'

'No, it's no' come yet, Sammie.' Mrs Nisbet distractedly gave him a hug. 'Now, you stay here, and keep an eye on the others and I'll gi' you some sweeties, eh?'

As she hurried in and closed the door and the children began howling for the sweeties then and there, Sylvie escaped up the stair as fast as she was able, followed by Isa, shaking her head and bemoaning the way some folk had to live.

'Five children and another one being born,' agreed Sylvie. 'Oh, the poor woman, I can't bear to think of it. At least, Ruth's no' in that state, Ma.'

'No' yet,' said Isa grimly.

In spite of Isa's criticism, Ruth's flat was in better condition than any other in the tenement, for there had been paint applied here, by Nicco and Ruth themselves. They had two rooms, a bedroom and a living room, which they had cleaned and decorated, and made

175

to look as attractive as possible. Ruth had blackleaded the stove, sewn new curtains, and rubbed up the second-hand furniture they had acquired, while Nicco had put up shelves and pictures, and made a cradle for the baby. After the scene below, it seemed to Sylvie, and even Isa, that Ruth's place was something of a haven.

Ruth herself seemed hollow-eyed and weary, but she had made an effort to look her best for her mother's visit, washing her hair and wearing a freshly ironed dress. As for Baby Gina, she reclined in her new cradle and cooed and gurgled like the best baby in the world, which of course, said Ruth, she was.

'Except that she's awake all night,' she added smiling. 'Och, Sylvie, get your sleep while you can, eh?'

'Put the kettle on, Ruth,' her mother ordered, picking up Gina and cuddling her. 'Sylvie, sit down and put your feet up. Oh, my goodness, it's nice to sit here, eh, after seeing thae poor bairns down the stair.'

'What poor bairns?' asked Ruth, moving the kettle over on the range and getting the teapot down. 'Oh, you must mean the MacSweens. Is the baby coming, then? I heard it was due any day.'

'Aye, it's coming and all the family's on the stair, except for the dad. If there is a dad?'

'There is. He's unemployed, but he's just got temporary work doing repairs for the council.' Ruth made the tea, sighing. 'Great relief for the time being.'

'Aye, you're seeing how the other half lives here, Ruth,' her mother remarked, as the baby sagged into sleep against her shoulder. 'Now, look in that bag I've brought – there's some of ma scones and a sandwich cake. And there's a matinee coat for the babby from Sarah MacAllan, and bootees and a bonnet from Millie. They'd like to come round.' Isa sniffed. 'If you'll let 'em.'

'Why not?' asked Sylvie lazily. 'Ruth's made this place very nice.'

'Aye, that's true. But it's no' the place for her, all the same.'

'As a matter of fact, I'm no' staying,' Ruth said quietly. She took the baby from her mother's arms and settled her back in her cot. 'Ready for your tea, Ma?'

176

Sylvie and Isa were exchanging glances.

'What d'you mean, you're no' staying?' Isa demanded. 'Where are you going, then?'

'Back to Ginger Street.'

'Ginger Street? Ruth, you're never going to live over the shop with Nicco's mother?'

'I am. She wants us to, now that I've got the baby and Marilena's living with Guido's folks.' Ruth poured the tea and handed the scones. 'Don't look like that, Ma. It'll be better than here.'

'Think so?' Isa stirred her tea vigorously, her face a study of conflicting emotions as she studied this new information. 'It's true, you'll have more room—'

'And a bathroom again,' put in Ruth.

'That's worth a lot,' Sylvie agreed.

'But is it worth living with the signora?' asked Isa. 'Ruth, you'll be under her thumb from the start, so you will!'

'I won't!' Ruth set her chin. 'I've made up my mind. She won't be running my life the way she used to run Marilena's. I've already made that clear to Nicco.'

'Aye, and then there'll be ill feeling and if you fall out, he'll be upset.'

'There won't be ill feeling. I'll be very careful to get on with her, and the thing is, when Gina's a bit older, she's offered to look after her, while I help Nicco in the shop. So, you see, I'll be out of her way.'

'You're going to try to go back to work?' Isa wailed. 'Och, it's no life with a babby!'

'I want to work again, Ma, and Nicco needs help, now that Marilena's gone. It'll only be part-time, anyway. You'll see, it'll all work out.'

'Of course it will,' said Sylvie, taking a slice of the cake. 'Ma, I can tell you're itching to get down the stair to start washing the bairns. Why don't you do that while I stay with Ruth?'

'Ma's going to wash the MacSweens?' cried Ruth, laughing. 'They won't know what's hit them!'

'Aye, well I'll have to see if the babby's come first,' said Isa. 'Else I might have to bring thae bairns up here, if you don't mind, Ruth.

Give me some soap and a can of hot water, anyway. If you could've seen their little faces, you'd have been down there yourselves, with a scrubbing brush!'

'Who would?' cried Sylvie, with a shudder.

Chapter Thirty-Three

When Isa had bustled away with her hot water, soap, flannels and old towels, Sylvie looked at Ruth and smiled.

'She hasn't changed, has she?'

'Changed towards me, though, thank the Lord.'

'Och, she never wanted to make a real break, Ruthie. It was just she felt she had to make her point. That's the way she is.'

'Made me very unhappy. So did Dad.'

Ruth's face had darkened, her eyes looking away from Sylvie. She was thinking back to the time when she'd gone to the Trinity flat after her honeymoon and been shown the door. At first, she hadn't been able to believe it. All the nightmare memories of the time her mother had threatened to throw her out seemed to have come true, yet she still couldn't take it in. But then her dad had followed her when she'd finally turned away, and told her, somewhat shamefacedly, that she couldn't expect any different treatment. Not after sneaking away to be married, the way she'd done. She'd really upset her ma, doing that, and him, too.

'I had to get married that way!' Ruth had cried. 'You wouldn't accept Nicco!'

'Aye, well, it's too soon yet for your ma to come round, Ruth. Mebbe if you were to try later, eh?'

'How much later?'

He'd shaken his head and given her another piece of advice. Better not contact Kester, eh? Fenella didn't approve of Ruth's marriage at all, and Kester wouldn't argue with her.

Ruth had been so angry, she'd been unable to speak. Fenella didn't approve? Her brother wouldn't take Ruth's part? Though Sylvie and Renata hadn't turned their backs on her, Ruth's familiar world had seemed so cold and alien then, only Nicco had been able to console her. He'd had the same reception, of course. Though he'd given his mother warning of his marriage, she had still been furious. Had refused to speak to Domenico, when he had once again looked after the shop, and for days had refused to speak to Nicco after his return from honeymoon. Things had settled down for him eventually, in that she had begun to talk to him again and insisted on making his lunch for him every day, as his new wife would certainly not be able to cook the things he liked, but for a long time he and Ruth had felt themselves alone. Alone against the world. Or, their parents, which amounted to the same thing. When they made love at night, they didn't think of it. They were still lost to the world, anyway, in a haze of delight that was so new and fresh and unexpected, they were transported away from every care. Until the morning came, when Nicco had to go to the shop and Ruth had to go to the chocolate factory where she'd found part-time work. Then the world returned and seemed a very hostile place.

Two things happened to bring change. The first was Guido's marriage to Marilena, following his return from London. This made Ruth feel better for Sylvie, and gave her some hope for her own future in Nicco's family. There were so many things against her in their eyes, but if Marilena were happy again and Sylvie were forgotten, that would at least be one grievance less. But imagine Guido's actually wanting to marry Marilena, after all he'd said! It had taken his time away from her to make him realise what he was missing. Such a beautiful, sweet, docile girl! He now declared himself a fool ever to have looked at anyone else, and if his family agreed with him, they didn't rub it in, being only too relieved that he was finally doing the right thing. As for Marilena, she was so ecstatic, planning her wedding, Renata told Ruth that she feared for her. Could any woman stay on such a plane without falling off and seriously damaging herself?

'Oh, yes,' Ruth had answered, smiling. 'I haven't fallen off yet.'

And Renata had smiled and carried on with her pasta-making

demonstration, for she was giving Ruth lessons in Italian cooking and Ruth was proving a star pupil.

The second thing that happened was that Ruth discovered she was going to have a baby. At first, she hadn't wanted it. After all, she'd taken Renata's advice and tried to take precautions, because the money she earned was useful and she really couldn't face bringing up a child in the tenement. But she'd fallen for a baby, anyway, and though Nicco said he was thrilled, and was probably speaking the truth, for Italians loved children, Ruth for a time sank into deeper despondency than ever.

But the expected baby brought breaks in the clouds she could never have foreseen. Her mother, for instance, arriving in Hebburn Place with flowers, a Coronation mug and full knitted outfit in white wool, suitable, of course, for boy or girl.

'Ma!' cried Ruth.

'Ruth!' sobbed Isa.

'Did Sylvie tell you?'

'Aye.' Isa blew her nose. 'Ma first grandchild, eh?'

'I'm so glad you came, Ma.'

'Couldn't stay away. Put the kettle on, eh? Then show me round.'

That was the beginning of the 'let bygones be bygones' period that brought the smile back to Ruth's face and the spring to her step, as Nicco was invited round to her parents' flat, and the frosty Fenella went so far as to be polite when she saw them, though her tolerance did not extend any further than that. Ruth didn't care. She knew her folks still weren't happy that she'd married an Italian, she knew they thought she should have found a nice Scot, but they had 'come round', they had accepted the situation, she was part of the family again and Nicco was no longer excluded.

After her mother's visit, came Carlotta's. Ruth, by then devoted to her new daughter, had been so astounded when Nicco's mother visited her in hospital, she could only feel humbly grateful, even though the signora had immediately observed what a pity it was that Nicco had not been given a son first. Never mind – she had fixed Ruth with those dark eyes of hers – the little granddaughter was certainly a fine and healthy child, in spite of having been born in hospital, and next time, God willing, Ruth would have a boy. Now, what was happening about Giovanna's christening? It must be arranged as soon as possible, and be Catholic, of course, with as a grand a ceremony as could be afforded. 'Tell your parents this must be so,' ordered the signora, 'we will all pay.'

Oh, my goodness, Ruth had thought, what's it going to be like, living with her? How would it work out? She couldn't help feeling nervous, but as she'd told Isa, she was prepared to make it work. She had to make it work, there could be no alternative.

'Better get these cups done,' Sylvie was saying, but Ruth, looking at her sister again, told her to sit down and rest.

'Feeling all right?' she asked solicitously, as Sylvie began to rub her back. 'Want a cushion?'

'I'm fine, thanks. It's just carrying all this weight, makes me feel so tired. I'm no' used to it.'

'It'll all go like magic, when the baby's born.'

'So you say.' Sylvie shook her head dispiritedly. 'I can't believe it'll ever go. When I look at my dancing dresses, I could bawl my head off!'

'Ah, everybody feels like that, but you'll see, you'll be slim as a wand in no time. Anyway, it's worth it, Sylvie, trust me!'

They both looked down at the sleeping Gina, and smiled.

'You're really happy, eh, Ruthie?' Sylvie whispered.

'Very happy,' Ruth said softly. 'Nicco and Gina are all the world to me. I know Ma still thinks I should've married some Scot, but if I can just be with Nicco and the baby, that's all I want.'

'I feel the same about Mark,' Sylvie said, after a pause. 'Mebbe he's no' as handsome as some, but he's so kind and gentle, you ken.' She laughed a little. 'Seems funny for a policeman, eh? But he's really good natured.'

'I'd say, we've both been lucky,' said Ruth, silently praying the luck wouldn't change.

'Have you girls no' washed thae cups yet?' cried their mother, coming in with Ruth's hot water can and a pile of damp towels. 'I bet you've been blethering, eh? Just like that Mrs Nisbet down the stair. Still, she's a good-hearted soul and doing all she can.'

182

'I'll wash the cups, don't worry,' said Ruth. 'Has the baby come yet?'

'Aye, a fine little boy. We put him in a drawer – makes a good cradle – and his ma's sitting up in bed, drinking tea, right as ninepence. Says she going to call him George – after the new King, you ken.' Isa set down the towels and went to wash her hands at Ruth's sink. 'Wonder what the King would make of Hebburn Place, eh, if he was to see it? Aye, well, he never will. Find me a bag for that laundry, Ruth, and I'll take it home. You've no time for doing extra washing, eh?'

'Did you give the kids a good scrubbing?' asked Sylvie, as Ruth obediently found a bag for the laundry, and Isa answered that indeed she had.

'My word, you should've seen the layers that came off! You'd never've recognised the poor little mites when I'd done! And I found a bit of cloth and changed last year's baby, while Mrs Nisbet started tearing up strips for the new one, but the bairns were howling that much, with all the washing and that, I ran round the corner and got them some sweeties and a few things for their tea, because I could see they'd no' much.' Isa was buttoning her jacket and putting on her hat. 'Ruth, if you've time, will you pop down and see Mrs MacSween? See if she needs a hand? It'll be a drop in the ocean, but we have to do what we can, eh?'

'You certainly do that, Ma,' Ruth said quietly. 'Of course, I'll try to help Mrs MacSween. At least, till I go.'

'And when'll that be?' asked her mother.

'Couple of weeks. We'd to give the landlord notice.'

'Say, if you want help flitting, then. You ready, Sylvie?'

'I'm just seeing if I've enough for a taxi,' said Sylvie, looking in her purse. 'You'll no' fancy carrying that bag of washing on the tram, Ma.'

'You and your taxis!' her mother said fondly. 'Your Mark'll be skint, the way you go on!'

'Sylvie's tired, Ma,' said Ruth, picking up Gina, who was stirring and ready to be fed. 'Thanks for coming, you two.'

'Keep in touch,' her mother told her, kissing Gina. 'Sylvie, let's away.'

'And I'll be in touch,' said Sylvie, hugging her sister around the baby. 'I'm so happy for you, Ruth. I mean, that things are working out.'

Just hope they are, thought Ruth.

It was some time before Nicco came home. His day was long and he was weary, but his face was alight as he came back from seeing the sleeping Gina in their room and gave Ruth a loving embrace.

'How've things been, *cara*? How did your mother's visit go?'

'Very well. Mrs MacSween's baby's come and Ma decided to wash all the children.'

'By way of celebration?' asked Nicco, smiling.

'Och, you know what's she's like.' Ruth was setting out knives and forks ready for their meal, a stew that was simmering on the range. 'I told her about moving to Ginger Street.'

'She's happy about that?'

Ruth hesitated. 'Not too sure I'll get on with your mother. To tell you the truth, neither am I.'

Nicco rose and went to wash his hands. 'You'll be all right, Ruth. I'm sure Mamma wants to be friends now, and you've been doing all you can to fit in. Even learning Italian and a bit of our dialect!'

'I wouldn't say I was very fluent yet.'

'The thing is, you're trying, you're showing willing.'

But is she? wondered Ruth, beginning to serve up the meal. In spite of all her brave words to her mother, the thought of moving to Ginger Street throbbed like a pain. But Nicco's eyes were anxious on her face and she gave a reassuring smile.

'*Buon appetito*, Nicco!'

He relaxed, smiling back. '*Grazie altrettanto*!'

They began to eat and for a pleasant while put Ginger Street from their minds.

Chapter Thirty-Four

It turned out that they had to sell their furniture. Ruth was upset.

'Is there no way we can keep it?' she asked Nicco. 'I mean, we might want it, and I've cleaned it all up and made it nice.'

'I know, *cara*, but there isn't room over the shop. My mother has too much furniture as it is.'

'Yes, but that's hers. This is ours.'

Nicco sighed and shook his head. 'I'm sorry, Ruth, I know how you feel, but we must be practical, the furniture will have to go.'

It was just one more pointer to the fact that their lives were to be absorbed into the signora's. Perhaps, if she'd held out for it, Ruth could have kept her little family in the tenement, but she knew it was no place to bring up Gina, not to mention the waste of money in paying rent. Also, Nicco's life was made more difficult by not living over the shop, nor could she be of help to him. Oh, in every way, the move to Ginger Street made sense. Only, Ruth didn't want to go.

The day came, however, when they closed the door of the Hebburn Place flat for the last time and walked down the stair, Nicco loaded up with cardboard boxes for the hired van, Ruth carrying the baby. They hadn't asked for help from Isa in the move, their excuse being that there really wasn't much to do once the furniture had been sold, but in truth, Ruth didn't want her mother dashing around at the Ginger Street flat and upsetting the signora. For the relationship between those two was distinctly cool and could take a turn for the worse, if the signora thought Isa was giving orders in her own flat. And Ruth could just see her mother doing that!

'Hang on a minute,' she told Nicco, as they passed the MacSweens' door. 'I want to say goodbye to Etta.'

'Ruth, are you away?' asked Etta MacSween, appearing in the doorway with the new baby over her shoulder. 'Och, I'm goin' to miss you, hen! You've been that kind, I dinna ken what I'd have done without you, thae first days when I had Georgie here!'

'I didn't do much, Etta. Mrs Nisbet was the one.'

'Aye, she was very good, but you took the bairns and minded 'em, and I got a bit of rest, did I no'?' Etta, who was only twenty-eight but looked forty, shifted Georgie on her shoulder, and bent to give Ruth a damp, heartfelt hug. 'And you thank your ma and all, when you see her, for cleaning up ma bairns! Och, what a worker, eh? I bet her place is like a palace!'

Ruth laughed and pressed some coins into Georgie's tiny fingers, as Nicco stood waiting. 'Take care of yourself, Etta, eh? And I'll come and see you, you know, I'm no' going far.'

'Aye, I'll do what I can.' Etta shook back her thin fall of hair. 'If I could just get Sammie to go to school, but he'll no' go and ma man's always away to work, there's ony me for iverything, you ken. Och, but I'll no' keep you blethering, you'll want away. All the best, then, all the best, Mr Ritty now, and you take care o' your wife, for she's a grand girl, so she is!'

'I know,' said Nicco, smiling, and as Mrs Nisbet and one or two other neighbours appeared to wave goodbye, he and Ruth left Number Thirty-Seven and the first short chapter of their lives together.

'We were happy here, weren't we?' asked Ruth. 'I'll try to go back sometimes, and see them all.'

'Sure you will,' Nicco murmured, as he threaded his way through the city traffic, but he was thinking of the van. 'Wish I'd one of these, Ruth. Nearly got one, you know. Thought I'd be like your dad and do deliveries.'

'Why didn't you, then?'

'Money was too tight. Never got round to serving snacks, either. Remember how I used to talk about doing the same as the Valdos?'

'We're doing better than some, I thought?'

'True, but the books are always full.'

'Books?'

He gave her a sideways smile. 'Credit books. When you help me, you'll know all about them. Somebody can't pay, they say, put it in the book.'

'Ah, you're talking about tick?' asked Ruth. 'I know about that already. Dad used to say plenty of folk wanted tick at Tomlinson's.'

'No doubt his customers don't ask for it? Lucky man, your dad.'

'Always called himself that,' Ruth agreed, with a smile, but her mouth was dry as she thought of the coming meeting with the signora. Be strong, she told herself, be firm. Start as you mean to go on. Glancing at Nicco, she could tell that he also was on edge. He might not be any help if there were trouble. After all, the signora was his mother. Very special to him. But so am I, thought Ruth, so am I!

Ginger Street. Here it was. Memory Lane. Everything so much the same. And the Riettis' shop – that was the same, too. Where were those two little girls looking in the window? Ruth could almost see herself and Sylvie, noses pressed to the glass, eyes going over the soor plums, the Highland toffee, the buttered brazils.

'Why, they're all still there!' she cried to Nicco, as he helped her out of the van with the baby. 'The jars, the boilings, I can see them all!'

'You've been back once or twice, Ruth – have you never looked at the shop?'

'No' really.' Ruth's eyes suddenly pricked with tears. 'I've never really been back.'

'It's home now,' Nicco told her, kissing her swiftly. 'Promise me you'll be happy here.'

'I promise,' she answered, but knew her promise was worthless. It didn't depend on herself.

The shop, of course, was closed, for they had chosen early closing day for their move. Now Nicco unlocked the door and said he would take Ruth up the stair, then start unloading. But Ruth was hesitating. She was looking round, gazing at the shelves she remembered so well, smelling all the different smells she remembered too, when Guido came running lightly down from the flat.

'Hallo, Ruth,' he said without smiling.

'Hallo, Guido.' She had seen very little of him since her marriage, had not even been to his wedding, for though she had been grudgingly invited with Nicco, she had thought it better not to attend. Now she made an effort to smile at the closed, handsome face he presented to her, but had the feeling he was only seeing her as sister to Sylvie and that she was already off to a bad start.

'What are you doing here?' asked Nicco, without warmth.

'Came to help. Mamma said it would be a good idea.' Guido jerked his head towards the stair. 'Marilena's up there already, dying to see the baby.' His face softened a little, and he put a finger to Gina's cheek, but when she began to cry, drew back with a laugh. 'Take her away, Ruth, take her up the stair, that's what they're waiting for!'

Oh, I don't think so, thought Ruth. At least, no' the signora. She's waiting for me.

Chapter Thirty-Five

She was. Dressed in her usual black, a touch of lace at her throat, Carlotta Rietti sat in her Italian room, her possessions around her, her daughter beside her, definitely the mistress of the house, definitely in command. Nothing new there, thought Ruth, advancing valiantly with her baby, just remember, be strong! But when her own eyes met the dark gaze of Nicco's mother and instantly fell, she knew it was not going to be easy to be strong.

'Mamma, here we are,' said Nicco with carefully assumed ease. 'Here's Ruth, with Gina.'

The signora inclined her head. She said nothing.

Nicco bent desperately towards her. 'Mamma, won't you speak to Ruth?'

Is this how it's going to be? thought Ruth, feeling the cold wind of hostility chilling her to her bones. His mother spoke to me in the hospital, why can't she speak to me now? Does she expect us to live in silence? Clinging tightly to Gina, as though to a talisman to keep her safe, she forced herself to smile at her mother-in-law and made the formal little speech in Italian that she had already rehearsed.

'Thank you for letting us come here, signora. I appreciate it. I hope we will be happy together.'

A shiver crossed the older woman's face. She put her hand to the white lace at her neck, and cleared her throat.

'I pray for that,' she answered slowly.

Marilena, whose own happiness had added a new dimension to her beauty, now decided that it was safe to greet Ruth and leaped up to kiss her on the cheek. 'Oh, it's so lovely to see you, again, Ruth! And you look so well! May I take the baby?'

'I will take the baby,' said her mother. She stretched out her arms and Ruth, after a moment's hesitation, placed Gina into them, praying that she would not cry for this grandmother, as she had cried for Guido. She didn't, only sent a wondering gaze over the new face bent over hers, a face that for the first time since Ruth's arrival, relaxed its lines.

'Yes, it is there,' the signora murmured, in her own dialect, gently rocking Gina on her knee. 'The likeness to your father, Nicco. I think I see it before in the hospital, now I am sure. See the nose? The brow? Do you not see it, then?'

'Mamma, it's too early to tell.'

'Babies change,' said Marilena, edging forward for her turn in holding Gina.

'What is your mother saying?' whispered Ruth, making a little vow to work even harder on studying the family dialect.

'That Gina is like my father,' Nicco whispered.

Ruth gave a faint smile. Better not say that her own mother had already claimed likeness to herself. If the signora saw Gina as a Rietti, she would surely accept her, and Ruth wanted her daughter accepted. But now the signora was moving on to discuss the christening, speaking English so that Ruth should be sure to understand. Why had this not already been arranged?

'Everyone is saying to me, Nicco, when is your grandchild's christening? What are you thinking of, to leave it so late?'

'I'm sorry, Mamma, it's just that with the move and everything—'

'Nothing is more important than a christening.' The signora glanced at Ruth. 'You agree?'

'Yes, of course. Nicco is going to see about it.'

'I hope so!'

There was an uneasy silence. It seemed that Nicco and Ruth had already failed their first hurdle. They glanced at each other and let their eyes fall, Ruth thinking, mutinously, that anyone would think Gina was the signora's baby, not theirs. Be strong, she reminded herself, be patient! And was relieved when Guido asked, restively:

'Nicco, shouldn't we be bringing up your stuff? I've taken time off work to be here.'

Since his return from London, Guido had given up the seasonal selling of ice-cream for his father and was working permanently for Gibb's biscuit factory. He was already a foreman and was ambitious to get on; might well do so, Nicco had told Ruth, if he could keep his politics out of his work. There was, however, no guarantee of that.

'OK, fine,' said Nicco. 'It's good of you to give us a hand, Guido. Marilena, will you show Ruth our room?'

'I was just going to take the baby!' Marilena protested.

'Leave the baby to me,' said her mother. 'Go with Ruth, Marilena.'

'Mamma is so bossy,' Marilena muttered, as she and Ruth reluctantly left the living room. 'She still tells me what to do, though I am a married woman!'

'Mothers are like that,' said Ruth. 'I think we are their children for ever.'

Marilena shrugged and showed Ruth into a large room dominated by a fine double bed with brass head and foot, a billowing snowy-white counterpane and mounds of lace pillows. There were rows of framed pictures of saints on the walls, draped white curtains at the windows, a mahogany chest of drawers with photographs of the family, and lamps with frilled shades on either side of the bed. Ruth stood very still, looking at everything, while Marilena walked around, straightening things and admiring herself in a hand mirror.

'*Bellissima*, eh?' she asked, over her shoulder.

'Marilena, is this your mother's room?' asked Ruth.

'It was. She has given it to you.'

'We can't let her do that. We can't take her room!'

Ruth's eyes were fixed now on the double bed, the signora's marriage bed. How could she and Nicco sleep there, thinking of his parents? How could they make love, thinking of those others, also making love? His father? Oh, God, his mother! No, no, it wasn't possible.

'I never wanted to take your mother's room,' she said frantically. 'I mean, it's hers, it's special. It was your father's room, too.'

'Yes, he died here,' said Marilena. 'But that's good, to think of the past, of family things. Mamma is happy to give her room to you. Please don't worry about it.'

'But where will she sleep?'

'In my old room. She has already taken all her things there, it looks very nice. And you need the space for the baby, you see.' Marilena fixed Ruth with her beautiful eyes. 'Oh, how lucky you are, to have the baby, Ruth! I am hoping I will soon be lucky too! Guido and I, we want a family straight away, for why should we wait?'

'You're only a bride, still,' said Ruth absently, for she was still trying to come to terms with the fact that she must sleep in the signora's bed. 'You've plenty of time.'

Marilena made a face. 'Everyone says that. Listen, later on, when your baby is older, she can go into Nicco's little room. It's only a slice of a place, really, but it will take a cot.' She began again to move dreamily round the room. 'I'm to have the family cot when I have children, Mamma has promised me. It's in the store room behind the shop, Guido is going to paint it.'

'Perhaps I could speak to Nicco about the room,' Ruth murmured, looking out of the window at Ginger Street. She could see Nicco below, unloading boxes from the van. Where on earth would all their things go? In the store room behind the shop? Suddenly, she wanted to burst into tears, but with a great effort, mastered herself and turned back to Marilena.

'I'd better go and relieve your mother of Gina,' she told her. 'She's due for her next feed.'

'Mamma would probably sit with her for ever,' Marilena said moodily. 'I haven't even held her yet, and I must go back to Aunt Brigida's, I'm needed in the café.'

'There'll be lots of times for you to hold her.'

'I suppose so.' Marilena put her hand on Ruth's arm. 'It's lovely to be friends again, Ruth, I have missed you.' She hesitated. 'And Sylvie.'

'You know Sylvie would like to see you,' Ruth said gently. 'Any time. What happened with Guido – that's all forgotten, isn't it?'

Marilena looked away. 'Not by Guido.'

'But Sylvie is married now, and expecting a baby.'

'I didn't know that.' Marilena's mouth drooped. 'So she is lucky, too? But it makes no difference, Ruth. Guido won't want me to meet her. When you see her, tell her I was asking after her. Tell her, I hope she's happy.'

'I will, Marilena. But I think I should have a word with Guido, you know.'

'No, don't, please don't. It would only stir things up, and I want him to forget.'

'At least, you can be friends with me.'

Marilena brightened. 'That's true. I'm really glad you're part of the family, Ruth. I do hope you'll be happy, living here.'

At least, somebody's glad to see me, thought Ruth, hugging her sister-in-law.

Chapter Thirty-Six

Marilena and Guido were long gone, and the unpacking finished, what there was of it, for Nicco and Ruth had not been able to keep many of their own things to hand. As Ruth had guessed, most had had to remain in boxes and be stored behind the shop, together with Gina's pram, though at least the pram would be used, whereas Ruth's books, pots and pans, cutlery and crockery would probably never see the light of day. Would she ever have a place of her own to put them out again? Don't even ask the question, she told herself. The present arrangement had to be made to work, and there was no point in wishing for something else.

No point, it seemed, in asking for another room, either. As Gina was settled into her cradle in the bedroom, Nicco told Ruth in whispers that there was no question of their having any other room. This was the one with the double bed, this was the one where they could put the cradle. He was sorry, but that was the way it had to be. Anyway, what was wrong with it?

'It was your parents' room, Nicco,' Ruth had answered miserably. 'We'll be sleeping in their bed.'

'People often do that, don't they?' Nicco kissed her comfortingly. 'Parents pass on, children take their beds, happens all the time. There's no need to be sensitive about it.'

'But then, your mother has had to give up her room. I'm sure she can't be happy about it.'

'She understands there's no choice.' Nicco laughed a little and

194

smoothed Ruth's hair. 'Unless you want us to sleep in a single bed? We could, of course.'

'No, it's all right.' Ruth pulled herself free. 'As you say, this is the only room for us. Just as long as your mother doesn't mind.'

'I tell you, she doesn't.' Nicco hesitated. 'Won't you try to call her Mamma, Ruth?'

Ruth turned from the mirror where she had been combing her hair. 'When she asks me,' she said quietly. 'I'll call her Mamma.'

The signora had prepared dinner for them, to which they now sat down. As Ruth's eyes went over the table in the living room with its stiffly starched cloth and good china, Nicco lit candles and said that this was a special occasion, they did not eat like this every day.

'We always eat well,' his mother said sharply in English. 'Ruth will see.'

'I'm sure,' Ruth said quickly. 'But this all looks lovely.'

'Please open the wine, Nicco,' was the signora's only reply.

When they had finished the antipasto and she had served the main course, however, she permitted herself to address a remark to Ruth. 'This is veal,' she told her. 'Cooked with spinach. You will not know this dish.'

'Oh, but Ruth does!' Nicco retorted. 'Renata has taught her how to make it – isn't that right, Ruth?'

'Not like this,' Ruth said hastily, seeing the signora's brow darken. 'Mine was nothing like this!'

'Renata!' echoed Carlotta. 'What sort of cook is she? Her mother trusts her to cook nothing, I can tell you!' She lapsed into her own dialect, gesticulating and flashing her eyes, as she outlined all Renata's faults, from burning omelettes to serving tough beef, to getting her hair cut short again and having no children! No grandchildren for Brigida! What was to be done with such a girl?

Ruth, who could understand only a fraction of the tirade, murmured that Renata had been very good to her.

'Yes, yes, maybe!' Carlotta drank her wine and fanned her flushed cheeks with a lace handkerchief. 'But if you have learn from Renata, I will teach you again. Better learn nothing at all, than from her!'

At the thought of being taught to cook by her mother-in-law,

Ruth sank into silence, and Nicco, catching her mood, gloomily drank more wine. When the meal was over, he said that he and Ruth would wash up and his mother could rest. Then they would have coffee.

'You and Ruth? What is this, Nicco? You wash dishes now?'

'I sometimes help Ruth, Mamma.'

'Never in my house! You work hard, Nicco, you are the bread-winner. You shall not work in my kitchen!' Carlotta herself began to clear the table. 'I will wash the dishes.'

'Signora Rietti, please sit down,' said Ruth. Her hands on the plates she was carrying were trembling, but her tone was strong. 'I do not need help, I can do this myself.'

Her mother-in-law stared at her for a long moment, then shrugged. 'We work together,' she declared. 'I show you where things go, *si*?'

'Thank you,' Ruth replied. 'I shall need to know.'

'I'm sorry,' said Nicco, when they were in their new room, preparing for bed. He stood watching Ruth as she changed Gina and put her back into her cradle, his face downcast. 'I let you down, didn't I?'

'Over the washing-up?' Ruth smiled wryly. 'No point in having an argument about it.'

'I should have said something.'

'Not on our first night with your mother, Nicco. It's best to try to be careful.'

'Careful! Why should we have to be careful? If I want to help you, I should help you!'

'Please, Nicco, keep your voice down. We're no' exactly alone here.'

'We'll never be alone.' He bit his lip. 'I wonder if we've done the right thing?'

'I was thinking of the baby, as much as your mother.'

They both looked down at Gina, whose eyes were closing. In the last week or so, she had taken to sleeping until 2 am. Fingers crossed, she kept to that here! Even though the signora was said to adore children, she would be in a sweeter mood, perhaps, if she did not lose her sleep.

'Let's get to bed,' said Nicco. 'I need to be near you, I need to hear you say you forgive me and my mother for making you unhappy.'

'You haven't made me unhappy, Nicco, and your mother's no' been too bad,' Ruth whispered, thinking that in fact she had. 'At least, she's talking to me. I didn't expect any more.'

They pulled back the elaborate bed clothes and climbed into bed, where they lay together, listening to Gina's even breathing, the sounds from the street, the odd creaks and noises of rooms at night.

'Tomorrow, I will tell Mamma I do what I want to do,' Nicco said firmly. 'I'll admit, I'm not used to telling her that, but I have you to think of now. There must be a new regime.'

'You've forgotten,' Ruth murmured, in between kissing his chest, 'This is her flat.'

'Well, I own the shop. She depends on me.'

'We must go gently, then. I'm sure, she'll get used to me, in time. And Gina will help us. Your mother loves her already, I can tell.'

'Love, that's the thing. I love you, Ruth, so much.' Nicco's eyes glittered in the dusk of the room, as he strained her to him. 'You're not too tired, are you?'

'I'm never too tired, Nicco.'

It was strange, when they came to make love for the first time in the signora's bed, Ruth never even remembered her earlier worries about it, nor even thought that the signora might be listening, which only occurred to her afterwards. A great relief washed over her that she'd overcome her fears without any conscious effort. It gave her heart to face the morning.

But in the morning, when Nicco had gone down to the shop, and Ruth and her mother-in-law were left facing each other across the breakfast things, Ruth's heart plummeted. How many long days would they face each other like this, before Gina was old enough to be left with her grandmother and Ruth could escape to the shop?

'What would you like me to do?' she asked, rising. 'I usually do my washing first, then I take Gina out for some fresh air.'

'Do what you wish,' Carlotta replied. 'But I think is better to clean the house before going out. Then, I want to teach you how to make pasta, and do not tell me Renata has shown you, for I have tell you what I think of Renata. Afterwards, we will write the list of guests for the christening and decide on the *compari*. I think we ask Marilena and Guido. You agree?'

Ruth, who would have preferred Renata and Federico as god-parents, decided not to argue. 'We must go gently,' she had told Nicco. For how long?

Chapter Thirty-Seven

The signora did not ask Ruth to call her 'mamma'. Of course not. Ruth had never thought for one moment that she would. The fact that her mother-in-law was talking to her and imperiously giving her cookery lessons she didn't need, was as much as could be expected. And sometimes, Ruth did try to see things from the signora's point of view. Not only had her son married 'out' of the community, he had also married out of the Church. Many Edinburgh Italians, even though Nicco's little daughter had been christened a Catholic, were disapproving of Nicco, and this reflected on his mother, or so she believed. It must appear to her that her wonderful son had spurned everything she held dear, from the feeling for home, to the religion that was a part of her life. There was no way, therefore, that the woman who had caused all this could be regarded as a member of the family. Never was the signora going to say to Ruth, 'Call me Mamma'. If she had been a forgiving person, she might have done, but she was not. Nor would she ever be, thought Ruth, who was finding it even more difficult than she'd imagined to adjust to life with Nicco's mother.

Slowly, slowly, she settled into a routine. Washing, housework, cooking, all performed under the signora's eye, unless she had been called upon to help her son. This happened only rarely. He did not like to ask his mother's help too often, treating her as though she were a piece of Dresden china when, in Ruth's view, she was actually as strong as a horse, but there were times when he really had to call on her and she had to leave Ruth to her own devices.

'Oh, what fun!' Ruth used to sing to Gina then, and dance round the kitchen with her, but of course, she couldn't waste too much time, because there was Nicco's lunch to get, or Nicco's dinner; meals for the three of them, in fact, though always described by his mother only as Nicco's. 'Nicco's!' Ruth would exclaim. As though she and her mother-in-law did not need to eat! 'But we're only women,' she'd say to Gina. 'We don't count. Now, when you grow up, you see that you do count!'

Time and again, Ruth could have picked a quarrel with the signora, but she had promised herself she would get on with her and keep the peace, for not to do so would only make matters worse. She therefore did all that the signora wanted, only taking time off when the lunch had been cleared away and washed up and she could push Gina out in her pram for a little while. Sometimes, they went to the Meadows, sometimes just down Ginger Street. Wherever they went, the air was sweet, because they were alone.

Sometimes, in Ginger Street, she would stop outside their old flat and look up at the windows, thinking of the carefree days when she and Sylvie and Kester had been children. But the days hadn't been so very carefree, she knew that in her head, it was only the passage of time that made them seem so. Hadn't she nursed a broken heart over Nicco in that very flat? Now she had Nicco, to have and to hold, and he was worth everything. Every long, dreary day with his mother giving her instructions, clicking her teeth, waving her arms, crying for strength to some saint when Ruth had not rolled out the pasta to her satisfaction, or let the rice catch on. No, she truly didn't regret having married and given up whatever else she might have had. Just couldn't help thinking of it, now and again.

Occasionally, she called on Etta back in the tenement and gave her a hand with some household chore. Sometimes she met old friends. Vi Smith, now Dochart, for instance, who was still in Ginger Street, though married to a baker, or Millie MacAllan, hurrying back from her dinner hour to the greengrocer's in Clerk Street, where she was an assistant. Millie's dark plaits were now replaced by Marcel waves, she had grown tall and rangily attractive and was walking out with Derek Niven, a boy Ruth remembered from school, who was now an electrician. 'Got a good job, you ken, no' on the dole,'

Sarah MacAllan had told Isa, for not being on the dole was the most important thing they looked for in a son-in-law, and Derek Niven was soon to become that. All the Millars would of course be invited to Millie's wedding, for the MacAllans were eternally grateful to Jack for rescuing Bob from the depths and giving him a new life.

Vi Smith, now Dochart, had been large as a schoolgirl and was still large as a young wife and mother. Stanley, her baby, was large, too, with a belligerent blue stare and a terrible way of roaring at regular intervals.

'Och, he's that strong,' Vi would say indulgently, once adding: 'Now your little thing looks as though she'd blow away in the wind, eh? You're no' bottle feeding her, eh?'

'No, I'm not bottle feeding her!' retorted Ruth. 'I'm nursing her myself – just waiting to get her weaned, so's I can help Nicco in the shop.'

'Fancy you being married to Nicco Rietti and back in Ginger Street, then,' Vi remarked with interest. 'And working in his shop! Now, I always thought you'd be a teacher or a secretary, or something.'

'Did you?' Ruth said shortly.

'Aye, you were always cleverer than the rest of us, eh? How d'you get on, minding your p's and q's with Nicco's mother, then? I'll bet she keeps you on the hop!'

'She's all right, we get on,' Ruth answered, gladly lying. 'Anyway, I told you, I'll soon be helping Nicco.'

'No' trying for another baby? Now, I thought sure you'd be wanting a boy.'

Coffee with Renata at her father's café was a small treat Ruth sometimes allowed herself, for she was always sure of a welcome, not only from Renata, but from Brigida and Vittorio too. They had long since forgiven her for marrying Nicco the way she had and were always keen to take Gina and hug her and spoil her, while Ruth let off steam to Renata. No one was more sympathetic than she, when Ruth outlined her problems with the signora.

'Honestly, if you could just hear her telling me how to boil water,

Renata! No, no, not that way, this way ! What are you doing, then? Where is the sauce for the meatballs? Are the onions not ready yet? I tell you, I'm ready to scream sometimes!'

'*Cara*, you don't need to tell me anything about my Aunt Carlotta!' Renata put back her head and laughed, then patted Ruth's shoulder. 'No, no, I shouldn't laugh, it's hard for you, I know, and you are doing so well, you amaze me, you really do! How come you're so patient?'

'I'm not patient underneath, Renata, but I have to keep the peace.'

'For Nicco, I suppose?' Renata poured Ruth more coffee. 'That's a woman for you, always doing something for a man.'

'Not just for Nicco. For all of us. There's Gina to think of, too. I did hope that having the christening just as Nicco's mother wanted would do me some good.' Ruth shrugged and smiled. 'Didn't make the slightest difference, surprise, surprise.'

'Ah, but Aunt Carlotta does adore Gina, Ruth! And if you were ever to have a boy—!' Renata clicked her fingers. 'You'd be top favourite, I promise you.'

'I don't think I want another baby yet.'

'Well, I don't blame you.' Renata glanced round at her mother who was cooing with Marilena over Gina, to the delight of various customers, and lowered her voice. 'But, the thing is, I'm really beginning to think I might weaken about it myself. Give 'em all what they're waiting for.'

Ruth's eyes widened. 'Renata! You're not expecting?'

'No, no, I'm only thinking. Well, to be honest, trying.'

'You won't regret it, I can promise you.' It was Ruth's turn to laugh. 'But your folks'll be over the moon!'

'Aye, and even Aunt Carlotta will not be able to find fault, eh? Can't let you have all the glory. Or Sylvie, come to that. But how is Sylvie these days?'

'Tired of waiting. The baby's due just before Christmas.'

'It'll be Marilena's turn next, though she's had no luck yet.' Again, Renata glanced back, but Marilena was completely absorbed in cuddling Gina. 'If Sylvie has a son and Marilena doesn't, Guido will probably cut his throat. No, only joking.'

But Ruth didn't think she could ever joke about Guido.

Chapter Thirty-Eight

Fascism. That was the great divide between Guido and Nicco. Even long ago, Ruth could remember their arguing about it. She hadn't been interested at the time, but she was interested now. Fascism had become a threat and she had come to realise that she should know exactly what it was. In Nicco's words, it was a political philosophy that was the reverse of democracy, that set the state over the individual, and gave one leader absolute power. 'No discussion, only obedience' was the motto. What more did you need to know about it, once you'd heard that? asked Nicco.

Yet, Mussolini, who had begun the movement in Italy back in 1922 and was now Il Duce, the political leader, was completely revered, far more than shadowy Victor Emmanuel, the figurehead king. Adolf Hitler, the Fuehrer, in Germany, had the same power and the same adulation. These two leaders had brought their countries out of the economic doldrums, made them important again, returned their national pride and self-esteem. These were things to be admired, it was true, but the cost, in Nicco's view, was too high. For regained power, for state efficiency – making the trains run on time, as was always said of Mussolini – the rights of the individual had been sacrificed. Any opposition was ruthlessly put down, the leader's word was law, and if you didn't like the law, you could face the firing squad, or the concentration camp.

'I can't see how Guido can support it!' cried Ruth, but Nicco had smiled wryly.

'Guido is carried away by Il Duce. He sees Italy as a world

power again, he sees all the wonderful things Mussolini has done for our country and for expatriates like us, and that's enough for him.' Nicco shook his head. 'I don't believe he ever thinks about the consequences of fascism. Other people here are the same. They're just grateful for being remembered, for being considered Italians again.'

'But you see things differently.' Ruth's look was troubled. 'I worry about that sometimes.'

'Why? You know I'm right.'

'Yes, you are, but you know what folk are like. They don't want you to be different.'

'Some agree with me.'

'I hope they do. I don't want you to be alone. I don't want you to be in danger.'

'Think Guido will rough me up?' Nicco laughed. 'As though I'd let him! He wouldn't, anyway.'

'He didn't mind hitting Mark.'

'That was different.'

'I hope you're right.'

Every Sunday, Carlotta and Brigida took it in turns to provide an elaborate lunch after church to which all the family and certain friends were invited. Ruth, of course, did not go to Mass, but felt bad that Nicco, because of his marriage in a register office, could no longer take Communion. Though she wouldn't change her religion, she had in fact offered to be re-married in church if that would make things easier for him, and he had gratefully accepted. Another sweetener for his mother? Hadn't worked, for the signora had only pursed her lips when Nicco told her of the quiet ceremony that would be arranged in the New Year, and said she hoped the priest would be happy about it.

'He is, Mamma, for I can go to Communion again, that's good, isn't it?'

She had shrugged. 'It's something,' she finally admitted.

Family and friends who came to the lunch over Nicco's shop one Sunday in December were delighted with the news, however, and kissed and embraced Ruth and Gina, which went some way to making Ruth feel accepted and perhaps a little better about never visiting her own family for Sunday dinner. She knew Isa simmered away in the background over this, just as Carlotta simmered in the foreground, even when she had her own way. Och, what a thing it was, trying to keep families happy! Somebody had to suffer.

There were always plenty of women to do the cooking at these family gatherings, to rush around with dishes of pasta and sauce and superb stews, warm fragrant bread and pungent cheese, while the men poured wine and smoked and waited to be served. As usual, Guido, drinking freely on that December day, decided to tackle Nicco.

'I was at the *fascio* last night,' he remarked, fixing Nicco with an intense blue gaze. 'I couldn't help thinking what a great thing it was for Il Duce to have done, to set up such clubs for us all over the land.'

'You've said that before, and I'm not denying it,' said Nicco.

'Worth saying again, Nicco, and again! Take the Casa d'Italia in Glasgow – it has everything anybody could want. Societies, activities, trade meetings—'

'That's true,' Federico, Renata's husband, agreed. 'And nobody did anything for us before Il Duce.'

'We were forgotten,' said Vittorio, filling up glasses. 'Out of Italy, out of mind, that was it. I remember how we used to feel. Now even the children get language classes and schools and holidays.' He shook his head. 'It's amazing.'

'I've said, I appreciate all that,' Nicco said, lighting a cigarette. 'And before you tell me, I do know everything that Mussolini's done for Italy. But, you have to admit, he was in the wrong over Abyssinia. He had no right to invade there.'

'He was restoring our empire!' someone cried. 'He had every right to make Abyssinia part of Italy!'

'Britain didn't think so. The League of Nations didn't think so.'

Guido grinned. 'The League of Nations? I don't think Il Duce need worry about that lot. Any more than Hitler worries.'

Nicco leaned forward, the blue smoke of his cigarette wafting across his face. 'Can't you see the danger, Guido? Mussolini has already signed a pact with Hitler to give arms to Franco in Spain. If

Hitler decides to take over Austria, and they say he will, Mussolini will support him, then it'll be Czechoslovakia and Poland and we'll be on the road to war!'

'War can be necessary,' said Guido. 'I'd be glad to fight for Italy. I suppose you wouldn't, Nicco?'

'Fight? For God's sake, how can you talk so easily of fighting? There's more to war than wearing a black shirt and marching with banners, you know!'

Guido's face went scarlet, he leaped from his seat, picked up his glass and stood with his arm raised over Nicco. For a split second, it seemed that he would hurl his wine and his glass into Nicco's face, and Nicco, bracing himself, closed his eyes. Then a woman screamed.

'Guido, sit down!'

It was Brigida, entering with a tureen of vegetables. She ran to the table, set down her dish, and grasped Guido's arm.

'What do you think you are doing?' she shrieked. 'This is Sunday, this is our family meal! Vittorio, why are you sitting there with your mouth shut? Why are you not controlling our son?'

'I haven't done anything,' Guido muttered, slowly taking his seat again. 'What's the matter with you, Mamma?'

'You were going to attack Nicco, I saw it in your eye!' Brigida burst into tears. 'Oh, Guido, why must you always behave like this?'

'What is going on?' cried Carlotta, sailing in from the kitchen like some great dark warship. Renata, behind her, was looking to Federico, but Marilena had already run to Guido and Ruth was at Nicco's side.

'Are you all right?' she whispered. The room was full of Italian voices speaking too fast for her to understand, she felt an alien, she felt afraid.

'Quite all right.' Nicco was on his feet, smiling reassuringly, putting out his cigarette. 'Don't look so worried, *cara*.'

'Guido has done nothing, Carlotta,' Vittorio was explaining. 'He lost his temper a little, that is all. There was nothing to worry about. Just sit down.'

'Sit down? You tell me to sit down in my own house? When

my son has been attacked? I heard what Brigida said from my kitchen!'

'I was not attacked, Mamma,' said Nicco soothingly. 'Look, I'm quite all right.'

'Of course he is!' cried Guido. 'I didn't touch him!'

'You had your glass in your hand,' put in Federico.

'So? What did I do with it? I didn't even throw my wine at him.' Guido scowled. 'Though I should have done, the things he says to me, the things he says about Il Duce!'

'Let's all sit down and get on with lunch,' ordered Vittorio. 'Carlotta, please to bring in whatever we're having, and I'll pour more wine.'

'No more wine,' said Carlotta shortly. 'Your son has had enough. I think he should leave my house.'

'Oh, God, another family row,' groaned Guido. 'For no reason at all. But I don't mind leaving. Marilena, get your coat.'

'Marilena, sit down,' said Vittorio. 'Guido, apologise to Nicco and your Aunt Carlotta. Then we stay and we eat and we all get on together, OK?'

Guido hesitated. He drew his hand across his mouth and shook his head. Marilena caught at his hand.

'Please, Guido,' she whispered. 'Please?'

'All right, all right.' He glanced contemptuously from Nicco to his aunt. 'Aunt Carlotta, I'm sorry if I upset you. Nicco, I apologise.'

'No need. I'm sorry I spoke to you as I did.'

There was a silence, during which Carlotta fixed her nephew with an icy stare. 'Very well,' she said at last, 'we eat.'

Summoning her troops with a jerk of her head, she departed for the kitchen, from where came fierce sounds of pots and pans being clattered about and more Italian voices raised. Only Ruth absented herself. Making the excuse that she had to check on Gina in the bedroom, she slipped away.

The baby was sleeping peacefully, the little blond wisps of her hair quite damp, her two pink fists raised above her head. 'Oh, Gina,' Ruth whispered, 'what are we going to do?' She would have liked to snatch up the unknowing child and keep her safe from all that lay ahead, but of course she couldn't do that, and she didn't know what lay ahead. That was the trouble!

'Ruth,' came Nicco's soft voice at her side. 'Come and have something to eat.'

'I'm just so worried!' she cried, turning to lean against him.

'Not about Guido? There's no need to worry about him, Ruth, believe me.'

'Not just Guido. The future, and everything,'

'Can't do much about the future, but I can promise you that you don't need to worry about Guido. He's hot-headed and a fool, but he'd never harm me.'

'How can you say that? He was going to harm you just now!'

'But he didn't do it, he drew back.' Nicco put Ruth's arm in his. 'He always will. Come on, the pasta's on the table, and I'm hungry.'

She was smiling faintly, allowing him to take her with him, when they both stood transfixed by the sound of a loud knocking on the shop door below.

'Who in hell is that?' asked Nicco irritably. 'Don't they know it's Sunday? We're closed!'

'You'll have to answer it,' Ruth told him. 'They don't seem to be going away.'

'It's stopped. Someone else has answered it.'

'Ruth!' came Marilena's voice. 'It's your brother. It's Kester, wanting to speak to you.'

'Kester?' Ruth's eyes grew wide with fear. 'Oh, God, it must be Sylvie! Something's happened to Sylvie!'

She went leaping down the stairs and was met halfway by Kester, who took her hands and said it was all right, Ma had sent him, nobody was replying to Nicco's shop phone.

'But what's happened, Kester, what's happened?'

'Sylvie's had her baby, a great strapping boy. Nine pounds four ounces, and she's fine!'

Ruth had to take Kester in to the lunch party, where they were met with solemn stares. Kester Millar here? Most of the Riettis hadn't seen him since Renata's wedding. How were they supposed to greet him?

208

'Here's my brother come to give me some news,' Ruth said self-consciously. 'My sister's had her baby. A fine, big boy. And she's well.'

There was the smallest of silences. Ruth's sister? That was Sylvie. They all remembered Sylvie and not with pleasant memories. But a baby was a baby.

'*Congratulazioni!*' they cried.

'Wonderful news,' said Renata, coming to hug Ruth.

'Oh, but she's so lucky!' wailed Marilena. 'Tell her, she is lucky!'

'*Complimenti*, Kester!' said Vittorio. 'Sit down, have a glass of wine, have some lunch.' And Brigida rushed to get a plate, while Nicco and Federico shook his hand. Only Carlotta sat without moving, her brow dark, as if she would have liked to say, 'Sylvie Millar's brother is offered a drink in my house? He is offered lunch? Whose house is this?' As for Guido, he said nothing at all.

Kester did not in fact stay for lunch, he had to get back, he told them, but he did accept a glass of wine so that they could all drink the health of the new bambino. Then, oh, joy, he offered to drive Ruth to the maternity home. Dad had already taken Ma in his old Morris Eight, but Kester had the van.

'Oh, will it be all right if I go, Nicco?' Ruth asked. 'I can take Gina with me, I won't stay long.'

'Of course, you go,' he told her. 'Stay as long as you like, and give Sylvie and Mark our congratulations and best wishes.'

'*Scusate!*' she cried to everyone, when she was in her coat and carrying Gina, wrapped in shawls. '*Grazie!*'

Then away she went with Kester to his van, floating on air, she and Gina, so glad to be free, just for a while.

'Oh, but Nicco,' she gasped, as he saw her into the passenger seat and was closing the door. 'You take care now, promise?'

'Ruth, how long are you going for?' he asked laughing.

'No, I'm serious,' she told him, only relaxing a little, as Kester drove her away.

'What was all that about?' asked Kester curiously.

'Nothing,' Ruth answered. 'Just a private joke.'

'A joke? Can't say we go in much for jokes, Fenella and me.'

Chapter Thirty-Nine

It was a tonic, to see Sylvie and Mark so ecstatic over the birth of their son. Is happiness catching? wondered Ruth. Perhaps some of this carefree joy would spill over on to her, though she'd already had her share of joy and was grateful. Hadn't she always said, all she wanted was what she had – Nicco and Gina? It was just that of late there had been so much to cause her woe.

Oh, but it was lovely to see happiness unalloyed! Ruth kissed her sister, who didn't even look tired, and hugged Mark, who did. 'A long night,' he told the visitors, grinning. 'But worth it, eh, Sylvie?'

'I've already forgotten it!' she cried, sitting up in bed in her pleasant little room in the maternity home somebody'd found the money to pay for. Had it been Dad? Ruth asked her mother. Surely Mark couldn't have afforded it?

'No, it was Mr Imrie helped to pay,' Isa told her. 'No' badly off, you ken, and that keen to be a grandfather. He's already been to see the baby, with Mark's mother. And what a fine bairn, eh? Nine pounds four ounces. Ma poor Sylvie!'

They all trooped along to the nursery where they were allowed to look at the as yet un-named Master Imrie, squirming behind a panel of glass, and Isa pronounced him a perfect image of Jack, while Jack said, no, he could see Mark, or was there not a touch of his own brother, Don?

'Actually,' said Mark, 'I think he's like my dad. Anyway, he's the best looking baby here, eh?' That went without saying.

*   *   *

When her family had departed, for it had been agreed that they wouldn't stay too long, Sylvie lay back, admitting then that she did feel a little tired.

Mark said he'd go, too, but he'd be back early next morning.

'You get some rest, Sylvie. Something tells me you're going to need it, dealing with Master Andrew!'

'Now, we didn't say for certain we'd call him after your dad, Mark. There's my dad to consider, too.'

'We could call him Andrew Jack.'

'Or, Jack Andrew. No, John Andrew. But I quite like Dugald.'

'Help!' said Mark. 'I'm off!'

'No, wait.' Sylvie touched his arm. 'I wanted to ask you, how did you think Ruth was looking?'

'All right. A bit tired, maybe.'

'Very tired, or anxious, or something. I worry about her, Mark, being with the Italians all the time. I know she loves Nicco, but it can't be easy, can it?'

'No, especially as Italians aren't exactly popular here at the moment, anyway.'

'Why? What have they done?'

'Nothing. It's just that they support Mussolini, and he's been acting the tough guy lately. Seems to have thrown in his lot with Hitler, too. Nobody likes that.'

Sylvie sighed. 'I've been so lucky, Mark, finding you, haven't I? No problems for us.'

'I'm the lucky one,' he said softly. 'Now you rest, like I said, and I'll be in tomorrow with your flowers.'

He gave her a last kiss, blew more kisses from the door, then marched away, watched by an admiring nurse bringing Sylvie an early supper.

'Oh, lovely!' said Sylvie, as the nurse set the tray in front of her. 'I'm really ready for this! Nurse, mind if I ask you, how soon do you think it will be before I can get back into my ordinary clothes?'

Isa had decreed that Ruth should return with her for something to eat. She'd had no Sunday dinner, had she? And she'd to keep her strength up, being a nursing mother.

'What your ma really wants is a chance to play with Gina,' said Jack, with a laugh.

'Well, I certainly don't get too many chances to do that, do I?' snapped Isa. 'When I think how much time that signora spends with my granddaughter compared with me, I canna help feeling annoyed.'

'I'm sorry, Ma,' said Ruth. 'You know the situation. I live in her flat.'

'Your choice, I believe.'

'It's a question of money.'

'Always is,' said Kester. 'Look, I can't stay for tea, Ma, sorry. Fenella will be waiting.'

'She'll be going to see the baby soon, I hope?'

'Oh, yes, sure. She's dying to see him.'

'Didn't see her there today.'

'There wasn't room in the van, was there? When I had to pick up Ruth.'

'Surprised she hasn't made you get a car of your own, she's got everything else she wants.' Isa turned to Ruth. 'You should see her new three-piece suite, Ruth. Real leather, with velvet cushions! Good enough for a hotel!'

'I've got to go,' said Kester hastily. 'Ruth, it was nice to see you. Come over some time, eh? We're no' far away.'

'That'd be lovely.'

'Lovely?' echoed Isa, as Kester drove off and they made their way to the Morris Eight Jack had acquired some time ago. 'You'll never get invited to Fenella's, Ruth, unless you invite yourself. I do! Now give me the wean on ma knee, you sit in front with your dad.'

How pleasant it was to be with her parents again, thought Ruth. Just like old times, except for the baby on her mother's knee. She did love Nicco, she would never give him up, but to be free for a while of the strain of being in his mother's home was a quite a treat, she couldn't deny it. And then when they got back to Trinity, there was the comfort of being waited on, with her mother telling her to put her feet up while the kettle boiled, rest while she could, she really did look pale.

'You'll have to think about weaning the baby, Ruth,' Isa told her, hurrying about with preparations for tea. 'It's too much for you, nursing her, you ken. If you can afford it, you start her on a bottle and a wee bit of cereal. You'll be a new woman, I'm telling you!'

'Think so?' asked Ruth. 'I'm planning to wean her early anyway, I want to help Nicco in the shop.'

'Like father, like daughter!' said Jack, looking up from controlling Gina who was wriggling on his knee.

'We've got quite enough in this family working in shops,' Isa told him. 'Ruth should have been a civil servant.'

'There's nothing wrong with working in shops, Isa. Kester's doing all right.'

'Oh, that's good,' said Ruth. 'The new shop's doing well, is it?'

'Pretty well. Slow in starting, maybe.' Jack played with Gina's fingers. 'But picking up.'

'I'll bring in the tea,' said Isa.

The December darkness had closed in quickly. They'd had the lights on since four and now tea had been cleared away, the fire was crackling cheerfully, there was no incentive to go home. Ruth stood up, though.

'Time to go,' she said lightly. 'It's been lovely, seeing Sylvie's baby, and everything.'

'Couldn't you try to get over to see us more often?' asked her mother, folding Gina's shawl around her. 'I could give you a rest, you ken. I don't like to see you looking so down.'

'It's just that I'm worried about the way things are going,' Ruth said, after a pause. 'I mean, there might be a war.'

'For heaven's sake, haven't you got enough on your plate, without worrying over something that might never happen?' Isa turned to Jack. 'Have you heard this talk of war, Jack?'

'Folk are wondering what Herr Hitler's got planned, and Mussolini, too. Italians here will have to be careful, there'll be plenty ready to blame 'em.'

'Blame them what for?' cried Ruth.

'Well, for being Italians, I suppose.'

'But they've lived here for years, Dad. Some were born here, like Nicco.'

'Aye, but they're still loyal to Italy, eh? That's what folk see. Mind you, I've heard that some are taking out naturalisation papers, if they're no' British-born. Might be safer.'

'Nicco isn't loyal to Mussolini,' Ruth said quickly. 'If war comes, things'll be difficult for him.'

'Well, let's worry about it if it happens,' Jack said comfortingly. 'Now, if you're ready, I'll take you home.'

'Funny, to be back in Ginger Street,' he remarked, when he'd stopped the car outside Nicco's shop. 'No different, eh?'

'No different.'

'Ever walk along and look at our old place?'

'Oh, yes. Always think of us, as we used to be.'

'No worries then, eh?'

'I don't know about that.'

'Well, I do. I'd an easy life in Ginger Street.' Jack drummed his fingers on the steering wheel. 'Just working for Tomlinson's, you ken.'

Ruth stared. 'I thought you liked being your own boss, Dad.'

'Aye, I do. Being your own boss means you say what's what, but it's your fault, you ken, if things go wrong. Got to think of that.'

'They're no' going wrong, are they?'

'No, no, I'm only talking.'

In the harsh light of a street lamp shining into the car, Jack's face looked older than Ruth remembered it. All those lines by his eyes and his mouth – had she seen them before? Or, were they new? But then he turned, the light fell elsewhere, and the lines vanished.

'Och, I'm no' complaining,' he added, after a moment. 'I've been lucky, eh?'

'You seem a wee bit tired tonight, though.'

'When am I tired?' He smiled. 'Just glad Sylvie's got through all right, that's all.'

'Me too. I know what it's like.'

'Aye.' Jack studied her face. 'Thing is, you're happy, eh?'

'Yes, I am.'

'I ken you've got your problems.'

'Who hasn't?' Ruth pressed her father's hand, thinking how rarely she had time like this with him alone. Yet his was a comforting presence. 'Dad, why don't you come in for a minute? Just to say hello?'

'What, now? Meet the signora again?' He made a face. 'You want me to?'

'I think it would be friendly.'

'OK. Just for a minute, then.'

'Why, Mr Millar,' said Nicco, opening the door for them. 'It's nice to see you.'

'Were you no' going to call me Dad?' asked Jack, shaking Nicco's hand. 'Ruth says I should just come up and say hello to your ma.'

Nicco didn't hesitate. 'She'd like that. Yes, please come up.'

But as soon as he had kissed Ruth and Gina, he called up the stair to give warning.

'Mamma, Ruth's father is here!'

'Signor Millar?' She gave him her hand, her eyes going over his blond hair, his handsome, cheerful features, and it seemed to Ruth that her expression relaxed as it never did for this man's daughter. 'Is long time since we met.'

'Aye, too long. How are you, signora?'

'Very well.' She shrugged. 'If you can say well. When I am alone.'

'Alone?' Jack looked perplexed. 'But you have all your family!'

'I have no Roberto,' she said gravely. 'You remember my Roberto, Signor Millar?'

'Of course. A very fine man. Yes, I can see you must miss him.' Jack's eyes went a little despairingly to Ruth, but the signora was herself rising from her chair.

'You will take some coffee, Signor Millar? And a little almond biscuit?'

'I'd like to, signora, but I really should get back. Just brought Ruth and the baby home, after seeing my new grandson.' Jack beamed. 'What a fine boy, eh? Ruth, did you say how much he weighed?'

'A grandson.' Carlotta sighed. 'You are so fortunate!'

'Mamma, you have Gina,' Nicco put in quickly, and as if on cue, Gina, in Ruth's arms, began to howl and the signora immediately took her and soothed her.

'Yes, I am fortunate,' she agreed, glancing up at Jack. 'This child is my great joy. But a brother will be nice for her.' Her gaze went to Ruth. 'One day.'

Jack made polite farewells, Carlotta favoured him with gracious smiles, then Ruth, a little amused at her father's reception, saw him out from the shop door.

'The signora admires you,' she told him teasingly. 'I never saw such smiles for anyone before!'

'A handsome woman, Ruth.' He shook his head. 'But difficult. I wish you'd your own place.'

'So do I!' She flung her arms around her father's neck and kissed him. 'Thanks for bringing me back, Dad.'

Chapter Forty

On 14 March 1938, Hitler and his army entered Vienna. Austria was his, and the Austrians, it seemed, were quite happy about it, for they gave him a wonderful welcome. The old Chancellor, who had not approved of the *Anschluss*, the union of Germany with Austria, had been persuaded to resign. His successor had welcomed it. Both German-speaking nations would now be as one. *Heil* Hitler!

Reading the news in the morning paper, Nicco's eyes glistened with anger. He pushed aside the breakfast things and spread the paper out in front of him, reading every word again as though he couldn't believe what had been set up in print for the world to accept. Then he folded the paper and raised his eyes to Ruth and his mother, both watching him.

'It's come, then,' he said quietly. 'The *Anschluss*.

'*Anschluss*?' repeated the signora. 'What is that?'

'Political union of Germany and Austria. It has happened. Hitler has marched into Vienna and everyone is happy about it. Especially Mussolini.'

'So?' His mother shifted her gaze to Gina, who was being fed by Ruth with small spoonfuls of baby food. 'A little more, my darling,' she called. 'To please your grandmother! There, there, is good, is sweet!'

'So, we are in a very dangerous situation.'

'Why, if everyone is happy?'

'They're not,' said Ruth. 'Nicco was joking.'

'Not about the Austrians. What a surprise, they've all turned into Nazis. Except those who are Jews, of course.'

'I don't see what it has to do with us,' the signora said placidly. 'We should think of the good news.'

'What good news?'

'Why, that Marilena is expecting! Have you forgotten already, Nicco?'

Since they'd heard of nothing else since January, Ruth thought that that was unlikely, but Nicco only shrugged and stood up. He had to open up, he said.

'I'll be down in a little while,' Ruth told him, adding to herself, thank God. Since she'd weaned Gina, she'd been able to get out of the flat for a few hours every morning. Though serving behind a counter and helping Nicco with his accounts would not at one time have been something to look forward to, now they represented a lifeline to which she clung with all the desperation of the rescued sailor. Even the air downstairs seemed different. Fresher, purer, hers alone, which of course it wasn't. But she must be grateful to her mother-in-law for looking after Gina, and she was grateful. Always. Even though she must keep her eye on the clock and be ready to run upstairs to help with preparations for 'Nicco's lunch', as the morning progressed. But that was a small price to pay for a change of scene from the flat.

Downstairs, as Nicco set about his preparations for opening the shop, Ruth tied herself into a white overall and checked the petty cash. She always looked forward to this quiet time before the customers arrived, when she could be alone with Nicco, and knew he cherished it too. That morning, however, he was preoccupied.

'You're thinking about Austria?' she asked him. 'You know when I said that time I was afraid of the future, and you thought I meant Guido? It wasn't Guido, it was this.' She took his hands in his, made him look at her. 'This is the beginning, isn't it?'

'I wish I hadn't said anything,' he muttered. 'Shouldn't have upset Mamma.'

'She wasn't upset. Didn't take the slightest notice.'

'Might have done.'

She swung his hands in hers. 'You don't mind upsetting me?'

His sombre gaze rested on her face. 'To you, *cara*, I speak the truth. Every time.'

'Nicco, that's why I love you.' They kissed long and deeply, then drew away, laughing a little at their own passion so early in the morning, with the shop door already unlocked and customers due at any moment.

'Anyone would think we were newly-weds!' cried Ruth.

'Well, we have been married twice,' said Nicco, beginning to open up a box of imported tomatoes. 'And I'm grateful to you for that, Ruth.'

'I was glad to do it,' she told him, thinking back to the quiet ceremony in January, when she and Nicco had been married in the Catholic church with only the family present. Aferwards, they had all had a meal at Vittorio's – the wedding day had been a Wednesday, of course – and Guido had drunk too much and been in disgrace again, until Marilena had sprung her news, after which it was impossible for anyone to be in disgrace. Heavens, the noise! Does everyone have to shout congratulations at once, Ruth asked herself? She'd been delighted for Marilena, of course, but had had a pretty shrewd idea what this news would mean for her and she'd been right. A constant barrage of exhortation from the signora that she too should have good news to announce. Weren't they all waiting for Nicco's son? It was true that Gina was still only a few months old, but by now her brother should certainly be on the way. Carlotta herself had never wasted time, and it was not her fault that several of her babies had miscarried, but she had at least been fortunate in having a son first. Now here was Marilena expecting and would probably have a boy. Would not Ruth feel upset if Guido was given a son and Nicco was not?

'No, no, I wouldn't!' Ruth had cried. 'I don't want to produce sons to order, I want to have my family when I want and where I want!'

After such an outburst, it was only to be expected that a hard frost should descend between her and her mother-in-law, and only Renata, still childless, had been truly able to sympathise. Nicco was Ruth's heart's delight, yes, but she couldn't say too much to him about his mother. The last thing she wanted him to feel was that he was the centre of a tug of war.

'Well, is it the beginning?' she called now from the counter.

'Beginning?'

'This Austrian business – is it going to be the start of trouble?'

Nicco straightened up from the tomatoes. 'Most people think so.'

'Except Mussolini?'

'He wants trouble. He's dying for a war, so he can prove how strong he is.'

Ruth fiddled with a pencil on the counter. 'You don't think Hitler might just stop now?'

Nicco shook his head. 'He'll go for the Sudetenland. That's the German-speaking part of Czechoslovakia. Germany's always wanted it back, after it was taken from them in 1919. After that – who knows?'

'You're very gloomy.' Ruth tried to laugh. 'This country's strong, so's France. They won't let Hitler do just what he wants.'

'Mussolini will.' Nicco came to the counter and looked seriously into Ruth's eyes. 'Folk'll turn against us here, you know. We Italians – we'll be considered Nazis.'

'Nicco, don't talk like that!' Ruth looked at the clock. 'There'll be customers in any minute. We'll have to try to look more cheerful.'

'Not easy.'

'Just remember, what you've been talking about might never happen.'

'We'll have to hope it doesn't.'

Their eyes met, then fell. The shop bell rang, and two Italian women customers came in, still talking to each other.

'*Buon giorno,*' said Ruth pleasantly, and was rewarded with their smiles.

Chapter Forty-One

While the signora took her afternoon nap, Ruth still liked to go out with Gina, making her usual visits to Etta or Vi, occasionally venturing further afield and calling on Renata or Sylvie, or her mother. Of these visits, Ruth least enjoyed meeting her sister, for it had to be admitted that Sylvie of late had become just a little too pleased with herself. It had to do with her move into a brand-new bungalow off the Queensferry Road, with a garden that went ALL round the house, and had two bedrooms and a separate little room for Ronald (as the baby had been named, Sylvie having preferred to call him after her favourite film star, Ronald Colman, rather than his grandfathers). Oh, if she tells me once more about that garden, I shall throttle her, Ruth would groan, sitting in Sylvie's front room, eating Sylvie's coconut cake, listening to Sylvie's latest list of things acquired, jobs done by Mark, progress made by Ronald. She knew she was just envious of what Sylvie had, which was not the house or the things in it, or Mark's prowess with a paint brush, but her independence. What would Ruth give for that? Smoothing Gina's soft hair, she felt she would give anything, except Nicco, of course, except Gina. Sacrificing her own independence was the price she paid for her husband and her child.

One person Ruth had never visited was Fenella. Though Kester had urged her to call, Fenella had issued no invitation and Ruth was not prepared to invite herself, the way Ma did. It was a surprise, then, one April day, to receive a little note in Fenella's childish hand, asking her and Sylvie to tea. Kester's idea, no doubt. The sisters knew he felt guilty about his wife's aloofness from his family; probably he had finally worn her down and she'd agreed to give a family tea party to shut him up. But when Ruth and Sylvie arrived at their brother's large Newington flat, they discovered that their mother was not present. It seemed having her husband's mother AND his sisters all in one day was too much for Kester's wife.

'I'm going to have your parents to Sunday lunch,' Fenella told Ruth and Sylvie, as she hung their jackets in a roomy hall cupboard. 'I thought it would be quieter for them, without the children.'

The sisters exchanged glances. As though Ma or Dad minded any noise Ronald or Gina might make! Still, it was just as well Ma wasn't with them; she could be pretty outspoken when she liked and never made much of an effort to pretend she liked her daughter-in-law.

'Come into the drawing room,' Fenella was saying, leading the way to a large, ground-floor room with fine, high windows and an elegant fireplace where a coal fire was burning. Again, Ruth and Sylvie exchanged glances. Drawing room, indeed! Anyone would think Fenella was one of the Scottish quality, the way she was talking. And living. How on earth could Kester afford this place, anyway? Had Fenella's parents helped out? They didn't live in quite this style themselves, but they might have offered to give their only daughter what she felt she ought to have. Sylvie, after looking round at the furniture obviously never sullied by childish fingers, cleared her throat and said:

'Fenella, I hope you won't think me rude, but I really think we might be better off in the kitchen. Ronald's a terror for bringing back his feed, and I'd hate to spoil this lovely carpet!'

'And Gina's crawling now,' put in Ruth. 'Gets into everything.'

Fenella's pale blue eyes flickered and she winced a little as she looked at the two babies bouncing in their mothers' arms. 'I see what you mean,' she said thoughtfully. 'Well, if you're sure you don't mind, I could easily take everything back to the kitchen.'

'That's right, and we'll help,' Sylvie told her. 'Believe me, it'll be for the best!'

The kitchen was just as Ruth and Sylvie had imagined it would be – large and immaculate, like Fenella herself. Not that Fenella was overweight, but she was certainly tall, with big hands and long feet. Her straight nose had slightly flaring nostrils, and her eyes, very good at displaying displeasure, had been inherited from her father, who always let you know what he was thinking, before he threw the chalk at you.

'I'm sure I don't know what my mother would say to this,' she murmured now, as she made the tea and laid a cloth over the scrubbed table. 'Entertaining in the kitchen – she'd have a fit!'

'Och, you're no' entertaining, when it's just us,' said Sylvie, perching on a wooden chair, with plump Ronald on her knee. 'But we really appreciate being asked round, don't we, Ruth?'

'We do,' Ruth agreed. She set Gina down on to the tiled floor and watched her rapidly make off, probably trying to put distance between herself and that other baby, now gnawing on a rusk. 'Mind if I shut the door, Fenella?'

'Oh, do,' Fenella replied uneasily. 'Heavens, you have your work cut out, haven't you? Running after the baby?'

'Does it put you off?' Sylvie asked kindly. 'I mean, having any yourself, when you see us?'

Fenella's fair brows drew together. 'I'm not put off, it's just that I've had no luck so far.'

'Oh, that's a shame,' said Ruth quickly. 'My husband's cousin is having the same problem.'

'An Italian?' Fenella poured tea and passed some buttered currant bread. 'So, how do you get on with these Italians, then? It must be very difficult.'

Ruth flushed. She was not going to spell out her problems with her mother-in-law to Fenella. 'I wouldn't say that,' she said quietly.

'Ruth gets on very well with her in-laws,' Sylvie said quickly. 'Except mebbe Signora Rietti, but we don't count her. Mothers never think anybody's good enough for their sons, eh? I'm sure I'll be just the same with Ronald when the time comes!'

Fenella busied herself adding hot water to the teapot and made no reply. But when she had cut into a Madeira cake that the sisters recognised as a type sold in their father's shops, she looked again at Ruth and asked her if she wasn't worried about the international situation.

'Isn't everybody?' asked Ruth.

'Yes, but with Italy siding with Germany, aren't you in rather an awkward position? My father says there might easily be a war, if Hitler invades Poland, and then your people would be on the wrong side.'

'My husband is not in favour of Mussolini,' Ruth said tightly.

'Oh? I thought all Italians here were fascists?'

'That's no' true. Some are, but most just love Italy and think the fascists are helping their country.'

'They go to that fascist club, don't they?'

'For social reasons. They like to meet and chat.'

Ruth's gaze was angry, Fenella's amused, as though she found Ruth's defence of Nicco's people not to be taken seriously.

'What nice cake!' Sylvie remarked tactfully. 'Is it one that Kester sells?'

'Yes, they're so good, aren't they?' Fenella answered coolly. 'Why bake yourself, is what I say, if you can buy?'

'Couldn't agree more,' said Sylvie, but her smile at Ruth indicated that Fenella had better not let Ma hear her talk like that. Give Kester bought cake, even the sort he sold himself? Never!

The sisters did not stay long after they had finished tea, making the excuse that they must get the babies home, though it was quite apparent that Ruth's reason for hurrying home was her annoyance with Fenella. She was barely civil when she said goodbye, leaving Sylvie to make their thanks while she strode away with Gina in her pushchair without looking back.

'Hey, wait for me!' cried Sylvie, who had put Ronald in a pushchair, too, though she'd earlier said he wasn't really big enough and Ruth had laughed and said Ronald was big enough for anything. But Ruth wasn't laughing now.

'Och, Ruth, you're no' taking any notice of Fenella, are you?' Sylvie panted. 'What she says is no' worth worrying over!'

'There are plenty of folk think like she does.'

'She doesn't think, she just repeats what her father says. Look, will you just slow down?'

'Sorry.' Ruth halted her fast march. 'Look, I know I shouldn't

224

care what Fenella says. It's just that, like I say, other folk are saying the same thing.'

'Well, what does it matter what folk say?' Sylvie began to walk on towards a tram stop. 'What harm can talk do?'

'There might be more than talk.' Ruth's troubled gaze moved from the traffic rattling past to her sister's face. 'The truth is, Sylvie – I'm afraid.'

Sylvie's eyes widened. Instinctively, she bent to pull the cover over Ronald who was already nodding off in his pushchair, as though any danger that was around should not touch him. 'How d'you mean, afraid?'

'Sometimes I think Italians might be attacked. You know, by people who don't care about the truth of things. And then there's Nicco. I'm afraid for him, too. For different reasons.'

'What sort of reasons?'

'Well, he doesn't mind speaking out, letting folk know what he thinks. There are some who don't like that.'

'You mean Italians? I thought you said most weren't really fascist?'

'I said some were.'

'Oh, Ruth!' Sylvie's eyes were anxious. Mark had talked once of the difficulties Italians might face with Scots. Maybe he would know something of the difficulties Italians might face with Italians. 'Shall I speak to Mark about it?' she asked Ruth. 'See if he could help?'

'Thanks, but what could he do? Until there's a crime, he can't step in, can he?'

'It was just an idea.' Sylvie sighed. In her view, Mark could solve any problem put to him. He was Police, he was Authority, he always knew what to do, but if Ruth didn't want her to speak to him, well, she wouldn't, of course. She put her hand on Ruth's arm. 'Look, try not to worry, try to put it all out of your mind, because it might never happen, eh? That's the way you've got to think.'

'Your tram's coming,' said Ruth, screwing up her eyes in the late afternoon light. 'I'll give you a hand in with Ronald.'

'Now, remember what I say, Ruth! Don't worry!'

In helping with the complicated business of getting Sylvie, the baby, and the pushchair on to the waiting tram, Ruth made no effort to answer her sister. What was the point? She knew and Sylvie knew that she was going to worry anyway. Of late, she'd done nothing else.

'Bye,' mouthed Sylvie from the window, as Ronald opened his mouth to bawl, and Ruth waved and managed to smile.

'That's it,' she told Gina, whose dark eyes were closing. 'Now we can go home.'

Nicco was at his counter when they arrived back, looking his usual calm, handsome self.

'Had a nice afternoon?' he asked, stooping to kiss his sleeping daughter.

Ruth made a face. 'You know what Fenella's like.'

'I don't, in fact. I've hardly seen her.'

And that's the way she wants it, thought Ruth. She put her hand over Nicco's and raised her eyes to his.

'You've been OK?' she whispered. 'Nothing happened while I've been away?'

'Why, what should happen?' he asked, laughing, and slid his hand from hers as a customer approached.

Ruth shook her head. 'I'll take Gina upstairs, see your mother.'

'Mamma's out. Went to Aunt Brigida's, to ask after Marilena.'

'Oh, Marilena, of course . . .'

Ruth, carrying Gina, ran up the stairs on light feet. What a bit of luck, the signora was out! She could have a little bit of time to herself in the flat, and pretend it was hers.

Chapter Forty-Two

Marilena's baby was born at the beginning of July. A boy. Of course. The Rietti family could not contain its joy. Vittorio went about with tears in his eyes and Brigida kept laughing and crying, even in front of patrons of the café, while Guido, a perfect peacock, strutted about, declaring his pride in having a son to anyone who would listen. As for Carlotta, she was a woman in a dream. Her daughter had had a boy! She herself had a grandson! What more could she ask? Except a son for Nicco. Ruth wished she could emigrate.

She was, of course, very happy for Marilena, who was so beautiful as a mother, it made the heart sing to see her, but, as Ruth told Renata, Marilena's joy was her burden. The signora would never leave her alone now.

'According to her, I should be expecting my second in September, if not before,' Ruth said gloomily. 'Everyone she knows has a baby every year, especially if they're trying for a son, and of course I am, I must be, mustn't I?'

'Take no notice,' Renata advised. 'It's all rubbish, anyhow. Nobody has a baby every year these days, and she's the one who's crazy about sons. Plenty of women are happy to have a daughter. I would be.'

'Oh, Renata, I'm sorry! I shouldn't be rubbing it in.'

'Don't worry.' Renata lit a cigarette. 'As a matter of fact, the way things are, I'm not sure that this is the time to bring children into the world anyway.'

They were both silent, remembering that Mussolini had renewed his allegiance to Hitler in May, and that there was talk he would soon be following the Fuehrer in his treatment of the Jews. Their familiar world seemed to change a little more every day, to crumble, darken, open as an abyss before their fearful eyes.

'Sometimes, Federico talks of going back to Italy,' Renata said, at last. 'Things might be bad for us here, you know, if there's a war.'

'But you wouldn't do that, would you?' cried Ruth. 'You wouldn't really go back?'

Renata shook her head. 'No, I don't think so. It's just the way Federico talks, when he's depressed.'

'Nicco would never go to Italy, he hates fascism.'

'Well, there's the difference. I told you Guido had persuaded Federico that fascism is right for us. Of course, at the moment, all Guido can think of is Vittorio Paulo!'

'Marilena's decided on the name?'

'Yes, and she's asked Federico and me to be *compari* at the christening, as we were at her wedding.' Renata laughed heartily. 'Aunt Carlotta will be furious all over again!'

This was true. When Guido came one evening to give her the news and to discuss the christening, the signora turned quite pale with rage and said he needed his head examining. To choose that insolent sister of his as sponsor for his child! It was bad enough that he and Marilena had been foolish enough to select her and Federico to be *compari* at the wedding, but to ask them to be godparents was really too much. Federico was not too bad, but Renata! What could be said of her? A woman who was always smoking, who chopped off her hair, who had no children of her own—

'She wants children, Aunt,' Guido put in nervously. Before his aunt's onslaught, all his pride in himself and his son had slipped away, and he was a boy again, found out in some mischief and resigned to a tongue lashing.

'So she says. Who's to say whether she is really trying, or not? Anyway, that is not the point. There are many more suitable persons you could have chosen, Guido, as I'm sure you very well know. Nicco, for example.'

Guido's eyes slid to Ruth. 'Yes, but Ruth will not mind me saying that we could not ask her.'

'Of course not,' agreed Carlotta. 'I could have taken her place.'

'Well, it's usually a married couple, as you know – at least, we wanted a married couple . . .' Guido's voice trailed away. 'It's done now.' He finished. 'We've asked them.'

'Very well.' His aunt rose. 'You wish a drink before you go?' she asked glacially.

'Thanks, no. I'd better be getting back.'

Guido was sidling off towards the door, when Nicco appeared, his work in the shop finished for the evening. At once Guido's bravado returned. He clapped Nicco on the shoulder, grinning, said he'd just come over to discuss the christening of his son, his heir, his contribution to the family.

'He bears the name,' he told Nicco, 'he is a Rietti. When my father is gone and I am gone, he will be here, he will run the business, he will take our family into the future. You should be thinking of these things for your side of the family too, Nicco. I tell you, every man should have a son!'

'Oh, that is true!' cried the signora. 'Have I not always said this? Ruth, have I not said this many, many times?'

Though Ruth had not understood all that was said in the family dialect, she had grasped the gist of it and as she went to Nicco's side, felt her old rage rising. Gina was the most perfect thing in the world. Why was she not enough? Nicco put his arm around her shoulders.

'If the Lord wants us to have a son, Guido, Ruth and I will have a son.'

'Yes, but you know what they say here?' Guido laughed. 'The Lord helps those who help themselves! Ruth should be in the family way already.'

'As I say,' said the signora with satisfaction. 'If another girl comes, so be it, we shall love her. But if a boy, oh, think how happy we will be!'

'*Buona notte*!' cried Ruth. 'I am going to bed!'

'Don't worry about it,' Nicco whispered, when he joined her. 'It's just an old-fashioned thing, wanting sons.'

229

'Guido is old-fashioned?'

'He's just getting at me, as usual. Ignore him.'

'I can't ignore your mother.'

'I know she's annoying, but she means no harm.'

'She wants to dominate me. That's all this is about. Gina isn't a year old yet, your mother knows we want more children and will probably have them, there's no need to go on at me. But she wants me to do exactly as she says, and I'm tired of it, Nicco, I've had enough!'

He lay beside her, his hand on her thigh. 'I know, I know, *cara*, but what can we do?'

'We could live somewhere else.'

'Where? We can't afford the sort of place you'd like. We don't want to bring up Gina in one of the Old Town tenements, do we?'

'I just want my own life, Nicco, to do things my way. Is it too much to ask?'

'Oh, Ruth!' He took her in his arms. 'I wish to God I could give you what you want, I do!'

She kissed him gently. 'I shouldn't complain, we've other things to think about. At least, you've been safe so far, that's all that matters.'

'Of course I've been safe! Who's going to hurt me?'

She shook her head, not wanting to spell out the threat, and turned away for sleep, hoping Nicco would do the same. He did. Neither of them felt like making love.

The following afternoon, as soon as the signora had gone to lie down, Ruth took Gina over to Vi Dochart's, and asked her if she would look after her for a couple of hours. 'Just want to look at the white sales in town,' she said quickly. 'And you know what it's like with a baby at the sales!'

'Aye, or anywhere!' Vi agreed fervently. 'My Stanley's an angel, till you take him shopping, then – watch out – he's a devil!'

'I'll do the same for you, if you like, Vi. Any time.'

'Aye, if I can find a few bob to spend! Now, don't you worry, hen, little Gina'll be fine wi' me. Why, she's falling asleep, already, eh?'

'I'll away for the tram,' said Ruth, loth to leave Gina, even with Vi. 'I'll no' be long – promise.'

'Take as much time as you like, Ruth. We're no' going onywhere!'

As much time as I like, thought Ruth, jerking along in the Trinity tram. How long does it take to ask your father for money? She felt bad about asking him, quite ashamed, in fact, but she had set her feet on this path and would not turn back. It was true what she had told Nicco, that there were more important things in her life than finding somewhere to live away from her mother-in-law. But not many. Nicco's safety, yes, and her family's welfare, but oh, God, was it wrong to ask for a place of her own as well? Only her dad could help her and here she was, on her way to asking him, fingers crossed as the stop for the shop came in sight, still crossed as she opened the door of Millar's High Class Groceries and Provisions. But her father wasn't there.

Feeling let down, she asked Bob MacAllan casually if her dad was not around.

'Gone over to Kester's. But your ma's in. Can you no' smell that jam she's making?' Bob rolled his eyes. 'Tell her to send a bit doon here, eh? I could just do with a jammie piece!'

'Me, too,' said Ruth, making her way to her parents' flat.

Chapter Forty-Three

The wonderfully sharp yet sweet smell of warm raspberries was filling the kitchen, as Ruth put her head round the door and called to her mother.

'Och, Ruth, you made me jump!' cried Isa, looking up from the last jar she was filling from a vast preserving pan on the stove. On the table were the rows of jars already filled, their splendid, dark-red contents still bubbling, their paper tops waiting to be put on, their labels in a pile ready to be written. 'What a nice surprise to see you, then, but where's Gina?'

'I left her with a neighbour – wanted to talk to Dad.'

'Talk to your dad?' Isa pushed damp hair from her brow, her eyes suddenly wary. 'What about?'

'Could do with a cup of tea,' said Ruth. 'Shall I make it?'

'If you like. No, wait – let's do thae tops and labels first. Get this lot finished, eh?'

'Lovely raspberries, Ma.'

'Aye, from that farm out Queensferry way where your dad used to work when he was a lad. Your granddad used to take him and his brothers in the holidays, if he could find the train fare, and they'd earn a few bob picking. Och, Jack said it was like being in another world! All that land and sea, and the air! Niver forgot it.'

'Dad picked these?' Ruth asked, surprised.

'No, of course not! Went in the car and bought the punnets already picked.' Isa wiped her flushed face and laughed. 'We're quality these days, eh? No picking for us!'

As she obediently helped to put tops and labels on the jars, Ruth thought her mother seemed a little out of sorts. Kept looking at her, strangely, as though she suspected something. Had she guessed that Ruth wanted money? In the hot kitchen, Ruth's cheeks flamed, and she kept her eyes down.

'Tell me what you want to talk to your dad about,' Isa ordered, when she had made the tea. 'It's no' about his health, is it?'

'His health?' Ruth was changing one anxiety for another. 'Why, he's no' ill, is he?'

Isa shrugged. 'I don't know what he is, but he's keeping something from me, I know that. You're no' married to a man all the years I've been married to him without knowing when he's got a secret.'

'Dad never has secrets from you, Ma.'

'I'm telling you, he's got something on his mind. Today, he says to me he was going to see Kester. I says, are you sure, and he says, of course I'm sure, where else would I be going? Well, I thought it might be the doctor's, because he had such a funny look in his eye, and he was that grey.'

'Grey?'

'Aye, he's lost all his colour.' Isa drank her tea and set down her cup with a shaking hand. 'I'm that worried, Ruth.'

Ruth came over and gave her mother a hug. 'Don't be, Ma, I'm sure Dad's all right. He'd have told you, if he wasn't, I know he would.'

Isa sniffed and patted Ruth's hand. 'Well, what did you want to see him about, anyway?'

Ruth sat down again, and fiddled with the teaspoon in her saucer. 'I don't like to say now.' She raised her eyes to her mother's. 'The thing is, I was going to ask him to lend me some money.'

'Ruth!'

'I don't want to, Ma, I hate doing it, but the truth is, I'm going mad, living with Nicco's mother. I have to find a place where we can be on our own, but all we can afford is another flat like we had before, and that'd no' be good for Gina. So, I thought, mebbe Dad could lend us a bit, to put down on a bungalow. I don't mean something like Sylvie's, but there are smaller ones going up that I thought we might be able to afford, if Dad would help us out. Just to begin with, you ken.' Ruth's eyes were fixed on her mother's with such a bright, hopeful look, Isa turned away.

'I don't know, Ruthie,' she said slowly. 'I don't know what to say to you. I've no idea if your dad could help you or not, you see. He's no' told me lately how things are going.'

'I thought he always told you how things were going?'

'Aye, well it's the same as the secrets, eh? You say he doesn't keep secrets, but I know he's got them. You say he tells me everything, and I'm no' sure whether he does or not. He's no' been himself lately, that's for sure.'

Mother and daughter were silent for some moments, then Ruth stood up.

'I'd better go, Ma. Looks like I shouldn't be bothering Dad just now, anyhow.'

'Don't say that. For all I know, he could help you easy. Wait a bit, see if he comes in.'

'I've left Gina, I'd better get back.'

'I'll give you some jam, then.' Isa leaped up, glad to be doing something. 'Mind, it's still hot. I'll lend you a shopping bag.'

But as she began to root in a cupboard for a bag, steps were heard outside the kitchen, and she looked back at Ruth.

'There's your dad now!' she cried. 'Lucky you waited!'

'Why, Kester's with him!' cried Ruth, and immediately thought never in her life had she seen her brother looking so ill. As for her father – had they really called him Lucky Jack? There was no luck about him, then. At least, not good luck.

Chapter Forty-Four

There was an ominous silence in the over-heated kitchen, still filled with its delicious smell of jam. Outside, the July sun beamed through the open windows, and the sound of Trinity traffic rose to their ears, but was not heard. No one tried to pretend that something bad had not happened. Jack and Kester knew that it had. Ruth and her mother knew it too, simply by looking at the faces of the two men. It took extraordinary courage for Isa to say, at last, that she would make a cup of tea, but then those familiar words seemed to sap Jack's strength. He sank into a chair, his hand to his head, while Kester, still standing, could look at no one.

Ruth cleared her throat. 'Dad – Kester – what's wrong?'

Her father looked up. He ran his hands through his thick fair hair, now showing one or two threads of grey. 'A lot,' he answered curtly.

'It's me,' Kester said hoarsely. 'I – I've taken some money.'

Isa, at the table, dropped a cup. The pieces lay at her feet and she stood looking down at them. 'Ruth,' she whispered. 'You'd better make the tea.'

It was some time before the story came out, during which they drank tea that had no taste and ate cake they didn't want, and all except Isa smoked cigarettes they almost immediately stubbed out, even Jack, who normally smoked a pipe. Finally, Jack cleared his throat and prepared to speak, while Kester sat stiffly at his side, a being apart, in the heart of his family.

'I'd had ma suspicions for a long time,' Jack said slowly. 'But I wouldn't let maself act. I didn't believe it could be happening. No' with Kester, ma own son.'

Kester gave a groan, that was echoed by Isa. Ruth felt numb.

'The thing was, the Marchmont shop was no' doing as well as it should've done.' Jack went on. 'I'd done everything right, taken every care, hadn't made the mistakes I made with Trinity. I kept asking Kester about it. He said it was early days. My God, early days! Aye, for him to beggar me!'

'Oh, Jack,' Isa moaned. 'I'm no' wanting to hear this!'

'Think I'm wanting to tell it?' cried Jack. 'The thing was, I'd borrowed a lot to get the Marchmont shop in the first place. I'd lost money here – well, you know, that, Isa – so, what could I do? I had to borrow.' He struck a match with shaking fingers and lit another cigarette. 'Then I found I couldn't meet the repayments. All the time, I kept thinking of Kester. There was the rent he was paying for that good flat. Where was it coming from? I asked him and he said Fenella's parents were helping out. That wasn't true, was it, Kester?' As Kester made no reply, but sat with his eyes closed, Jack put down his cigarette and roared. 'WAS IT, KESTER?'

'Jack!' shrieked Isa.

'No!' cried Kester, shuddering. 'It wasn't true. For God's sake, Dad, why are you telling it this way? Why'd you no' just say I'm an embezzler? I fiddled the books, I pretended we'd bought stuff when we hadn't, I pocketed the profits, I did everything to get money to make Fenella happy. We couldn't start a baby, she was very low, I wanted to make her happy. I thought I could do it with money. When it wasn't enough, I went racing.'

'Racing?' Ruth repeated.

'Aye, at Musselburgh.' Kester gave a dreary laugh. 'What a fool, eh? I thought I could make a killing. Every time I bet, I thought I could do that. They say that's what gamblers always think, but I'd never gambled before, I didn't know. To start with, I was lucky, I backed winners. I repaid some of the money. That was before the auditors came the first time.'

'Aye, that's what fooled me,' groaned Jack. 'I thought I'd been wrong.'

'You weren't wrong,' said Kester. 'I never had good luck again. The landlord put our rent up, Fenella bought some more furniture, and more clothes. I took more money, I went back to the races, I lost. Every time, I put money on a horse, I lost. I didn't know what to do, I owed money on the furniture, I owed money to the bookies, a fellow come round, said if I didn't pay up, I'd have to face the consequences. I decided I'd shoot myself.'

'Oh, God,' whispered Ruth, but her mother's face was stony, and Jack was staring at the floor.

'Couldn't do it.' Kester went on, with another of his laughs. 'No gun. So, I went to Dad.' He sat back, breathing hard. 'Now you know everything, Ma. I suppose you want me to go to prison.'

'Don't be a fool,' she said shortly. 'What I want is to tell you I've niver been so ashamed of anybody in this family as I am of you. When I think of how your dad's worked, and I've worked, to give you and your sisters a decent life, and of what we started from and where we are now, and that you were willing to risk it all just for that wife o' yours, I could bawl ma eyes out, Kester. Aye, I could scream the place down, but what good would that do? Nothing. But you should be on your knees, Kester – aye, on your knees – before your dad, asking his forgiveness – but even if you do that to me, I'll niver forget what you've done to him and me. Niver, as long as I live!'

Kester, ashen-faced, sat still as a dead man in his chair, while Jack stood up and began to pace the kitchen. Ruth, not daring to glance at the clock, went to him and took his arm.

'Dad, what happens now?' she asked gently. 'Will you lose the shop?'

'Aye, the Marchmont one.' He pressed her hand. 'Mebbe it was always too much for me, eh? I'd these grand ideas, being a second Sir Thomas Lipton, and all of that. Mebbe I was a fool.'

'Why should you no' have had grand ideas?' cried Isa, hurrying to him. 'I always talked you down, but you were doing well, you'd have been all right, if it hadn't been for Kester.' Her voice faded, choked with tears, and turning from Ruth, Jack put his arm around her.

'We'll weather this, Isa, don't worry. I'll be able to keep on the

Trinity shop. I'll pay back the bank and thae damned bookmakers. But it'll take all we have. There'll be nothing to spare.'

'Oh, Ruthie, I'm sorry.' Isa stretched out a hand to her. 'We can't do anything for you.'

'For Ruthie?' asked Jack. 'Why, what did you want, Ruth?'

'Nothing, Dad, it's all right. I'm OK.' Ruth looked back at her brother, still sitting without moving at the table. 'But what's going to happen to Kester?' she asked in a low voice. 'Oh, look at him, Dad! He won't have to go to prison, will he?'

'Would I prosecute ma own son?' asked Jack tiredly. 'I'll tell you this, though, he'll have to leave.'

'Leave?' repeated Isa. 'What do you mean, leave?'

'Leave the shop.'

'But you're selling the Marchmont shop, anyway.'

'I mean the Trinity shop. I canna give Kester a job at all.'

As Ruth and her mother stared at Jack with horrified eyes, Kester got to his feet and came towards his father.

'You're sacking me?' he asked thickly. 'Sacking me, Dad? You can't. You can't do that. What'll I do? What'll I tell Fenella?'

'Oh, you're going to have to tell Fenella a lot o' things you'd rather not,' Jack said roughly. 'You're going to have to leave that flat you're in, you're going to have to sell that furniture you bought on the never-never, you're going to have to find another job. And if you don't find one, she might have to go to work herself, if she knows what work is.'

'She can't work, she's married,' Kester said dazedly.

'Och, we're no' talking professional stuff here. She can work in a shop, or a factory, she can find something.'

'Jack, it's too much,' Isa said sharply. 'You canna take Kester's job away. I'm niver going to forgive him for what he's done, but I don't want to see him and his wife on the street, all the same. Say he can work at the Trinity shop!'

'And put Bob out of a job?' asked Jack. 'Or Arthur Fowler that I took on when Kester went to Marchmont? I'm already going to have to part with Terry MacDuffie, Kester's assistant, and he's got two bairns, so that's bad enough.' Jack shook his head. 'I'm no' being vindictive, Isa, I would give Kester another chance if I could, but

238

if he's the one that caused this mess, he's the one that pays, is the way I see it.'

Another silence fell, as the four of them stood together, locked in misery. Then Ruth said quietly that she must go, she'd left the baby.

'Aye, Ruth, you go.' Her mother kissed her. 'Keep in touch.' Her voice trembled. 'For God's sake.'

'I've got the van,' said Jack. 'I'll drive you back, Ruth.'

'No, no—'

'I'll drive you,' he repeated. 'You get your hat.'

'And your jam!' cried her mother. 'Here – I've found a bag – give it to the signora. Say it's good Scottish jam.'

'Kester,' Ruth whispered, touching his hand. 'I don't know what to say to you.'

He shook his head, he couldn't speak.

'It'll work out, Kester. Things do.'

'Come on, if you're coming,' said Jack, rattling keys, and Ruth, feeling an empty shell of the woman who had walked in to her parents' flat not so very long before, went with him to the van.

Jack drove fast, dodging in and out of traffic in a way Ruth had never seen him do before, only speaking when they were almost back at Ginger Street.

'How d'you feel?' he asked, then.

'Awful. I know I shouldn't say it, but I feel so sorry for Kester. His world's in ruins. What's he going to do?'

'He should have thought of that before he took money that wasn't his.'

'He did it for Fenella, Dad.'

'And how often could I have robbed a till for your mother? For you bairns, when we'd barely enough to buy shoes?' Jack's eyes flashed, as he stared ahead at the traffic. 'Do you no' think I'd have liked to make all of you comfortable? Rent a nice flat? Buy you nice clothes? Everybody wants to do their best for their family, but they don't start thieving to do it!'

Ruth bit her lip, her eyes filled with tears. 'No, Dad, you're right, of course. It's just that Kester's weak – and we never knew it.'

239

'Never knew it,' Jack agreed heavily. 'Och, it's mebbe my fault as much as his, Ruth. I should've known what he was like, I should have taken more care. But I thought I could trust him.'

'Of course you did.' Ruth blew her nose. 'At least, you're not ill, Dad. Ma was worrying about you, thought you were hiding it from her.'

'Did she?' He gave a faint smile. 'Well, we've got our health, it's true – hello, what's up, then?'

'What is it?'

They had turned into Ginger Street, they were almost at Nicco's shop.

'There's an ambulance,' Jack whispered.

'An ambulance?' Ruth was on the edge of her seat, her face a mask of fear. 'Outside our shop? Dad, is it outside our shop?'

'I don't know, canna be sure.'

Jack was slowing down, stopping, as Ruth wrenched open the van door and leaped out.

'It is!' she shrieked. 'It's at our door!'

Chapter Forty-Five

Her father was calling to her, 'Ruth, come back! Come back!' But nothing was going to stop her from reaching that ambulance. Though it might have been for a customer in the shop, a neighbour, or the signora, somehow she knew it was for someone close to her. Gina, or Nicco. But how could it be for Gina, who should have been with Vi Dochart several houses away? It was for Nicco.

He was being carried from the shop on a stretcher by two ambulancemen, watched by his semi-hysterical mother and half the population of Ginger Street. His face was covered in blood, his eyes were closed.

'Oh, my God,' groaned Jack, and held Ruth close, as though he could spare her from seeing, but she was breaking from his arms, and crying her husband's name, bending over him, trying to touch him. An ambulanceman held her back.

'Make way, now, stand back, there. We're in a hurry.'

'I am going with him!' screamed the signora, in English. 'Let me through! Let me through!'

'I am going with him,' declared Ruth, swaying on her feet, but still trying to be at her husband's side.

'I am his mother!' cried the signora.

'I'm his wife!' cried Ruth.

The signora's eyes on Ruth's face were blank.

'I must go,' she whispered. 'Is my right.'

'You can both of you come,' said the ambulanceman, who had a creased, kindly face. 'Aye, in with you, then, and let's away.'

'Dad, will you go to Vi Dochart's house and take Gina?' Ruth asked feverishly. 'It's her old house – you remember – where the Smiths lived?'

'It's OK, Ruth,' cried Vi, running up with Gina in her arms. 'I've got her here. I was looking out o' the winder, when I saw the ambulance stopping at your door. I thought, Oh, Lord, who's that for? Then I saw you arrive and I told Cameron to take ma Stanley, so here's Gina, and she's fine. But I'll keep her, Ruth, you've no need to worry!'

Ruth, hugging Gina, burst into tears, then put her back into Vi's arms, with broken words of thanks. 'My dad'll take her to ma mother,' she whispered. 'I don't know how long I'll be, I don't even know what's happened.'

'Thae fascists got him!' someone in the crowd of onlookers shouted. 'Aye, come in the shop, so they did, and hit him with bars!'

'Aye, but no' Scots, you ken, Italian fellas from London, they say.'

'Blackshirts!' someone spat. 'What the hell they doing here, then?'

'Come on, come on, hen,' called the ambulance men. 'Up with you now, if you're coming.'

'Dad!' cried Ruth imploringly, as the doors were closed on her.

'Don't worry, I'll take care of everything!' he shouted, and the ambulance roared away.

'Where's it going?' asked Jack. 'Which hospital?'

'Infirmary,' the crowd told him. 'They'll soon fix the laddie, eh? Mebbe no' as bad as it looks.'

'Mebbe,' said Jack grimly.

In the ambulance, Ruth and her mother-in-law sat on small side seats and kept their eyes on the battered face of Nicco.

'Where were you?' the signora asked, at last. 'We look and could not find you. I say, where is Ruth? Where is my grand-daughter?'

'I'm sorry, I should've said, I'd gone to my father's, I left Gina with Vi Dochart.' Ruth leaned forward, her hand to her dry lips. 'What happened to him, signora? Were you there? Did you see? Please tell me what you can!'

The signora's eyes were dark and blank. 'I am upstairs, sleeping. Suddenly, I wake, I hear voices below, not voices I know. Terrible voices, shouting to Nicco. Someone screams – a customer, I think, and I run down. Then I see my Nicco. People are bending over him, but they say the men have gone, the men who hurt him. Oh, God, oh, God!' She began to breath fast, weeping uncontrollably. 'Oh, see! See what they have done to him! Will he die? Have they killed him?'

The ambulanceman travelling with them put a blanket round the signora's shoulders and spoke to her soothingly. 'It looks worse than it is, hen, you'll see. A lot o' bleeding, but no' so bad, I'm telling you. Dinna worry.'

'But he's unconscious!' cried Ruth. 'If it's no' so bad, why is he unconscious?'

The ambulanceman bent over Nicco. 'He'll be a bit concussed, you ken. But I think he's coming roond, he's opening his eyes.'

The signora caught her breath, Ruth's heart bounded, as Nicco's eyes slowly, painfully opened. For a moment, it seemed he could not see, then he whispered, 'Ruth?'

'I'm here, darling. And here's your Mamma, too.'

The signora began to murmur in her dialect, crying great soft tears over Nicco, until the ambulanceman made her sit back and said they were approaching the hospital, both women must be calm, let them do their job.

'Si, si,' cried the signora. 'We stand aside, we let you do your work, only save my son!'

Then began the waiting. Ruth and the signora sat together on a wooden bench, watching but scarcely seeing, the routine traffic of the Infirmary's casualty department, each locked in her own apprehension, sharing the same anxiety, but taking no comfort from the other's presence. Ruth's mind was all on Nicco, she couldn't spare anything for his mother.

'Like a cup of tea?' someone asked them, and they drank the tea, the signora sighing over it and staring bemusedly at the arrowroot biscuit that was presented with it.

'Oh, my Nicco . . .' she murmured, then her eyes flashed with recognition. 'Here is Vittorio!' she cried. 'And Brigida, and Guido!'

'And Renata and Federico!' said Ruth. 'Oh, how wonderful of them to come!'

Suddenly, the whole casualty department seemed full of Italians and the sound of wailing and cries of sympathy. There were huggings and fallings on to shoulders, kisses and hand wavings, more tea was brought and drunk, and though nurses shook their heads and put their fingers to their lips, the waiting patients and their relatives only brightened, pleased to see a little liveliness, treating all the activity as a kind of play.

Nor were the Italians the only ones to bring support, for soon Jack was there, comforting Ruth and telling her that Gina was safe with her mother, and then a little hush did fall, for Sylvie's husband, Mark, arrived, in uniform, and accompanied by a constable.

'Mark!' cried Ruth. 'What are you doing here?'

'Official business,' he told her quietly. 'Sylvie's desperate with worry for you, can't come herself, because of Ronald, of course, but she sends her love. Now, I've got to find somebody who'll tell me how your husband is and whether we can interview him. This is a serious matter.'

'Is serious, *si*,' said the signora, detaching herself from Brigida and approaching Mark. 'And if you wish to speak to someone who know about it, I say, he is standing there!' She pointed with a shaking finger at Guido. 'Ask him, if you please, who has hurt my Nicco!'

Chapter Forty-Six

Guido, staring at his aunt, had turned white.

'Ask me?' he cried. 'Ask me what, Aunt? I don't know anything about this attack on Nicco! How could I? Is it likely I would try to hurt my own cousin?'

'Carlotta, what are you saying?' asked Brigida. 'That my Guido knows these criminals? How can you say such a thing?'

'How can you?' thundered Vittorio, moving to stand next to his son.

'He nearly hurt Nicco once before, if you remember,' said Federico quietly. 'There was that incident with the glass.'

Guido's pallor turned to scarlet, his eyes flashed brilliant blue. 'What incident? I was never going to hurt Nicco with that glass and you know it. As for these men who attacked him today, I have no idea who they are, except that they came up from London. Somebody said they had London accents. Plenty of guys from Mosley's Union of Fascists come up here, it doesn't mean I know them!'

'Perhaps you'd like to come down to the station and tell me what you do know, Mr Rietti,' Mark said politely. 'We can't talk here.'

'No, you certainly can't!' cried a senior nurse advancing on them in obvious displeasure. 'This is a hospital, Sergeant, and there's been too much noise as it is. If these people can't keep quiet and stop causing disruption, they must leave.'

'I apologise, sister,' Mark said humbly. 'Is there any news yet of Mr Nicco Rietti? I have to question him about an attack.'

'The doctor is coming to see the relatives now. Please inform everyone here that they must keep quiet, or be prepared to leave.'

'I am leaving anyway,' Guido said to Mark in a ferocious whisper, 'and I am not coming down to your station. If you want to interview me, you can arrest me, but I've done nothing wrong and I will not be questioned by you! Of all people,' he gritted, 'not by you!'

'You might have no choice,' Mark said mildly. 'But we'll leave it for now. I think I know where to find you, Mr Rietti.'

Guido, trembling with anger, began to walk away, but as he passed his Aunt Carlotta, he stopped.

'I swear to you I had nothing to do with the attack on Nicco,' he said slowly. 'Please believe me, Aunt.'

'Go, go,' she said irritably. 'I will say I believe you, but all I want now is to hear about my son. Please go, Guido!'

The news was better than they had hoped, yet not good. Nicco's nose had been broken, his jaw had been damaged, he would need extensive stitching to various cuts, and was suffering from mild concussion. He would be kept in hospital for a few days for observation and treatment, and would not be fit enough to be interviewed by the police that evening.

Jack had asked if Ruth and the signora could see him.

'For a few minutes only,' the young doctor had replied. 'A nurse will take you to him.' He had glanced at the rest of Nicco's relatives hanging on his every word, and said he was sorry, no one else could see the patient. As for the sergeant, he would have to come back tomorrow.

Mark, making his goodbyes to Ruth and Jack, said he would continue his investigations in Ginger Street, and return to the hospital in the morning.

'Try not to worry,' he told Ruth. 'He's in good hands here, and we'll do our best to find out who was responsible for what happened.'

'And I'll say the same,' Jack murmured. 'Don't worry.' He bent to kiss Ruth's cheek. 'Does it all seem a long time ago since we were talking to Kester?'

'A lifetime.' She gave a sob. 'Oh, God, Dad, what a day this has been!'

'Ruth!' cried the signora sternly. 'Come! They are waiting to take us to Nicco.'

Nicco was in a side ward in the casualty department, waiting for his stitches. His face had now been cleaned of blood and in that way he looked better, but bruises were rising around his eyes, his mouth was swollen, and to the two women who loved him, he seemed scarcely recognisable.

'Oh, Nicco,' wept his mother, and Ruth, sinking down beside his bed, could only take his hand. When he opened his mouth to speak, they told him not even to try.

'But we'll see you tomorrow,' Ruth whispered. 'And you'll feel better, then, won't you, darling?' Her eyes filled with tears. 'Oh, I knew this would happen, I always knew! I should never have left you!'

'You should not,' said the signora.

Nicco shook his head and tried to say a word. It sounded like 'shop'.

'Never mind about the shop, we can manage – Renata said she'd help, or we can ask Domenico.' Ruth held tightly to his hand. 'Please don't worry, Nicco, just get well. Get well!'

They kissed his brow, his mother and his wife, and left together, as the doctor and nurse came in to begin his treatment. In the waiting room of the casualty department, everyone except Guido was watching out for them and they gave their news in subdued tones, keeping a wary eye open for the sister. Jack was still there and said he'd drive Ruth back to her mother's where she was to stay the night with Gina, while the signora was to stay with Brigida.

'I'll be over first thing to open the shop,' said Ruth.

'And I'll be over later,' said Renata. 'So that you and Aunt Carlotta can both go to the hospital.

The signora kissed her briefly. 'That is kind, Renata. But are you sure you know what to do? Ruth, leave all instructions.'

They all went out into the summer evening, glad that Nicco was no worse than he was, yet so eaten up with apprehension for the future, the beautiful light around them might have been darkness.

Chapter Forty-Seven

Nicco was young and strong. Though his nose was never going to look quite the same, he made a quick recovery from his concussion and his various cuts and bruises, and was soon pronounced well enough to leave hospital. His mother and the family went to church to give thanks, and Ruth was with them in spirit, but for her and Nicco there was no real rejoicing. Too much fear still encompassed them. Too much dread still filled their minds, that the shop bell would ring and three men in black would appear again, sticks behind their backs, violence in their hearts.

But these men were faceless. Nicco couldn't remember anything about the attack except for his first sight of the men in the doorway. He had known they meant trouble, had stood his ground, had shouted to his customers to run. That was all he knew.

'I'm sorry,' he told Mark Imrie, who said not to worry, concussion often caused slight amnesia, the faces could come back to him and if they did, the police had photos of troublemakers in Edinburgh and London he could check. A fleeing customer had not seen the men clearly but had heard them speak and said they had London accents, so in all probability they'd been members of Sir Oswald Mosley's British Union of Fascists, come to Scotland to recruit members and stir up trouble. Of course, if they were Londoners, they'd be back south by now and, as Mark ruefully admitted, if they were ever caught, it would probably be by the Metropolitan Police.

'Thing that bothers me,' he said carefully. 'Is how would

Londoners know about you, Nicco? You know your mother accused your cousin of having a hand in this?'

'I simply don't believe that,' Nicco replied. 'I'm family. Guido might get mad at me, he'd never hurt me.'

'Someone gave those guys your name, Nicco. And Guido knows London fascists.'

'Other Italians here know my views, it didn't have to be Guido who put those fellows on to me.'

'He certainly denies it,' said Mark, who had had a difficult time interviewing Guido. 'Without some evidence, there's no' much I can do.'

'You can leave him out of it,' Nicco said earnestly. 'It would split this family from top to bottom, if Guido was mixed up in this.'

Isn't your family already split from top to bottom? Mark wondered, but said nothing. As for him, he would keep an open mind on Guido, and hope that Nicco's memory came back. If they ever caught the men responsible for his attack, they'd find out then who'd given them Nicco's name.

The attack on Nicco had put Kester and his troubles out of Ruth's mind. Sylvie had said he was pretty low, and when he visited Nicco in the hospital he looked so ill, Ruth's heart went out to him, but that had not been the time to talk. When he came again to see Nicco after his return home, she asked him later to walk with her and Gina to the Meadows. It was a beautiful summer's afternoon, Domenico was looking after the shop, Ruth could spare a little time, if Kester could. Come on, then!

'Oh, I can spare the time,' he told her grimly. 'I'm no' working at Marchmont now. In fact, I'm no' working at all.'

'Kester, what's happening?'

'Dad's put Bob MacAllan in charge till the shop's sold. He's given me the sack, like he said he would.'

'I can't believe he'd do a thing like that!'

'He says he can't afford to pay me. The other fellows must keep their jobs, and I'm the one to go.' Kester shrugged. 'Makes sense, Ruthie. I'm to blame for what's happened, right enough.'

They sat on a bench and Ruth let Gina out of her pushchair while

Kester watched without interest, his red-rimmed eyes narrowing in the sun. He had lost weight, thought Ruth, and seemed a stranger. Remorse, misery, they could change a person, as much as sorrow, as much as fear. No doubt, she didn't look the same, either.

'I don't like to ask you,' she said, after a pause. 'But how has Fenella taken this?'

Kester gave her a sharp glance. 'She's supposed to be sticking by me.'

'Supposed?'

'Well, she is. But I think it's to do with keeping face. Doesn't want to let on that she's made a mistake.'

'Oh, Kester!'

'Och, I've got to admit it. I let her down. I let everybody down. She's a right to feel fed up with me, and so have her folks, as they've made pretty clear. You can imagine how they feel.'

'Yes, I can, but Fenella's isn't her folks. If she loves you, she'll try to understand why you did it. Was all for her, anyway.'

He shrugged. 'The only good thing is that her dad's going to help us keep on the flat and the furniture. Oh, and Fenella's getting a job.'

'A job?' Ruth stared. 'What sort of job?'

'Helping out at a kindergarten. A friend of hers is opening one in August. Fenella's going to be working mornings.' Kester smiled grimly. 'Looks like she'll be the breadwinner, eh?'

'You'll find something, Kester, don't despair!'

'Oh, yes? Seen the unemployment figures lately?' Kester sat back, as Ruth set Gina on her knee and retied her sun bonnet. 'Know what I'm thinking of doing? Joining the army.'

'The army? Never!' Ruth could have laughed, except that she didn't feel like laughing. But Kester in the army? No, she couldn't imagine it. 'You're not seriously thinking you could be a soldier?'

'Why not? I'm going to try for the Argylls.'

'A Highland regiment?'

'We've got connections – Dad's mother was a Campbell, if you remember. Anyway, I think they'll take me, they're going to be desperate for men as soon as the war comes.'

'We don't even know there is going to be a war. Some of the

papers say Mr Chamberlain won't let it happen. He thinks Hitler doesn't want war.'

'You can believe that if you want to. I say, we'll be at war some time next year. So, I might as well join up now, if they'll have me. Get three meals a day and all found, just be prepared to take a bullet when convenient.'

Ruth sat, gazing down at Gina on her knee, her eyes filling with tears, until Kester put his hand over hers.

'Just joking, Ruthie.'

'You're not joining up?'

'I mean, about the bullet.'

'It could be true,' she said, wiping her eyes. 'About the bullet.'

They walked slowly back to Ginger Street, Kester pushing Gina, and outside the shop, said goodbye.

'You'll let me know what happens?' asked Ruth.

'Sure I will.'

'What do you think Ma and Dad will say, if you join the army? And Fenella?'

'They'll all say, best place for me. No' keen to see me at the moment, anyway.'

'Ma and Dad'll forgive you, Kester, and Ma didn't want you to lose your job, remember.' Ruth hesitated. 'Fenella will forgive you, too.'

'I've been a bloody fool, and I have to take the consequences, that's all there is to it.' Kester kissed Gina's cheek, then Ruth's. 'Look after Nicco,' he said in a low voice. 'And yourself. I was sorry, you ken, you couldn't get Dad to help you move.'

'Ma told you about that?'

'Aye. Rubbed it in, to make me feel worse.'

'It doesn't matter. After what happened to Nicco, it doesn't seem important.'

'I'm sorry, anyway. I'll be in touch.'

She watched him walk away down Ginger Street, his head low, his shoulders stooped. Didn't look like a soldier, did he? Perhaps the Argylls would turn him down? They would not turn him down. Probably he was was right, the army was going to need all the men it could get before very long, whatever Mr Chamberlain said.

Chapter Forty-Eight

For a little while, though, at the end of September 1938, it looked as though Kester had been wrong. Neville Chamberlain, the British Prime Minister, returned from a meeting with Hitler in Munich holding up a piece of paper guaranteeing 'peace with honour'. That was one way of describing the promises held out by the treaty Hitler had signed with Great Britain. Another description was 'peace in our time', which didn't sound quite so permanent. Never mind, there was to be peace not war, that was all most people cared about. If the Sudetenland, the German-speaking part of Czechoslovakia, had to be handed over to Hitler, so be it. Seemed a small price to pay for peace, especially as the people of the Sudetenland wanted to be back with Germany. Only a minority in Europe wondered if there might be more to pay at a later date.

Ruth was one who was happy and relieved. No war. It seemed too good to be true, but it was true. Mr Chamberlain had the treaty. Italians in Britain need no longer worry about being pulled two ways if war came, and Kester, who was now doing his basic training, could have his three meals a day, courtesy of the army, and not worry about meeting bullets. Ma needn't worry about that either, though she was still in a state about Kester's joining up.

'Och, we were too hard on him, your dad and me,' she told Ruth. 'Poor laddie, he never meant to cheat the shop, it was just because that wife of his wanted so much, you ken. And you should see her now! Rattling round in that big flat her dad's shelling out for, going out to work, cool as a cucumber! I don't believe she's even missing Kester!'

'I think she is genuinely fond of him, Ma.'

'Was, maybe. No' longer.'

'Well, don't worry about him any more. Kester's found something that he wants to do, and now there's going to be no war, he'll be safe enough.'

'Don't worry?' Isa sniffed. 'That's all there is in this world, Ruthie – worry. I worry about Kester and I worry about your dad. He's still no' got a buyer for the Marchmont shop, you ken, and we'll be in Dickie's Meadow, if we don't get rid soon. Then there's you and your poor Nicco. Think I don't worry about you?'

'We're all right,' Ruth said uneasily. 'Nicco's quite recovered, except for remembering the attack. We're managing well.'

'Aye, but look at that bump he's got in his lovely nose! Och, what a terrible thing it was, eh, that he should get hit like that? And Mark still thinks Guido had something to do with it, you ken, but he says he'll niver be able to prove it. Not found anybody, have they?'

'No, but Nicco swears Guido is innocent.'

'That's just Nicco's sweet nature. I'll bet the signora has her suspicions.'

'We don't discuss it, Ma.'

That was true. For the sake of family harmony, Carlotta now kept her views on Guido to herself, and while Marilena was always round visiting with her beautiful baby son, Guido himself was seldom seen. No doubt he was still involved with his fascist friends, but he wisely kept himself out of his aunt's way, which was no loss to Nicco or Ruth.

'Cheer up, Ma.' Ruth still urged her mother. 'Think of Sylvie. At least you don't have to worry about her.'

A relieved smile lightened Isa's face. 'You're right, Ruth. Sylvie's the lucky one, just like your dad used to be. Everything's worked out for her.' Isa's smile faded, and she sighed. 'If only they could've worked out for you and Kester, eh?'

'Things are all right for me, Ma. I told you, Nicco's made a good recovery and that's what matters to me. I don't care about another place to live now. As long as I've got him, I can manage where I am.'

'That's good, then. It's a waste o' time, being discontented, if you canna change things.'

Neither Isa nor Ruth mentioned Ruth's ever-present fear that the men who attacked Nicco would come back.

Time went by, however, and they did not come back. The fear began to fade. World peace was still holding, too, and at long last, Ruth began to think that she might try for another baby. The signora had been keeping quiet lately, perhaps because she'd given up hope of influencing Ruth, yet Ruth all along had wanted another child. She just wanted it to be in her time and on her terms, and now that it looked as though she might get her way, began to have little fantasies about telling the signora and waiting for her astonished joy. But she never did tell her, for no second baby came along. And then in March, everything changed, anyway, when Hitler occupied the rest of Czechoslovakia.

Ruth never forgot that morning when she came into the kitchen for breakfast the day they heard the news. Everything so pleasant, so normal. Gina crooning to herself in her high chair, the signora pouring tea, Nicco turning off the wireless. Then Nicco raised his eyes and Ruth read their message. They spelled disaster.

'What's happened?' she asked quickly.

'Just been listening to the news.'

'Hitler again!' exclaimed the signora.

'What's he done?'

'He's on the march again. Take a look at the newspaper.'

Hitler had marched on Prague. He had not been satisfied with the Sudetenland, he wanted the rest of Czechoslovakia, too. All his promises were words on the wind; the treaty he had made with Chamberlain was so much waste paper. What Hitler wanted, as he had made contemptuously clear, was not peace, but war.

'Next will be Poland,' said Nicco. 'Then this country and France will declare war.'

'What about Mussolini?'

'Ah,' said the signora, rising to slice a crusty loaf.

Nicco shrugged. 'He'll declare war, too. On somebody.'

Ruth asked quietly, 'What will happen to us?'

Nicco shook his head, glancing at his mother, who had her back to him. 'Later,' he mouthed, and Ruth, tying on Gina's bib, smiled at her and felt ready to weep.

'What will happen to us?' she asked again, when she and Nicco were alone in the shop.

'You know what'll happen. We'll be thought of as foreigners and fascists, though we're not. We'll have to be prepared for a rough time.'

'You can't be sure that Hitler will attack Poland. He might only want Czechoslovakia.'

'He wants the lot,' Nicco said impassively. 'He wants Europe, he wants the world. So does Mussolini. They're both crazy.'

'There must be something we can do to stop them, Nicco. This country can't just stand back and let things happen.'

'No, but we're not prepared.' Nicco opened his cash drawer and stared unseeingly at the coins within. 'There'll be a mad rush to arm now, but it'll be too late.' He laughed shortly. 'At least there'll be an end to unemployment.'

'I'm thinking of Kester. He's already in the army.'

Nicco hesitated. He reached for Ruth's hand. 'You realise I'll probably be called up if war comes?'

The blood left her face. 'Called up? No, that's impossible. You're Italian!'

'I'm British born. So was my father. Vittorio came over as a little boy, but my dad was born here.'

She was stricken. 'I never thought you could be asked to fight, Nicco!'

'Well, I don't know the ins and outs of conscription, but I think I'd come into the category they'd take. I wouldn't mind, anyhow. Except for leaving you.' He kissed her fingers. 'It'd be hard on you, Ruth, managing here.'

With his mother. Just herself and the signora, running the shop together. Oh, God! In all her nightmares, Ruth had never considered anything as bad as that.

'Would Guido have to go, too?' she asked after a pause, during which she tried to pull herself together. 'I don't see him fighting for the British.'

'Guido has no British nationality. He was born in Italy, because Aunt Brigida's mother wanted her to have her baby at home, in the village.'

'Nicco, what about your own mother? She'd never get over it, if you went to war against your own country!'

'Mussolini's Italy is not my country, Ruth.' Nicco moved to unlock the shop door. 'Anyway, we don't know yet what Mussolini will do. I could just be fighting the Nazis.'

'I feel so bad about this,' Ruth said slowly. 'I just never imagined you'd have to leave me.'

'We're not even at war yet.'

'You know it's only a matter of time,' said Ruth.

Chapter Forty-Nine

In a way, it was a relief when the war actually came. They were all at Vittorio's on 3 September 1939, when Mr Chamberlain made his announcement on the wireless at 11.15 am. After a long, tense summer, filled with diplomatic activity and aggression that had included Mussolini's invasion of Albania, Hitler had marched on Poland and annexed Danzig. Britain had sent an ultimatum, threatening war if he did not undertake to retreat, but, as the prime minister told the country, no such undertaking had been received by the deadline of 11 am, consequently, Britain was at war with Germany.

A silence fell when the broadcast ended, broken only by Marilena's little son's chatter and Gina's singing. Then everyone except Ruth and Nicco began to talk at once. Vittorio and Brigida, Carlotta, Guido, Marilena, Renata, Federico – all waved their hands and shook their heads, as they gave their opinions of what would happen next and where their future would lie.

'We should have gone home!' cried Federico, his large, usually calm face a mask of anguish. 'We should have gone back to Italy! You realise my father's business will go under? Who will buy ice-cream machinery now?' A thought struck him, as he hastily drank some wine and wiped his lips. 'Maybe it's not too late, maybe we can still go? The last thing we want is to be stuck in an enemy country!'

'This is not an enemy country!' Renata told him angrily. 'This is our home, not Italy. I am not leaving.'

'So, that's your loyalty to your mother country, is it?' Guido cried. 'I know who's a good Italian, Renata, and it isn't you!'

'I am facing facts, Guido. I love Italy, but I love this country, too. If you're so keen, why don't you go back yourself?'

He hesitated. 'It's not so easy. I don't know what I could do.'

'Guido, you are not going anywhere,' Carlotta told him. 'Nor is my Marilena. We have made our home here, and here we stay.'

'The truth is,' said Vittorio, wiping his moist brow. 'We have two homes, this country and our own country. That's our good luck and our problem. What do we do now?'

'Italy hasn't declared war on Britain yet,' Nicco said carefully. 'Why don't we wait to see what happens before we start getting agitated?'

'People here won't wait for Italy to declare war before they take it out on us,' Guido snapped. 'They already hate us, just for being what we are.'

'That's not true,' Nicco told him. He picked up Ruth's hand, as she tried her best to understand all that was being said. 'I think Ruth here is the proof of that.'

'Oh, yes?' sneered Guido. 'And how long did it take her folks to accept you, when you were first married?'

'Shut up, Guido,' Renata said evenly. 'I have some news that might be of interest.' She laughed, tossing back her hair, which she had once again grown for the sake of being in fashion. 'I've been told that rationing will come in as soon as possible after the war starts, and that there are going to be books with different colours for children and expectant mothers. Blue, I think, for children, and green for expectant mothers.'

'For God's sake, what has this got to do with anything?' shouted Guido.'

'Well, guess who's going to need a green ration book?' Renata's eyes were bright on her family, as the news sank in. 'Yes, yours truly! What a time to pick, eh?'

'Renata! Renata!' Her parents embraced her, her husband kissed her, everyone kissed her, even Guido, and no one said what everyone thought that of all the times to have a baby, wartime was undoubtedly the worst. But a baby was a baby, and to Italians, that was all that mattered. Happy, happy, Renata, then, even if she was going to need a green ration book.

After a more cheerful lunch than anyone had expected, Ruth and Nicco said they had to go. Ruth needed to see her parents, everyone would understand? Her brother was already in the army, her folks would be particularly worried.

'Oh, sure, Ruth, we understand,' said Vittorio. 'A daughter should be with her parents on a day like this.'

Brigida nodded and even Carlotta made no objection, but Guido's face was dark.

'There's worry for us all,' he called after Ruth and Nicco, as they left for the tram. 'Not just for guys in the British Army!'

'That goes without saying,' Nicco shouted back. 'Are you saying Ruth shouldn't see her folks?'

Guido shrugged and turned away.

Sylvie and Mark were already at the Millars' flat, having been asked round for Sunday lunch. Young Ronald, now known as Ronnie, was spinning himself about, getting under everyone's feet, while the grown-ups watched with melancholy eyes, brightening only a little when the visitors arrived. Jack and Mark, both smoking pipes, were wearing Sunday suits; it seemed they had, unusually, attended kirk that morning.

'Aye, they say God's always popular when there's a war on,' said Jack, smiling uneasily. 'The kirk was full and we'd no' even heard the announcement then.'

'I can't believe it's happening,' said Sylvie, her voice trembling. 'They said the Great War was the war to end wars.'

'That's a laugh,' Mark murmured.

'Want a cup of tea, Ruth?' asked Isa dolefully.

'No, thanks, Ma, we've just had a big meal at Vittorio's.'

'I've made ma cherry cake. You'll take a bit, Nicco, eh?'

'Thank you, that would be very nice, Mrs Millar.'

'You should call me Ma. Jack, I think I'll put the kettle on, anyway.'

'Good idea. First thing to do, when war's been declared.'

Sylvie and Ruth went to help their mother, leaving the children to play together under the eyes of their fathers.

'Poor bairns,' said Ruth, glancing back at them. 'What's their future going to be?'

'What's Kester's?' asked Isa, setting a tray with her best china cups. 'He's already in the army, he'll be first to fight.' Tears came to her eyes. 'Lord knows when we'll see him again!'

The sisters were silent.

'Thing is, nobody'll be safe now,' Isa went on, taking out a plate for the cherry cake. 'To think I've lived to see the world come to this! They say we're all going to be issued with gas masks.'

'Even the weans?' cried Sylvie, her face paling at the thought of her Ronnie needing a gas mask. 'Why, they'll never send gas down, will they?'

'We can expect anything from thae Germans, Sylvie. Bombs, gas, anything. Have you no' seen the air-raid shelters the men have been digging in Princes Street?' The kettle boiled and Isa made the tea. 'Only good thing is that Jack's too old to go to war this time, and Mark might be needed for the polis, eh, Sylvie?'

'I don't know, can't be sure.' Sylvie glanced at Ruth. 'How about Nicco?'

Ruth bit her lip. 'He can be called up. He's British born.'

'Called up?' Isa raised her eyebrows. 'Over his mother's dead body! She'd niver let him fight Italians!'

'Italy hasn't declared war yet,' Ruth said sharply.

'Oh, it will, that's for sure. I'll bet yon Mussolini can hardly wait.'

Turning into Ginger Street, on their way home, Ruth suddenly stopped. Nicco, pushing Gina, now fast asleep, walked on, then stopped too, and looked back.

'Ruth?'

'Just look at it,' she whispered. 'Sunday evening in our street. Quiet. Just the same as always.' Her voice thickened and tears filled her eyes. 'How long for, Nicco?'

'Ginger Street needn't change because we're at war,' he told her gently.

'There could be air-raids tomorrow. Everyone says they'll be starting any day.' She clutched his arm as he came back to her, still holding on to the pushchair where Gina slept. 'Nicco, when will you have to go?'

'Might be soon. Some of the younger men have been called up already.'

'What will your mother say, if you go into the British Army?'

'She'll have to understand the situation. My father fought for the British in the Great War, you know.'

'Italy didn't side with Germany then.'

'That's true.' He sighed. 'Well, there's the Pioneer Corps. She might expect me to join that.'

'What is it?'

'Sort of non-fighting unit. They dig ditches and repair bridges, that kind of thing.'

'You'd be safe, then?' Ruth's spirits were rising.

'You want me to spend the war digging ditches?'

'I want you to be safe!'

'Ruth, I have to fight. I don't want to, I don't want to kill anyone, but I have to fight for this country against fascism. I can't let other men do it for me.'

She searched his face, so dear to her, so handsome still, in spite of the change in the straight nose. He minded about that nose, she knew, had often seen him running his finger down the bump. But nothing would change his looks for her. They were set for ever, as they had been when they were children. Only now, it grieved her to see his fine, expressive eyes so filled with pain. For herself, perhaps, and his mother. For Italy. 'We have two homes and two countries,' Vittorio had said earlier that day. And Nicco had had to make his choice between them.

'It's hard for you,' she said quietly. 'I won't make it harder. You do what you think is right, Nicco.'

'You always seem to know what to say,' he said softly and kissed her lips. 'But it's going to be hard for you, too, what I'm asking.'

'You mean, look after things?' She tried to sound brave. 'I'll do my best, Nicco. Other women'll be doing the same.'

He hesitated. 'And there's my mother. Will you look after her too? For me?'

It was Ruth's turn to hesitate. 'If she'll let me,' she said at last.

They held each other, until Gina, deprived of the motion of her pushchair, stirred and began to cry.

'Whatever happens, we'll love each other,' Nicco said solemnly. 'Hang on to that, Ruth.'

'Whatever happens, Nicco.'

They began to walk down the quiet street, Nicco pushing Gina, Ruth murmuring to her, until they reached the shop, when Nicco unlocked the door and they carried Gina up the stairs to where the signora was waiting.

Part Four

Chapter Fifty

Isa, walking down Princes Street with Jack, caught at his arm.

'Jack, Jack, listen! No one o'clock gun!'

'How can I listen if it's no' firing?' he asked testily, but his eyes went up to the Castle, from where the one o'clock gun had fired a time-signal ever since he could remember and now was silent. Just one more thing, eh, to remind them that they were at war? Along with the air-raid shelters in everybody's back greens, not to mention Princes Street itself, and the sticky tape on the windows, the barrage balloons in the sky, the black-out regulations that meant he'd had to make fitments for all his shop windows, and Isa's having to sew thick curtains for the flat. And what was it all for? Nothing seemed to be happening. The siren had gone off once and they'd all rushed down to the shelters, thinking their last hour had come, then had all come up again when not a plane had been sighted. Och, should be grateful, eh? But it made you uneasy, all this phoney war, as the papers were calling it. Because you knew what was coming. Hitler was never going to let this country off, not on past showing. There'd be a blitzkrieg planned for them, all right, they'd just have to wait and get through it when it came. In the meantime, there were British soldiers already on their way to France, so it was said. Thank God, Kester didn't seem to be among them.

'Folk say you can get used to anything,' said Isa, as they left Princes Street for a small café off Leith Street, where they'd decided to have something to eat before going to Ruth's. 'But I'll niver get over seeing all thae kiddies marching off for evacuation. Poor wee lambs, eh? With their gas masks and labels and all. Ruth said she burst into tears, watching the Ginger Street children going away, and she was that glad she didn't have to send Gina.'

'They were only going to Peebles,' Jack remarked, running his finger round his collar, for the café was warm on that September afternoon. 'And their mothers'll have 'em all come home again before the year's out, what's the betting?'

'That'd be a mistake, if the bombing starts.'

'Sometimes folk have to learn the hard way.'

'Let's no' talk about it,' Isa said with a shiver. 'Now, what'll you have, Jack? Better choose something good while they've still got it.'

'Aye, they say they're going to bring in a maximum charge of five bob for restaurant meals. Suits me, seeing as I've no' got two pennies to rub together these days.'

'Och, don't talk so daft!' Isa cried, but her eyes on Jack were uneasy. He'd taken to talking like that lately on their little outings when they came into town on early closing day. She'd always been the one to worry about money, could never quite realise that things had eased, but now to have open-handed Jack penny-pinching again brought home their new situation. Which was, in fact, too much like their old one for her comfort. 'Come on, what'll it be?' She pressed. 'The girl's waiting. I think I'll have the haddock.'

'And I'll have the shepherd's pie,' said Jack. 'Nice and cheap.'

Later, at the tram stop, waiting to go to Newington, Isa was fidgety; as she freely admitted, she never could stand waiting for anything.

'Why we couldn't have gone to Ruth's in the car, when we've still got a bit of petrol, I don't know,' she said crossly, but Jack only rattled coins in his trousers pocket and stared fiercely ahead.

'I'm saving that petrol for emergencies, Isa. And when it's gone, it's gone, and that'll be the car on blocks for the duration.'

'Och, I could cry, so I could!' wailed Isa. 'Just when we get to the stage of being comfortable, everything gets taken away! It's no' fair!'

'There's folk a damn' sight worse off than us at the moment,'

Jack told her. 'Think yourself lucky you're no' in Poland. Anyway, there's plenty been taken away from me, without the war interfering.'

'That's all water under the bridge. No point blaming Kester now.'

'I'm no' blaming Kester. Just wishing to God I could've got the Marchmont place sold before the balloon went up. Who in hell's going to buy a grocery shop now?'

'Language, Jack, language! Here's the tram – have you got the coppers ready?'

'Aye.' As they took their seats on the hard benches of the tram, Jack said sulkily, 'Tell you one thing, Isa, I've lost ma luck, that's for sure. Might've had a good run for ma money, but it's over now. Sometimes wonder if I'll even keep the Trinity shop going, I'm no' joking.'

Isa stared at him, her colour rising, her eyes snapping. 'Look,' she whispered, 'you're supposed to be going over to Ruth's to give her advice on keeping open, so don't you dare start making out you can't keep open yourself! You're just feeling sorry for yourself, Jack Millar, and that's no' like you. Snap out of it!'

'It's true I'm no' maself.' Jack folded the tram tickets into tiny pleats. 'Who is these days? But I'll do ma best for Ruthie, you've no need to worry, Isa. She's going to need all the help she can get, when Nicco goes away.'

Nicco had received his calling up papers and was soon to join a Border regiment. Jack had congratulated him, said how much they all appreciated what he was doing for Britain.

'No' easy for you, eh? And I don't mean just going off to fight.'

'You're thinking of my family?' A shadow had passed over Nicco's face. 'You're right, telling them wasn't easy.'

They'd been sorrowful as much as angry, except for Guido, of course, who had been pleased to find another excuse for quarrelling with Nicco. 'Why do you do this thing to us?' his mother had asked, holding her head. 'You have the right to do some other work, if you do not want to fight your countrymen, yet now you join a British regiment! How can you face it, Nicco? Killing Italians? Maybe getting killed yourself, making us all suffer!'

'I know it's hard to understand, Mamma—'

'Oh, do not give me all the arguments, Nicco. You want to fight fascism, you want to make everyone free. You forget all the good things Il Duce has done for us, for Italy. Maybe he has been wrong, trying for an empire, I don't know, people make mistakes, but he has done his best for our country, I know that, and I never thought you'd go against him.'

'Mamma, he's not declared war yet. I'll be fighting Nazi Germany. Surely you can't object to that?'

She had simply burst into tears and said that when Nicco was lying dead on a battlefield, she would be able to object to that, perhaps? See what his aunt and uncle thought of him, anyway! At least, Guido and Federico had the right idea, they would never join the British Army.

'They were not born here, Mamma, they won't be called up. But if Italy enters the war, they will be interned.'

'And safe,' sobbed his mother. 'Ah, your Ruth is right not to have a son and be caused the heartache you have caused me!'

It had been easier to face Guido than his mother, Nicco admitted to Jack, for he didn't care so much what Guido thought of him. Yet, when Guido told him he'd split the family right down the middle, the words had gone home. He'd had no answer, for he knew what Guido said was true. It was just another thing he'd had to balance in his mind against what he felt he had to do, along with leaving his family, but there'd never been any real doubt where his duty lay. Ruth had understood. The others would just have to forgive him. He couldn't picture it, their forgiveness; maybe after the war, it might happen. But he couldn't picture the end of the war, either.

'What really hurts me is leaving Ruth with all the worry of the shop,' he told Jack. 'She's very capable, but you know what it's going to be like, with rationing and new regulations. How will she manage?'

'She'll manage, nae bother, Nicco. Got a very good head on her shoulders, has Ruth. Worked for a lawyer, if you remember, and was trying for the Civil Service.'

Nicco lowered his eyes. 'I remember. She gave it all up for me.'

'Women have to do that, eh? Don't go blaming yourself, Nicco.'

'I feel bad about leaving her.'

'Everybody feels bad about leaving their wives. I remember how I felt last time round, when I had to leave Isa. Main thing is, you're going away to do a job that has to be done. You just remember that, Nicco, and don't go worrying about how Ruth'll manage. I'll keep an eye on her, anyway.'

'I'd be very grateful—' Nicco hesitated. 'Dad.' He finished.

Jack grinned. 'Good lad. Here's what I'll do – I'll come round next early closing day and have a chat about what's new. Soon put her in the picture, eh?'

Here he and Isa were, then, on the next early closing day, advancing up Ginger Street that seemed so strange. No men, except old men; no children, except babies. Ruth had said that Vi Dochart's husband had already left the bakery and was 'somewhere in France', and Millie Niven's husband was in the navy, up at Scapa Flow in the Orkneys. Aye, they were alone, those little girls Jack and Isa had known in the old days; grown-up, married, but alone, and though Sylvie still had her Mark, it would not be long before Ruthie was alone, too.

Chapter Fifty-One

Ruth and Nicco were ready and waiting when Jack and Isa arrived, but Gina was having her afternoon sleep and the signora had her hat and shawl on. She asked if Mr and Mrs Millar would excuse her, she was going along the road to see her daughter, they were taking Paulo to the Meadows. No doubt Mr and Mrs Millar would have many, many things to discuss with Ruth – she turned a dark look on Nicco – who would have so much to do when her husband had left her for the war.

'Her husband,' Isa repeated, when the signora had gone. 'Oh, dear! Are you no' your ma's son any more, Nicco?'

'Isa!' rapped Jack. 'Don't talk like that.'

'Don't worry.' Nicco shrugged. 'It's true enough, I'm in disgrace. You know my mother's views.'

'Wait till you go away,' Isa told him. 'You'll be her son again, then.'

'And still my husband,' said Ruth, wincing. 'What shall we do? Talk before tea?'

'Aye, we'd a bite to eat in town, we'll have our tea later.' Jack settled himself, cheekily, in the signora's chair. 'Now, Ruth, looks like you're going to be in charge of the shop before very long. How d'you feel about it?'

Her face was pale, showing the strain of waiting for her own personal blow to fall, which was Nicco's leaving her. Everything would be secondary to that, thought her watching parents, but there was no doubt that running the shop in wartime circumstances when she had never actually run it before would prove an ordeal. All over the country, women were facing just such ordeals, as Ruth herself knew, and would be the reason why she replied now:

'Oh, I think I'll be able to manage, Dad.'

Nicco pressed her hand and she gave him a quick, appreciative glance from her shadowed, grey-blue eyes.

'You'll have got yourselves registered with the Food Council?' asked Jack.

Oh, yes, Nicco had done that, and they knew all about the ration books being issued in January, and what would be rationed first – sugar, butter, fats, bacon, and such. Cigarettes and sweets would be scarce, so profits would fall from those sales, and ice-cream would probably go completely off the market, which would mean many Italian businesses would go under.

'You were never dependent on ice-cream, though,' Jack commented. 'Or cigs and sweeties come to that.'

'Not dependent,' Nicco agreed, 'but they'll be a big loss.'

'Aye, but what you're going to need to keep this shop going are registered customers. Folk who'll deposit their ration books with you. Think you can get them, Ruth?'

She looked at him uneasily. 'That's my worry, Dad. This has always been an Italian shop. Now, Nicco says we won't be able to get Italian supplies any more, so we'll be dependent on ordinary groceries.'

'Which you've always stocked.' Jack pointed out.

'Yes, but you can buy them at the Co-op stores. What's to stop folk registering there, where they'll get the dividend?'

There was a silence, during which Jack frowned and took out his pipe and tobacco pouch.

'Och, Jack, you're no' lighting that thing, are you?' asked Isa. 'What will the signora say?'

'She's no' here.'

'She'll smell it when she comes back.'

'We can open the window. You let me smoke it while I can get the baccy, eh?' Jack lit his pipe and puffed on it for a while. 'It's a tricky one, that,' he admitted. 'You'll have to hope that folk will stay loyal. If they didn't shop at the stores before, they probably won't now.'

'I agree,' said Nicco.

'I've no worries about folk leaving me for the stores.' Jack went on. 'But what I've got to face is that once I was special and now I'm not. All the things I stocked to make maself different will be going off the market for the duration.'

'We were special, too,' Nicco said sadly. 'Now the suppliers say there's no chance of getting shipping space for my sort of food, even while Italy's neutral.'

'With German U-boats around, imports are going to be a problem, anyway,' commented Jack. 'We canna manage on what we grow ourselves, so we'll have to get supplies from somewhere. No' from Italy, though.'

'You think our Italian customers will stay loyal, even when we can't get Italian foods?'

'If they can't get Italian stuff anywhere else, they might as well stick with us and take what they can get,' said Nicco.

'That makes sense,' Jack agreed. 'I think you'll get your customers, Ruth.'

'I'll need Scots, too.'

'Folk from Ginger Street,' Isa told her. 'Why, we've got friends here that go back years. They'll no' let you down.'

There was a silence, broken by Nicco. 'Some folk don't like Italians these days,' he said quietly. 'I think we have to accept that.'

'Ruthie's a Scot!'

'I'm not.'

'You're joining the British Army,' snapped Jack. 'What more do they want?'

'I think my friends'll support me,' said Ruth, but she looked uncertain. 'I'll still be selling our good vegetables, anyway, and eggs.'

'One egg a week, remember,' said Jack. 'That's what they say we'll be allowed.'

'One egg a week!' Isa was horrified. 'How'll I do ma baking?'

'You'll have to improvise.'

'Without eggs?'

'They say there'll be dried eggs. Mebbe dried milk, too.'

'Och, it's a nightmare!'

'What about bread, Dad?' asked Ruth. 'They're no' planning to ration bread?'

'Not so far as I know.' Jack shook his head. 'Could come later. I bet by the time we win this war, everything'll be on the ration.'

'By the time we win this war,' Ruth repeated. She gave a long shuddering sigh. 'But will we?'

Isa leaped to her feet. 'I hear Gina! I'll get her up. Ruth, you make the tea.'

After the first Scottish tea ever provided in the signora's home, Isa set Gina down from her knee and said they must be going. Sunday evening was her time for writing to Kester, took her an age, so it did, for letter-writing did not come naturally to her, but Kester loved to hear from her and she would never let him down. What was the betting that his Fenella didn't bother putting pen to paper for him, eh? But you had to keep the poor lad happy when he was away from home, and who knew how long it would be before Kester got sent somewhere dangerous?

While her mother was chattering on, Ruth's eyes were on her father. While he had been talking about rationing and regulations, he had been quite animated, for food provision was his job, it was what he'd done all his life, and he could always be relied upon to know what was what. But now their talk was over and he was putting on his coat to go home, he seemed low in spirits again, as he had been when Kester's dishonesty had first come to light. It saddened her beyond measure to see him looking so down, and almost old, her dear dad who had lost his luck and could do nothing about it. What made things worse was that Kester would never be able to right his wrong but could only offer more anxiety, this time through no fault of his own.

'What's up, Dad?' Ruth asked softly. 'Is it the Marchmont shop?'

'Aye. It's like a ball and chain around ma neck, Ruth, it's pulling me down, so that I canna think straight. Did get one offer and it fell through. Since then, no takers.'

'He's done all he can,' said Isa, 'Paid off thae bookies, you ken, and cut things to the bone, but till he gets rid o' that shop, he'll stay in debt.'

'If it hadn't been for the war, I might have had a hope,' Jack muttered. 'But that's put the tin lid on it for me. I've been that low, I was telling your ma, I couldn't even say for sure if I could keep the Trinity shop going.'

'Dad!'

'Aye, it's true. Well, if your sales are going to be down, mine'll be no different, eh? And I've the wages to pay, and all ma overheads. I've pretty well used up the capital I had left, so if I don't sell Marchmont, I canna see any way out.'

Ruth's eyes went to Nicco, who put his hand on Jack's arm.

'I feel bad,' he said quietly. 'Here we've been telling you all our troubles, when you've enough of your own.'

'But I'm staying here, Nicco, I'm no' going off to war.' Jack managed a grin. 'I'll sort this out, no need to worry.'

'Dad, how would you feel about renting?' asked Ruth.

'Renting?' He laughed shortly. 'Now, who's going to want to rent a grocery shop when there's a war on? About as many as would want to buy it, I should think.'

'It doesn't have to be a grocery shop, does it? What you've got is premises, Dad, and premises are wanted these days.'

'Oh, yes, who by?'

'Well, the army, for one. I saw an advert in the paper the other day seeking premises to rent for a recruitment office. Then, there's the ARP – they're wanting a place on that side of town for their air-raid post. Your shop'd be just the thing, Dad!'

'It's worth a try,' put in Nicco. 'Shall I get the evening paper?'

'Renting,' said Jack slowly. 'It could be the answer. If the building society'll let me do it. They might, in view of the circumstances. Then I'd have something to pay off the mortgage with, anyway. Aye, get the paper, Nicco. As you say, it'll be worth a try, eh? Why'd I no' think o' renting maself?'

'Because you can only think of grocery stores,' said Isa smartly. 'Takes an eye like Ruth's, to see that a shop needn't stay a shop!'

When her parents had left, Jack looking happier with the ARP advert in his pocket, Nicco drew Ruth to his arms and kissed her.

'I was worried about you,' he told her quietly. 'I needn't have been.'

'Don't say that. You haven't even left yet.'

'You'll be all right, when I go. I'm a lucky man to have someone like you to rely on.'

But Ruth wasn't so sure. 'There's the door, Nicco.' She left his arms and tidied her hair. 'Your mother's back.'

The signora was looking tired and fretful. As she took off her hat and shawl, she groaned audibly, and Nicco shot to her side.

'What's wrong, Mamma?'

She straightened a cushion on her chair before sitting down, then sniffed the air. 'Signor Millar has been smoking his pipe?'

'Just a bit, Mamma.'

She shrugged. 'What does it matter? Everything is falling around us, what is a little tobacco smell? Nicco, your cousin has lost his job.'

'Guido? Why?'

'The biscuit factory is closing. They cannot get what they need to make the biscuits, so they transfer to balloons.'

'Barrage balloons?'

'Yes, yes, the things in the sky.' His mother waved her hands irritably. 'They are to make balloons and parachutes and all things of that sort. But Guido will not make them, so there he is, unemployed, and my Marilena is without a breadwinner.'

'Can't he work at the café?' asked Ruth.

'At the café? When Vittorio can scarcely keep going as it is? There will not be enough money to pay Guido, I can tell you.'

'I don't understand,' said Nicco. 'There must be places where folk can eat away from home, the government will have to see that cafés get their supplies.'

'Italian cafés, Nicco? It is like the biscuit factory. Vittorio cannot get what he needs. And only Italians will come to him, anyway.' Carlotta's mouth drooped and she gave another shrug. 'The Scots do not wish to eat at Vittorio's any more.'

275

'*Nonna, Nonna*!' Gina cried, stretching her arms to her grandmother, and the signora, her face softening, stooped to sweep the child to her knee. She smoothed Gina's fair hair and laid her cheek against the small face. 'My comfort,' she whispered. 'Little Gina, little Paulo, my only comfort.'

Nicco, watching, sighed deeply, and Ruth, her relief at cheering her father quickly fading, began to clear away the tea things.

Chapter Fifty-Two

The days passed, and Ruth, strangely, no longer wanted to hold them back. Nicco had to go, therefore it was better he should go, so that she could learn to adjust to her new life, face whatever she had to face. So the arguments went in her head, but in her heart was just a gaping wound, lightly covered while Nicco was with her, ready to bleed when he went away.

There was some action in mid-October, when German planes bombed the Forth Bridge. It seemed to be only an isolated incident, though a taste of what might follow, but true tragedy had already struck two days earlier when the battleship, *Royal Oak*, was sunk by a U-boat at Scapa Flow. Over eight hundred men were lost, including Millie Niven's young husband, Derek, and while the country went into national mourning, Ginger Street wept for its own private loss.

'Good job I'd no bairns, eh?' Millie said to Ruth and Vi, her voice rough with tears, 'At least, there's nobody to cry for their dad.'

'Oh, Millie!' They clung to her, crying with her, relieved to be able to do that, for they could think of nothing to say.

'Och, I feel so bad,' Sylvie told Ruth, dabbing at her eyes with a wet handkerchief when she heard the news. 'Here's me with Mark no' even in the war yet, though he says he wants to go. It isn't so easy, being a policeman.'

'Be glad he's still with you,' said Ruth. 'Don't worry about being brave, or what folk think. He's doing his job, anyway, think of that.'

'Aye, but you ken how it is. Ma told me that women used to hand out white feathers to men who weren't at the front in the first world war.'

'The cheek of it!' Ruth said contemptuously, 'At least, there'll be nobody to do that today. Women are going to be called up, too, if they're single, and why not? I wouldn't mind going.' Her voice trembled. 'I think I'd rather go, in fact, than wait at home, wouldn't you?'

Sylvie touched her sister's hand. 'When does Nicco have to report to Berwick?' she asked gently.

'Pretty soon. End of the month.'

'And then you'll be running the shop?'

'It'll keep me occupied, and Dad'll help me out if I get stuck.'

'How about that nice looking Italian guy who used to give you a hand?'

'Domenico? He's in the Pioneers Corps, with his brother. Their café's closed.'

'Och, what a shame! This war's changing everybody's lives!'

Oddly enough, not always for the worse, Ruth thought later. Folk who'd led deprived lives throughout the 1930s were suddenly finding themselves needed and with money in their pockets. The labour nobody had wanted before was now at a premium, and for those not required to join the armed forces, there were jobs going everywhere. And Etta MacSween had taken one.

'Why, Etta, how well you look!' cried Ruth, calling one day at the tenement, to find Etta just leaving. She looked a different woman, young and attractive, with her hair permed and her face made-up, her eyes clear and shining. 'What's happened to you?'

'Got a job,' Etta told her proudly. 'Making parachutes at Gibb's old biscuit factory. Hen, you'd niver believe how much I'm getting!'

The old biscuit factory, thought Ruth, where Guido had refused to work in its new capacity. He had found another job now, though, with one of the breweries, where Federico had joined him, his father having temporarily closed his business.

'I'm just on ma way out now, I'm on afternoon shift.' Etta was continuing. 'Want to walk a bit o' the way wi' me?'

They walked together up the Canongate, Ruth pushing Gina, who was looking about her with lively interest, Etta chattering away like a running stream.

'Ma man's away to the war, and ma two eldest are in Peebles, you ken, so I says to Mrs Nisbet, will you take a few shillin' to mind the others while I get maself a job, and she says any time, honey, so here I am, in work again, and I tell you, Ruth, I niver felt better!'

'I can't believe the change in you, Etta. You look ten years younger!'

'Aye, that's going out, you ken, and having no more weans.' Etta laughed, showing new false teeth. 'I says to ma man, if you come home on leave, we're taking care, eh? I'm no falling for any more babbies, and he says, suits me. So, fingers crossed!' Her laughter died. 'Just as long as he does come home, eh? Och, but it's grand to see you, hen, and your little girl. Is she no' lovely? How's Mr Rittie, then? And how's your grand wee shop?'

'The shop's fine, but Nicco's joining up pretty soon. I'm going to be running the shop myself.'

'Fancy! Och, but you're like your ma, you can do onything. What say I come and get ma messages from you and we'll have a bit crack, eh?'

'I'd love that, Etta, but I'm too far away for you to do your shopping with me.'

'No' so far from the factory, I can do ma messages on the way home.' Etta shook her head. 'Och, you dinna ken what it's like, to have a bit cash to play with, when you've niver had it before! I've bought all the bairns new shoes and new clothes before the stocks run out and they put clothes on the ration. And Mrs Nisbet is washing wee Georgie and the others at home ivery day, till they dinna ken where they are! Now you remember me to that ma of yours – what a whirlwind, eh? I say they should put her on to fighting Hitler – she'd settle him, I'm telling you!'

The little encounter with Etta had cheered Ruth for a while, until she began to wonder why money could not have been found before to help folk like the MacSweens, when it could be found now for anything to do with the war. She wasn't an economist, maybe it hadn't been possible, the whole problem had no doubt been a lot more complex than she knew. Maybe it didn't do, anyway, to believe that all the misery of the 1930s need never have happened. Just as long as it didn't happen again.

Another who had profited from the war, even if indirectly, was Jack. He had taken Ruth's advice, checked with his building society and let his Marchmont premises for use as an ARP Wardens' Post. What a relief! He too was like a different person when he told Ruth that the deal had gone through. Youthful again, and with the air of a man whose luck had turned, whose burden had been laid down.

'Aye, you're a clever lassie, Ruth, to think of that letting. It's made all the difference to me, and to Kester and all. He'd been fretting, you ken, about landing me in the soup like he did, and there seemed to be no way out. Now this rent'll just tide us over and we can stop worrying.' Jack's grin faded. 'About that, anyway.'

'What's the news of Kester, Dad? Has he got a posting?'

Jack hesitated. 'He rang me on the shop phone. Said he'd be getting Christmas leave.'

'Why, that'd be lovely!'

'Maybe. I just got the impression – don't ask me why – that he might be going somewhere after that. France, for instance. 'Course, he couldn't say, on the phone.'

'You might be wrong, Dad.'

'I remember the last time,' he said flatly. 'We all ended up in France.'

'Things are different now.'

'If you want to defeat Germany, you've to go to Europe, and if you go to Europe you start with France.'

Ruth didn't say any more, but it seemed to her that with war only just begun, the time for defeating Germany must be a very long way off.

Chapter Fifty-Three

The night before Nicco had to leave, he and Ruth made love. They thought it would be something special, their last time together – filled with urgency and joy – but sadness hung over them and coloured their pleasure, so that they were relieved when it was over. For the first time, too, Ruth had thought of Nicco's parents in the bed that had been theirs, of their making love, conceiving children, and of how all that had come to an end. Nicco's father had died, in that same bed, and for years, his mother had slept there alone. Will that be me? thought Ruth. Will Nicco never return, and this bed be only mine?

In the morning, she watched him dress.

'Somehow, I always thought of you going off in uniform,' she told him.

He looked at her in surprise. 'How could I wear uniform? I have to be kitted out at the depot.'

'I know, it was silly. Just thought of you in Scottish trews.'

'Scottish trews!' Now he laughed. 'It'll be khaki battledress for me.'

'Oh, Nicco!'

He came to her where she sat on the edge of the bed, still in her nightdress, and they kissed with a passion they hadn't known in the night.

'How am I going to leave you?' Nicco groaned, caressing her, but it was too late now for passion. They could hear the signora moving round the flat, and Gina calling from her own tiny room.

'Come on, I've got to get ready,' said Ruth. 'And make your breakfast.'

'I expect Mamma will be doing that.'

Breakfast was a silent meal, except for Gina's prattle, which was a mixture of Italian and English. The three adults looked at her a good deal; it saved looking at one another. And she was a pretty child, with her father's dark eyes and her grandfather's blond hair. It was too early to say whether her little button nose would be turned up or straight, but it didn't matter, anyway. She was always going to be one to turn heads, that was for sure.

'Dada going away?' she asked Ruth, when she got down from her chair. No one had told her that her father was leaving, but as children do, she had sensed what was happening. 'Gina go, too?'

'No, darling, Dada has to go on his own. He'll come back when he can.'

Gina's lip trembled. 'Dada not go away!' she cried.

Nicco picked her up and held her close, while his mother with set lips cleared away the breakfast dishes.

'I'll do those,' said Ruth.

'No, I will,' said Carlotta.

Nicco had decreed that no one was to go with him to Waverley. Saying goodbye at stations was one of life's little cruelties. Better by far to say goodbye with no onlookers, then just march away.

'I agree, is better,' said the signora, but when he came into the kitchen in his coat and cap and set down his canvas bag, she burst into such paroxysms of tears, Ruth took Gina's hand and quietly left mother and son together. Gina was puzzled, wanting to know why *Nonna* was crying so much, when Dada would soon be coming home.

'Well, we're no' sure when he'll come, you see, and then he'll still have to go away again. He has work to do, very important work, and we must let him do that.' Ruth blew her nose. 'And no' make a fuss.'

'It's *Nonna* who's making a fuss,' said Gina.

Ruth's turn to say goodbye came when Nicco's mother, her eyes red-rimmed and her mouth now trembling, stood apart with Gina, and Nicco came to take Ruth into his arms. It was a brief parting, the quicker the better, Ruth said. Just a last kiss and a last exchange of looks, then Nicco was unlocking the shop door and standing by, to let his first customers in.

'Yours now,' he said to Ruth, with a faint smile. 'Good luck, *cara*.'

'Good luck to you, Nicco!'

'Aye, good luck, Nicco!' some of the shoppers echoed, but two of the Italian women did not speak. They don't approve, thought Ruth, which was no surprise, she and Nicco had already experienced that sort of reaction from some Italians who would not accept his going to war. But for the first time, it occurred to her that she would not be able to count on all the members of the Italian community for custom. Oh, God, did it matter? If only Nicco could come safely back to her, she didn't care how many registered customers she had.

'Have you got your tram fare?' she asked Nicco in the street.

'Have you the rolls I made for you?' asked his mother.

'I've got everything.' He looked from one to the other, then kissed them both, and Gina, too, in his mother's arms. 'I won't say goodbye again,' he got out. 'I'll just go now. Don't watch me.'

But they did. They watched him march away, as he'd said he'd do, to the corner of Ginger Street, then when he looked back, they waved. For a moment, he hesitated, then was gone. A silence fell on the two women, and even the child. Ruth, after a moment, put her hand on the signora's arm, but the signora turned away into the shop.

'Come, you have customers,' she told Ruth. 'This lady wishes to have potatoes weighed.'

'Och, hen, it doesnae matter aboot the tatties,' said Mrs Fyfe kindly. 'You go and have a good cry, it'll do you good.'

But Ruth said no, she'd get on with it. Had to start somewhere, eh?

'That's the ticket,' someone said, but when Ruth had finished weighing the potatoes and put them in a brown paper bag someone else asked, 'D'you hear there'll be no paper bags soon?' The signora was already on her way up the stairs, holding Gina's hand.

'Mammie, Mammie, come on up!' cried Gina.

'Later, Gina!' called Ruth, opening up the till. 'Mammie's got work to do.'

Chapter Fifty-Four

When Kester came home for Christmas leave, it was with the news that he had been posted to France with his battalion. Jack said, 'I told you so, I knew he'd go to France, everybody goes to France.' But he was wrong about that, as Nicco's posting was to prove in the spring.

He'd had no idea of any posting when he too came home at Christmas, which Ruth in retrospect was glad about, for to have known about it would have spoiled her little daydream that he wasn't going anywhere. Kester, however, was going somewhere and pleased about it. He wouldn't at all mind joining the British Expeditionary Force when he went back from leave, he told his family. He wanted some action; hanging about in his own country was only prolonging the agony. If you were in the army, you had to fight sooner or later, and he would prefer it to be sooner.

'Soldiers I knew were never that keen on battle,' Jack murmured to Isa, whose eyes were already full of fear. It was bad enough that Kester should be going to fight at all, but that he should almost seem to be welcoming the danger, was, she declared, 'beyond her'.

'What's the matter with him, d'you think?' she asked Ruth and Sylvie on Boxing Day. They had each spent Christmas Day with their in-laws, which normally would have infuriated Isa, but she had been so eaten up with worry over Kester, she had accepted the arrangements without a word. After all, she'd had Kester himself for Christmas dinner, even if she'd had to have Fenella as well, and with rationing not yet arrived, Jack had managed to get her most of the things she wanted. Aye, they'd had a lovely chicken, and the pudding had been one of her best, though she said so herself, and they'd all made the most of it in case they shouldn't have another. So, now, on Boxing Day, there was just the bird to finish up cold, with a good boiled ham, which meant she could concentrate on getting the girls to tell her what they thought about Kester. Luckily, he wasn't there. It was Fenella's mother's turn to entertain her daughter and son-in-law. So while Jack, Nicco and Mark talked war and the children played in the living room, Isa poured tea for her daughters in the kitchen and looked at them with bright, hopeful eyes.

'I don't know what you're worried about, Ma,' said Sylvie, studying chocolates in a pre-war box from Jack's stock. 'Kester seemed OK to me when I saw him on Christmas Eve. Drinking a fair bit, but that's nothing new. Probably needs a jar or two, being married to Fenella. I expect she's been going on at him since he came home.'

'You think so?' asked Isa.

'No,' said Ruth. 'Seems to me, he's still feeling guilty.'

Isa groaned, and added hot water to the teapot. 'He said he was feeling better since your dad'd let the Marchmont shop, but he's no' better at all. He canna get over what he did, and it's all my fault.'

'Now, how d'you work that out?' asked Sylvie, biting into a strawberry cream with a little shudder of delight.

'Well, I was too hard on him, you ken. Soon as I heard what'd happened, I really let fly, I said I'd niver forgive him for what he'd done to your dad and me – aye, and a whole lot of other things I don't want to remember. You were there, Ruth, you heard me. I was awful hard on him, eh? And he took it badly, I could see, went that white and still, I thought he was going to faint. But he should've known I didn't mean it. I mean, I always forgive you bairns, whatever you do, now is that no' true?'

And sometimes we forgive you, thought Ruth, but aloud she said sincerely, 'Ma, you'd a perfect right to talk to Kester the way you did. What he did was wrong, and he lost Dad the Marchmont shop and a lot of money as well. Anybody'd be angry with him.'

'Aye, but poor laddie, he niver meant to do it, and he couldn't

286

be more sorry.' Isa poured more tea. 'What can he do to make up? He's no money, he canna pay us back. Well, we don't want him to, now that he's in the forces and away to France.' Her eyes filled with tears, as she passed the girls the milk jug. 'What's money, eh? When you think of your son in the war?'

'Try no' to worry, Ma,' said Sylvie. 'Mark says there'll be no fighting in France for ages.'

'And how does Mark know what's happening in France?' Isa asked with asperity. 'He's still here, last I heard.'

'The police get to hear what's going on,' Sylvie answered defensively. 'And Mark doesn't want to avoid the war, you know. The police are needed at home.'

'No, I know, Mark's a brave fellow.' Isa's eyes went to Ruth. 'And so's Nicco, Ruth. It took a lot of courage to do what he did.'

'That's true,' said Sylvie. She glanced at Ruth. 'So, how's Christmas been, then?'

Ruth understood her. How had Christmas been, with the family? Difficult, you might say, at least to begin with.

After the first ecstatic moments when Nicco had folded his mother in his arms, she had emerged displeased to see that he was wearing his uniform and outraged that he was under orders to do so. Even on leave? It was ridiculous! He was to go to Midnight Mass in uniform?

'Half the church'll be full of fellows in uniform,' he told her. 'The country's at war, everybody has to be ready for action.'

'Not every country is at war,' she had answered coldly. 'And what will Brigida say when you walk in for Christmas dinner dressed as a soldier? What will Guido say?'

Nicco bit his lip. 'I'm not interested in what Guido says, Mamma. He has his views, I have mine.'

All the same, when they were alone, Ruth asked Nicco if he couldn't put on his civilian clothes, just for Christmas Day?

'I know it's orders, and all that, and I think you look wonderful in your battledress, anyway—'

'As if it matters what I look like!' he cried.

'But, who's to know, if you wear your civvies, darling? And it would help to keep the peace. And it is Christmas.'

His gaze on her had melted and he had taken her in his arms. 'Couldn't we skip dinner at Brigida's and just stay in bed?' he asked, kissing her over and over again.

'What wouldn't I give! No, we have to go, Nicco. Everyone's coming – Renata and Federico, and Federico's parents, and Guido and Marilena, and one or two folk who've nowhere to go for Christmas. It's only Guido who might be difficult. Everyone else is so glad to see you, dearest, as I am!'

When they'd surfaced again from a long embrace, Nicco had said, all right, he'd take a chance on it, but if the military police picked him up, Ruth would have only herself to blame. To which, Ruth had said if they did, she'd come and bail him out with money from the till.

'No bail in the army,' he told her cheerfully, and she'd taken his arm.

'Are you managing?' she'd asked softly. 'Truly? I know you say you are in your letters.'

'Truly, I'm managing. It's been better than I thought. They're a decent bunch of chaps in the regiment. No one's called me Wop yet.'

'Oh, Nicco!'

'Never mind me. Are you managing yourself? Truly? I know you say you are in your letters.'

She laughed. 'Truly, I'm managing. But it won't get difficult till the New Year. When the ration books come.'

'You think you'll find the customers?'

'Yes, but don't let's talk about it. Let's no' spoil this time together, eh?' They kissed again, lingeringly, then parted, to find Gina.

'You don't know how much I've missed you!' Nicco cried, swinging his little daughter up high, but she looked down at him without a smile and said:

'I do know, Dada, I've missed you.'

It had been a great relief for Ruth to see Nicco wearing his dark suit

288

for Brigida's Christmas dinner, and to observe his mother's pride at her son's wanting to please her. No red-capped military policemen appeared on their short walk down Ginger Street to Vittorio's café, and there the welcome was genuinely warm for Nicco from everyone except Guido.

'So, here's the gallant soldier,' he sneered. 'Won any medals yet?'

'Guido!' exclaimed his mother, and Renata, vividly attractive in a dark red maternity dress she had made herself, smartly told her brother to behave himself.

'It's Christmas, the season of goodwill, in case you've forgotten, Guido!'

'Not much goodwill about when there's a war on,' he snapped.

'Whose fault is it that we have a war?' asked Federico's father, Signor Martinello. 'Those Nazi fellows! Mussolini should never have got Italy involved with them, is what I've always said. Why did the King let him do it?'

'Il Duce does what he thinks best,' said Federico. 'Victor Emmanuel knows that.'

'Best for him? Or us?' Bruno Martinello was a large man with heavy features and dark brows, but it seemed to Ruth that he had shrunk a little since the last time she'd seen him. His wife, Lucia, a woman of Carlotta's style and strength, also appeared to have changed, being less forthright, less sure of herself. Strange, in a woman who had been likened to Carlotta!

They were both devastated at the closure of Bruno's ice-cream machinery business, Renata whispered to Ruth. Of course, it would only be for 'the duration', as people had taken to saying, but who knew how long that would be? In the meantime, Bruno had nothing to do and was not making money, which was terrible for him because, like Federico, he was the most generous of men. Liked to be there for those in the family who needed him, liked to be able to say, 'don't worry, I'll see you're all right'. And now he was not all right himself and nor was Lucia. Apart from all their financial problems, they were worried about Federico. Bruno, like Vittorio, was no fascist, but like Vittorio was worried about a son who was. Probably, both Guido and Federico would be interned.

'It might no' come to that,' Ruth said, trying to offer comfort she knew was no more than words.

Renata shrugged. 'A poor start for the baby, if it does. And how am I going to manage for money? Dad's café might not survive, my father-in-law's business has closed. I can see me working in the parachute factory before long.'

'You'd leave the baby with your mother?'

Renata's face relaxed into a smile. 'She can't wait! Oh, but Ruth, here am I babbling on about my problems, and there's you, with Nicco away and the shop to run! How's it going to be for you, when all the rationing comes in?'

'Don't remind me. I'm trying to put all that out of my mind and just enjoy Christmas.'

Her eyes found Nicco and rested on him, as her heart leaped and bounded with love, and the thought of the night to come.

How had Christmas been? Ruth stirred her tea and smiled at Sylvie.

'Wonderful, really,' she answered finally. 'And it's not over yet.'

Chapter Fifty-Five

Ah, but January had to follow Christmas and January was miserable. First, there was Nicco's quiet departure, no fuss allowed, for he was only going to Berwick, after all, though again, for Ruth, it might have been the moon. Then Kester had to be seen off at Waverley, to the accompaniment of tears and waves from the women and a stiff upper lip from Jack, and with his departure on a train filled with troops, it seemed as though the war had really begun in earnest. No more phoney war, if one of the family was on his way to France, whether or not there would be immediate fighting. There would be fighting, sooner or later, as Kester himself had said. Oh, God, would it be sooner? was the unspoken question, as Kester's family left the station, and even Fenella was crying into her handkerchief.

Ruth returned to Ginger Street feeling ill-equipped to deal with the life that awaited her. The sight of her brother's dispirited face at the train window coming so soon after her farewell to Nicco, had so wrenched her heart she felt almost sickened by the prospect of worrying about customers, nagging over supplies. Yet she knew such thoughts were only the product of depression. Her work, if not as vital as Nicco's and Kester's defence of the realm, was still important. Whatever happened, folk had to eat, and she'd better not forget that what they ate should come from her, or the business would go under.

Marilena had been minding the shop for her and looked up now with a concerned smile, as Ruth came in and hung up her coat on the peg at the back door.

'Oh, Ruth, how was it, saying goodbye to poor Kester?'

'Pretty awful.' Ruth sat on a stool behind the counter and looked around the shop, which was far from busy. Already, her shelves were emptying of all the fascinating Italian foods Nicco had liked to stock, and of other goods, too. Where were the folk to buy what she had, anyway? Ration books were about to be issued and though a surprising number of Scots had promised their custom, an equally surprising number of Italians was keeping out of her way. Ruth ran her hands through her thick brown hair and sighed, at which Marilena put her arm around her shoulders.

'Why don't you go up and have a cup of tea, Ruth? You look so tired.'

'I will, if you don't mind carrying on a bit longer.'

'I don't mind, it's not exactly hard work.' Marilena shrugged. 'The shop's like the café.'

'You mean quiet? You think your uncle will manage to keep going?'

'If he can find different things to serve. Pies and peas, maybe, stuff of that sort.'

'Pies and peas?' Ruth smiled faintly. She couldn't imagine Vittorio and Brigida serving up ordinary fare, but if they had to, they would. All over the country, folk were doing things they'd never done before, just to survive.

'I want to tell you, Ruth, that I think you're being very brave,' Marilena was saying quietly. 'It must be so terrible for you, with Nicco away, and for your sister-in-law, too, now that Kester's gone. I don't know what I'd do, if Guido had to go.'

'Guido will not be going to war, Marilena.'

'But he might be interned, Ruth. He might have to go to a camp somewhere.'

'On the Isle of Man?' Ruth could not keep the edge from her voice. 'Hardly a danger zone!'

Marilena flinched. 'I know you don't like him, Ruth, because of what happened to Nicco, but Guido had nothing to do with that, I swear to you! He and Nicco don't get on, and Guido doesn't agree with Nicco's views, but he'd never hurt him, or let other people hurt him. Please say you believe me!'

292

Ruth, who didn't know what she believed, said of course she didn't think Guido had caused the attack on Nicco. But there was no denying that he was a fascist and might have to face the consequences.

'I know, I know. I just pray every night that Italy stays neutral.'

Poor Marilena, thought Ruth, climbing the stairs. Her prayers were certain to go unanswered.

Since Ruth had taken over the shop, the signora usually cooked the evening meal, and very modest it was. Gone were the days of her elaborate cooking, for she could no longer get the ingredients she required. Even if she could, Ruth knew she would not think it worth while to make special efforts for a couple of women. All the same, Ruth, speaking Italian as well as she could, had to make an effort to compliment her mother-in-law, and thank her for doing the cooking.

'You work in the shop,' the signora said grudgingly.

'I wanted to talk to you about that, if you would not mind?'

Her mother-in-law graciously inclined her head.

'Well, the problem is that we need to get people to promise to be our customers and let us have their ration books.'

'We have plenty of customers.'

'We did, we had Italians and Scots, but it's the Italians who are not promising to register with us. Some have said they will still shop with us, even though we can't get Italian provisions, and others – well, they don't seem to be coming to us any more.'

The signora set down her fork. 'Who? Who is not coming to my Nicco's shop?'

'I don't know their names—'

'I think I do!' The signora's eyes were alight with anger. 'I know these people! They have said to me, why is your Nicco in the British Army? Why did you let him join? He is not faithful to Il Duce! They say this to me, his mother! As though I can tell my son what to think! My son has a right to think as he likes, I told them, we live in a free country, is that not so?'

'Oh, that's so,' Ruth agreed, putting up her hand to cover an incredulous smile.

'But now you say they do not come to the shop? Italians not to come to an Italian shop! It is disgraceful, not to be endured. Ruth, you will leave this to me!'

'Gladly,' said Ruth.

As soon as the meal was over, the signora leaped to her feet and put aside the black-out curtains to look down on Ginger Street.

'Too dark,' she muttered. 'I can't go out tonight.'

'Oh, you can't!' Ruth exclaimed. 'You can't see anything in the streets at night.'

'Tomorrow, then. Tomorrow, I will take Gina and we will make some visits.' The signora gave a fierce smile. 'Then we shall see – who comes to my Nicco's shop!'

It took only a day or two, following the visits to the Italian community of the formidable lady in black, accompanied by the fair-haired child, for certain Italian customers to return very quietly, very sheepishly, to Nicco Rietti's shop. What her mother-in-law had said Ruth was never told, nor did she enquire. The only thing that mattered was that her customer numbers were up and when the ration books were issued and she was clipping out and sending away coupons, was able to feel some confidence in the future. Thank the Lord for the signora!

Sometimes, in the evenings, when she was doing her ironing and listening to *It's That Man Again* on the wireless, she would snatch covert glances at her mother-in-law, whipping away at her lace-work and snorting with impatience because she couldn't find Tommy Handley and the ITMA show funny. She wasn't so bad, really, Ruth would think. They were rubbing along together pretty well, all things considered. Yet still she had never been invited to call her mother-in-law 'Mamma', still they held each other at arm's length. Perhaps always would.

'This is Funf speaking,' whispered a voice from the wireless, and Ruth grinned at the comic German accent of the supposed spy.

'Funf?' the signora repeated, drawing her brows together. 'Funf is German for five. Now, what is funny about that?'

'Well, it's hard to explain. All the voices are funny, you see. Funf's a German spy and keeps ringing up Tommy Handley who's in one of the war ministries. And then there's this charlady and all different people coming in an out, taking off officials and that sort thing.' Ruth was smiling indulgently. 'Och, it's just something to laugh at!'

But the signora was quite lost. 'You British are strange people. Scots, English – all very strange, all laughing at strange things. And in a war, too!'

'I certainly don't feel like laughing very often,' said Ruth. 'But it's good to laugh sometimes, if you can.'

To that, her mother-in-law made no reply.

Chapter Fifty-Six

Everyone was now well into wartime routines. Putting up the black-outs every night, queuing every day for this and that, accepting at frequent intervals that something else had been put 'on the ration'. In March, for instance, it was meat.

'A shillingsworth a week?' cried Isa. 'Jack, how'll we manage?'

'Och, we lived on less than that when we were young,' he said cheerfully. 'How often did we get meat when we were bairns?'

'Aye, but we're used to something different today, you ken. You'll have to do your best for me wi' Jim Simpson, eh?'

Jack said he'd see what he could do, but Jim Simpson, the butcher, was going to be a very popular man, from the sound of things.

'Why, so are you popular, Jack!' Isa smiled. 'With your packets of tea here, and your bits of sugar there!'

'I'm no' into the black market, though,' he answered loftily. 'If I've a wee bit of something to spare, I'll help a customer out, nae bother, but I don't hold with making money out of shortages.'

'No' like some. Jack, how's our Ruth managing, d'you think? She always says she's fine, but I worry about her, you ken, she's got that much to do.'

'She's doing well, really well. Got the hang o' the rationing, working out supplies, everything. Nicco'd be proud of her, and so am I.'

'Where d'you think Nicco'll get posted? France, like our Kester?'

They thought of Kester, whose letters gave so little away, but who seemed to be leading a fairly quiet life. Until Hitler got moving again, eh? Jack, who knew that a good deal of Isa's loudly trumpeted worries about food were a smokescreen for her true worries about Kester, said he'd no idea where Nicco would be sent. How could he have? But one thing was certain, he, like Hitler, would be on the move soon.

It was in April that Hitler invaded Denmark and Norway, and in April that Nicco telephoned Ruth at the shop to say that he was coming home on leave the following weekend.

'Is it embarkation leave?' she asked, turning cold.

'Can't say anything now, *cara*. I'll give you all the news when I see you. Do you love me?'

'I love you, Nicco.'

It was embarkation leave, she thought, putting the phone down, it must be, she'd been expecting it. Nicco was going to France, and she must be brave. Oh, God!

'Is it France?' she asked, when he came into her arms at the station, for she had insisted on meeting him at the station, while Marilena once again looked after the shop.

'No, it's not France.' He was holding her so close, she could feel the buttons of his uniform pressing into her chest, but scarcely noticed.

'Where, then? Norway? They say troops are going to Norway. Nicco, tell me!'

He drew a little away, the better to see her face. 'It's India.'

'India!' She was baffled. India? When the country was fighting a European war, why would a soldier be posted to India? But relief succeeded surprise. India was a long way away, but it would be safer than France. Oh, yes. No Germans in India.

'No Germans in India!' she cried.

'No Italians, either,' Nico said gravely. 'If they should come into the war, they won't be where I'm going.'

'No, but why are you going, anyway?'

'One of the battalions is already there. Some of us are forming a relief detachment.'

'It all seems so mysterious. I can't imagine what you'd be needed for – in India.'

Nicco shouldered his kitbag and laughed. 'The British are in India, or hadn't you heard? So, they need the army. There are always troops around somewhere.'

'Not for fighting?' Ruth asked quickly.

'Various duties.'

'Fighting?' she persisted.

'I shouldn't think so. More like patrols, guard jobs, that sort of thing.'

She was reassured. India was better than France, they'd been lucky. As for the distance that would separate her from Nicco, she needn't think of that for the moment.

'Let's treat ourselves to a taxi,' she said, taking his arm. You can't take that great pack on the tram!'

'Looks like a terrible queue for taxis, sweetheart.'

'Terrible queues for everything these days, Nicco.'

A wave of relief swept over the Rietti family when Nicco told them that he was being posted to India. India? Why, he was practically not in the war at all! And would certainly not be fighting Italians, should Il Duce decide to enter the war. What a relief! There were celebrations at Vittorio's café, where everyone put up with the makeshift menu and divided their time between slapping Nicco on the back and admiring Renata's baby daughter, Emilia, just four weeks old. Even Guido held his fire for once, and Carlotta, so proud of her son who had managed to please the family and himself, sat like royalty at the top of the table, being served by Brigida and Marilena, and actually smiling in a way no one had seen for years.

'She's even managed not to say again that it was a pity Federico hadn't got his son,' Renata whispered to Ruth, who smiled in recognition. 'But I think she's just so stunned I had a baby at all, she's letting me down lightly.'

'We're all just so glad Nicco's no' going to France,' said Ruth. 'It might be quiet there now, but everyone says that's where the battles will be.'

'And your brother's there. Oh, poor Kester! Your mother must be in a state.'

'You sort of learn to live with it. I was preparing myself to do that, as a matter of fact. I was so sure Nicco would be sent to join the Expeditionary Force.'

'Can't be sure of anything, which is just as well. I mean, where are the air-raids they said were coming? And why hasn't Il Duce made a move? Federico says he's waiting to see which way things go.'

It seemed to Ruth that they were going Germany's way, but she didn't say so. Hitler's victories to date could go to the back of her mind, along with the thought of those miles of sea and land that would divide her from Nicco. This party at Vittorio's was like Christmas all over again, and she would just think of that. Her lips curved in a secret smile, as she looked forward to making love to Nicco again when night came, and of the long, long days of his leave.

Of course, the days weren't long, they were short. They flew past like dreams impossible to be caught, so that before Nicco had unpacked his kitbag, he seemed to be packing it up again. Then came the same wrenching farewells, the desperate eyes, the tears, as at previous partings, only now there was the awful knowledge that it would be years, not months, before they met again.

'Take care, take care! Oh, God, take care, all of you!' cried Nicco. And as he looked at Gina and wondered how old she would be, how much she would have changed before he saw her again, he thought for a fleeting moment that he would rather be going to France. But that was foolishness. You might get leave from France, you might also die in France, and he wasn't expecting to die in India.

'I wish you'd let us come to the station,' fretted Ruth, but he was already giving his last hugs, to his mother, to Gina, to herself. 'Or, taken a taxi,' she added, as they pulled themselves apart. 'Look at you, with that great kitbag!'

Away he went, the kitbag on his shoulder, and it was all just as it had been before. Watching and waving and turning back with hearts of lead.

'He will be safe,' Ruth murmured to his mother. 'He will come back.'

But the signora went into her room and closed the door.

Chapter Fifty-Seven

There was talk of Fenella volunteering for the WRNS, the Women's Royal Naval Service. Sylvie laughed and said to Mark:

'Fancies the uniform!'

'So do I fancy a uniform,' he answered glumly.

'You've got one.'

'You know what I mean.'

'She's no' joining, anyway,' Sylvie said uneasily. 'Changed her mind, I expect, when she found there was more to it than looking smart.' When Mark made no reply, Sylvie, peeling potatoes for their evening meal, chattered on. Actually, Fenella wasn't too bad these days. Visited Isa regularly and had been quite friendly. 'Of course, Ma says it's only because Dad lets her folks have a few extras, they're registered with him, you ken—'

'I should be away,' Mark said, not listening. 'You've heard what they say about bairns asking, what did you do in the war, Dad?' What the hell would I say? I stayed at home?'

'You're doing your job, Mark. Someone has to do it, we can't be left without any police.'

'There are others who can do it. I don't want to be in a reserved occupation. I'm going to try to volunteer. Maybe for the RAF.'

Sylvie put the potatoes into a bowl of cold water and gathered up the peelings, which had to be saved for a man they knew with a pig. All part of the war effort.

'You do understand?' asked Mark.

'Yes, I can see how it is for you, Mark.' Her lip trembled. 'I'm just being selfish. I want you safe.'

'Can't always just think about being safe.'

'I can,'said Sylvie, 'for you.'

May, the 'merry month', lived up to its reputation that year, for the weather was beautiful. But no one had the heart to enjoy it when Hitler's troops were running through Europe like some dreadful disease. Holland, Belgium and Luxembourg had all been invaded. On 15 May, Holland surrendered. Britain's new prime minister, Winston Churchill, tried to give the country heart, but on 28 May, Belgium surrendered. France was threatened and Allied troops were being encircled by the enemy, they had no choice but to withdraw. While the future had never looked darker for the British across the Channel, the great evacuation from Dunkirk got under way.

These were the worst days of their lives, said Isa. Was it wrong, to think only of your own laddie, when there were all thae thousands of men to be rescued from the beaches?

'Only natural,' Jack told her. Somehow, he was keeping going, serving in his shop, waiting for the phone to ring. Fenella was officially Kester's next of kin, she would be the one to hear any news. But in those beautiful days at the end of May, she heard nothing. Sylvie and Ruth spent all the time they could with their mother, for Isa was refusing to eat and constantly blaming herself for Kester's plight, which she knew herself was absurd but which seemed to give her a twisted kind of relief.

'Aye, if he's gone, it'll be because of me,' she would say. 'He's lost his will to live, because of what I said to him, he thinks he'll niver be forgiven, he thinks there's no hope.'

'Ma, you know that isn't true!' Sylvie would wail, and Ruth, who'd had to leave the shop to the signora or Marilena, would make more tea and recklessly spread the butter ration on scones or teacakes to tempt her mother, all to no avail.

'Leave her, leave her,' said Jack. 'She's getting through this her own way. You canna do anything for her until the news comes through.'

But no news came.

The signora was being very sympathetic over Kester. Anxiety over a son was something she understood, and she would frequently urge Ruth to visit her mother and tell her of the Rietti family's feeling for her at that time. Even Guido came round to express his concern for Kester, his old mate from the biscuit factory, which touched Ruth more than she could say. Marilena was right, there were good things about Guido. Och, everyone was being so kind. Renata and Federico, Vittorio and Brigida. And Ruth herself had to think of others apart from her family. Poor Vi Dochart, for instance. She too was waiting for news, of her husband, Cameron, and would come into the shop, white-faced and red-eyed, just for something to do, she said, keep her mind off what was happening. Keep her mind off! That was a joke, eh? Who could keep their minds off what was happening at Dunkirk?

For a time, it seemed, nothing was happening. The beaches were crammed with British and French troops being bombed and hit by shrapnel, waiting for the boats to take them off, but there were no boats. Suddenly, there they were. Destroyers, yachts, little boats, life-boats – anything that could sail had been pressed into service, and the men raced across the sands to get aboard, hearts in mouths, as the planes circled overhead and the shrapnel still fell. But over 330,000 men made it home over several days, and the retreat became in a way a victory, even though a terrible truth was now beginning to dawn on Britain. The Germans were about to conquer France, they were just across the Channel; soon, very soon, they would be preparing to invade. First would come the Blitz, then the troops, then Britain would become another scalp to hang round Hitler's belt. So, it seemed, if the people let themselves think about it, but first there were all these men to welcome home, snatched from death or prison camp. One of the rescued men was Cameron Dochart, and another was Kester Millar.

The relief was almost too great to bear. It was as though their dread had held them up, and when there was no longer dread but only joy, they wavered and collapsed. Not for long, though, for Cameron, who had come through unscathed, was due home on leave and Vi must welcome him, while Kester, who had a lacerated right leg and was in a military hospital in Kent, had to be visited. Fenella, of course, would go, but so would Isa and Jack.

'Try to keep us away!' cried Isa.

'No one's going to do that,' Fenella replied calmly. 'But what about the shop?'

Bob MacAllan, poor Bob, who'd lost his son-in-law in the *Royal Oak* disaster, would take care of the shop, no worry about that.

'And I'll bake Kester a cake,' said Isa, fidgeting round her kitchen, for she couldn't keep still. 'You get me some eggs, Jack, and some fruit, eh? Cherries, or something?'

'Cherries? Where am I going to get cherries?'

'Well, currants, then, anything. Come on, I ken well you've got stuff stashed away that you niver let on about. Why am I always at the bottom of the list for extras?'

'Shoemaker's wife niver has shoes,' said Jack, laughing as he often did now, in spite of the war news. 'Och, I canna belive we've been so lucky, eh? Kester's alive!'

Ruth and Sylvie saw the travellers on to a train so crowded with service people, both men and women, there was scarcely an inch of room to stand, never mind sit. But, true to form, Isa managed to squeeze herself into a seat between two ATS girls, embracing her bag and the box with Kester's cake, while Jack and Fenella stood in the corridor, lighting cigarettes to add to the smoke that wreathed every passenger, waving to the sisters, as the train slowly ground away from the platform, picked up speed, and vanished from sight.

'At least, it'll be daylight for most of the way,' said Sylvie, as she and Ruth turned away. 'They say it's awful at night in the trains, with all the lights painted blue, making everybody look ill.'

'And most of 'em feeling ill, too, I expect, being packed together like sardines.' Ruth took a deep breath of happiness. 'But isn't it wonderful that Ma and Dad are on their way to Kester? Some good news at last!'

'I've got some news and it's no' good,' said Sylvie. 'At least, no' for me. Mark's thrilled to bits.'

'He's away?' asked Ruth, fearfully.

'Will be. They're letting him join up, he's got an interview board with the RAF next week.'

'Oh, Sylvie! When does he have to leave?'

'If he's accepted, it'll be soon.' Sylvie shook her head. 'It's what he wanted, to get to the war, and I can't complain. Only makes me the same as everybody else. Only thing is, I thought I was luckier.'

As she gave a small sob, Ruth put her arm around her and suggested they should go for a cup of coffee at the station buffet, cheer themselves up.

'Och, no, it'll be too crowded, and I need to get home. A neighbour's minding Ronnie, but he'll be missing me. You could come and have something at my place, though, if you like?'

'Thanks, but I'd better get back, too. Shouldn't leave poor Marilena with the shop for too long.'

'The signora OK these days?'

'No' too bad, though we'll never be close. I've given up expecting that.'

'And Nicco?'

Ruth's face lit up. 'Writes as often as he can, but the letters take so long to come, you'd wouldn't believe it. Seems fine, though. Standing up to the heat.'

'Well out of Europe, anyway.'

'That's what I say.'

Some days later, at a few minutes after five o'clock on 10 June, Mark, still feeling pleased with himself that he might soon be away, received a telephone call from a superior officer. When he had listened for a few moments, he put the phone down and summoned his sergeant to call the constables for a briefing. His face was white, and several times he ran his finger round his collar, where the sweat was beginning to gather.

Chapter Fifty-Eight

Ruth was closing up the shop, humming to herself. She couldn't say that she felt happy, for that would be too strong a word, but she thought she might admit to being cheerful. Fenella, Isa and Jack had arrived back from Kent the night before and Isa had come round that morning, full of news of Kester, all of it good. He hadn't told them much about his actual escape or of the hardships he'd suffered before it, though they could guess the details, but the wonderful thing for them, Isa said, was that he had become their old Kester again. It was as though his closeness to death had put things into perspective for him, and though he still felt guilt over what he'd done, he was no longer letting it colour his whole life. He'd been lucky, he'd come though a terrible ordeal with only a damaged leg that would soon heal. Now, it was up to him to set things right when the war was over, and in the meantime be grateful for the new chances he'd been given. And cut down on the drinking too!

'Aye, he looked us in the eyes and he told us we'd be proud of him one of these days,' Isa murmured, shedding a tear or two. 'So we said we were proud of him already. I asked him to forget all thae hard things I'd said before, and he said they were only what he deserved, but he'd no' sulk around any more, and do what he could to make up. Then your dad told him to give over worrying about making up and just get better, that was all we wanted.'

'Och, it's such a relief he's all right!' Ruth held her mother close. 'And more his old self too. Did he say how long he'd have to be in hospital?'

'He's no' sure. Might be a few weeks. When he's recovered enough, he'll be coming home on leave.' Isa sighed. 'And then it'll be back to active service, I suppose.'

They were silent for a moment, thinking what that active service might be. Fighting the Germans in Britain itself? Isa and Jack had seen some of the anti-invasion practices that were being carried out in Kent. The Home Guard digging trenches, setting up guns, and turning round signposts, to 'confuse the enemy', while some folk they'd met in the hospital had been given leaflets telling them what to do, if the Germans actually arrived. Jack had said afterwards, that it would be the Germans who'd be telling everybody what to do, if they arrived – and how!

Ruth had asked about Fenella. Och, she'd been very nice with Kester, Isa had grudgingly admitted. 'Brought him a load of magazines and some chocolate, where from, goodness knows. But he liked my fruit cake best! He said he'd no' had anything so good since he went to France!'

It had given Ruth a pleasantly warm feeling inside, to think that her brother was not only safe, but free from the depression that had burdened him for so long. Now, as she went about her routine duties of locking up and tidying the shop, it seemed to her that just now and again, even during a war, you could get good news. And that gave you hope, didn't it? Hope that one of these days, there'd be good news all round. The war would be over, Nicco would be home.

'Ruth!'

At the sound of her name, Ruth swung round. Her mother-in-law was standing at the top of the stairs, her face yellowish, her dark eyes seeming black against her pallor.

'What is it?' cried Ruth, running up the stairs. 'Is it Gina? Has something happened to Gina?'

But Gina was running towards her, arms outstretched. Nothing had happened to Gina.

'It is Il Duce,' gasped the signora. 'He has declared war. He has declared war against Britain and France.'

Ruth stood very still, holding her child in her arms. So, what they had feared had come. They had hoped against hope that it would not, but here it was. She could feel the colour draining from her face, knew she must be looking as pale as the signora, while Gina played with the string of beads round her neck.

'You heard it on the wireless?' she asked, with dry lips.

'Yes. On the six o'clock news.'

The six o'clock news. Everyone listened to that. Everyone would now know the situation.

'When will it happen? When will we be at war?'

'From midnight tonight.'

'From midnight.'

In just a few hours' time, their whole world would change. The two women on the stairs, gazing into each other's eyes, knew it and were powerless, there was nothing they could do.

'Come and eat,' the signora said, at last. 'Come, Gina, eat.'

After the meal, at which the adults had only picked, Ruth put Gina to bed, read her a story, then drew the curtains against the light of the June evening. Everything seemed so normal, yet was already so different. Already, in the flat, their home, there was the feel, the taste of fear, setting their lives apart from all that they had known before.

'There was something else on the news,' said the signora. 'The Germans have crossed the River Seine.'

'They'll soon be in Paris?'

'In days, the man said.'

'So France will fall.'

It didn't mean a great deal. They'd been prepared for it since Dunkirk. Defeat might be staring them in the face, but all they could think of was Mussolini's war.

'I hear something!' cried the signora suddenly.

'The phone in the shop,' said Ruth, listening. They couldn't always hear it when it rang after hours, but their ears must have been sharpened by the fear that gripped them.

'Answer it, Ruth!'

'Yes, I'm on my way.'

With shaking fingers, Ruth unlocked the flat door and ran down the stairs to the shop. The telephone was on the wall behind the counter; it was still ringing. She hesitated, then grasped the receiver.

'Ruth, is that you?' The voice was Mark Imrie's. 'Listen, I have some bad news. Guido Rietto has been arrested.'

'Oh, no!' Ruth's knees sagged and she sank to a stool. 'When?'

'Earlier this evening, at the *fascio*. All the men there were taken into custody. I've told Guido's family, and I thought I should tell you.'

'Thank you, Mark. What – what will happen?'

'I'm not sure, but his name is on a list we have of known fascists. He'll almost certainly be interned.' Mark's voice was strained; he cleared his throat. 'I can't talk now, but I just want to say to you to take special care at the moment. Have you got shutters for the windows?'

'Shutters? No. I'll be doing the black-outs when it gets dark. But what do you mean, Mark, what's wrong?'

'We've had reports of some activity against Italians in Leith Street. There may be trouble coming your way, too. Be sure that everything's secure, then go upstairs and don't come down. Ruth, are you listening? Have you heard what I've said?'

'Yes, yes, everything's locked. I'll do the black-outs and go upstairs now.'

'Good. Take care, then. I'll try to be in touch.'

Mark rang off and Ruth replaced the receiver. Her hands were already slippery with sweat, her heart thumping. She ran to the window and looked out, over the tops of the empty sweetie jars. All seemed quiet in Ginger Street, which was not yet dark, though the light was fading. She tried the door, which was securely locked, and was on the point of running back upstairs when the signora came down towards her.

'Who telephoned, Ruth?'

Ruth put her hand to her damp brow. 'The police. I'm – I'm sorry to say – Guido has been arrested.'

'Arrested!' The signora began to wring her hands. 'When? Why? Tell me, tell me!'

'The police have been to the *fascio* and taken the men who were there. Guido's name was on some list they've got, he will probably be interned.'

'I cannot believe this! He has done nothing wrong! Why should his name be on a list? What list?'

'Let's go upstairs, we'll be safer upstairs, the police said.'

'Safer?'

Ruth was trying to think of some way of soothing her mother-in-law without frightening her, when a series of loud knocks on the shop door made her jerk with fright herself. But it was Marilena. They recognised her voice.

'Ruth! Ruth! Let me in! Let me in!'

'Oh, God, Marilena, what are you doing here?' cried Ruth, letting her into the shop and re-locking the door behind her. 'It isn't safe!'

'Mamma, Mamma!' Marilena threw herself into her mother's arms. 'They have arrested my Guido! He has been taken to the police station! They rang the shop, they said they've taken all the men from the *fascio*!'

'We know, Marilena, we know.' Mother and daughter rocked together, tears streaming down their faces, as Ruth, on pins, stood watching, longing to get them out of the shop and up the stairs.

'Marilena,' she said at last. 'It's terrible what's happened, but we did think Guido would be interned, didn't we? We always said that. Now you have to think of yourself. It isn't going to be safe on the streets for Italians tonight. You'd better come up to the flat with your mother and me.'

'Come up to the flat?' Marilena's tear-stained face was horror-stricken. 'I have to get back to my Paulo! I can't stay, I only came to be with Mamma a moment, to tell her about Guido. Please, I must open the door.'

'You can't go, Marilena, I tell you, it could be dangerous!'

'There is no one out there,' said the signora, from the window. 'See, the street is empty. Unlock the door, Ruth, Marilena and I are going to Vittorio's. Marilena, wait, while I get my shawl.'

'Please, don't go out!' begged Ruth. 'My sister's husband told me, we must just go upstairs and stay there!'

'Who is going to attack ME?' asked the signora, from the stairs. 'Let them try! Now, I fetch my shawl.'

'Come with us, Ruth,' said Marilena. 'Let's all go to the café. We'll be safe there.'

'I can't come, I can't leave Gina, she is asleep.'

'Oh, poor Gina, poor little girl, sleeping like an angel, with all these terrible things happening!' Marilena was trembling, holding fast to Ruth's hand. 'When do you think I will be able to see Guido?'

'Tomorrow, I should think. Try not to worry, just get to the café as quickly as you can. Tell your father to clear the place, then go upstairs. Will you do that, Marilena?'

As the signora came sailing down, her black shawl around her head, her eyes snapping, Ruth unlocked the door, and watched the mother and daughter move away up the street. It was true that there was no one about, but the signora wasn't even hurrying. Marilena kept pulling her arm, she kept shaking her arm free. Heavens, what a spirit she had! Ruth ran back into the shop, put up the black-out frames and locked up again, intent now on getting herself up the stairs and into the flat, where she would barricade herself in and sit outside Gina's door all night, keeping watch. She had scarcely had time to look in on her daughter, before she heard the sound of voices outside.

Voices! For a moment, she stiffened, her fears running riot, then she ran to her bedroom window and looked down. A small crowd of men was below, all strangers to her. They were shouting things she couldn't hear, didn't want to hear, and she hastily drew back, out of sight. Please God, she prayed, let them go! But there came the sound of crashing glass. They were breaking the shop windows. Ruth, behind her curtain, did not move.

Chapter Fifty-Nine

After long moments, she looked down again at Ginger Street. The men had gone. Doors and windows were opening, neighbours were looking out, but the men had gone. To Vittorio's? Oh, God. She must phone, see what was happening, see if she could help. But what could she do? She had Gina to think of. Gina?

Ruth shot away to check on her daughter. Sleeping like an angel, Marilena had guessed, but now Gina was awake and crying.

'Frightened, Mammie, frightened!'

'Nothing to be frightened of, darling, Mammie's here. See, here's Rabbit, too.' Ruth found the faithful old soft toy and put him into Gina's outstretched arms. 'Just wait there a minute, now, Mammie has to check something. Be back in a flash!'

Down the stairs Ruth ran, and into the shop. She switched on the light, then instantly snapped it off again. The black-out frames had been dragged down, tossed to the floor, she daren't show a light. Would she be able to see? She was able to see. 'Oh, no, no,' she moaned. 'No!'

Glass was everywhere, all over the floor, over the groceries on the shelves, over the counter, over the potatoes in their bin. Both large windows had been shattered. Every glass sweetie jar had been broken. The few packets that had been on display had been opened and the contents thrown about, and the old advertisements for ice-cream and cigarettes had been hurled into the shop to join the glass fragments Ruth was crunching underfoot.

As she stood looking round at the devastation, rage replaced her

312

fear. To do this to innocent people! To do this to folk who were not the enemy, who, in fact had a loved one in the British Army! She longed now to confront the mob who'd done this, to scream and shout at them, hurt them, as they'd hurt her, but she knew that even to try that would have been foolish. She had Gina to think of, she must get Gina away, right away from Ginger Street, for there was no guarantee that the mob would not come back.

First, she tried to ring Vittorio's, but there was no reply. Next, she tried to ring her father, but didn't expect a reply and there was none; her folks rarely heard the shop phone from their flat, and had no phone of their own. Finally, she took a broom and swept a pathway through the glass to the front door.

Now, she thought, breathing hard, we'll go to Fenella's. Of all the family, she was the last person Ruth would want to go to for help, but her house was nearest yet not in Ginger Street, and that was what mattered.

Dressing Gina was a nightmare. The more she tried to hurry, the less Ruth could fit the plump little feet into socks and shoes, or do up buttons, but at last, Gina was ready, strapped into her pushchair, excited now and bright-eyed, trying to understand all the new things that were happening. 'Naughty!' she cried, when she saw the broken glass in the shop. 'All broken!' And Ruth, unlocking the door which was no longer going to keep anyone out, echoed, 'Naughty, yes, bad people have done this, but we'll clear it all up tomorrow.'

It was still not quite dark and she could see people she knew huddled together in the street. Some called to her – Vi Dochart, for one – but she didn't stop, she didn't want to stay in Ginger Street where a mob might find her. No, she must press on, reach Fenella's, only then would she be able to relax. Thank God, it wasn't far. Just down the main road, with its trams and people hurrying home before black-out time, then round the corner into the Grange. See, Gina, here was the house, Auntie Fenella's house, they would be safe now.

Fenella took her time answering the doorbell.

'Who is it?' she called at last through the letterbox.

'It's Ruth and Gina, Fenella. Can you help us out?'

'Help you out? How d'you mean?'

'If you could just open the door, Fenella, I could explain.'

There was the sound of the chain being removed and bolts drawn back, and Fenella appeared on the doorstep, looking beyond Ruth and Gina, up and down the street.

'What's happened?' she asked slowly.

'Some people have broken the shop windows, we had to get away.' Ruth's voice was trembling. 'Aren't you going to ask us in?'

'I've heard what's been going on. A neighbour came round, told me not to go out, in case any gangs came this way. There are crowds in Leith Street and other parts of the city. The police had to be called.'

'I'd heard about Leith Street. Where else?'

'Leith Walk, Union Place, Broughton Street – I don't know them all. But there've been terrible scenes.'

'All Italian shops being attacked?'

'Yes.' Fenella's face was expressionless. 'We're at war with Italy, you know.'

'And folk think shopkeepers are going to hurt them?'

'I always said it was a mistake to get mixed up with foreigners. Now we can all be put at risk.'

'You mean you? You think I'm putting you at risk?' Ruth could feel her anger rising again and clung desperately to her self-control. 'May I remind you, Fenella, that my husband isn't a foreigner and is actually in the British Army? Are you going to ask us in, or not?'

Fenella took a step backwards. It seemed she might be going to give way and let them in, but suddenly, still looking beyond them, she cried with obvious relief, 'Why, look who's here, Ruth, it's your parents!'

'Ma!' screamed Ruth. 'Dad!' She had never been more pleased to see anyone in her life before, and ran to them, half-crying, half-laughing. 'Oh, it's so good to see you! Oh, you don't know how good it is! But what are you doing here?'

'Looking for you,' said Jack. 'Soon as we heard what was going on in the city, we took the tram and came over.'

'We've seen the shop,' said Isa, taking Gina from her pushchair and cuddling her, and Rabbit, too. 'Och, what a sight, eh? If I could get my hands on the fellows who did that to your windows, there'd be murder done, I'm telling you!'

'Thought you might try to come here,' said Jack confidently. 'Thank God for you, Fenella, eh?'

Ruth glanced back at her sister-in-law, who lowered her eyes. Neither she nor Ruth said a word.

'Come on, then,' cried Isa. 'Let's away in and get this bairn to bed. Jack wants to go round to Ginger Street and board up your windows, Ruth. Anybody can get inside now, you ken. Quick, Fenella, put the kettle on.'

It was wonderful for Ruth, back at the shop, to have her father's solid presence, but all the time he was rooting round for wood in Nicco's stores, finding a hammer and nails, and cheerfully banging away at the window frames, Ruth was eaten up with anxiety for Vittorio's café. She'd tried phoning again, but there was still no reply, and she told Jack that as soon as she'd swept up the shattered glass, she'd have to go up the street to see what had happened.

'Aye, we'll go together, soon as I've finished this. It's no' marvellous, but it'll hold till I get a glazier round in the morning.' Jack shook his head. 'It's lucky you've no' been looted already.'

'Folk in Ginger Street wouldn't loot.'

'Folk in Ginger Street didn't break your windows. It's thae other madmen you've got to think about, going round smashing up half the city for no good reason.'

'Dad, why did they do it?' Ruth cried passionately. 'Some of the Italians here have lived in Edinburgh all their lives, they thought the Scots were their friends!'

'It's no' just here it's been happening, Ruth. I phoned the polis station. They said Italian shops and cafés have been attacked all over the country. The Italians are the enemy, you ken.'

'That's no' true, Dad. The Italians here aren't the enemy!'

'Aye, but some folk don't see it that way. It's like it was in the Great War, when little German shops had their windows broken, just like yours. Folk go crazy sometimes.'

Ruth shivered. 'Let's go soon, Dad. See what's happened to Vittorio's place.'

'Just let's get this notice done first.'

'What notice?'

Her father was busy writing on a piece of cardboard he'd found. 'This one. See what it says?'

'Oh, Dad! Business As Usual? You're never expecting me to open tomorrow?'

'I am, then! You show thae devils what you're made of, Ruth. Away now, and let's tack it up outside.'

Business As Usual. Ruth smiled at her father's defiant handiwork. Yes, she'd show them! She'd open the shop as usual, and be damned to the vandals. But would any customers come?

Chapter Sixty

Northern summer nights are rarely completely dark and, though there were no streetlights to pierce the black-out, when Ruth and Jack reached Vittorio's café, they could see what they had feared to see. Every window broken, chairs and tables flung into piles of shattered glass, menus tossed into the gutter. Of the family, there was no sign, and the upstairs windows were, of course, shrouded in black curtains.

'Place looks like it's been hit by a bomb,' Jack muttered. 'They'll niver have enough wood to board up thae windows.'

'Knock on the door,' said Ruth. 'They'll be upstairs.'

'You can walk in, if you want.'

'No, let's knock.'

A couple of neighbours came up, as Jack banged on the door, and stood staring in at the devastation.

'Terrible, eh? And thae Riettis such nice folk, and all! Who'd do this?'

Jack shook his head. 'Anybody at home?' he cried.

An upstairs window opened. A trembling voice asked, 'Who is it?'

'Ruth and her dad. Come to see how you are.'

'Ruth? A moment, please.' The window closed.

'That's Brigida,' Ruth whispered. 'Oh, poor soul, she sounds in a state.'

As the neighbours wandered away, Brigida appeared at the door and with her was Carlotta. In the darkness, their faces shone with

317

ghostly pallor and they held each other fast by linked arms, as though they would fall if they should part.

'Oh, Ruth,' whispered Brigida. 'Something terrible has happened here.'

'I know, they've done the same to the shop. My dad and I've been clearing up.'

The women glanced at Jack, but did not say his name.

'I don't mean this,' said Brigida, staring at the devastation in her husband's café.

'Not this!' Carlotta said with contempt.

'What, then?' asked Ruth desperately. 'What else has happened?'

'Vittorio has been arrested!' cried Brigida, and burst into tears. 'Federico and Bruno, too. Every Italian man is being arrested. The police will go on on all night till it is done.'

Ruth and Jack were taken upstairs to the living room, scene of so many cheerful meals and celebrations, wine drinkings and toasts. Now, dimly lit and very still, it was like a room of mourning, with Marilena sitting, waxen-faced, on a sofa, Renata next to her, and on a chair, with her head bent, Lucia, Renata's mother-in-law. When Renata saw Ruth, she came to embrace her, and they clung together.

'Tell me what happened,' Ruth said quickly.

It seemed that the authorities had long ago made plans for what would be done when Italy declared war. They had a list of names of known fascists who would be arrested at once – Guido's name would be on that list and maybe Federico's too. The fascist clubs would also be raided as a priority and any men present who were members would be taken into custody. After that, the police would go from house to house, arresting all Italian males between seventeen and sixty, who had lived in Great Britain for less than twenty years. A friend of Vittorio's had come hurriedly to the café and given them this information, which had been been passed to him from someone in London. He had advised Vittorio to run away, he was about to do that himself, but Vittorio, being over sixty, had believed himself safe. He had not been safe.

'Why did they take him?' cried Ruth. 'Why take Federico's father?'

Renata shrugged. 'They made a mistake. I daresay a lot of mistakes will be made tonight.'

'But everyone's been here for more than twenty years!'

'If you are a member of the *fascio*, it doesn't matter how long you've lived here, you'll still be arrested. They are looking for true fascists. They think they might be working for Italy.'

'Spies, you mean?' asked Jack. 'I suppose it's possible.'

Lucia raised her head and looked at him with stormy eyes. 'My Federico is no spy! He is no fascist! All he did was admire Il Duce, and we all admire Il Duce!'

'Guido isn't really a fascist, either,' cried Marilena. 'He would never want to hurt people, like the Nazis do!'

But Guido had admitted to his fascism, thought Ruth, and so had Federico, there was the problem. She touched her father's arm.

'I think we should go now, Dad. I must get back to see how Gina is settling.'

'You're not sleeping at the flat?' asked Renata.

'No, at Fenella's. The shop windows are shattered and all the things broken and thrown about. We've been trying to clear up.'

'And for people who do these things, my son is fighting a war?' asked Carlotta fiercely.

'No,' Jack told her quietly. 'For people like you and me.'

She was silent, as he took Brigida's hand and said he wished he could do something to help. He knew a glazier, a personal friend, who might be able to replace Ruth's windows. Should he ask him to come to the café?

'No, no,' Brigida answered wearily. 'What does it matter about the café? We are closing it. All I want is to have my husband home.'

'We are going to the police station tomorrow,' said Renata. 'We all want our husbands home.'

Ruth thought of them next morning, as she opened up her battered little shop. Brigida and Renata, Marilena and Lucia, all desperately converging on the police station, along with other Italian wives trying to see their husbands. But the country was at war, aliens had to be interviewed and if they represented a danger, interned. Oh, but only then! Surely Vittorio was no threat, nor poor Bruno. Mistakes will be made, Renata had said, and had been made already.

Ruth, leaning on her counter, longed for Nicco. He would know by now that Italy had declared war on the country he was fighting for, and must be feeling torn apart, so far away, so helpless to do anything for his family. And his family, like other British Italians, was torn apart, too, by divided loyalties. Yet now it seemed they were being given no credit by the authorities for any loyalty to Britain at all.

The shop bell pinged and Ruth raised her head. A customer? No, several. Vi Dochart, Sarah MacAllan, old Mrs Fyfe, Mrs Dobson, Mrs Burns, and others Ruth couldn't see for sudden tears misting her eyes.

'Hello, hen! How are you?' Vi cried, and the others began wandering round the shop, making a running commentary as they went. 'What a thing, eh, thae devils doing all this to the shop? What's the polis doing? Nothing, as usual! Och, the shame of it, attacking folk like you, that niver did any harm. What've you got left, though? Any rations this morning? I'm desperate for ma butter and a bit bacon!'

'I think we're all right except for potatoes,' Ruth said. 'They're all covered in glass, I'd better no' sell them.'

Then she did burst into tears and the women gathered round and said was there nobody to make a cup o' tea? Poor lassie! No need to cry. Thae folk who did this to the shop'd be strangers and would get short shrift if they put their faces back in Ginger Street, so they would. People in Ginger Street were friends of the Italians, friends of Ruth's, she need niver think any other!

'Glass?' cried a voice outside, and a man in white overalls appeared at the door. 'Mind yourselves, ladies, let's get started, then.'

'All back to normal in no time, eh?' asked Sarah MacAllan cheerfully, but Ruth blew her nose and shook her head. Back to normal? She didn't know about that.

320

Chapter Sixty-One

The Italian wives did see their husbands, but very briefly. Marilena and Renata were able to hand over a few toilet articles and a change of clothes to Guido and Federico, then were asked to leave. Vittorio and Bruno, arrested at home, had been allowed to pack a small bag and needed nothing. Except their freedom. The imploring looks in their eyes haunted their wives all the way home. When Carlotta asked how the men had been, Lucia and Brigida could only sob, and were soon joined in tears by Marilena, but Renata sat, dry-eyed, with her baby on her knee, and spoke to no one.

'Guido says he is to be interviewed by Inspector Imrie,' Marilena said, when she was calmer. 'And you know who he is, don't you? Sylvie Millar's husband! What justice will my Guido contract?'

'Ruth has told me that Mark Imrie is a good man,' said Brigida. 'I pray he will be fair.'

'The police are not always fair,' Lucia muttered, drying her eyes. 'The women today – some had stories to tell of the way the police behaved when they arrested their men.'

'We were lucky, then, they were polite to us,' said Marilena. 'But I don't trust Mark Imrie. What will he do to Guido?'

Across the city, over a table in a police interviewing room, Guido and Mark Imrie faced each other, while a constable stood at the door. Mark, though he gave no sign of it, was feeling considerable apprehension; dealing with Guido Rietti was something he would have liked to avoid. No doubt Guido knew that. When his eyes met

Mark's, they had taken on that hard blue glitter he liked to affect, and were also a little amused. He had been allowed a cigarette, and as the smoke from it drifted across his face, he smiled.

'Well, Inspector, now you've got me where you want me, eh? Or, think you have.'

'I don't understand you,' said Mark.

'Come on, you've always wanted to get back at me, haven't you? We both know why.'

'All I want you to do, Signor Rietti, is answer my questions truthfully.'

'Or, else?' Guido leaned forward. 'I know the way police behave. All police.'

'Not here,' said Mark. 'We have rules to follow.'

'There've been some complaints about the way folk were arrested last night. Did you know that?'

'Yes, I know it, and I'll be looking into it.' Mark's voice roughened. 'Just leave the questions to me, Signor Rietti.'

Guido sat back. 'You talk about rules. You weren't supposed to arrest any men over sixty, so why's my father been arrested, then? And Signor Martinello?'

'It may have been they had no proof of their ages. Mistakes happen. I'll be looking into their arrests.'

Guido grinned. 'You're going to be pretty busy, Inspector, looking into so many things!'

'We know you are a member of the *fascio* here,' Mark said equably. 'Do you admit to membership of the British Union of Fascists?'

Guido stopped smiling. 'Yes, what of it? I joined when I was in London. Is that where you got my name?'

'So you're a committed fascist?'

'Yes. Committed, and proud of it!'

'You would be willing to work for the party against the democratic government of this country?'

Guido hesitated. 'I don't say that.'

'But you go along with the belief that the state should be ruled by one powerful leader?'

'Of course. And in Italy, that leader is Il Duce.'

'And all individuals must obey the leader?'

Guido nodded. 'Absolutely true.'

'So, if Il Duce told you to work against this country, you would do so?'

'You're trying to trap me, Inspector. I knew you would.'

'I'm just trying to establish whether you're an enemy of the state. That's my job.'

'I'm a fascist, that's all I'm prepared to say. If you want to send me to the Isle of Man, that's up to you.'

'I can't say where you will be sent eventually. To begin with, you'll be going to Lancashire.'

'Lancashire? I thought all aliens went to the Isle of Man?'

'A decision will be made when you reach the centre in Lancashire.' Mark stood up. 'That'll be all for now. The constable will take you back to the cells.'

Guido's face was dark. 'Where else could I be sent?' he pressed. 'I don't want to be sent abroad, I want to be able to see my wife and son.'

'I've told you, I can't say where you'll be sent. It will be up to the people in Lancashire to decide. Constable!'

As the policeman at the door stepped forward, Guido gave Mark one last scowl. It was plain that meeting him again had brought back memories of what Guido considered his humiliation at Mark's hands, and that he was brooding over it, even at a time when his whole future was in doubt. The constable touched his arm, told him to get a move on, and Guido finally, reluctantly, turned and went out. Thank God for that, thought Mark, now I've got to see his father.

The news for Vittorio and for Bruno Martinello was good. As they had both lived in Scotland for more than twenty years and appeared to have no real connection with the fascist movement, Mark told them they were free to go home.

'Home?' cried Vittorio. 'I can't believe it! You mean it, Inspector? You mean it?'

'You are not a fascist, Signor Rietti, and over sixty anyway. You should never have been arrested.'

'There are plenty of men over sixty in the cells, Inspector, some who've lived in Scotland for many years.'

'Yes.' Mark admitted uneasily. 'Mistakes have been made.'

'And what of my son, Inspector? And Signor Martinello's son?'

Vittorio asked the questions, but both he and Bruno already knew the answers. Their sons must face internment, there was no argument that could be made against it, though they did not expect their wives to see the situation that way. When the first euphoria of their husbands' homecoming had subsided, both Brigida and Lucia declared that their sons must be allowed home too. Why should they be sent to Lancashire, and then to some unknown destination? They had done nothing wrong, only supported Il Duce. Ruth must go to the police station and speak to her brother-in-law, make him send Guido and Federico home.

Of course, Ruth did not go to the police station. While their mothers were passionately crying for their release, Guido and Federico had already been moved to Lancashire, from where Federico was sent to the Isle of Man, and Guido was sent to Liverpool to set sail aboard the SS *Arandora Star* for Canada. He never reached it. On 2 July, the ship was torpedoed off the coast of Ireland by a German U-boat. Over 400 Italian men were amongst those who lost their lives. It was some time before his family knew if Guido had been one of them.

Chapter Sixty-Two

As soon as news came of the tragedy, the Rietti family was, of course, distraught. Marilena, though she did not yet know if she had lost Guido, was inconsolable. Vittorio, who had been considering re-opening his café, fell ill with a summer cold that turned to bronchitis and had to be nursed by a weeping Brigida, while the windows of the café remained boarded up. Renata came every day to see Marilena, who would only turn her head away from her cousin, because Federico was safe in the Isle of Man and her Guido could be at the bottom of the ocean and they didn't even know. As for Carlotta, her face was tragic. She could scarcely bring herself to speak to Ruth, who, because she was not Italian, could not possibly understand what Italians were going through at that time.

'I do understand, I do!' Ruth would cry, but her mother-in-law would only shake her head. This was Italian grief, Ruth was outside it.

Perhaps I am, thought Ruth, but the loss of the *Arandora Star* still occupied her mind and presented the kind of question that was soon being asked of the authorities. Why had so many men drowned, and should they have been on the ship in the first place? It was beginning to be apparent that many of the Italians on board were not the fascists they were thought to be, and many were over-age, too. Mistakes had been made when they were selected to be sent to Canada, along with German prisoners-of-war and Jewish refugees, and further mistakes came to light when it was revealed that the ship had had too few lifeboats and nobody seemed to know how to organise the evacuation when the torpedo struck. Many of the Italians could not swim and stood little chance of surviving without boats, and what boats there were were sometimes so badly lowered, they hit men already in the water. An official enquiry was promised from the government, but that would be for the future. What Italians wanted to know, there and then, was who had died and who had been saved? Not knowing only increased the relatives' suffering, but information was slow to be released. This time, no one asked Ruth to speak to Mark Imrie; she thought of doing that herself.

It seemed to her that it would be best to see him at home, rather than at the police station, and arranged to call one evening at the bungalow off the Queensferry Road. Sylvie had set chairs in the garden, for the weather was still fine and warm, and had managed to find some lemonade. All so civilised, thought Ruth. Who would think there was a war on? Yet Mark was preparing to join an RAF unit very soon; he had been accepted for training as a non-commissioned navigator and was up to his eyes in last-minute work at the station. Ruth had been lucky he'd been able to snatch even one evening at home.

'I'm very grateful to you for seeing me,' Ruth told him. 'I wouldn't have troubled you, but the Riettis are in such a state, not knowing what's happened to Guido. Well, all the Italian families who had folk on that ship feel the same. Why can't they be given news?'

'It's difficult, Ruth.' Mark hesitated. 'You have to remember that bodies are still being washed ashore. I don't think it's known yet who is dead.'

'But there were survivors who were picked up by another ship, weren't they? Why can't their names be released?'

'There's been some confusion about some of their papers. Some swapped with others, to be with family, that sort of thing. Getting out accurate lists takes time.'

'Can you do anything to help, that's what I've come to ask?' Ruth finished her lemonade and looked around Sylvie's peaceful garden. 'You can't imagine what it's been like for the Italian families lately.'

326

'I can. I know it's been hell for them, and I know they must think this tragedy is just the last straw.' Mark shook his head. 'I can't promise anything, can't get out proper lists, or anything, but I'll try to find out about Guido. I do know that the injured were taken to various Scottish hospitals. He could be in one of them.'

'The one ray of hope is that he could swim. He used to go to the Glenogle swimming baths with Kester, and sometimes Portobello.'

'I expect he'd be a good swimmer,' Sylvie said in a low voice. 'Poor Guido.'

There was a silence, until Ruth said she must go. Sylvie walked with her to the gate, after Mark said he'd be in touch.

'It's terrible, to think of Guido being drowned, Ruth.' Sylvie swung the gate to and fro. 'He was such a lovely dancer, eh? But I'm really thinking of Mark.'

'Mark?' Ruth stared.

'Something could happen to him, just like it happened to Guido. Then I'd be like poor Marilena.'

'We don't know yet what's happened to Guido,' Ruth said uncomfortably. She knew that she was considered lucky bcause her own husband was out of things. But who knew how long that would last? Giving her sister a quick hug and a kiss but no words of comfort, for she knew of none that would not sound hollow, she hurried home. No doubt Mark would do his best, but she had no great hopes that he would find anything out, or that it would be good news, even if he did. Which was why, when he came round to the shop a few days later, she looked at him with no expectations at all.

'Ruth, aren't you going to ask me why I'm here?' he asked her gently.

She glanced at the customers who were studying the uniformed Mark with interest, and suddenly felt overwhelming fear. He had come in person. To break bad news?

'It's good news,' he said quickly, reading her thoughts. 'Guido's alive.'

She made him go up the stairs with her to tell the signora, who was sitting watching Gina play with a basket of clothes pegs, her face a mask of strain. As soon as she saw Mark, she rose to her feet, summoning all her dignity, all her strength, to meet the challenge of his news.

'Is Guido?' she whispered.

'He's safe!' cried Ruth. 'The Inspector has come to tell us. Guido's been injured, but he was picked up and taken to hospital. He's going to be all right!'

For a moment, the signora's face seemed to disintegrate, as she relaxed her efforts at composure, then her mouth straightened and the muscles around her eyes tightened; she was herself again. '*Grazie*,' she said simply, and shook first Mark's hand, and then Ruth's. Ruth knew that if they had been Italians, her mother-in-law would have been weeping by now and flinging her arms around them, but it didn't matter, they didn't need a show of emotion. That little word, '*grazie*', said everything that came from the signora's heart.

'Let me take Gina downstairs,' said Ruth, picking up the little girl and her pegs. 'You go to the café and tell Marilena and everyone.'

'Then we go to the church and give thanks to God,' said the signora, taking up her shawl. 'He has been good to us.'

'And you've been good, Mark,' Ruth told him, as the signora, in spite of her bulk, moved from the shop with astonishing speed. 'I can't thank you enough for what you've done.'

'I was glad to do it. Should maybe have gone directly to the wife, she's next of kin, but I thought I'd frighten her out of her wits, arriving in uniform.'

'No, it's better to let my mother-in-law tell her and Guido's folks. Then they can celebrate together.' Ruth's own look was serious, however, as she moved with Mark to the shop door. 'But I suppose it'll only be a temporary celebration, won't it? Guido will still have to go to Canada?'

'I don't think so. I'm told he probably won't be fit enough to make a long ocean voyage for some time. Looks like he'll end up in the Isle of Man, after all.'

'Oh, Mark!' Ruth kissed his cheek. 'That's such a relief, I can't tell you!'

'Nothing to do with me, but I'll take the credit for it,' he said, smiling. 'Nice to know I'm no' always the bogeyman!'

'Bogeyman? You're the nicest policeman I know.'

'I'm the only one you know, aren't I?'

'Take care,' she said quietly. 'And good luck.'

'Good luck!' echoed Gina, and as Mark left them, still smiling, the customers at the counter smiled too, and said what a bright bairn Gina was and what a nice fellow the policeman seemed.

Sometimes things work out for us, thought Ruth, and did not try to look into the future. Better not.

Part Five

Chapter Sixty-Three

Sitting in Sylvie's garden on a summer's day in 1942, Isa was reflecting on the recent past and thinking they'd been lucky. That was what Jack had said, after the Battle of Britain, and the family had agreed with him. When the bombs had begun to fall on London and other cities in late summer, they'd thought as everyone had, that the raids were a prelude to invasion. Next would come the troops, for that was Hitler's way, that was how he'd always conquered. But the troops had never come. The RAF defeated Hitler's air force as early as October, and though the raids continued until 1941, there was no longer any danger of German occupation.

Aye, Jack had been right to say, 'Have we no' been lucky?' Especially, living in Edinburgh, which unlike Glasgow and so many other cities, had suffered so little in the bombing. They'd a lot to be grateful for, and that was the truth. Thinking of the hundreds who'd died in the raids, firemen as well, and the thousands who'd lost everything they had, folk in Edinburgh felt a certain guilt they'd got off so lightly. But what could you do? Send your sympathy and thank God it wasn't you. Och, but it would take years to get things back to normal, and your heart went out to the poor folk who'd suffered. Nothing much could be done until the war ended. If it ever did.

Would the war ever end? It seemed to Isa on that tranquil summer's day in Sylvie's garden, so far from the worst of things, that it only seemed to be spreading, covering the whole world in a great

333

suffocating cloud. Greece, North Africa, Russia, the Far East. Everywhere you looked, there was fighting. In December 1941, America and Britain had declared war on Japan, following Japan's attack on the American navy at Pearl Harbor. Germany, already at war with Russia, had declared war on America; Italy had done the same. Britain had declared war on Finland, Hungary and Rumania. Japan had marched into Burma and North Borneo. Seemed, as soon as you opened your paper, there was news of someone else going to war, or being marched on, or being bombed.

'You think it canna get worse, and then it does,' Isa told Sylvie, who had arrived with the tea. 'And all the men scattered. Your Mark in thae planes, our Kester working with tanks – he'll be next for the desert, I daresay, fighting thae Italians. Good job Nicco's no' there, eh?' Isa shook her head. 'You ken who's best off? Thae two that don't deserve it. Yon Guido and Federico. Safe as houses over in the Isle of Man!'

'Houses aren't particularly safe at the moment, Ma,' Sylvie answered, passing a plate of slices of the national wholemeal loaf that was all anyone could buy. 'Sorry, I've no scones. D'you want some jam?'

'Aye, I'll need some jam to get that bread down. Now, you ken well what I mean about thae two fellows, eh? It just doesn't seem fair to me, that they should be so well off over there, when our lads are under fire.'

'Where else could they be, Ma? They won't fight for us. You're no' suggesting they should be allowed to fight for Italy? Anyway, it can't be much fun for them, being interned.'

'Fun? Who's expecting fun these days!' Isa drank some tea, to take away the taste of the jam she said, which, though it had come from Jack's shop, had been made, she'd bet her life, from anything but fruit and sugar. 'And isn't it true that their wives are allowed to visit them, then? With the bairns as well? Think how long it's been since poor Ruth saw Nicco!'

'And I've seen Mark,' sighed Sylvie. Every time she looked up at the sky, she thought of him. He was in Lancaster bombers now. Would he be on 'ops'? Would he be going over Germany? Every

334

time the doorbell rang, she prepared herself for a telegram. Every time she listened to the news, she expected to hear of planes having been shot down and to learn that one was Mark's. All these feelings were so usual to her now, they might have become dull in their impact; instead they cut her with sharper and sharper blades and she knew there would be no respite until she had Mark home again. Now, she called to Ronnie, playing at the bottom of the garden, to come and have his jammie piece.

'You're right, Ma,' she murmured. 'There's no end to it. I just take one day at a time, to get through.'

'That's the way,' Isa agreed, smiling on her grandson, who seemed not to mind at all the taste of the jam on his bread and margarine.

Chapter Sixty-Four

It was true, that Renata and Marilena had been allowed to visit their husbands in internment on the Isle of Man, but these visits were never happy. Both men were depressed, staring out from behind barbed wire at a world rocked by a war in which they could take no part. Italians, their fellow-countrymen, were fighting desperately alongside the Germans in Libya, while they were imprisoned, helpless and frustrated, deprived of any purpose. Though they appreciated being able to see their wives, in a way the visits only made them feel worse, for the women were free to leave, taking the beloved children with them, while they, because they were men, must stay where they were, behind the wire.

'I tell you, I sometimes feel like cutting my throat,' Guido told Marilena dramatically on one occasion, and took perverse pleasure in seeing her eyes widen with terror.

'You wouldn't, you wouldn't!' she cried. 'Oh, think of Paulo, Guido! Think of me!'

'It's all right, I'm not going to do it. Just feel like it sometimes.'

'But you're safe, Guido, that's the thing to remember. Even your leg's better now, and that's wonderful, isn't it?'

Guido's leg, badly broken when he was hit by wreckage after the sinking of the *Arandora Star*, had taken months to heal. There had even been a time when he would shake his head and say that he would never dance again, but the fears had passed and the breaks had mended. Still, he could not shake off his malaise, and even if the war should come to an end, felt he would never forgive the British for inflicting this imprisonment on him.

'It's your own fault,' Renata told him crisply. 'And the same goes for Federico. Always complaining about being here, but you could get out any time you like, if you'd just agree to help the war effort.'

'The British war effort?' Guido asked coldly. 'Is it likely I'm going to do that? We Italians here have no intention of doing war work.'

'It wouldn't be fighting, just farm work, or clearing up bomb damage. Next time they ask you if you'd be willing to help, say yes. Why don't you?'

'We're not discussing it, are we Federico?'

But Federico's eyes slid away from Guido's. 'I've been thinking of it,' he said in a low voice.

'You what?'

'I want out, Guido. It's getting me down, being here. I don't think I can stand it much longer. When the next tribunal sits, I'm going to say I'll join the Pioneer Corps.'

'Thank God,' said Renata softly. 'Guido, are you listening?'

'I'm listening, all right, but I'm not understanding.' Guido's face was white with rage. 'Do you realise what you'll get from the guys here, if you do that, Federico? You'll be going against all that we believe, you'll be making a mockery of the stand we've taken.'

'I've been thinking about what I've believed, Guido.' Federico gave a bitter smile. 'I've had the time to think, in here. And I'm not sure now if I believe in Il Duce any more. The things he did for us, OK, they were good. But think about the other things. The way people have suffered, because of him, that can't be right, you know.'

'Well, how convenient!' spat Guido. 'Just when you need to renounce Il Duce to get out of this camp, you find you want to renounce him, anyway! Who are you trying to fool, Federico?'

'Leave him alone!' snapped Renata. 'He's doing the right thing. Why should he waste his life in here for something he doesn't believe in any more? He's needed outside. I need him!'

'You won't even see him if he's in the Pioneer Corps!'

'He'll get leave and it'll make all the difference to me. Times are pretty miserable for us, Guido. The café's closed for the duration, Mamma's had to find a job in a factory canteen and I'm working sewing parachutes. I've had to ask Federico's mother to see to Paulo.'

'Everybody has to work, Renata. There's a war on, so they tell me.'

'Yes, well Federico can work as well, instead of being stuck behind barbed wire!' Renata, breathing hard, turned back to her husband. 'You get out of here, Federico, after the very next tribunal, OK? And you, Marilena, talk some sense into this brother of mine. Get him out of here, too.'

Marilena's lips parted, she put out her hand. 'Guido,' she began, but he flung back his head and would not look at her.

'No, Marilena, I won't do it. Don't ask me.'

While Renata groaned in exasperation, Marilena let her hand fall. She knew better than to say any more.

She said a great deal to her mother, though, on her return from the Isle of Man.

'It's terrible, Mamma! There's Renata so lucky, with Federico coming out of the camp, and me so miserable, with Guido staying in! I never even knew about these tribunals, he never told me, but seems if you promise to do work for the war effort, they let you out. And he won't do it! Won't even think about it!' Marilena burst into tears. 'Can you believe it?'

'Of course I can believe it,' her mother answered sternly. 'Guido is only doing what he sees as right, and a lot of Italians would agree with him. You'd have agreed with him yourself not so long ago.'

'Maybe, but things have changed. I can't think the same of Il Duce any more, now that he's making Italy fight with the Germans. That's how Federico feels. Why can't Guido feel the same? Why can't he see that it's wrong to conquer other countries all the time? Why can't we all just live in peace?'

'You're talking about things you know nothing about,' her mother told her. 'It's not for you to tell your husband what to do. If Renata's Federico wants to give up his beliefs in Il Duce, that's up to him, but Guido is sticking to his principles and you should admire him for it.'

'Mamma's always the same,' Marilena murmured to Ruth on her way out through the shop. 'Always thinks a man knows best!'

'Unless he disagrees with her,' Ruth answered, smiling wryly. 'She didn't think Nicco knew best when he wanted to join the British Army.'

'I think she's accepted that now.' Marilena's gaze was compassionate. Ruth seemed weary, and why wouldn't she be? Working so hard in the shop all the time, coping with Mamma, waiting for letters from a husband at the other end of the world. 'How is Nicco, Ruth?'

'Pleased he's made corporal. But I don't hear from him very often these days and when he does write, he can't say much.' Ruth pushed back the hair from her brow and shook her head. 'I get the feeling he is involved in fighting, though. Tribesmen who don't want the British, maybe.'

'At least, he's not fighting Italians.'

'Fighting's fighting,' Ruth said shortly. 'You can still get killed.'

'Couldn't he get leave?' asked Marilena, after a moment. 'I mean, soldiers do get leave, they can't keep going for ever.'

'Oh, he gets local leave, but he can't come home. Not from India.'

'We thought it was so wonderful when he was posted there, didn't we?'

'Had its price. Like everything.' Ruth straightened her shoulders and smiled. 'Sorry, I'm getting gloomy. Never does any good. Let's see if I can find a sweetie for Paulo, then.'

Never did any good to get gloomy, that was for sure, but sometimes she couldn't help it. When Marilena had left her, Ruth's smile died and though she kept herself busy, serving her customers, she could not raise her spirits again. Maybe when she got another letter, she'd feel better. At least, then, she'd have confirmation that Nicco was still alive. In the meantime, no news was good news.

The shop phone rang when she was locking up. Always sent her heart to her mouth, in case it was somebody telling her something she didn't want to hear. But it was only her mother.

'That you, Ruthie? Listen, I've just had Fenella round here. She's joined the WRNS, after all! Aye, she's away down to Portsmouth in September, can you credit it?'

'Always did fancy the uniform, Ma.'

'But now there'll be nobody at home when our Kester comes back on leave.'

'Is he coming back on leave?'

'No.' Isa's voice was suddenly choked with tears, and Ruth realised she was now getting the true message of her mother's call. 'The battalion's going abroad. Niver said where, but I guess it'll be North Africa, eh? They'll be going to fight that awful man, the one they call the Desert Fox. Rommel.'

'Had to happen, Ma. Try no' to worry.'

Oh, what a waste of time it was, coming out with words like that, thought Ruth, putting down the phone.

Chapter Sixty-Five

Kester's battalion did fight Rommel, at the battle of El Alamein, which ended in victory for the Allies. The newsreels at the cinema were the most cheerful things anyone had seen for months, and Isa was always sure she could see Kester in them somewhere, leaning against a tank, smiling, waving a cap in the air, at which Jack would tell her no' to be so daft, that wasn't their Kester! All the same, it had been a great victory for the Eighth Army and all involved, and General Montgomery was a great man. Sent the Desert Fox running, eh? Aye, the Germans and the Italians were in retreat, heading for Tunisia. This could be the turning point of the war.

Federico, preparing to leave the internment camp, said the same thing to Guido.

'That battle – El Alamein – could be the turning point, Guido. The Germans and Italians are in retreat. You'd better start making your plans.'

'What plans?'

'For what you'll do, if Italy loses.'

'Who says Italy is going to lose? All right, they've lost this battle. What's one battle? You're saying Rommel's going to give up because he's lost one battle?'

'I'm saying that the Germans are not as good as they thought they were, and they've taken on more than they can handle with Russia. Il Duce should pull out while he can.'

Guido looked at Federico with dislike. 'You mean, run away?'

'I mean, try for peace.'

'You mean, run away. Il Duce will not run away.' Guido turned away his head. 'If you're going, Federico, just go.'

'Come with me, Guido! Come on, why not? What's the point of staying here, listening to bad news?'

Federico put his hand on Guido's shoulder, but Guido instantly shook it off.

'Don't touch me!'

'Guido—'

'I said, don't touch me. Don't speak to me. I don't want anything more to do with you.'

'Guido, you can't talk to me like that. I'm married to your sister—'

'Forget it. You've split the family, just like Nicco did. Only you're worse than Nicco, because he never pretended to be a fascist and you did.' Guido's lip curled. 'When I remember how you used to pretend to admire Il Duce, say how much he was doing for us, how we should all follow him, it makes me sick to see you now. Crawling to the British, just to get out of here! Federico, you should be ashamed!'

Federico, standing like a child being admonished, flinched from Guido's words as from blows. 'I can't believe you are talking to me this way, Guido. My brother – my friend!'

'No friend. No friend ever again.' Guido turned his back. Over his shoulder, he called, 'Goodbye, Federico. That's my last word to you.'

After a long agonised moment, Federico turned and left him. It was time to go, anyway, the transport was waiting. Soon, he would be back on the mainland. Not travelling towards Renata, of course, but on his way to the depot for the Pioneer Corps. It would be some time before he would be allowed leave for home and the way he felt then, he didn't want it. Not if he were to meet other Italians who would treat him as Guido had treated him, see him as a disgraceful, 'bad' Italian, a man with no loyalty to his leader. Yet he had no loyalty now for Mussolini. For once in his life, he had made up his own mind and would stick to it. Come what may, he had done what he saw as right, and would not regret it.

*   *   *

Guido, left with his fellow-fascists, also harboured no regrets. At least, none he would acknowledge, just as he refused to acknowledge that he was going to miss Federico. He'd always been fond of his large, generous brother-in-law, and there was no doubt that his presence had made internment more bearable. Yet, with his conscious mind, Guido dismissed Federico with contempt. Everything he'd said to him was true, he never wanted to see or speak to him again. Underneath the top layer of consciousness, though, lay the sharp pang of loss, and he now lit one of his few, precious cigarettes, to help him defy it.

As though he wouldn't have given anything to be leaving this camp with Federico! Oh, God, yes. To be free, to be with Marilena again when he could get leave, to make love, hold her, hold his little son. Of course, he wanted that. Everyone in the camp wanted the same, to be free, to be able to see their families. But they had principles. They followed Il Duce and were loyal to him, they were loyal to Italy, and being loyal to Italy did not mean digging trenches or clearing bomb damage for the British. Those who chose such a way to freedom, would never again be considered true Italians, and if they could live with that, so be it. He, Guido, would never be in that position. Whatever happened.

When he had smoked his cigarette to its end and reluctantly thrown it away, he wondered why those words had come into his mind. 'Whatever happened.' What meaning could they have had? Defeat? For Il Duce? He swept the thought away.

Chapter Sixty-Six

In spite of all the triumphant newsreel pictures she kept seeing, Isa was beginning to worry. Kester had been so lucky ever since Dunkirk. How long could his luck hold out?

'I went right through the Great War,' Jack reminded her. 'Nothing happened to me.'

'Aye, but that doesn't mean Kester'll do the same.'

'He'll be OK. He's got my luck.'

Not altogether, for he was wounded at Tunis. While the Allies were celebrating a great victory, at which thousands of Italian and German prisoners were taken, Kester was being sent back home to a hospital near Glasgow.

'Aye, it's me in trouble again,' he wrote home himself. 'Shot in the right leg, same as before. Here's hoping I've still got it, when you come.'

'Oh, no!' cried Isa in horror. 'Oh, Jack, he'll no' lose his leg, will he?'

How could Jack answer that? All he could say was that they should be thankful Kester was alive, and back in his own country.

'Oh, but to lose a leg!' moaned Isa. 'He's no' the sort to manage, eh? He niver could put up with anything, could Kester.'

As it turned out, he didn't have to put up with the loss of a leg. He might have to walk with a limp, but some luck still clung to him, he would not require an amputation.

'Oh, yes, I've been lucky, all right,' he told Ruth, when she visited him, but there was a dark look in his eye that made her heart sink. 'Lucky Kester, that's me.'

'Is there something else?' she asked hesitantly. 'Something you haven't told us about?'

'Well, seems my name's John now.' He laughed and tossed a letter across his bed. 'According to this.'

'John? What are you talking about?'

'Never heard of a Dear John letter? I got one yesterday. Read it. Go on, I want you to.'

Ruth opened the letter. 'Kester, it's from Fenella. I can't read a private letter from your wife.'

'First line'll do. Go on, read it. OK, I'll read it for you. No, I'll recite it, I know it by heart.' Kester raised himself slightly in his bed, not moving his leg under its cage, and fixing his eyes on Ruth's face, whispered:

'"Dear Kester. This is going to be a very difficult letter to write, and I can't tell you how sorry I am to be writing it now, but you know these things happen, and I hope you'll understand . . ." Need any more?'

'No,' Ruth answered grimly. 'That's enough. Who's she met?'

'A naval officer, of course. An English lieutenant, down in Portsmouth. Just couldn't help herself, was completely bowled over, he felt the same.' Kester laughed again. 'What could she do? As she says, it happens all the time.'

'Oh, Kester, I don't know what to say. It's terrible for you, really terrible! To get news like that when you're injured, as well!'

'She didn't know I was going to get injured, I suppose, when she fell for this guy.'

'She knew when she wrote to you. Have you told Ma?'

'Not yet. Thought you might tell her.'

'Me? Oh, Kester, she'll blow up!'

'She'll no' be sorry, though. None of you'll be sorry. Will you?'

'It's no good trying to pretend we liked Fenella.'

'Aye, well, maybe we were always wrong for each other. I was just so crazy about her, though. And she seemed keen on me.'

'I think that's true.'

'In the early days.' He shrugged. 'Now it's next stop the divorce courts.'

'Divorce?' Ruth's eyes widened. 'Kester, she's asked you for a divorce?'

'What else? Can't marry the English officer if she's still married to me, can she?'

'Ma will never recover. Am I supposed to tell her about the divorce as well?'

'You could say it won't be till the war's over.'

'If you weren't in a hospital bed, I'd never agree!'

'I'll soon be out, wearing my hospital blue suit and my red tie, leaning on my stick. Quite the hero, eh?'

'Oh, Kester!'

'You realise I'll no' be going back? No more fighting for me. They don't want dot and carry ones in the army, you ken.'

'At least, you're alive,' Ruth said, after a pause. 'And we know where you are. I never know what's happening to Nicco.'

'Oh, Ruthie, I'm sorry! Here am I, thinking about myself again, when you've got your own worries. Don't you hear from Nicco, then?'

'Now and then. He writes when he can. Always says he's well, never says what he's doing. Sometimes has a bit of leave. Reading between the lines, I think he might be on the move again.'

Kester nodded. 'Burma, probably.'

'Burma? Why do you say Burma?'

He flushed a little. 'I – I don't know. It's another field of operations, that's all.'

'The Japanese have taken Burma,' Ruth said slowly. 'You think Nicco will be fighting the Japanese?'

'No! Honest, Ruth, I've no idea where Nicco might go. I don't know why I said Burma. He could go anywhere. Don't you start to worry about the Japanese.'

'Who's starting?' asked Ruth. 'I already am.'

It took her mind off Nicco to have to face her mother and give her Kester's news. As predicted, Isa 'blew up', and Jack wasn't happy, either. That terrible girl, that beanstalk, taking up with another man while their Kester fought for his country, and then had to lie in a hospital bed and get a letter like hers! What sort of girl could she be? Hard as nails, cold as charity, as selfish as they come! He was well shot of her, eh, and if she should ever put her head round THEIR door, well, she'd better watch out, that was all! But why hadn't Kester given them this news himself, the foolish laddie?

'Didn't want to upset you,' said Ruth.

'Aye, well, there's no way we wouldn't be upset, is there?' cried Isa. 'So what's he going to do? He's no' going to give her a divorce?'

'After the war.'

'He is going to give her a divorce? Oh, my God, what a thing to happen. We've niver had a divorce in our family before. Think of the disgrace!'

'Disgrace for her folks, too,' said Jack. 'They won't be pleased.'

'When the new son-in-law's a naval officer?' asked Isa smartly. 'You can bet they'll get over the divorce quick enough when they hear about him! They'll probably pay for it, eh?'

'Well, I'm no' paying for it,' Jack declared. 'If Fenella wants it, she can pay for it. Come on, I'll walk you to the tram, Ruth.'

The July evening was warm and sticky, and Ruth fanned herself with her hat as she and her father stood at the tram stop.

'Better no' tell the signora about the divorce,' Jack advised. 'Wait till it happens, eh?'

'Don't worry, I don't make trouble for myself!'

'Might have something else to worry her soon, though, if the papers are anything to go by. Been reading about old Musso lately?'

'No, I never have time to read the papers. What's happened to him?'

'Nothing yet, but seemingly the Italian people are getting fed up with him. He's lost an army in Africa, hundreds of his men were taken prisoner at Tunis. Now he knows the Allies will invade Italy to reach Germany, and he's scared stiff.'

'You're right, the signora would be upset about that. I'm sure she hasn't heard.'

'Another thing no' to tell her, then.' Jack grinned. 'Sometimes, you ken, yon signora reminds me of your mother.'

'Well, I've just told Ma about Kester's divorce.'

'When he didn't have the nerve. Och, mothers just care a lot, that's all. Mebbe too much.'

'You care, too, Dad.'

'Aye.' He kissed her cheek. 'Here's your tram, then. Keep smiling, eh?'

But in the tram, packed in with other passengers, Ruth thought about Nicco. Couldn't keep smiling, then.

Chapter Sixty-Seven

Rumours were beginning to circulate amongst the Italian community that plotting against Il Duce was going on in the mother country. It must be so. Why else should Churchill and Roosevelt send a message to the Italian people? News of it had filtered through to those abroad, and the wording had struck chill to Italian hearts.

'Consult your own self-respect and your own interests and your own desire for a return to national dignity,' the message had read. Decide whether 'to die for Mussolini and Hitler, or live for Italy and civilisation'. What could the intention of such a message be, except a call to rise against Il Duce? And it must already be known that there were those in Rome who were ready to do that.

'Oh, Mamma,' cried Marilena. 'Those words could have been written for Guido! But will he listen?'

'He will never listen,' said Brigida, as Carlotta sat without speaking, her brow furrowed, her hands tightening in her lap.

'He's been the same since he was born,' said Renata. 'What he wants to do, he does, and nothing else.'

'Do we want him to listen?' Carlotta cried suddenly. 'Who are these people to tell Italians what to think?'

'I've heard it said that Il Duce is no longer popular at home,' Vittorio remarked. 'The people are weary of this war. Some never wanted it in the first place.'

'We're all weary of war, Vittorio, but I don't see the British rising against Churchill!'

*   *   *

There was no rising against Mussolini, but something more extra-ordinary. On 25 July 1943, he was sent for by the so-called figure-head king and dismissed from his post. As he left the palace, he was arrested. Marshal Badoglio, once Commander of the Italian army but never a true fascist, became prime minister.

Italians round the world were stunned. Il Duce arrested, out of power? It didn't seem possible. There were those, in fact, who refused to believe it. Carlotta, for instance, declared the whole thing to be a fabrication by the enemies of Il Duce. Guido said the same. There had always been people willing to discredit the leader, that was well known. All they were doing now was issuing false statements. Mussolini had not been dismissed, had not been arrested. When he appeared, to refute these lies, folk would be able to see the truth for themselves. Many of Guido's fellow-internees took the same view. How could they do other-wise? Mussolini was the rock on which they had stood for so long, it wasn't possible for them to accept that he had become shifting sand.

Worse news was to come for them. On 8 September, the new prime minister announced to the world that Italy had surrendered to the Allies. Il Duce was not to be given a chance to redeem himself. For him and all Italians, the war was over.

'Surely, Guido will come home now?' Marilena cried, and this time even her mother agreed. Guido must agree to leave the camp, there was no longer any point in his staying. But Guido was as one pole-axed. He and his friends could no longer think what was the best thing to do. It was true, everything seemed over for them, all that they had worked and suffered for, had been in vain. Why not, then, get out? They were painfully trying to come to some conclusion when fate took another turn at the wheel. Mussolini had been imprisoned in a remote mountain resort. On 12 September, in brilliant adventure story style, men of Hitler's SS rescued him and flew him off in a light aircraft, to unite the fascists of North Italy against the Allies and those who had betrayed him. It was a truly incredible feat and set Guido's heart alight with pride and hope.

'You see!' he cried in triumph. 'We were right all along! Il Duce is still our leader, we shall still follow him!'

He wrote at once to Marilena, telling her that he would not be asking to be released from internment at the next tribunal. He and others loyal to Il Duce would stay on until the fight was done. Soon he and Marilena would be reunited, but honourably, which was what, being good Italians, they both wanted. He was her everloving husband, Guido, and sent kisses to her and Paulo.

'I'm sorry, Marilena,' said Ruth, when she had been shown the letter. 'You'll just have to accept Guido for what he is.'

'A man of principle!' cried Marilena. 'That's what Mamma says, and it is true.'

A man of principle, but mistaken, thought Ruth. She said no more to Marilena, who was coping as best she could. Weren't they all?

Chapter Sixty-Eight

'Telegram for Rietti!' called a telegraph-boy, putting his head round the door of the shop.It was almost closing time on a March afternoon in 1944. Millie Niven had looked in for her messages on her way home, and Kester, who had been invited round for his tea, was sitting on a chair at the counter with his legs stretched out and his stick to hand. He and Millie had been having 'a bit crack', as Millie called it, they not having met for years but remembering each other from early Ginger Street days, while Ruth packed the shopping basket. They'd talked of Nicco, who'd been promoted sergeant, and Kester had been admiring and said three stripes would never have come his way, to which Millie had told him he should have had a medal, so he should, him with his bad leg and all! It was just a pleasant afternoon, Ruth rememberd afterwards, there'd been nothing special about it. Until the telegraph-boy came.

Telegram for Rietti. The words seemed so loud, the shop so quiet. Kester and Millie, turning pale, looked at Ruth, who set down a packet of tea. The boy advanced towards the counter.

'Rietti?' he asked again.

'I'm Mrs Rietti,' said Ruth. She put out her hand and the boy put the orange envelope into it. He was very young, she saw, and had freckles. His eyes were already not meeting hers.

'Want me to open it, Ruth?' Kester asked hoarsely.

'No. No, thanks.'

It didn't take a second to open the envelope, didn't take a second to read the words.

'Any answer?' asked the telegraph boy.

'No answer.' Ruth fumbled in her cash drawer. 'Here, this is for you.' She held out a coin, but he shied away.

'That's OK, I dinna want onything, that's OK.'

'Poor boy,' she murmured, as he hared from the shop. 'What a terrible job, eh? Bringing such news.'

'What news?' Millie whispered, but Ruth shook her head. The shop seemed to be going round, she couldn't keep track of it.

'I have to go to the signora,' she said, and turned and walked waveringly up the stairs.

Kester picked up the telegram, as Millie watched with large eyes.

'What does it say, Kester?'

'Regret to inform you—' he began, and she gave a little shriek and clung to the counter to steady herself.

'Oh, no, no, Kester, no! Is Nicco dead? Do they say he's dead?'

'He's no' dead, he's missing. "Missing from patrol."' Kester's voice trembled. '"Every effort will be made . . . will keep you informed . . . as soon as any news . . ."' He put down the scrap of paper with its small and terrible pasted-together words. 'Oh, God, Millie, what can we do?'

'Nothing,' she said sadly. 'Nothing at all. I know.'

Upstairs, in the living room, Gina, now getting on for seven and tall, was helping her grandmother to set the table. Uncle Kester was going to have his tea with them and *Nonna* had been lucky at the butcher's and made meatballs, so Uncle Kester was very lucky, too, because they didn't always have meatballs for tea. They would all have to speak English when he came because Uncle Kester didn't know much Italian, though Gina was teaching him some words whenever she saw him. He made aero-engines now in a factory that had once been an ice-rink, and sometimes Gina would daydream that it still was and she could skate there and be like that film star Ma had let her see at the pictures once. Only she never mentioned that to Uncle Kester, who had to walk with a limp since he hurt his leg and would never be able to ice-skate, or dance, or anything. He'd had to leave the army because of his leg, and another daydream of

Gina's was that her father would hurt his leg too and come home from the Far East. Surely he wouldn't mind giving up ice-skating or dancing, to get away from the jungle?

'What is it?' Gina's grandmother asked, and when Gina turned her head she saw that her mother was standing in the doorway, not moving. She looked strange.

'Gina, just go downstairs and see Uncle Kester a minute,' she said quietly.

'Is Uncle Kester here already?' Gina's face lit up. 'Why'd he no' come upstairs?'

'He's coming soon. Just you go down and say hello.'

'I'll tell him we've got meatballs!' cried Gina and raced away to the stairs.

'What is it?' the signora repeated. She had already turned white, for she had read Ruth's face.

'It's Nicco. He's been posted missing in Burma. They sent – a telegram.'

The signora swayed. She raised her hands and stretched them before her, as though to ward off what she'd heard, and gave a long cry of anguish.

'Ruth!' The cry resounded. 'Ruth!'

Ruth hesitated, only for a moment, then she sprang across the room and took Nicco's mother in her arms, held her as their tears came and mingled, and for the first time said, close to her face, 'Mamma.' They had kept themselves so long apart; they were together now.

Everyone came to the flat over the shop to comfort Ruth and Carlotta. Kester had made telephone calls, Marilena had run for Renata, Jack had gone round to tell Sylvie. This was a nightmare for them, the first news of possible loss since the anxieties over Guido and Kester. But Guido and Kester had survived and it had been too much to hope that that kind of luck would hold. It seemed it hadn't, but then they didn't know. They might not be mourning a loss. Nicco could still be all right. That was why there were no tears permitted as the family gathered, producing whatever they could find for an impromptu supper – soup, cheese, spam, corned beef, to add to Carlotta's meatballs. There must be no tears until they knew for sure, that Nicco wasn't coming back.

The youngest child of the family, Renata's Emilia, who was not quite four, was already asleep on Gina's bed, but Gina herself was watching the preparations with bewildered eyes, along with her two cousins, Paulo, who was five and Ronnie who was six. Paulo had his father's blue eyes, but looked in every other way like his beautiful mother, Aunt Marilena, while Ronnie, who was fair and solid, looked like his father, Uncle Mark.

'We were going to have meatballs,' Gina said, studying the table. 'But then we heard that my Dad was lost.'

'Lost?' repeated Ronnie. 'Where?'

'In the jungle.'

'Can't they find him?' asked Paulo.

'I don't know.' Gina's lip trembled. 'Uncle Kester says they will.'

'That's all right, then.' Ronnie was also studying the table. 'Can we still have the meatballs?'

Gina took out a small handkerchief and blew her nose. 'We'll have to see,' she said, in her mother's voice.

'Oh, look at them!' whispered Sylvie. 'Bless them, they can't understand what's going on.'

Marilena looked at Ruth's sister, so pretty, so fair, and remembered how she had once cried over her and Guido, and wondered why she had. It was all so long ago, all seemed so unimportant now.

'Ruth is trying not to say too much to Gina,' she told Sylvie. 'Because Nicco might be found, you know.'

'Oh, I know, I know!'

'It's my mother I'm worried about, she looks so ill.'

Sylvie looked across to the signora, who was sitting next to Ruth. Both looked ill, in fact, with shining white faces stretched by fear, but it seemed to Sylvie that there was a strange peace between them. This has brought them together, she thought. Oh, how sad, that Nicco might never know.

Over the meal, where everybody had a taste of everything and wondered that they had such appetite, Vittorio asked Kester in a whisper what he thought were Nicco's chances. It was known that his unit was now part of an Indian Division fighting the Japanese in Burma. That'd be terrible country, eh? Anybody could go missing in the jungle, and then be found? To go missing wouldn't necessarily mean – well, the worst?

'Och, no,' Kester agreed quickly. 'I've no experience of jungle fighting, but I should think it happens all the time – I mean, men losing contact with patrols, and that.'

'So, you say we shouldn't start to worry yet?' asked Vittorio.

Kester looked across the table and met Ruth's desolate gaze. 'We shouldn't start to worry yet,' he answered firmly.

Ruth lowered her eyes.

When the meal was over, the washing up done and the kitchen tidied, people began to get ready to go home. There was nothing that they could do to comfort Carlotta and Ruth, but they had been there with them, shown they shared their suffering, and maybe that was something.

'Yes, yes, it helps,' Ruth told them, as she and the signora were embraced and kissed. 'It was good that you came, we appreciate it.'

'Now, you'll come over to us?' Isa asked anxiously. 'Come whenever you can, bring the signora, don't stay at home on your own.'

'Ma, I've the shop to look after, I'll be all right.'

'Aye, but when your work's done, that'll be the time to be with other folk. Kester'll be with us, remember, and he's good with Gina.'

It was true that since the break-up of his marriage and his leaving the army, Kester had taken to spending more time with his sisters, particularly Ruth in Ginger Street, and had become something of a father figure to Gina.

'I'll see you, Ma,' Ruth told her. 'Don't worry about me. I'm no' giving up hope for Nicco.' Her voice shook. 'Until I have to.'

'That's the way.' Isa wiped her eyes. 'I feel so bad, you ken,' she added in a low voice. 'That I didn't want you to marry Nicco. And him so good to you, such a grand husband in every way.'

'Ma, it's all right, don't say any more, all that was a long time ago.'

'Aye, but I still feel bad.'

The nights would be the worst, thought Ruth, as they prepared for bed as usual. During the day, there'd be work, there'd be people; at night, just themselves alone, trying to sleep, knowing it wasn't possible. Even Gina was tossing and turning that first night when Ruth looked in on her, not truly awake, but perhaps in nightmare land, seeing the father she didn't really remember lost so far away. Ruth straightened her covers, and picked up Rabbit, who was still the dear companion, now so worn with loving, his fur had almost completely gone. 'There, sweetheart,' she murmured, placing Rabbit into Gina's arms, then went with loaded heart to her own bed.

Some time in the small hours, she gave up the struggle to sleep and padded into the kitchen, where she found the light on and the signora making tea. Turning her great sad eyes on Ruth, she set another cup.

'You too?' she asked.

'Me too. How can we sleep, Mamma?'

'We must.' The signora poured Ruth's tea. 'We must carry on as usual. It is what Nicco would have wanted.'

'Tomorrow. Not tonight.'

'Tomorrow, I go to the church.'

Yes, that would be a comfort. Prayer. Seemed like that was all they had.

Chapter Sixty-Nine

The weeks went by and there was no news of Nicco. The war seemed to be going well for the Allies, with success in Italy and the Russians advancing into the Ukraine and Rumania, but all of that passed Ruth and Carlotta by. They lived for the post, for telephone calls, even for telegrams, but all that came was a letter from Nicco's Commanding Officer. It was meant to be cheerful, maintaining that every effort was still being made to trace Sergeant Rietti, and Ruth was grateful for all the good things said about Nicco, how he was well-liked and respected and considered a valued NCO, but the letter depressed her all the same. It seemed to her to be the sort a CO would write after a man was dead.

She kept busy in the shop, where all her customers, Italian and Scots, were so kind and sympathetic. Millie and Vi, Etta MacSween, all her old friends, would come in for their messages, never ask about Nicco, only let their eyes express their feeling which she would return. After all, they had their problems, too. Millie had already lost her man, Vi's husband was fighting in Italy and Etta's was training for the next big offensive. Aye, all hush-hush, you ken, but everybody knew it was going to be France. Maybe no' yet, but it was on its way, and that would be the end of it, eh? The end of the war in Europe, thought Ruth, but not the Far East. Folk never mentioned that.

She saw her parents regularly and once even took the signora, which sent Isa into a frenzy of house-cleaning and cooking. The visit went off well, with Carlotta admiring everything and taking an interest in Jack's shop, but really feeling happier with Brigida and Vittorio, where she could let down her guard. Sometimes she told Vittorio he should open his café again, but he said he didn't feel up to it, they could manage on what Brigida earned at the factory canteen. Marilena was working at the canteen, too, now that Paulo was at full-time school. She rarely visited Guido, but when she did, reported that he was just the same, waiting for Mussolini to pull something out of the hat.

'And he'll wait a long time for that!' cried Renata. Nothing had been heard of Mussolini for quite some time.

Kester told Ruth she should go out, try to take her mind off things. Maybe go to the pictures with him? Rita Hayworth was on in *Cover Girl*.

'Oh, I don't think so, thanks,' said Ruth. 'I can't really be bothered. Why don't you ask Millie?'

'Millie? We're talking about you.'

'Never mind me. Look, ask Millie. She never goes out, just seems to go to work.'

'Still thinking of Derek, that's why. Can't see her wanting to go out with me.'

'It's getting on for five years since Derek died. I don't think she'd mind going to the pictures with you.'

Kester hesitated. 'I'd never be able to take her dancing.'

'Thought you were only offering the pictures?'

'Aye, well, I am, I suppose.' He gave a crooked grin. 'Still officially a married man, you ken. We're no' trying for divorce until the war's over.'

'Do you feel a married man?'

'No! Fenella's made it plain enough she only wants her naval guy.'

'Well, then.'

Kester wasted no more time, asked Millie to see *Cover Girl* with him and when she accepted, arranged to take her for a five-shilling meal as well. That was the first of their regular outings together and everyone was pleased to see the two saddened young people enjoying themselves again. Sarah MacAllan said it was about time her poor girl got some fun out of life. Isa said it did her heart good to see her Kester putting the beanpole out of his mind and turning to a sweet girl like Millie, who'd fit in with the family and be a real asset, eh?

'Ma, they're only going out together,' said Sylvie. 'No' married yet.'

'Aye, they'll have to wait for the divorce, but, you'll see, they'll make a match of it. When the war is over.'

'When,' Sylvie murmured, thinking of Nicco and poor Ruth, and of Mark. Like most people, she couldn't imagine the war ever being over, wouldn't let herself even dream of peace.

It was a day in April when the letter came. Gina brought it up the stairs before breakfast, a buff-coloured envelope marked OHMS. When Ruth saw it, she felt the floor come up to meet her and had to sit down.

'Mamma,' she said faintly. 'I think this is it.'

The signora stayed upright by the table, not able to speak.

'Is it about Dad?' asked Gina worriedly.

'It might be.' Ruth ran her finger along the flap of the envelope and took out the single sheet of paper it contained. For a moment, the lines ran together, her eyes couldn't focus, then the words rearranged themselves and gradually, wonderfully, made sense. Her eyes filled with tears as she put down the letter and struggled to her feet.

'He is dead?' asked the signora heavily.

'He's alive! Mamma, he's alive! Gina, your Dad's alive!'

They all three clung together, sobbing as they had never sobbed in the long weeks when they didn't know if Nicco was alive or dead. But he was alive. Found some time before by Gurkhas and taken to an army hospital, slightly injured and suffering from malaria, but only recently identified. He was making a good recovery, but would have to remain in hospital some time before returning to his unit.

'Malaria, that's bad,' the signora said slowly. 'And what is the injury?'

'I don't know, something slight, that's all they say. But, oh, Mamma – Nicco's alive!'

'I go now to the church to give thanks,' cried the signora, taking her shawl. 'Then I tell Marilena and Brigida and Vittorio!'

'And I'll tell everybody at school!' carolled Gina, dancing round the kitchen. 'I'll tell Sister Monica and Paulo, and everybody!'

'I'll ring Ma and she can tell Kester and Sylvie,' said Ruth. 'Oh, I think I'll have to eat something – I feel so strange.'

'Yes, yes, eat something,' her mother-in-law told her. 'All this is taking your strength.' She threw her shawl around her shoulders. 'But this evening, I am certain, Vittorio will ask us all to go round there, to celebrate. He still has some wine, you know. Oh, yes, in his cellar. We shall all be drinking wine tonight!'

Later, after Ruth had opened the shop and told her customers, been hugged and slapped on the shoulder, she read and re-read the letter from the War Office. Wonderful, wonderful letter! She could have kissed the man who'd put the careful phrases together, who'd given her back her Nicco! It was only when she'd folded it and put it in her bag, that she remembered the letter's final sentence. Sergeant Rietti 'would have to stay in hospital some time before returning to his unit'. Returning to his unit? Did that mean he was just going back to fight? Not coming home? He'd been lost in the jungle, had been very ill with malaria, and he would still be 'returning to his unit'? Oh, God, it could all happen again. He was still in danger. Why couldn't they have sent him home? He'd been out there so long. Surely, he could come home for a time, then be posted somewhere else? No, it couldn't happen, she knew it. He was with a battalion, he must stay where he was.

Ruth closed her eyes and for a moment felt sick at heart. Only for a moment, then she rallied. This was a great day, one of the best of her life. Nicco was alive. She mustn't forget that, mustn't be ungrateful. Whatever the future brought, today, he was alive.

'Say a prayer for me at the church, Mamma,' she said under her breath. 'Because I'm giving thanks. Nicco is alive.'

Chapter Seventy

One evening in April 1945, Marilena came to the shop on her way home from work and asked Ruth if she would do her a favour. Of course, Ruth told her, if she could.

'Well, then, will you come with me to see Guido?' Marilena asked in a rush, as though she were afraid Ruth would say no, which was, in fact, Ruth's first inclination.

'You mean, go with you to the Isle of Man? Marilena, I can't do that, I can't leave the shop.'

'Aunt Brigida and Uncle Vittorio don't want to go, they hate seeing Guido behind the wire, but Uncle Vittorio will help Mamma to look after the shop for you, if you'll come. It'll only be for a couple of days.'

'What about Renata? Doesn't she usually go with you.'

Marilena shook her head. 'Not since Federico left and Guido quarrelled with him. But the thing is, Ruth, I'm feeling so guilty. I haven't seen Guido for so long and I'm worried about him.'

'Worried?'

'Well, because the war's nearly over and I don't know how he'll take it.'

Ruth's mouth tightened. 'He should be glad to see the Nazis defeated. Here's the rest of us giving thanks, and he's upset? It's crazy!'

'I know, I know, but it's all to do with Mussolini. He thought Mussolini was going to make Italy powerful again, he thought it was right to be a fascist. Now, he sees the Allies winning and nobody

362

knows what Mussolini's doing, and I'm just so worried he won't be able to cope.' Marilena's eyes were large and haunted. 'Maybe he won't even come home when the war is over.'

'Of course he'll come home!'

'I don't know, I can't be sure. I just know I have to see him.' Marilena grasped Ruth's arm. 'Say you'll come with me, Ruth, please. I need you.'

'Would you take Paulo?' Ruth asked doubtfully.

'No. I did take him when he was younger, but I don't want him to see his father as a prisoner now. Aunt Brigida says she's due some holiday, she'll take him from school.'

'And I suppose I could get Vi to help with Gina, if Mamma is looking after the shop.' Ruth sighed. 'Looks like you've persuaded me, Marilena, but I can't say I'm looking forward to the trip.'

'I never look forward to it,' said Marilena with a shudder.

It was true that the war in Europe was nearly over. The battles since D-Day, when the Allies had invaded France, had been hard fought, and there had been some bad times, particularly when the Germans began sending rockets over London, but now everyone was waiting for Berlin to fall to the Russians and the Germans to surrender.

'Can't believe it, somehow,' Kester said to Jack. 'The Germans always seemed so strong.'

'Took on Russia, that was their mistake.' Jack was filling his pipe with precious tobacco. 'But what's going to happen in the Far East, Kester? How are we going to beat the Japanese?'

'I honestly don't know, Dad. It's going to be difficult. They're so ruthless, and so bloody good at jungle warfare. That war could go on for years.'

'Poor Nicco,' said Jack, after a pause. 'Still out there.'

'At least he recovered, after he went missing.'

All they knew about that episode was that there had been some sort of ambush and Nicco, leading a patrol with one of the officers, had gone looking for some men who'd become separated from the rest and become separated himself. The others had been found quickly, but it had been some time before Gurkhas had come across

Nicco. When he came home, he might be able to tell them more. If he could remember. If he came home.

'Poor Ruth,' said Jack. 'Carrying the place on all these years on her own. Now Marilena wants her to go to the Isle of Man to see Guido.'

'Should tell her what she can do with that idea!'

'Och, you know Ruth. She's going.'

If she had been travelling anywhere else, Ruth might have enjoyed the little break, for she'd hardly had more than a few days away from the shop since Nicco joined the army. But, to go to the Isle of Man, see the old boarding houses and hotels all cordoned off with wire, as Marilena had described, and the men who had chosen to remain there rather than fight fascism – no, that was not Ruth's idea of a holiday. She was doing it for Marilena, and Marilena alone, for she could not summon up much sympathy for Guido.

After the long train journey, they took a room in a small boarding house in Barrow, from where they were to take the boat to Douglas. Marilena said she had stayed there before and had not been popular; the landlady didn't like accommodating Italian women visiting internees on the Isle of Man.

'I'd like to hear her say something to me!' declared Ruth.

'She won't say anything to you, you're not Italian.'

After their breakfast of scrambled dried egg and toast, Ruth said she'd slip out for a paper. They'd heard no news since they left and no one in the boarding house had spoken to them, but there might be more news of the German surrender.

'All right,' Marilena agreed dispiritedly. 'I suppose Guido will have to know about it some time.'

She was drinking a second cup of tea, when Ruth came back, the paper in her hand. Her face was cheesy white and she looked sick.

'Ruth, are you not well?' cried Marilena, jumping up from the table.

'I'm all right.' Ruth glanced around at the two or three other people in the dining room now looking at them. From the door, the landlady watched with darkening brow. 'Marilena, will you come upstairs for a minute?'

'What is it? What's happened?'

'Just come upstairs – quickly.'

In the small twin-bedded room they had shared, Ruth told Marilena to sit down. 'There's something in the paper that's upsetting,' she said, breathing hard. 'It's a picture of Mussolini.'

'Oh, God, what? Show me, Ruth, show me!'

Ruth unfolded the newspaper and Marilena looked at the picture. At first, she couldn't take in what it showed, then she realised she was looking at two bodies, those of Mussolini and his mistress. They had been shot and put on display in Milan. She gave a cry and collapsed sobbing into Ruth's arms.

'Oh, no, no! Oh, no, Ruth, it's too horrible! Oh, God, what happened? Il Duce – dead? Like that? Oh, Ruth, Ruth!'

Ruth brought her water and rocked her like a child until she grew calmer. 'It is horrible,' she murmured. 'They needn't have done that, the people who shot him – put him on display.'

'Who? Who shot him?'

'Partisans, anti-fascists. Apparently, he'd been living near Lake Garda, and had been trying to escape to Switzerland. He was in a convoy, hidden on the back seat of a car, and the partisans stopped the convoy.'

'And they just shot him?'

'They took them to some villa, Mussolini and the woman, and shot them both, after what they called a trial. That's what the paper says, anyway.'

Marilena sat on the edge of her bed, shivering. 'What shall I tell Guido?' she whispered.

'Let's hope he knows already.'

He did know. They could see that as soon as they saw him, sitting alone in an interviewing room that might once have been the dining room of the guest-house in pre-war days. Beyond it were the rolls of barbed wire, and beyond the wire, was the sea. Guido had his back to it, his face was in shadow, but they could see that his blue eyes were empty of all expression. He had put on weight in captivity, and his handsomeness that had always been flashy now seemed overblown. As she looked at him for the first time in years,

Ruth could no longer imagine him dancing. But then he would no longer feel like dancing.

'Guido,' Marilena said timidly. 'How are you?'

He shrugged and said nothing.

'I've brought Ruth to see you.'

'But not Paulo.'

'Not this time. But you'll soon be out of here, Guido. You'll soon be home!'

'Will I?'

'Shall we sit down?' asked Marilena. 'We've got some things for you—'

'Today's paper, I suppose?'

Marilena licked her lips. 'You – you want it?'

'I've seen it.'

Ruth cleared her throat. 'Guido, I've never agreed with your views, but I know you must be feeling terrible today, and I'm sorry.'

Guido's dull eyes flashed with the old blue fire. 'You have no idea how I'm feeling,' he said curtly.

'Well, seeing those pictures, of your leader must have been upsetting.' Under that blue stare, Ruth felt she was floundering. 'I mean, he shouldn't have been shown like that, he shouldn't have been shot, without a proper trial.'

Guido leaned forward and looked into Ruth's face. 'He deserved all he got, and more,' he said distinctly. As Marilena drew in her breath, he turned to her. 'How was he found? Hiding in the back of a car. Il Duce! What was he doing? Running away!'

'You could scarcely blame him for trying to save himself,' Ruth said uneasily. 'Look what happened to him, after all.'

'He was supposed to be saving Italy!' Guido cried. 'He was giving us back our power, our place in the world! But it never happened, did it? When Hitler rescued him and he had a second chance, we stood by him, we thought he'd still save our country. But he did nothing and when things went wrong, he hid, and then he ran. Hid in a car under a bundle of coats, for God's sake!' Guido's face twisted, there were tears in his eyes.

There was a long silence. Ruth and Marilena sat with averted eyes, as Guido sank his head in his hands.

'He did do a lot for Italy,' Marelina said at last, 'everyone says so.'

Guido looked up, dashing away his tears. 'I thought so once. All over now, though, isn't it? All we dreamed of?'

'What are you going to do?' Ruth asked quietly.

'What can I do?' he asked thickly. 'I've thrown away five years of my life. What does a man do then?'

'Pick up the pieces? Salvage what you can?'

'Go back to Scotland, you mean?'

'Where else?' cried Marilena. 'Guido, we've waited all these years for you! Please say you'll come home. For my sake, for Paulo's sake!'

'I might do better in Italy,' he said slowly. 'You and Paulo could come with me.'

'No, there's Mamma, and your parents, Guido. I don't want to go to Italy, my home's in Scotland!'

'There'll be trouble in Scotland, Marilena. Don't think that every-thing'll be forgotten when the war's over. Folk have long memories. They'll know who did what and who believed in Mussolini and who didn't.'

'It'll be up to us to make sure people forget all that,' Ruth said sharply. 'We'll have to learn to live in peace with one another, or what's the war been for?' She stood up. 'And Nicco's war's not over. He can't choose to come home, like you, Guido.'

He lowered his eyes. 'I feel bad about Nicco, Ruth. He's had a hard war. Thank God they found him that time, in Burma.'

She looked away. 'I think I'll wait outside now, leave you and Marilena to have some time together.'

As she went out, she saw from the corner of her eye, Marilena move towards her husband and take his hand.

Chapter Seventy-One

Allied victory in Europe was officially proclaimed on 8 May 1945. Hitler had already committed suicide, Berlin had surrendered to the Russians, all German forces had surrendered unconditionally to General Eisenhower. It was time to celebrate.

'Oh, Jack have we no' got anything to drink?' Isa asked Jack, when they had listened to the evening news bulletins on the wireless.

'Aye, I've kept a bottle of port, and a half of whisky.'

'Whisky?' cried Kester. 'Dad, you never told me you'd still got whisky!'

'Only a half, you ken.'

'I say we hang on to that and open the port,' said Isa. 'I'll get the glasses. What a day, eh? Did you think you'd ever see it?'

'Not at Dunkirk,' answered Kester. 'Though when we knocked Rommel for six at El Alamein, I thought we might.' He took the glass of port his father gave him and held it up to the light. 'Looks good. Make a toast, Dad.'

'What'll I say?'

'To victory!' cried Isa.

'In Europe,' amended Kester.

'Aye, better no' forget Nicco,' said Jack, and they were silent for a moment.

'I'm so scared of thae Japanese,' Isa whispered.

'Let's no' think of the Japanese,' Jack told her. 'Come on, raise your glass, now. To Victory in Europe!'

'To Victory in Europe!' echoed Isa and Kester.

They all drank, set down their glasses, and looked at one another.

'I wish the girls were here,' sighed Isa. 'Maybe we should go round to Sylvie's? Or Ruthie's?'

'The city'll be packed,' said Kester. 'You'll no' be able to move. Everybody'll be out on the town tonight.'

'Well, you're not.'

'I'm just going.' He grinned. 'Said I'd pick up Millie and we'd go out and see what's what.'

'Millie. Och, Kester, I wish you could marry that girl! She's such a sweet lassie, and would fit in so well with us. When are you going to do something about your divorce?'

Kester's cheerful look faded. 'Soon as I can. I've been on to Fenella and she's as keen as me to get things started.'

'Cost a bonny penny, eh?' asked Jack. 'I say Fenella should pay, but if you need a loan, Kester, I'll see what I can do.'

'Thanks, Dad, but I should be OK. I've managed to save a fair bit since I started at the factory.' Kester moved to the door. 'Whatever it costs, it'll be cheap to me.' He straightened his shoulders, put on a grin again. 'I'm away, then. Don't wait up, I'll be late.'

Isa hurried after him, as he went painfully down the stairs.

'Kester, you take care now! Remember that leg of yours, in all thae crowds!'

'Och, for pete's sake, Ma, I think I can take care of myself at my age!'

'Let him alone, Isa,' said Jack, drawing her back. 'You know he hates you fussing.'

'Aye, but it's such a tragedy, Jack. To be so lame, and so young.'

'Be more of a tragedy if he'd no' come back.'

'You don't need to tell me that,' she answered quietly.

After some moments, during which they sat together, each lost in thought, Isa leaped up and said she'd make a start on the cakes she'd promised for Ginger Street's victory party. Strictly speaking, of course, she and Jack were Trinity, but Ruth had said it didn't matter, folk were coming from all over the place, and anyway they probably still thought of themselves as belonging to Ginger Street, didn't they?

'Aye, we do!' Isa had told her. 'So, what do you need for the party?'

'Anything you can spare, and if Dad and Kester could put up some trestles, we'd be very grateful. We're short of men to help.'

'Same old question, what do we do if it rains? It was no' so good for the Coronation parties back in 1937, I remember, but we niver came over to Ginger Street that time.'

'And I was in Hebburn Place. But it'll no' rain for the victory party, Ma. Everything's going our way.'

How cheerful Ruth keeps, Isa had marvelled. You'd never know she was eaten up with worry over Nicco.

Chapter Seventy-Two

It did not rain for the victory party. As soon as the May morning dawned, the grown-ups were out in Ginger Street, looking up at the sky and giving one another thumbs-up signs, for the sun was climbing high and it looked as if they could agree with Ruth, everything was going their way. By the time Jack arrived after lunch with a pick-up van and the trestle-tables hired from one of the church halls, the flags were out, the bunting was strung between the houses, and the women were standing by, ready to pin red crepe paper to the tables as soon as Jack and Kester got them up. There were paper hats, too, made by Vi Dochart, who was good with her fingers, and little bags of sweeties and the awful 'blended' chocolate that the grown-ups had sacrificed their sweet points for, but no crackers. Heavens, the children'd no' mind, they were already tearing up and down the pavements, playing tag and shrieking with laughter.

From her upstairs window, the signora was looking down on the festivities. She was dressed in black as usual and seemed to have made no concessions to the spirit of the day, which had disappointed Ruth but not surprised her. Many of the Italians were still reeling from the shock of Mussolini's death; they would attend victory parties, no doubt, and be glad to celebrate the end of the Nazis, but would be subdued, it was only to be expected. It was not even certain, in fact, that Carlotta would come to the party. She was frowning now at the sight of Gina, running about with Paulo and Ronnie and the other children in the street.

'You permit Gina to play like this?' she asked Ruth, who, with her mother and Sylvie, was cutting sandwiches.

'Well, it is a special day, Mamma.'

Isa and Sylvie exchanged glances, but said nothing.

'I think perhaps she should come in now,' the signora said. 'Those boys are rough, even Paulo.'

'My Ronnie's no' rough!' Sylvie exclaimed. 'He loves to play with Gina.'

'He is a boy, Gina is a girl, I do not like to see her playing boys' games.'

'They'll all be sitting down soon, for their tea,' Isa said soothingly. 'That's what they're waiting for! And speaking of tea, who's doing the cups of tea for the grown-ups?'

'Brigida and Marilena, from the café,' Ruth told her. 'They're filling the teapots from the urns, just for today.'

'The café,' sighed the signora. 'Shall we ever see it open again?'

'Of course you will,' said Sylvie. 'I'm sure Signor Rietti will open it, now the war's over.'

'The European war,' Ruth said under her breath. Did nobody spare a thought for the Far East and the ongoing conflict there? Sometimes, as she prepared for this party, she thought of herself as one apart. The only woman whose husband was still fighting. But at least, there'd been better news lately. The Japanese were slowly being beaten back in the Pacific and in Burma, and for the first time, a light was shining at the end of the tunnel. The Allies were still a long way off another day like this, though, and she was still a long way off seeing Nicco again. With renewed vigour, Ruth applied herself to the potted meat and fish paste sandwiches, schooling herself to be as glad as everyone else, because this was VE Day.

Thank the Lord, Millie, who might also have been set apart in victory only more tragically, had Kester now to cheer her, though poor young Derek must be in her mind today. Oh, but it warmed Ruth's heart to see Millie and her brother so happy together, after all their sorrow. Thank goodness, Ma had come round to the idea of the divorce, once she'd realised she'd be exchanging Fenella for Millie as a daughter-in-law, though what the signora would say when she heard about it was not a thought to dwell on. While Sylvie stole a sandwich and said she hoped nobody'd mind, she was starving, and Isa said, why didn't they make a cup of tea NOW, Ruth went to join her mother-in-law at the window.

'You'll come down to the tea, Mamma?' she asked softly.

'I think not, Ruth. It is not for me, this party.'

Ruth put her hand on the signora's arm. 'I know you're thinking of Nicco,' she murmured. 'And I am, too. But this party's for the children. This is their day, you know, because they can look forward to growing up in time of peace.'

The signora's shadowed eyes rested on Ruth's face. 'That is what we want for them,' she agreed.

'So, come down and be with them!' Ruth opened the window and the soft May air filled the room. 'See, we're lucky – there's no' even a wind.' As the signora still hesitated, she added, 'You've made your almond biscuits, after all.'

'With no proper almonds!' Her mother-in-law sniffed. 'That essence, it is not the same.'

'They'll be lovely. Come on, Mamma, say you'll come.'

'Very well, if you wish it. I can help Marilena with the tea.'

'No, no, you must sit down, we'll serve the tea.' Ruth glanced back at Isa and Sylvie. 'Shall we take the sandwiches along now? Mamma is coming with us.'

Mamma, Isa repeated to herself. Would you credit it? Our Ruth calling the signora Mamma? Nicco, come home quick and see the miracle!

The children were gathering round the tables, the mothers fussing, seeing that each had a paper hat and a plate, and that there was no scuffling or squealing or snatching at the sandwiches before everyone had been given a seat. Certain of the older residents were given seats, too: Mrs Fyfe and her arthritic husband, Mrs Burns, some of the signora's Italian friends, and of course the signora herself, who always gravitated naturally to the top of any table.

Millie was there, standing with Kester, and Vi, watching over her Stanley, who was already scrapping with Sylvie's Ronnie over where he wanted to sit, and Etta MacSween and Mrs Nisbet had come over from Hebburn Place at Ruth's invitation, with four of Etta's six children. Seemed Sammie and Junie, the eldest, had already left school and got jobs at factories, which was very hard to believe, just as Ruth could scarcely believe that the hefty boys eyeing the sandwiches had once been 'last year's baby' and 'wee Georgie'.

'My, you're looking well!' cried little Mrs Nisbet to Ruth. 'All your hard work suits you!' But her eyes were already straying to Isa, who was hurrying about, carrying jellies and watching out for the tea coming from the café. 'And is that no' your ma over there? Och, I still remember that day wee Georgie was born and she come down and give me a hand. Now, I must just have a word with her, eh?'

'You're looking well, too,' Ruth told Etta, who, like most of the women was wearing a cotton dress with puffed sleeves, and had done her hair in upswept style. 'Work still suiting you, then?'

'Aye, keeps me smart as paint, eh?' Etta flashed her precious teeth and laughed, but there was an anxious sharpness about her eyes that Ruth did not miss.

'Everything's OK, isn't it, Etta?'

'Fine, for now, hen, but what happens when they dinna want any more parachutes? I reckon that time's coming pretty soon, now the war's over. I'll ha' to find maself another job.'

'Well, you will. There'll be plenty of jobs, with so much to do, to get things straight again.'

'Aye, well, I'm no going back to the old days,' Etta said fiercely. 'I'm no going to be looking round for ivery mouthful again, I can tell you! There'll have to be work for ma man and me, and thae politicians'll have to remember it. There's an election in July and I'm voting for any guy who promises me that.'

'Quite right, but I don't think you've any need to worry.' Ruth crossed her fingers. 'Those old days won't come back. Come and have a cup of tea.'

Vittorio and Brigida, accompanied by Renata and Marilena, were hauling over a trolley loaded with cups and teapots, round which the grown-ups immediately gathered.

'I could do with this,' said Jack. 'Who'll be mother?'

'I will pour,' Brigida declared. 'Renata, take this to your Aunt Carlotta.'

'Always first,' Renata murmured. 'That's Aunt Carlotta.'

'Now, now,' said Vittorio. 'Your aunt works hard, she deserves respect.'

'Made some delicious biscuits,' Ruth said, smiling. 'Almond essence, or no almond essence.'

'Wait there,' ordered Renata. 'I want to ask you about Nicco.'

Everyone was asking about Nicco, but what was there to say? The outlook was brighter, there was that light at the end of the tunnel. But Ruth didn't want to talk about it, in case the light went out.

'It must be difficult for you,' Millie told Ruth, when they were standing a little apart. 'I know how you feel.' As Ruth's eyes went to Kester, deep in conversation with Mrs Fyfe's grandson, home on leave from the airforce, Millie said quickly, 'Oh, I've got Kester, and that's wonderful, but I canna help thinking – well, today, anyway – of poor Derek.'

'I knew you'd be thinking of him,' Ruth said softly. 'It's only right he should be remembered, especially today.'

'Aye, well I do love Kester, you ken. I just hope he understands. About Derek.'

'He does understand, Millie. He's learned a lot lately, my brother, been through things the hard way.'

Millie hesitated. She put her hand on Ruth's arm. 'Mind if I ask you – d'you think he's really over Fenella?'

'Of course he is. Why, you know he is, Millie!'

'Aye. It's just that she's so elegant, you ken, and tall and blonde—'

'She was never right for him,' Ruth said firmly. 'He did fall for her, it's true, and she was keen on him, but it was never the sort of thing to last. You're different, you see, you're what Kester needs. You two are going to be very happy.'

'Oh, Ruth, thank you for saying that.' Millie suddenly kissed her cheek. 'You always seem to know what to say.'

The tears sprang to Ruth's eyes. Nicco had said those same words to her years ago, at the beginning of the war. It was strange, she could remember everything he'd said to her, but sometimes not the sound of his voice. Just as his face evaded her mind's eye and she had to look at his photograph to bring it back. Turning away from Millie, she poured more lemonade for the nearest children. Always find something to do. That was her mother's motto, and it worked. Usually.

The street party was gradually coming to an end. The children, wearing their paper hats, were slipping away to chase each other up and down the pavements again, as their mothers began to clear away the debris of the tea and Jack and Kester took down the trestle-tables. Older residents of Ginger Street, saying they'd had a grand day, were making their way home, while the signora and her Italian friends went back with Brigida and Vittorio.

Marilena and Renata, the clearing up finished, stood with Ruth and Sylvie, watching their children play a last game, while Isa chattered to Sarah, and Millie helped Kester and Jack to load the trestles on to the pick-up van. Already at the end of Ginger Street, Etta and Mrs Nisbet were waving goodbye, Etta's children milling round them, opening up their sweetie bags and choosing what to have.

'It's been a wonderful day,' said Renata.

'It has,' Sylvie agreed.

Marilena seemed far away, her brow clouded, her finger at her lip. 'Now the war's over, when do you think—' she began, but Renata sighed and interrupted.

'Marilena, we've no idea when Guido will be coming home. You ask me that pretty well every day.'

'But there's no point in keeping anyone on the Isle of Man now. They should just let them out. Why don't they?'

'These things take time, there are formalities. You'll just have to be patient, like the rest of us. We're all waiting for the men to come home.'

And thanking God they are, thought Sylvie, who still couldn't believe she needn't worry any more. Well, that wasn't quite true. Mark had come through his hazardous 'ops' with scarcely a scratch, though Sylvie guessed there had been things he had never told her about. Supposing after all that, he should be killed crossing the road?

Could happen, couldn't it? She knew she would not be at peace until he was back home and in her arms. Smiling wryly, she had to admit that that made her no different from all the other women waiting for their men's demob numbers to come up.

Chapter Seventy-Three

The British general election was held on 5 July, but as votes from service people had to come in from all over the world, the results were not declared for three weeks. As they began to be announced on the wireless, they were astounding. Seat after seat appeared to be falling to Labour. Jack, listening with Isa and Kester, said he couldn't believe his ears.

'Labour gain, Labour gain, Labour gain? What's happening? Winnie's niver going to lose, is he?'

It seemed incredible, but Winston Churchill, the man who had stirred the hearts of the British in their 'darkest hour', the Prime Minister who had led the country to victory, seemed to be on the point of losing his job.

'Och, it's no' possible, the country'd niver do that to him,' declared Jack, who had always voted Tory because he believed the Conservatives were the party to look after the small shopkeeper. 'They'd niver chuck out the man that won the war for them!'

'The fighting men won the war,' said Kester. 'Folks like me.'

'Aye, but he led you, Kester.'

'OK, say he did, he's still no' the man to win the peace. Guys coming back want something different from before the war, Dad. They're no' wanting to see the Means Test back again, and folk on the dole. I know how they think, I'm the same. I voted Labour.'

'So did I,' said Isa. 'I think ordinary folk'll get a better deal from them. I'm sure Mr Churchill is a great man, but Kester's right. We need somebody different, now the war's over.'

'All Labour'll do is nationalise everything,' Jack groaned. 'They'll have no time at all for folk like me, with small businesses to run.' He ran his hands through his hair. 'What a future we'll have, eh? And the rations have gone down already, you ken. Three ounces of bacon, instead of four, and margarine cut as well.'

'That's no' Labour's fault, seeing as they're no' in power yet!' cried Isa.

'No, but it's a sign of bad times ahead.'

Winston Churchill would certainly have agreed, as he went to the palace that evening after Labour's landslide victory, to hand his resignation to the King. It was a bitter blow for him, his personal 'darkest hour', perhaps, but as Clement Attlee, the new Prime Minister remarked, now was the beginning of a new era for Britain. Churchill was regarded by the commentators as the man who had finished his job, wonderful though it had been; now it was time for other people to do theirs.

At breakfast the following morning, Kester was ecstatic, Jack for once in despair.

'You can cheer, Kester, but wait till you have to run a shop again, and see how you do!'

'I'll no' be running a shop again, Dad.'

Isa, ladling out porridge, stopped to stare. 'You planning to stay on at the factory, Kester? What happens when it goes back to being an ice-rink?'

'I've been going to tell you for some time, what I had in mind,' Kester said hesitantly. 'You know there's all these courses planned for ex-servicemen? Help them catch up on qualifications for civvy life? Well, I'm going to apply to do an engineering course at Heriot-Watt.'

'Heriot-Watt College?' echoed Jack. He looked stunned. 'You niver said, when you were at school, that you'd like to go to college.'

'Only thought of it since I've been working on the aircraft engines. I got interested, thought maybe I could do something technical. Of course, I don't know if I'll be accepted. Then I'll have to get the grant.' Kester took a spoonful of his porridge. 'But it'll be worth a try.'

'I think it's a grand idea,' Isa said with decision. 'I'm all for it, Kester. Why, you'll be a professional, eh? You'll have a proper career!'

'I always thought you'd come in with me,' Jack said slowly. 'Millar And Son. That's what I thought we'd be. And I got you the new shop—'

Kester went scarlet. 'And look what I did for the new shop! Didn't exactly cover myself with glory, did I?'

'Water under the bridge, Kester.'

'Water?' He laughed shortly. 'Just about drowned me. No, I think I'm best out of your business, Dad. And if I do get as far as finding a good job in the end, I want you to know that I'm going to pay you back everything I took from you. That's a promise.'

'Oh, hell, don't talk about it,' his father muttered. 'Where's the salt for ma porridge, Isa?'

'Right there in front of you.' Isa was still staring admiringly at her son. 'Och, Kester, I'm so pleased with you over this. And getting engaged to Millie, and all. Things are going to work out for you, you'll see.'

'Fingers crossed,' said Kester.

Across Edinburgh, Sylvie was locked in the arms of Mark, home on leave and just off the London train, and in the shop in Ginger Street, Ruth was reading a letter from Nicco. It made her sick and faint, she could hardly find the strength to climb the stairs to speak to her mother-in-law. Hadn't this all happened before? Hadn't she felt like this when she'd heard the news that Nicco had been reported missing? But weakness could stem from many things, and joy was one.

'Mamma, Mamma!' she cried. 'Come quickly! There's a letter from Nicco. He's in India, the war in Burma is over. He's safe, Mamma, he's safe!'

But not coming home just yet. Within a day or two, news came that Japan had turned down an ultimatum that had been sent to them by the Allies, urging them to surrender or face destruction of their country. They were not like Germany, they indicated, they were not 'on their knees', they would fight to the end. VJ Day, Victory over Japan Day, was still some way off in the future, it seemed; no one knew how far.

Chapter Seventy-Four

When Guido and Federico finally arrived home, it was to criticism from different sections of the Italian community, Federico for coming out of internment to help the British, Guido for not coming out of internment and refusing to fight fascism. 'Seems somebody'd be upset, whatever we did,' Guido said moodily. 'Well, I did what I thought was right at the time, and if it was wrong, it's nobody's damn business but mine!'

'And what do you want to do now?' Vittorio asked patiently, on a day in early August. 'Something temporary till the biscuit factory opens up again?'

'Biscuits!' groaned Guido. 'Do I want to spend my life making biscuits?'

'You were very ambitious once, wanted to climb the ladder.'

'Just at the moment, I don't want to do anything.'

'Oh, that's fine!' cried Vittorio. 'Seeing as you haven't done anything for the past five years!'

'Vittorio, don't make trouble,' Brigida said hastily. 'Guido just needs time to adjust. Isn't that right, Guido?'

He shrugged, and lit a cigarette. Marilena, who had been sitting silently by his side, looked at him anxiously.

'Federico's going to take a temporary job in a factory,' she told him. 'Just until he can start up the ice-cream machinery business again. Then he's going to run it for his father.'

'Is he?' Guido blew smoke and looked at it with narrowed eyes. He had made his peace with Federico when he returned home, admitted he was in the wrong to speak to him as he did when he left the camp, but they both knew it might be some time before their old friendship was restored.

'What would you say to opening up the café?' Vittorio asked, after a pause. Guido raised his eyebrows.

'Me?'

'Yes, you. I'm too tired, I feel too ill.'

'Oh, not ill, Vittorio,' wailed Brigida. 'Tired, not ill. Do not say ill!'

'I did say tired. These have been long, long years, these war years.'

'You're right about that,' said Guido. His tone was sharp, but he was giving his father his full attention. 'You're not ill, are you, *Papà*?'

'No, just tired. I meant tired.' Vittorio ran his hand impatiently over his brow. 'But I think the time has come to open up again. Marilena is keen.'

'Would we get Italian supplies?' asked Guido.

'Not at first, but we could do what other cafés are doing – just offer what's going. I think we'd do well enough.'

'We'd have Italian customers, but would the Scots come back to us?'

'I think so. We have to bury the past, Guido.' Vittorio's gaze was steady. 'You know that better than most.'

Guido took Marilena's hand. 'You want this, Marilena?'

'I do, I really do, Guido. I think we could make a go of it, and we'd be together.' Her eyes glistened with pleasure at the thought. 'Think of it!'

'Me under your eye all the time?'

'Yes! Oh, say, yes, Guido. Say yes to your *Papà*!'

'All right, if it's what you all want. I'm willing to give it a go.'

Marilena threw her arms aound him, his mother threw her arms around him, Vittorio was smiling, when Renata appeared at the door to the flat, with Federico and Emilia.

'Hey, hey, what's the celebration?' asked Renata. 'Somebody had good news?'

'Guido is going to take on the café,' Brigida told her proudly.

'*Papà* doesn't want to open again, but we think it's time. What a waste it would be, if we threw away all that we'd worked for!'

'That's true,' Renata replied, but her gaze on her brother was cold. She had not yet forgiven him for upsetting Federico. 'I must say, though, I never thought you'd want to take on the café, Guido.'

'Why not? I can run it as well as anyone else.'

'Yes, well, I'm glad you've agreed. It will be a load off poor *Papà*'s mind.'

'Might be difficult, to begin with,' Federico remarked.

'Everything is difficult at the moment,' Guido snapped. 'But one has to make a start.'

'The war is over,' put in Brigida. 'Things can only get better.'

'One war is over, one's still to win,' said Renata. 'Which reminds me – did you hear the news at six? A terrible bomb has been dropped on Japan.'

'Another bomb,' sighed Vittorio. 'What good will that do?'

'This is different. This is an atomic bomb.'

'An atomic bomb?' The signora repeated, when Ruth told her the news. 'What is different, then, about an atomic bomb?'

'President Truman told the American people that it was two thousand times more powerful than the largest bomb ever dropped.'

Her mother-in-law shuddered. 'And it was dropped on a city?'

'Hiroshima.' Ruth's voice was filled with terrible awe. 'Apparently, much of it was destroyed in seconds.'

'And the people?'

'Destroyed, too.'

The two women were silent, considering the matter.

'Why so powerful a bomb?' the signora asked at last.

'To bring the war with Japan to an end. If the Allies don't use something like this, there'll have to be an invasion and thousands of troops will be killed.' Ruth was silent for a moment, thinking of the men who could die. Maybe Nicco? He could easily be sent to Japan from India. She cleared her throat. 'They say the Japanese soldiers would rather commit suicide than surrender, you see.'

'Then they will not surrender after this bomb?'

'Maybe not,' said Ruth and with a troubled look went away to collect Gina, who had been playing at a friend's house. She truly didn't know what to think about the latest development. Everyone wanted the war to end and everyone knew that Japanese soldiers were cruel and merciless, but the new bomb had killed civilians, there was the problem. On the other hand, what was the difference between this bomb and the bombs of the London blitz, or the bombs dropped on Germany? Size, numbers killed, that was all. No moral difference, then, for bombs shouldn't be dropped at all. Yet, in her heart, Ruth felt there was a difference. Maybe with this new technology, there were dangers they didn't yet know. Please God, prayed Ruth, may the Japanese surrender.

It took another atomic bomb to make them do that. This time the bomb was dropped on Nagasaki, with the same devastating results as at Hiroshima. Leaflets were dropped over Japan, again urging surrender before more bombs destroyed the whole country. Two days later, the Japanese government, surprising many, indicated that they were prepared to surrender, and on 14 August accepted Allied terms. VJ Day had come at last.

Chapter Seventy-Five

Celebrations in Britain were a little more subdued than for VE Day. Americans went wild, but then in a way the war in the Far East had been 'their' war, in a way it had not been Britain's. Japan had destroyed the American navy at Pearl Harbor, something they would never forget and had always sought to revenge. Now, revenge had come and revenge was sweet, and the British did feel that, too, but to a lesser degree. The eastern theatre of war had seemed rather remote to them, except to those with British relatives serving there, who had lived with the thought of it as part of their daily lives. So it had been for Ruth and her family, and their celebrations were from the heart.

Though crowds did gather at Buckingham Palace on 15 August, there were perhaps not so many street parties as for VE Day, and no plans were made to hold another in Ginger Street.

'We'll have our own party!' cried Ruth. 'All come to us, and we'll celebrate, all right!'

'No, no, come to the café,' said Vittorio. 'I'd like to do something, for my nephew's sake.'

But on the afternoon of 16 August, Brigida came running round to the shop to say that Vittorio was not well, they had had to call the doctor. There could be no party that evening.

'What is it, what is it?' cried Carlotta, clutching her sister-in-law. 'Oh, dear God, he is not going to be like my Roberto, is he?'

'It is his heart, it is weak,' Brigida sobbed. 'I knew he wasn't well, always so tired, not wanting to open the café, I should have called the doctor before. Now, he gives Vittorio pills and says he must take care, must rest, not climb stairs. I said, we live upstairs, what are we to do? The doctor says, I cannot tell you, you must work something out. Work something out, Carlotta! What can I work out, I ask you? Where can we go?'

'Oh, my poor sister!' cried Carlotta.

That evening, instead of celebrating, Ruth and Carlotta, with Gina carrying flowers, went round to see Vittorio, who was lying on the sofa complaining that far too much fuss was being made of him.

'What is it I have? A touch of angina. It is nothing, it is what many people of my age have. Why is everyone looking at me as though I am dying?'

'*Papà*, all we are doing is asking you to take care,' said Guido.

'But how is he to take care, when we live up the stairs?' cried Brigida.

'Mamma, Federico and I live on the ground floor,' Renata said quietly.

'So?' asked her mother, her blue eyes very bright.

'So, we want you and Papa to come and live with us. We have discussed it and we think it would be the answer. We have a spare room and we can make it nice. What do you say?'

'Leave the café?' asked Vittorio.

'Yes!' shrieked Brigida. 'Oh, Renata, you are my angel! And Federico, too! What can I say? To take us into your home, to help your poor father! Come here, let me hold you, both of you!'

But while Brigida was kissing and embracing Renata and Federico, Vittorio, very pale, was shaking his head.

'Leave my café? How can I do that? It is my work, my life!'

'*Papà*, you have already asked me to run the café,' Guido said gently.

'And it hasn't been open for years,' said Brigida. 'You won't miss it, dear Vittorio, I promise you, and we will be with our daughter and our son-in-law, and sweet Emilia. Come, now, look happy and be glad we have somewhere to go.'

'I could have helped Guido—' Vittorio began, but Guido shook his head.

'No helping, *Papà*. You have to take life easy from now on. Doctor's orders.'

'And how will I live my life with nothing to do? I am not a man to sit about the house, taking naps, reading the paper!'

'You will give us your advice, *Papà*, and we'll take it.'

'I will certainly give it,' Vittorio growled.

'Renata, it's good of you, what you're doing,' Ruth told her later. 'Are you sure it'll work out?'

'Oh, yes. *Papà* is no trouble and I think Mamma will let me do things my way in my own home.' Renata, flushed with wine, laughed. 'Hope so, anyway!'

'It's wonderful, how when it comes down to it, Italians always put the family first. I do admire you for it.'

'Family comes first and last and all the time for us, Ruth. I don't know if that's a good thing, or not, but that's the way it is.'

'With you, it's a good thing,' Ruth told her. She went to find her mother-in-law and said they must be going, there was Gina to get to bed, she had school in the morning.

'Oh, I don't want to go home yet!' wailed Gina. 'It's a special party, I shouldn't have to go to bed early.'

'Early? Look at the clock!' cried Ruth. 'Anyway, we have another little party tomorrow at Grandma Millar's. Uncle Kester'll be there, and Millie, and Auntie Sylvie and Uncle Mark and Ronnie.'

'But, when will we see Dad? The war's over now, why isn't he home?'

'It'll take a long time for him to come home. He'll have to come by sea and that takes weeks.'

'So, when will he be home?'

'I don't know, Gina. Maybe the autumn.'

'The autumn?' Gina made a face. 'Oh, that's ages away! Ages and ages! It's no' fair, everybody's dad is home except mine!'

'Be glad he is coming home at all,' her grandmother told her sternly. 'What are a few weeks to wait, when he might never have come home to us again?'

387

Chapter Seventy-Six

'Ages and ages away,' Gina had said of her father's homecoming. So it seemed to Ruth, who was finding these last weeks more trying than all the long years of separation. 'The longest mile is the last mile home.' Wasn't there a saying, or a song, with those words? They were true, anyway. The nearer you got to the end of the road, the more impatient you were. As long as he was really coming, though, she felt she could bear the wait; as long as the end of the road really was in sight. And it should be. As the last weeks of summer went by, she knew that Nicco, on the troopship, was coming nearer and nearer to home. One of these days – she caught her breath – he would just come walking in.

Sometimes, she would look in the mirror and study her face. Had she changed? Would he recognise her? Oh, heavens, he would surely recognise her! There were little lines by her eyes and mouth, though, that had not been there when he went away. Would he have changed? It was some time since he'd sent a snapshot, and he'd looked rather the same then, except that he'd lost weight. Och, they'd both know each other, all right. But what of making love? Her thoughts tended to veer away from that. So many years – why, they'd be like strangers. But all over the world, women must be facing that problem when their men came home, and would no doubt be solving it. Sylvie was already saying she felt she was in the family way again. No' sure, of course, but what was the betting she ended up having one of these 'boom' babies the newspapers were forecasting? It came into Ruth's mind that she and Nicco might have one of those 'boom' babies, too, but they hadn't had much luck starting a second baby when they'd tried before. If they still weren't lucky, and if the rules were relaxed about married women doing professional work, as folk were saying they would be, now that women had done so much in the war, maybe she might even get herself that good job she'd always wanted? If Kester could train to be an engineer—

What was she thinking of? Ruth leaped away from her imaginings. Let's get Nicco home first, before the day-dreaming, she told herself. Oh, God, let me just get Nicco home!

One evening in September, she was standing at her counter waiting to close the shop. Only Mrs Burns was left, still rooting round among the onions, insisting on squeezing each one to see if it was soft, breathing hard, as Ruth stood, shifting from one foot to the other. Sometimes, she glanced at the phone. Why didn't it ring? Nicco was going to call from Liverpool when his ship docked. She'd been looking at the phone for days, and of course, it had never rung. Not even for a business call.

'All right, Mrs Burns?' she asked at last. 'Want me to find you some paper for those?'

'Aye, hen, but I might just take a tattie or two, while I'm here. Just a couple o' pound, you ken, there's only me at home.'

'I'll weigh them, Mrs Burns,' Ruth said, thinking, poor old thing, all alone, now her husband was dead and her son moved away. She was picking out the potatoes, her hands all soil, when the shop bell rang, and she looked up.

A man stood in the doorway. A tall, bronzed man, in a soldier's uniform with three stripes on his sleeves. Very thin, especially in the face, where the cheekbones stood out and the dark eyes seemed unbelievably large. When he took his cap off, she could see two wings of white amongst the glossy blackness of his hair, just as his mother had. For she knew this man's mother, she knew this man.

'Nicco,' she whispered, and let the potatoes fall from her fingers. 'Nicco?'

The shop spun, and old Mrs Burns's face seemed to go sailing by. 'Are you all right, hen?' she was croaking, but Nicco was there, Nicco was catching her.

'Oh, Ruth!' he was crying. 'Oh, Ruth, I'm home!'

Mrs Burns had gone, with her potatoes and her onions, smiling and saying she was all of a fluster, seeing Mr Rietti come back from the war, and Ruth and Nicco were in each other's arms, not moving, just letting joy flow over them, just coming to terms with this moment they'd thought they might never see. But at last, they stirred and held themselves away, the better to look into each other's faces.

'Why didn't you phone?' Ruth asked breathlessly. 'I'd have been ready for you, and now look at me, all a mess from Mrs Burns's tatties—'

'You're beautiful, Ruth, just as I remember you! You haven't changed at all!'

'Neither have you, but you're so thin – so very thin, my darling!'

'And white,' he said, smiling. 'See my white hair? I'm an old man.'

'It's just those two wings, like your mother's.' Ruth grasped his arm. 'Nicco, you must come upstairs, see Mamma and Gina! Quick, they've waited so long!'

'Gina,' he repeated, and then with a quizzical smile, 'Mamma?'

'Mamma,' Ruth nodded. 'Oh, Nicco, there've been some changes here!'

Mamma had not changed. There she was, the same as ever, his indomitable mother, crying over Nicco, kissing him and thanking God, laughing, then crying again. But who was the tall, serious girl, with the shoulder-length fair hair and great dark eyes so like his own? She was looking at him warily, thinking maybe he looked different from his photos, older, stranger? Her dada? She didn't seem sure.

Nicco held out his arms to her, as soon as his mother had let him go, but his daughter didn't come running.

'Gina, here's your father come back,' said Ruth.

'And we have nothing for his supper!' cried the signora dramatically. 'We should have had a nice meal ready, all the things

390

he likes! Why did you not let us know, Nicco, when you were coming?'

'I was going to ring from the station,' he told her, his eyes still fixed on Gina. 'But then I saw there was a train due to leave that would connect with one for Edinburgh, and I ran for it and caught it, and when I got to Waverley, all I could think of was getting home. I took a taxi and here I am.'

'Kiss your Dada, Gina,' Ruth said, a little anxiously.

'I say Dad now,' she declared, her eyes still cautious.

'No, say Dada,' he pleaded. 'Just this once. The way you used to do.'

She burst into tears and ran to him, and he swept her up in his thin arms as he used to do, and somehow she was his little girl again and he was her dada. All the lost years were fading. The family was together again, quite complete, and this time there would be no partings. No partings. That was what the end of the war meant, and for the first time, the idea of that really sank into Ruth's mind. Nicco was home and home to stay. As he unpacked his presents of bangles and scarves of Indian silk, to the accompaniment of cries of delight from Gina, she gave herself up to happiness.

While the signora pleasantly occupied herself in putting together a meal for Nicco (no changes there, thought Ruth smiling wryly, the dinner was still Nicco's dinner, and the women would join in), he and Ruth made a start on giving the news by telephone that he was home. While Gina clung to him, looking into his face, smoothing back the white wings in his hair, Nicco announced himself to Jack, whose astonished voice crackled round the room, and then to Isa.

'Och, Nicco, I canna believe it! You're really home? Back from the jungle? Thank God, thank God! Here's Kester!'

And Nicco had a word with Kester, promised to meet, said there'd be a welcome home get-together, as soon as he got in touch with his folks.

'Did you get my letter about your Uncle Vittorio?' asked Ruth. 'He's got a bit of a heart problem—'

'A heart problem?'

391

'It's not too serious, but the doctor wanted him on the ground floor, so he and Brigida have moved in with Renata.'

'Moved in with Renata? No, I never got that letter. Who has the café, then?'

'Guido and Marilena. That had already been decided.'

Nicco lowered his eyes. 'Of course, Guido's home from internment. How is he?'

'All right now.' Ruth hesitated. 'He was a bit down when he first came back. Over Mussolini, you ken.'

'I can imagine.'

'He's quite changed about Mussolini, though. Has seen the feet of clay, I suppose you could say.'

'That's something,' Nicco said quietly.

'And he's really been much brighter since Uncle Vittorio asked him to take on the café. It's been closed for so long, there's a lot do, and Guido's been doing it all himself. Painting and plastering, mending the floor – I've never seen him work so hard.'

'Sounds as though he's a different man.'

'I think he is. Anyway, you'll be seeing him tomorrow. The café's going to be re-opened next week.' Ruth kissed Nicco's cheek. 'We can have a party for you before that.'

'Wonderful.' He yawned and stretched. 'But now, what I need is a bath. Any hot water, Ruth?'

She ran the bath for him herself, exclaiming again at his thinness, as he stripped off his uniform. 'Nicco, you're skin and bone! What are we going to do to fatten you up?'

'If I know Mamma, she'll see to that. Don't worry, it was only the heat made us lose weight – and maybe the food.'

'I'm sure there's a lot you're no' telling me, Nicco.'

'No, no.' He gave a sigh of pleasure, as he slipped into the water. 'Now I know I'm really home. In my own bath, with my own Ruth soaping me. This is worth coming all the way back from India for!'

'Who says I'm soaping you?' she teased, but as she ran her hands over him, the tears came to her eyes. She fell to her knees and took him, wet as he was, into her arms.

'I'm getting you soaked,' he whispered.

'I don't care, I just need to hold you, it's been so long, Nicco, so long!'

Later, she changed her damp blouse and fetched his 'civvies', which he said he intended to wear, and watched him dress.

'Can't be your handmaid every day, you know,' she told him, trying to laugh, to sound light-hearted, but he held her close, as strung up with emotion as she. They kissed and clung together, until Ruth said she'd better go, what would Nicco's mother think of them, cuddling in the bathroom?

'She's too busy cooking to notice.'

'Mamma notices everything,' said Ruth, and again Nicco repeated softly, 'Mamma?'

Over the meal, that was of course one of the signora's best, though she said she didn't know how, as it had been concocted only with prayers and imagination, Ruth hesitantly asked Nicco if he wanted to talk about his years away. It was all right if he didn't want to, some men didn't, apparently.

'I'll be one of those,' he said, after a pause.

'You have seen terrible things?' asked his mother.

'All soldiers see terrible things.'

'But, Dada, won't you tell us about the time you were lost in the jungle?' asked Gina. 'Please, please, just a little bit.'

He smiled indulgently. 'I don't remember much about it, sweet-heart. I was ill. Half the time I didn't know where I was going, or what I was doing.'

'But did you have to eat awful insects? Did you see snakes, and creepie-crawlies?'

'Saw snakes and creepie-crawlies all the time, but don't ask me what I ate, I don't know. I must have eaten something, because it was a long time before I was found. Days, I think, or was it weeks? The crazy thing was that I was looking for other people, when I got lost myself.'

'You were lucky the Gurkhas found you, and not the Japanese,' Ruth remarked, shuddering inwardly at the thought of Nicco a pris-oner of the Japanese. By now, everyone knew how their prisoners had been treated.

'Yes, I was raving with malaria, apparently, and had a broken arm. Got taken to hospital, but couldn't say who I was. I must have taken off my identity tag in delirium.' Nicco shook his head. 'One of the men from the patrol was in the same field hospital. He eventually saw me and recognised me.' He smiled at Gina, who was hanging on his words, remembering them all to be repeated at school the next morning. 'That's all there is to it. Let's not speak of it any more.'

'Let's not,' agreed Ruth. 'But tomorrow, when you're no' so tired, we'll tell you all that's been happening here.'

'Maybe I am a bit tired,' he agreed. 'If you don't mind, I think I'll go to bed.'

His mother came to him and embraced him. 'Goodnight, my son,' she whispered. 'And welcome home.'

'I won't be long,' said Ruth.

She needn't have worried about the love-making. It was all as easy and heavenly as though Nicco had never been away, as though they had just slipped back into bed that time he had kissed her when she was sitting in her nightie, and he was due to leave her.

'Oh, never go away again!' she cried at intervals throughout that first night he was home. 'Never, never leave me again!'

'I'll have to go back to my unit,' he told her, holding her close. 'I'm not demobbed yet, only on leave.'

'Nicco, I won't let you go!'

'Come on, it won't be for much longer, and I'll only be in Berwick.'

'As far away as India, the way I feel now.'

But, really, she was at peace. She knew he was truly home, not in danger, not going to leave her again, as he had had to leave her before. When they finally fell asleep together, they were more serene in joy than they had ever been.

Chapter Seventy-Seven

Nicco was lavish in his praise for all that Ruth had done to keep the shop going in his absence. She'd been marvellous he told her over and over again, but even more marvellous had been the way she'd managed to win over his mother. Now, how had that happened?

'I go away, and she is as cold as ice to you. I come back, you are calling her "Mamma", and she is all honey whenever you're around.' Nicco kissed Ruth lightly on the lips. 'Now, tell me, *cara*, how was it done?'

'It was when we heard the news that you were missing. Somehow, we both found that we cared about each other. I wanted to comfort her, she wanted to comfort me. That was how it was.'

'You are both good-hearted, you see. Yes, my mother, too. Underneath the frost, she is warm.'

'You could have fooled me once, but yes, I see it now. After all, she is your mother, Nicco – she must be good-hearted!'

'And Guido – he seems strangely friendly towards me,' Nicco said thoughtfully. 'Makes me uneasy.'

'Och, don't be so cynical! He was really upset when you were reported missing, you know.'

Nicco looked unconvinced. 'If you say so. I must admit, though, he does seem to be trying to make a fresh start, and that can only be good.'

'It's what has to happen,' Ruth said earnestly. 'When I talked to him in the Isle of Man, after Mussolini had been executed, he was very depressed. He seemed to think there'd be wounds that would never be healed in the community, and everyone would remember what folk had done. I told him that that'd be wrong. People shouldn't remember old grudges, or who did what in the war. It's all over now.'

'There will be some parts of it that are never over,' Nicco said, after a pause. 'They must be lived with, in the mind. Endured.'

'I know what you're thinking of,' Ruth said after a pause. 'I didn't mean that the camps and what happened to the Jews should be forgotten.'

'What about the things that happened here?' Nicco's mouth tightened. 'Italians are not going to forget the night of June the tenth, 1940. They're not going to forget the 'Arandora Star', or the way some men were treated on the ships to Canada or Australia.'

Ruth was silent.

'Do you think I can forget how it was for you and Gina, the night the mob broke all the windows in my shop? Or that my uncle's café was wrecked?'

She shook her head. 'I haven't forgotten any of it myself. All I'm saying is that we have to try to get on with one another, haven't we? Those things happened in the war, and now the war is over. Couldn't we make a fresh start?'

Nicco sighed. 'Like Guido, you mean? Perhaps you're right.'

'Well, he is giving it a try.'

'He is, and I should meet him half way. More than half, if you like. Let's hope all goes well for the café, Ruth.'

'Official opening on Saturday, but our party's on Friday,' she said cheerfully. 'Everybody'll be there.'

'My poor Marilena,' the signora remarked, the day before the party, 'So much work for her, so much cooking!'

'Oh, but we're all going to help,' said Ruth. 'That's understood.'

'Yes, for the party, but for the café, no, she will be on her own. It will be too much, I think.' Carlotta's eyes slid from Ruth to Nicco. 'Especially, if there is another baby. She is trying for one, you understand.'

'That will be difficult,' Nicco agreed. 'But Aunt Brigida will help.'

396

'Yes, but Brigida is still working at the factory.'

'That'll soon come to an end.'

'Maybe. But even so, Brigida has Vittorio to look after. She is not free.'

'And you are.' Nicco's eyes rested on his mother. 'Mamma, are you trying to tell us something?'

'I shall just be up the road.'

'Up the road?' Ruth stared. 'At the café, you mean?'

'At the café. The truth is, Marilena wants me to move there. Perhaps not for ever, but while I can help, you see. Do some cooking, maybe help with Paulo, and if there is a new baby, God willing—' The signora raised her hands. 'I shall be needed,' she said simply.

Nicco and Ruth exchanged glances. For a moment, they were speechless.

'Mamma, I'm stunned,' said Nicco, at last. 'This is your home, it is the home you shared with *Papà*. Now, you say you wish to leave?'

'I shall be sorry to go, of course, but at this time, you understand, I must put Marilena first.' The signora again looked from Nicco's face to Ruth's. 'Please say you understand!'

'Of course we do, Mamma,' Ruth said quickly. 'We know Marilena needs you and you have to think of her.'

'As I say, I shall not be far away, and I shall not forget my dear Gina. She will still see her *nonna*!'

They all three hugged one another, Ruth thinking that she was fast becoming as emotional as an Italian, for there were tears in her eyes as she thought of her mother-in-law leaving her marriage home. At one time, it would have been the answer to her prayers to have the flat to herself, but now that she no longer cared about that, life played one of its little tricks and gave her what she had wanted.

'Is Mamma really happy about it?' she asked Nicco later. 'It will be such a wrench for her, to leave her old home.'

'Ruth, you know Mamma. If she didn't want to do it, she wouldn't be doing it. It's true, that Marilena will need her, and she's confident now that you can take care of me, so she thinks it safe to go.'

'Nicco!'

He laughed. 'That's the way she will see it, *cara.*' He folded her into his arms. 'It won't be too bad, will it, just the two of us, and Gina?'

'It won't be too bad,' she solemnly agreed, marvelling at the way things sometimes worked out.

Chapter Seventy-Eight

Isa was getting ready for the party, squeezing herself into a pale green woollen dress she had made in 1939 and moaning that clothes were still on coupons and that she had put on weight.

'Which is more than poor Nicco's done, eh? Did you ever see such a skeleton? I scarcely recognised him, to tell you the truth, with that white hair and all, but Ruth canna see any difference. That's love for you, eh?'

'I'm pretty grey myself,' said Jack, studying his hair in the mirror. 'You still love me, Isa?'

'Great soft thing! I'm like Ruth, I canna see a blind bit of difference! But is it no' funny, the way things work out, then? I mean, who'd have thought the signora would ever leave her home and go to live with Marilena at the café? Nice for Ruthie, though, to have the flat to herself, eh?'

'Wonder what Guido thinks?' murmured Jack.

'Who cares what he thinks?' Isa took up the silk scarf Nicco had given her and tied it becomingly at her neck. 'It's about time that young man did something for somebody in his life.'

'Thought he was supposed to be turning over a new leaf, anyway.'

'Maybe.' Isa put on her lipstick and dabbed at it. 'How do I look, Jack?'

'Canna see any difference,' he said, laughing. 'No, I mean it. You're just as pretty as when you wore your blue dress for our wedding.'

'I'd niver get into it now,' she sighed.

*   *   *

Sylvie, also getting ready for the party, was having better luck than her mother, fitting into a pink dress she had worn on her honeymoon.

'JJ's best, this was,' she told Mark, who was back on leave, even if only with a twenty-four hour pass. 'Remember when I used to work there? Seems like another age.'

'Sweetheart, it was another age.'

'I'm not that old! Anyway, I can still get into this. Though I was thinking I'd soon be putting on weight and now I won't be.'

Mark came and kissed her neck and then her lips. 'I'm sorry it was a false alarm, Sylvie, but we've got all the time in the world to try for a baby. Meantime, you look gorgeous.'

'And you look thin. No' so thin as Nicco, but no' like your-self.'

'Thank God for that!'

'Well, I'm going to have to fatten you up when you get home for good, though what with, I don't know. The rations are worse than ever. If it weren't for Dad, I'd be sunk.'

'Hey, I'm nearly a policeman again.' He shook his finger at her. 'Better not tell me about any under the counter stuff.'

'Och, what's a bit of butter now and then?' she asked carelessly. 'Dad's no black marketeer.' When she had finished putting on her make-up, she glanced over her shoulder at Mark, who was buttoning up a jacket that was in his eyes pleasingly too big for him. 'Hope it's no' going to be too awkward for you tonight, Mark.'

'Awkward?'

'Well, you know, seeing the Italians. I mean, didn't you have to question Nicco's uncle and Renata's father-in-law? Then, there's Guido.'

'I was doing my job. I had to question them. And I let them go.'

'You didn't let Guido go.'

'He was different. He knew he'd have to be interned.'

'He was always different. But Ruth says he's a changed man since he took on the café.'

'Any change would be for the better,' said Mark in a low voice.

*　　*　　*

400

'All ready to go?' asked Nicco, from the bottom of the stairs.

'Ready!' cried Gina, skidding down towards him. 'Look, Dada, I'm wearing your scarf!'

'We're all wearing your scarves,' said Ruth, pointing to her own. 'Mamma as well.'

The signora, pausing at the top of the stairs as she liked to do, gave one of her rare smiles as she adjusted the brightly coloured scarf at the neck of her black dress.

'*Che bella Mamma*!' cried Nicco, and she bowed. 'We'll all be so smart at the party,' Ruth told Nicco, as he locked the shop door and they began to walk down Ginger Street towards the café.

'Except me. I look like a scarecrow in this jacket.' He gave a rueful smile. 'Reckon I could fit another fellow in here.'

'You look fine, don't worry.'

'I want to hold Dada's hand!' said Gina, and walked ahead with him, smiling proudly as they passed people they knew, and Nicco, turning back to his mother and Ruth, called:

'You see, I'm still Dada at the moment?'

'Until Gina wants to be grown-up again,' Ruth said to the signora in a whisper.

'But how happy Nicco is to be with her, his little daughter,' Carlotta answered, with a sigh. 'How many years he has lost!'

How many years we've all lost, thought Ruth.

Chapter Seventy-Nine

She'd been right, that everybody would be at Nicco's welcome party, squashed into Guido's newly decorated premises. Almost the whole of Ginger Street had been invited, including all Ruth's customers, plus the Riettis' Italian friends, Mrs Nisbet, Etta MacSween and her husband, Frank, and the Valdo brothers, back from the Pioneer Corps, who had found someone to look after their own café for the evening. Then there was the family, of course, and the in-laws, and Millie, soon-to-be-family, and her parents, soon-to-be in-laws, all adding up to a crowd so big that Carlotta exclaimed on arrival,'Where will everybody sit?'

'I've set up small tables, Aunt,' Guido told her, rushing by, at which a frown creased her brow.

'I think one long table is better,' she called after him.

So you can sit at the head, he thought, but in keeping with his reformed character, only smiled. But the smile immediately faded, as he found himself looking into Mark Imrie's eyes.

'Hello, Guido,' Mark said pleasantly.

Guido looked from him to Sylvie, who was flushing, but then the café was very warm.

'Good evening, Inspector,' said Guido. 'You will excuse me – as you see, I am very busy this evening.'

'Won't keep you, then.' Yet Mark had laid a hand on Guido's arm. 'Just want to say I wish you well in the new venture. And by the way, my name is Mark.'

'The room looks terrific, Guido,' Sylvie said, her voice unnaturally high. 'You've done a really grand job. Marilena must be thrilled.'

They all turned to look at Marilena, greeting guests, and looking so beautiful in a deep blue dress, with one of Nicco's scarves floating at her throat, that Sylvie said impulsively, 'Oh, she's so lovely, Guido!'

'I think so,' he said gravely. 'Nice to see you both.'

As he glided away with all his old agility, his injured leg now fully recovered, Mark and Sylvie visibly relaxed and circled on to say hello to Kester and Millie, who were with Vi and Cameron Dochart and Millie's parents, Sarah and Bob. Jack came up to talk to Bob – as though he didn't see him every day! thought Isa, moving to speak to Brigida and Vittorio, who were still looking round the café that had been theirs with astonished eyes.

'When I see what he has done, I ask myself, is this my Guido?' asked Vittorio. 'I tell you, he is a changed man!'

'I always knew he would do well,' said Brigida, her eyes suddenly filling with tears. 'He made mistakes, but he has come through, and the café will be a great success, you will see.'

'Especially now Carlotta is going to help Marilena,' said Isa. 'That must be a big relief all round.'

Brigida dashed away her tears; her blue eyes sparkled. 'I too will be helping,' she said loftily. 'When rationing permits, I shall be making ice-cream again.'

'And no one makes ice-cream like Brigida,' said Vittorio.

She smiled. 'Well, to be honest, Carlotta and I used to make it together in the old days, you know. Oh, what a time it took, too! The milk mixture was boiled and then left to cool, then we put it in a drum which we turned by hand—'

'Oh, Mamma, not the old ice-cream stories again!' cried Renata, arriving, with Federico. 'I'm sure Mrs Millar doesn't want to hear all that stuff!'

'Yes, I do, it's very interesting,' Isa protested, but Renata, looking very attractive in her favourite red, only laughed and said when the ice-cream was made again it would be with Federico's father's machinery, as it had been since the 1930s. And as soon as he possibly could, Federico would himself be making machinery, just like his *papà*.

'That'll be the day,' said Federico. 'We used to say, when the war is over, we'd do so and so, but what do we say now?'

'We just hope for the best,' said Isa.

The women of the Rietti family were now melting away to the kitchen, to help Marilena serve the food they had already prepared, and Guido was telling people to take their places at the tables he was now putting into position, they would be eating very soon.

'Let me give you a hand,' Nicco said, taking one of the tables with Guido.

'Sure you're up to it? You've lost a lot of weight.'

'I'm capable of lifting something this size!'

'Sorry.' As they set the table down, Guido suddenly put his hand on his cousin's arm.

'I'm glad to see you back,' he said huskily.

'Thanks. I'm glad you're back, too.'

'You know what my war was like.'

'No need to go into that now.'

'I'm trying to put the past behind me.' Guido's look was suddenly piercing. 'I never was a Nazi, you know. I did support Il Duce, but not Hitler.'

Nicco nodded, but said nothing; there seemed no point in saying then that Guido could not have supported one without the other. After a moment Guido's look softened.

'And there's something else I want to say.'

'Yes?'

'I want you to know that I never had anything to do with that attack on you. I'm willing to swear it.' Guido flung up his arms. 'On anything you like.'

'No need to do that, Guido, I believe you.'

'You do?'

'Yes. I never thought you were behind it.'

Guido whistled softly. 'Everybody else did.'

'I knew you wouldn't actually injure me.'

'Came pretty close to it once or twice.'

'But always stopped in time. That's what I told Ruth. I said, we're family.'

404

A smile lit Guido's face and he looked the handsome boy Nicco remembered from their childhood. 'Family,' he repeated. 'That's right. We're family.'

He slapped Nicco on the back. 'Eat well, cousin, get some weight on!'

'Guido!' screamed Brigida from the service doorway. 'What are you doing? The food is ready, those tables should be in position!'

The cousins, exchanging grins, rushed to finish setting up the tables, and a few moments later, Marilena and the rest of the Rietti women began to serve the celebration dinner.

Everyone said afterwards that it had been a triumph of ingenuity and skill, an Italian meal made from British wartime ingredients that would surely be as memorable as its occasion. Of course, Carlotta's friendly butcher had done his best for her, and Jack had dug deep into the reserves that he kept for favoured customers. Then, Vittorio had his contacts, too, and his wine, and by the time the guests had eaten the meal and drunk the wine, they were in a very pleasant state and ready to listen to any speeches going. Except that there weren't any. Nicco himself stood up and thanked everyone for coming, but said he really didn't want anything said to him, it was enough for him to see everyone there and to know that they welcomed him home. So, now, if they would just raise their glasses, they could wish Guido and Marilena all the best in their new venture in running the café. Everyone stood, everyone raised their glasses.

'To Guido and Marilena!' they cried, and clapped, as Guido bowed and Marilena burst into tears.

'Let's all have coffee!' cried Vittorio. 'Real coffee, too, courtesy of our dear Ruth's father, here, Signor Millar!'

'Who's he?' asked Jack, turning red, and Isa knocked his arm and said, in a whisper, 'I never knew you had any coffee beans, Jack!'

'Well, you'd rather have tea, anyway, eh?'

'I'm having coffee tonight, though. Coffee's special.'

'Marilena, that was a wonderful meal,' Kester told her, as she came round with the coffee. 'When Millie and me get married, you'll have to do the food.'

Marilena blushed. 'You know I can't take the credit, Kester. But when are you two getting married, anyway?'

They shook their heads. 'Next year, we hope,' said Millie. 'Seems you have to be prepared to wait, for a divorce.'

'Doesn't matter.' Kester put his hand over hers. 'We've found each other, eh?'

'Oh, Guido, isn't it lovely to see Kester and Millie so happy?' Marilena asked him, as she passed him in between tables. 'After all they've been through?'

'It is,' Guido agreed. 'My old mate, content at last. Wish they could have done something for his bad leg, though.' Subconsciously, Guido rubbed his own.

People were beginning to leave, shaking Nicco's hand and all the Riettis' hands, the Italians kissing and hugging and everybody making their thanks. What a night, eh? It was like something pre-war, so it was. Though Etta told Ruth she'd never known anything as grand pre-war. Och, no! They didnae have do's like that where she'd been brought up!

'Now, you take care of yourself, Mr Ritty,' she told Nicco earnestly. 'And get some meat on your bones, like ma Frank here. Was it thae Japs got you so thin, then?'

'No,' Nicco answered, smiling. 'Just the heat. And I wish you'd call me Nicco.'

'Coulda done with a bit o' heat when I was in your country, Nicco,' Frank MacSween told him. 'Sunny Italy, eh? No' in the Italian campaign, it wasnae!'

'Dinna be so rude, Frank!' Etta exclaimed. 'Take no notice, Mr Ritty – I mean, Nicco. I'm sure Italy's a lovely country!'

'It is,' said Nicco. He slipped his arm round Ruth's waist. 'One of these days I'm taking Ruth to see it.'

'Be sure you come over on Sunday,' Isa urged Ruth, as she and Jack made their goodbyes. 'I've got some eggs and I'll make Nicco a nice Yorkshire pudding. You'll no' be going to Brigida's any more for your Sunday dinner, will you? Now she's with Renata?'

'I expect Marilena will keep the tradition going, soon as Mamma moves in, but we'd like to come to you this Sunday, Ma, thanks.'

'Take care of yourselves,' said Jack, kissing Ruth and shaking Nicco's hand again. 'It's been a long pull, eh? Grand to have you back, Nicco.'

Kester and Millie left, with Bob and Sarah, Bruno and Lucia. Now there were only Sylvie and Mark, apart from the Riettis, who would be doing the clearing up.

'Can't believe the war's all over, can you?' Mark murmured to Nicco.

'It's not quite all over, I'm not demobbed yet,' Nicco told him.

'Nor me. Still waiting for my demob suit.' Mark grinned. 'Wonder how it'll be, to be back for good?'

'Can't imagine it. All I know is, I'll thank God I am.'

'You can bet I'll do the same!'

'Look what I found the other day, Ruth,' said Sylvie, rooting in her evening bag. 'This old photo! Do you remember it? I'd put it in my copy of *Gone With The Wind*. Remember how I used to cry over that? When Scarlett comes home to Tara and finds there's nothing left?'

'Oh yes,' Ruth said absently, as she studied the little snapshot Nicco's father had taken so long ago. 'We both cried, didn't we?'

'I thought one time it'd be like that here, you ken, everything bombed to blazes and us picking over the ruins.' Sylvie shivered. 'We were lucky, eh? That didn't happen to us.'

'I remember when Nicco brought this down just before we flitted,' Ruth was murmuring, half to herself. 'He said it was to remind us of Ginger Street when we were away, but I was cross with him, I pretended not to care. And all the time I'd have given anything for a photo of him to keep.'

'Would you?' asked Nicco tenderly, looking with her at the little group taken outside the shop – himself, his mother, Marilena and Sylvie. 'But you weren't in it. I remember feeling sad.'

'What, when you'd given me the push?' asked Ruth, laughing.

'I never gave you the push! You were just too young.'

'I'm no' so young now.'

'Don't let me interrupt you two billing and cooing,' said Sylvie. 'But we're going now. Why don't you keep that photo, Ruth? Mark, come on, say goodbye to Guido and everyone. We've Ronnie to get to bed, remember.'

'Now for the clearing up!' cried Renata, when all the guests had gone. 'Not you, Nicco and Ruth. You go on home, poor Gina here is half asleep.'

'I'm no' half asleep, I'm wide awake!' cried Gina. 'And Paolo's no' in bed yet!'

'Bed for you, all the same,' said Ruth. 'If you're sure you can manage, Renata? Marilena?'

'We're sure,' Marilena told her. 'Mamma, you've done enough, you go, too.'

'No, I will stay a little longer,' said the signora. 'Brigida and I will talk.'

'Oh, yes,' sighed Vittorio. 'They will talk. Get off home, Nicco, while you can!'

But first, his mother had to hold him and to shed a few tears as she thanked God again that her son was home.

'Come on, Mamma—' he said awkwardly. But she held up her hand.

'No, no, you must allow me my tears.' The drenched eyes turned to Ruth. 'See, your wife has wept, too. We have wept together.'

'That's true,' Ruth murmured.

'Go home with Nicco and I will join you.' The signora pressed her hand. 'Gina, come kiss your *nonna* goodnight. You will be in your bed when I return.'

'Nobody would imagine we'd be seeing Mamma again this evening,' Nicco remarked, outside in Ginger Street. 'I thought she wasn't going to let me go.'

Ruth watched Gina, dancing ahead of them along the pavement, determined to prove she wasn't tired. 'It's an emotional time, you can't blame her for wanting to make a fuss of you.'

'And a fuss of you,' Nicco said with a smile.

'I wouldn't call it a fuss.' It was Ruth's turn to be embarrassed.

'Means a lot to me,' he said softly. 'That you and Mamma get on.'

'And me.' Ruth took his arm. 'Do you think it proves something?'

'Families can accept folk who are different? I'd like to think so.' He pressed her arm in his. 'I'd like to see the barriers coming down.'

They walked on, still watching the dancing Gina.

'She'll go out like a light, as soon as she gets to bed,' Ruth whispered after a pause. 'Lucky it's Saturday tomorrow, no school.'

'Work for us, though.'

'Work for me. You can rest, get your strength back.'

'*Cara*, I don't need to rest. I like to work.'

'Time enough when you're demobbed.'

'In my new demob suit?' He laughed. 'I think I'd better not get one to fit, if I'm going to be fattened up by all you women.'

'My mother's Yorkshire puddings?'

'And my mother's ravioli. Listen, did you keep that photo Sylvie found?'

'Of course. It's a souvenir.'

'Fancy you thinking I'd given you the push!'

'I know what I know.' Ruth halted. 'Oh, but Nicco – look! Look at Ginger Street!'

'Ginger Street?'

'No black-out! Ever since VE Day, I've been thinking how wonderful it is, just to be able to leave the curtains open, let the lights shine out. It's a sort of symbol, isn't it?'

'I suppose it is.'

She glanced at his profile. The ending of a war was going to mean much more to him than lights shining in a street. Yet they did spell peace.

'Peace,' she murmured, as they walked on. 'It's a lovely word, Nicco.'

'Has to be more than that.'

'It will be.'

'Maybe.'

'Oh, Nicco!'

'I've got my hopes,' he said quickly. 'Of course I have. People have just got to make things work, that's all.'

They stopped again and kissed, briefly, but Gina was looking back, swinging on the shop door handle, and they went to her. Nicco took out his key and opened the door.

'Up you go, sweetheart, and into bed with you.'

'Chase me, then!'

'Ah, I'm too tired.' He leaned against the door, sighing heavily.

'You're not, you're pretending.'

'All right, I'm pretending!'

He chased Gina up the stairs, as she ran ahead, laughing, but Ruth paused for a minute on the step, and looked back at the lights of Ginger Street.

'Come on!' cried Nicco and Gina. 'Come on, where are you?'

'Coming,' answered Ruth, and closed the door.